WHO ARE YOU?

Bright red blood seeped as the arrow pressed deep, the black-feathered chest heaving. The large, hooked beak strained toward Isaac's feet as an eye glared up to him. He stood, watching his reflection in the glossy, black orb. Then the beak opened, gasping, tongue fluttering, as if trying to speak. A long, airy, gargled breath met the moist sea air.

"Hhhooo aarrhhh yooohh?" Hushed and low, it resonated through the ship, sending chills that ran deep and cold. A shadowy face appeared within the hawk's black eye—faint, but real. Then the eye clouded white and slowly turned to stone.

www.lorianstones.com
email: lorianstones@gmail.com

TSP

TREESTONE PUBLISHING
Northfield

ISBN-13: 978-1482542257
ISBN-10: 1482542250

TOMBS OF DROSS

The Lorian Stones

BOOK ONE

LEW ANDERSON

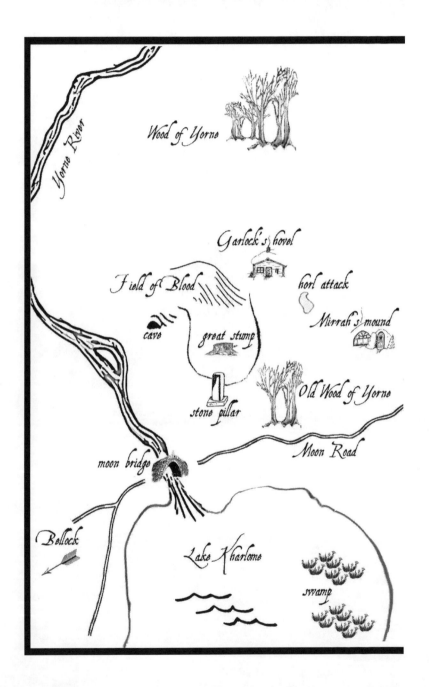

Wood of Yorne to Kharlome

Old Wood of Yorne

parlord attack

Kharlome

Kharlome Peerch Road

Isle of Mass

Hether Dawn

Kharlome Marm Road

Black Road

Skone Lor

N
W   E
S

To Isaac, Zachary, and Brielle
May you always have the joy that a good story brings

To my amazing and beautiful wife
Thank you for encouraging me to explore this new realm

Special thanks to my gracious editors,
Rachel Anderson, Elizabeth Potter, and Isaac Anderson
And to Dmtri Beeby, for valuable input that
helped set the course

TABLE OF CONTENTS

PREFACE

"Throughout history there have been accounts of people who spontaneously disappear, only to reappear just as suddenly in a different place. Researchers speak of the different dimensions of time—past, present, and future—existing next to each other as parallel universes." *Mysteries of the World* (Parragon Books, Ltd., p 300)

True stories do not always fall into pleasantly organized plot structures like those in novels and books of the sort. They rather must be told as they unfolded, as the events that made them memorable occurred in the realms of time. So it is with this adventure—it can only be told as it happened.

PROLOGUE

"Loria has fallen. The earth wails, the hooves thunder, the wind scatters. You must take your brother and the girl. Flee to Yorne. Find the pillar of stone—it will protect you."

A tall lad stood before his father as smoke rose from the valley far below.

"Keep this safe." His father handed him a knife with script upon the handle. "Protect the girl, she is your sister now. Travel only by night. Speak only the common tongue. When the time is right, you will return." They touched foreheads, the father's hands upon the lad's shoulders. "The pillar is hidden so listen carefully. From the great stump, on the Field of Blood, walk south to the tree of Loom. When you see a wall of chiseled stone, enter only through the arch." The man looked side-to-side, leaning close to his son. "When you see the pillar white... speak only these words..."

1 THE WHITE STONE

> "'By the moors of Myrrh...
> The stone cutters...
> In candle light...
> Carved the letters...
> On pillars white.'"

A teen boy stared into a pillar of stone. The words appeared in rhythmic waves like long-drawn breaths awakening things of old. Zac pulled the wool hat off his head. "Hey guys, come look at this."

"Yeah, right."

"Serious. I'm seeing words."

He read more.

> "'In the Wood of Yorne...
> In time of need...
> Of darkened night...
> The pure will read...
> The pillars white.'"

The last lines lingered as if calling to him. "Isaac, come

look. It's freakin' weird."

A girl came up. "I like it, Zachy—sounds mysterious."

"I wasn't reciting, Breeze. I saw words."

Three teens stood before a pillar of white, carved with sharp black lines of unknown script. The pillar stood alone in a small marble courtyard surrounded by a crumbled wall of stone.

Isaac, the oldest, reached up and touched the top. At fifteen, he stood six feet if he stretched, a thin boy, but strong. His brother, Zachary, still staring into the pillar, was two days into being thirteen. Brielle, or Breezy, stood beside him, a whole inch taller, although she would not be thirteen for yet another six weeks. A lanky girl, and sometimes clumsy, she loved to venture with the boys, as she and Zac had been friends since ever belonged to forever.

Isaac narrowed his eyes at the pillar. "Why is this here?" He glanced at Zac, "You weren't reciting?"

"I wasn't... honest."

The boys were exploring the property behind their family's farm. Having recently moved from the city, they would hike into the woods as often as possible. Breezy, who now looked down at the white marble floor, always came along. Although mid-November, in a wood of large oaks, maples, and elms, she noticed the lack of leaves and debris inside the courtyard. Glancing back to a narrow archway overgrown with brush and thorny vines, she pulled at a twig entangled in her amber waves of shoulder-length hair.

"How'd they get in here to rake leaves? Not where we crawled in." She pulled harder at the twig. "Zouch!"

Isaac turned, surveying the crumbled wall lined with birch trees and brush that made the tangled archway the only possible entrance. He scanned the clean floor, and then watched a leaf drift down outside the wall. "It's too clean," he muttered. Then, as if on cue, they all looked up. The older trees grew high overhead, vying for sunlight as the young birches stretched over the wall, forming a cathedral of branch and bough, dangling the last of the autumn leaves.

"Feels ancient," Zac said. "Who would come and clean?"

Breezy got the twig out and gave it a toss. It sat alone on the stone floor. Isaac had his hands on his hips.

"It's like nothing falls in here."

"Force field?" Zac had his head bent back. "Maybe leaves get vaporized."

Isaac rolled his eyes.

Breezy pressed her nose close to the pillar, her arms wrapping halfway around. "I don't see anything, just the funny black lines."

A watery white with translucent shades, the pillar had faint strands of red that wove through like veins in rock. It rested on a thick slab of pure white stone. Carved into the entire pillar's surface were symbols and strokes of rich black, contrasting the translucent stone. Appearing to be under a clear coating yet not, the writing spread out with no indication of left to right or top to bottom, its graceful curls and elegant lines mixing with strong bold marks and deep set symbols.

"Kind of beautiful." Breezy cocked her head. "You really saw words?"

"Sort of came from inside. I didn't make it up."

Isaac leaned in close. "What language is this? Sort of looks like... nah. Maybe it's... nah." Isaac knew a lot of things about a lot of things, but for this he obviously had no clue. "A script with pictographs..." He fiddled with his right ear as he studied the lines.

Zac stepped back. "Feels sacred, like we should leave, but it's kind of cool."

"Yazzers." Breezy rubbed her head, spreading fuzzed hair in all directions. "A bit of eerie, a hint of creepy, with a tweak of... hey!" She pointed to the floor. "Look—a circle." Just visible in the marble floor was the faint outline of a circle around the pillar and slab.

"How'd we miss that?" Isaac said.

"Girls see things that boys don't." Breezy flashed a smile with eyes twinkling. She had very unique eyes, one bright blue, the other a brilliant jade—beautiful, but unfortunately seen by most at school as freakish and weird. She once wore sunglasses to class, but that only made matters worse. She hated her 'freakish' eyes. The boys told her they were beautiful, but it came up every time she had a bad day.

Zac got down on his hands and knees. "More writing."

"Wish I could read it." Isaac liked science and math, games like chess, problems with solutions. He narrowed his eyes again, scrunching his nose. Breezy called it his 'thinking face.'

Zac sat on the slab, chin propped on his fists. "I bet in the summer you can't even see this place. Be a great hideout."

"It's got to be a monument," Isaac said, "a grave or something. But who comes to clean?"

"Think they'd mind?" Breezy asked.

"The dead guy won't." Isaac chuckled.

"Is this our land?" Zac asked.

"Thought so, but we better head home." The sun dropped behind the trees and the air turned chilly. Isaac went toward the archway; concluding it was all just an elaborate tombstone. "Staying for supper, Breeze?"

Breezy pulled her hair back with one hand, preparing for the squeeze through the archway. "Can't. Mom said be home for supper. Wish I could."

Isaac tried to clear the archway, quickly giving up and crawling through. Breezy followed.

Zac stood, staring at the pillar. "I really like this place."

"Come on, it's getting late."

He looked back one more time before squeezing through the archway. A yearning, warm and wistful, pulled at his heart. "Feels like—"

"Come on!"

Leaves crunched as they walked and talked, following a dry riverbed. A large black hawk drifted overhead, circling a few times before moving on.

"Should we tell your mom and dad?" Breezy asked. "They might say we can't go there."

"Why tell 'em anything?" Isaac tossed an acorn at a squirrel clinging to the side of an oak tree.

Zac pointed up. "Look." A large red-tailed hawk swooped low and rested on a limb up ahead, watching unconcerned as they walked towards it. Not until they came beneath did it push off, gliding toward the setting sun.

"Why not tell them?" Zac kicked a branch. "If we shouldn't be there, then we shouldn't be there, right?"

"Whatever." Isaac tossed another acorn to a squirrel scurrying about in the leaves.

"Mine'll believe whatever I tell 'em," Breezy said. Then in loud radio announcer style, "Which ya think would be great... but makes me feel like... like moldy cheese on a... scootenberry sandwich."

Zac chuckled. "What's a scootenberry sandwich?"

"I don't know." She giggled then got serious. "I say we tell 'em." They agreed to tell their parents but no one else.

Coming out of the woods, they crossed a pasture, passed by the old barn, squeezed through a small gate, and arrived at the house. Breezy got her school pack and strapped it to her bright red scooter.

"So tomorrow then?" She put on her helmet and swung her leg over the scooter with a road-warrior look in her eye. She could have just stepped through to sit, but to her it was more. "Gotta scoot." She flashed a silly smile, waving as she sped down the dirt driveway, wobbling much but mostly in control.

The story of their discovery did raise some interest. The boys' dad said he would go sometime and see. Their mother just listened. At Breezy's home, they weren't sure they were getting the story quite right and were just glad she was outside having fun. That night the boys talked about the pillar, the inscriptions, and the absence of leaves.

"You didn't make it up and weren't reciting something?"

"No, it was there in the stone."

"How?"

"I don't know. I was looking at it, then the light changed

and I saw the words."

"Hologram?"

"Don't know." Zac got into bed. "Maybe it's... ah, probably nothing." He turned out the light as Isaac stood in the doorway.

"Yeah, probably nothing."

· · · · ·

In a room of stone, built inside an ancient city wall, a teen girl tossed in her sleep. A small stone jewel hung about her neck as her long, black hair tangled inside her sheepskin bed. A fire crackled as she twitched, muttering soft moans, dreaming of a time now past.

> "'Hidden by veil, the pillars and power,
> Hidden from evils that destroy and...'"

A young child twirled a lock of her black hair. "I do not know this one, Father?" She rubbed the stone jewel that hung loose about her neck.

"'Devour'—a very old glyph. See the tail like of a serpentine." The child nodded, her black spirals bouncing in the fire's light.

> "'evils that destroy and... devour.
> The times they will turn...'"

She yawned, rubbing her eyes.

"Seems the time has turned for bed," came a woman's soft voice.

"Oh, Mama, I can do it. Father, please let me read more."

"You have done well, but Mother is right." He stroked her thick hair. "Remember, no one must know of what you learn."

"I know, Father."

The child sat near an open fireplace, a large book with tattered pages spread across her lap. An oil lamp of bronze flickered overhead. Her mother sat near the soot-darkened hearth as the fire's light danced upon the cabin walls. Large fur rugs covered chairs and floor, holding back the winter's cold.

"One more, Father, please?"

"The last for tonight—this one here—'tis said to be on the Lorian stone of Yorne."

She adjusted the book, lightly touching the worn edges. Excitement filled her heart as she leaned over the yellowed pages. The cabin seemed to hold its breath, awaiting the words to come.

> "'In the Wood of Yorne...
> In time of need...
> Of darkened night...
> The pure will read...
> The pillars—'"

Suddenly a thunderous boom rattled the cabin door.

"Open, or burn!" A loud voice shouted from outside.

"Hide the book!" Her father rose, a tall man with a ponytail, long and braided. Again the door shook with pounding thuds. The mother reached for the book just as the door burst with a deafening crash. An evil rushed in with the winter's cold, spreading out across the cabin floor. Snow flurries blew as warmth clashed cold. A huge man, over seven feet, dressed in chain mail and furs, filled the doorway. Protruding from the center of his forehead came a horn, three or four inches long, wide, curling upward like of a ram.

With instant movement he clutched the father's throat and yanked him through the doorway. Another man, even larger, pressed through into the cabin. The woman rose in protest but fell silent with one blow. This man, dressed like the first, towered over the trembling child, the book still open across her lap. He stared down at the black lines of forbidden script.

"Fools." He spoke from the side of his mouth as if his jaws were fixed shut. The calloused nub of a severed horn centered on his forehead. He scooped up the book and tossed it into the fire. Hoisting the girl under one arm he gave the command to burn it all.

He paused to watch the flames engulf the hallowed pages. The child peered through her twisty bangs. Frozen in terror, eyes fixed on the book, she heard her mother's screams, her father calling out. She saw the flames move inward, surrounding the precious script, advancing till one last piece remained. Through quivering lips, she softly read the last of the sacred lines.

> "'To the stone of Yorne…
> With blackened letters…
> Through battles grim…
> And broken fetters…
> Three ones will come…'"

The teen girl awoke with a start, her chest heaving. She looked around the small, cold room as chills covered her skin. She held the stone about her neck, loosening her tangled hair as the fire popped, sending a tiny ember onto the hearth by which she slept. "They will come…" she whispered, staring into the dying flames. "Three ones will come…"

2 LOST

"I was waiting aaaall day." Breezy stood with Zac after school, watching the gray sky pour down a freezing rain.

"Me too. We'll go tomorrow." Zac had thought about the pillar all that day, eagerly waiting for the school bell to release him. But tomorrow brought more of the same. He began to wonder if it had really happened. Would the pillar even be there? Was it a magical moment? Anxious doubts, even worries scurried through his mind like mice on a marble floor. The rain turned to sleet and then to snow.

He woke early on Friday to the phone's endless ringing.

"Zac? You up? It's one of life's most gloooorious moments." Breezy spoke like an actor in a Shakespearian play. "Not only is the earth covered in a beeeeeautiful rrrobe of white, but it's a snow-day!" Then speaking fast, "Supawesome or what? Are you guys up? Can I come over?"

Breezy's mom dropped her off, and the teens sat eating breakfast, planning their trip into the woods. The storm had passed, and the world became a wonderland of 'floating flakes of fluff,' as Breezy called it.

"Thank you, Mrs. Alders," she said as the boy's mother brought some pancakes. Although she had known Mrs. Alders before she could walk or talk, she had recently taken up the habit of calling adults by their last name. 'Makes 'em feel good,' she had told the boys.

Isaac readied his backpack. "I'll bring matches and paper for making a fire."

"I brought hot chocolate," Breezy said with a muffled burp. "Hmm, that was delicious."

The boy's father stepped into the kitchen. "The burp or the pancakes?"

"Hi, Mr. Alders. We're going out into the wild, white wilderness of wonder and… whatever." She flung her arms up, giggling.

"Hey Dad, listen to this—I almost got it." Zac cleared his throat.

> "'Tell me not in mournful numbers,
> "Life is but an empty dream!"
> For the soul is dead that slumbers,
> And things are not what they seem.
> Life is real, life is earnest—'"

"Not the whole thing, please." Isaac said.
"Crabby crustacean."

His father gave a nod. "Just the latest," and Zac cleared his throat with exquisite flare.

> "'Trust no future, however pleasant,
> Let the dead past bury its dead.
> Act—act in the living present,
> Heart within, and God overhead.
>
> Lives of great men all remind us
> We can make our lives sublime,
> And, departing, leave behind us
> Footsteps on the sands of time.
> Footsteps that…'"

He groaned. "I got the last lines but not that one." His father put his hands on Zac's shoulders. "Well done, that twenty bucks is getting hot."

"It's not fair," Breezy said. "You guys are so smart. Even if my dad offered a hundred bucks, I couldn't learn that poem."

"Perseverance," Mrs. Alders said, "not smarts. You will find your—"

"It's just a poem. It's not important." Isaac rolled his eyes.

"It's not just a poem," Zac said, "it's Longfellow's *Psalm of Life*."

"Whatever. Let's get going."

"Today is going be so wah-some." Breezy stood, bumping the table, nearly spilling everything. "It's going to be the most wonderfully, awesome day." She held her head high and arm out, like a statesman giving a congressional address. Zac laughed.

Isaac put everything into a large plastic bag before shoving it into his pack. When they had donned their gloves, hats and goggles, they set out looking like an expedition to the North Pole.

The wood became a drastically different world from the other day. They each had a sense of wonder as they tromped through the snow-laden woods, longing to return to the pillar and courtyard of white.

Following landmarks, they found the courtyard and squeezed through the thorny archway. When Isaac came through after Zac and Breezy, he found them just standing, mouths open wide.

"What the…?"

Everything was just as they had remembered, just as they had last seen it. "No snow…" Isaac whispered. "How can there be no snow?"

Zac looked up. "Force… field…?" This time the words came out with awe.

Breezy dropped her hood and lifted her goggles. "I don't…

think… this place is normal." She walked over to a lone thorny twig on the marble floor, holding it for the boys to see. "From my hair."

The courtyard was clean without a sign of snow having ever been there. It had been snowing the whole time they hiked. It was snowing now as they stood in the courtyard, but not a single flake fell inside its walls. The stone wall lay covered in snow, yet the marble floor was dry. They walked toward the pillar in fearful awe; a magic or mystery was here in this place.

"If it's a memorial," Zac whispered, "it's not an ordinary one."

He walked up to the pillar wondering if he would see the words again. He pulled off his glove, running his bare fingers over the smooth shapes and delicate curls. He looked deep into the stone, following a white meandering vein that led to a red swirl far into the center. The swirl became words, which again came like ancient breaths. He read them without speaking.

'To the stone of Yorne…
With blackened letters…
Through battles grim…
And broken fetters…
Three ones will come…'

He pressed his hand against the stone as the red swirl disappeared. Then, as if being shocked, he jerked his hand away.

"What's up?" Breezy watched him, her hair fuzzed out from beneath a blue-green headband.

"Shouldn't this be… stone cold?" He did not say anything about the words. They looked at Zac and the pillar as they took off their gloves.

Breezy hesitated, and then pressed her open hand against the stone. "It's warm." She put her hand to her cheek then pushed back her hair. "Not like a stone in winter."

"Hot spring?" Isaac had his thinking face on. "Ancient

marker over a sulfur spring, a lava tube, a—?"

"Would that keep the snow out?" Breezy took off her headband.

Zac put his hand on the pillar again. The warmth was good. He sat on the step and faced the archway. Pulling out a frozen brownie from his pocket, he thought to tell them about the words but without knowing why, he kept it inside.

Despite the puzzling pillar, they sat watching the snow float down outside the wall, enjoying the unexplained warmth. Like children watching a snow globe, they sat staring into the surreal wonder of this warm new world within the cold snowy wood.

Munching and talking, trying to solve the mystery, they touched the pillar a few more times. Zac looked for more words but only saw the mysterious black script.

Finally, they decided to walk about and look for clues. Isaac paused in front of the brush-tangled archway. He searched the outer wall for a better exit point. "This way," he said, as he climbed over the crumbled wall, pushing his way through the brush and birches.

Once again Zac looked back at the pillar as Isaac and Breezy scrambled over the wall. Something tugged at his heart... something ancient... something winsome... his chest warmed.

Breezy helped him over then walked around to the archway twirling, her arms outstretched. "Isn't it beautiful—the snow, the woods? So quiet... so... sereeme."

"You mean serene," Isaac said.

"No, sereeme—it's extreme serene." She gave Zac a silly look and was in the middle of continuing her twirl when something passed overhead, darkening the sky above.

"Whoa! Did you see that?" Zac stared up through the trees, his mouth open wide.

"Just a little," Isaac said. "What was it?"

Breezy whipped her head back, dropping her hood. "What? I didn't see anything."

Zac stretched his arms out. "A monstrous black hawk or eagle, the size of an airplane."

"Must have been a hang glider." Isaac searched the sky.

"Who'd be hang gliding in the snow?" Breezy looked at him funny.

"That was no hang glider," Zac said. "That was a real bird—beak, head, claws, feathers—huge!"

"It wasn't a bird. It was a glider or a small plane."

"You didn't see it. I saw it. Was the biggest hawk or eagle ever."

"It wasn't a hawk." Isaac knew Zac was not lying, but he knew it could not have been a bird. Then again—the courtyard.

"A U.F.Oooooh..." Breezy swayed with gloved fingers pointing out from her head like antennae. "Come on guys, you're freaking me out. Let's hike around."

Zac continued looking up through the trees, shaking his head and uttering disdainful comments toward his brother as only snowflakes appeared in the endless sky of white. Walking on from the courtyard deeper into the woods, they dropped into a valley and found an outcropping of sandstone into which an ancient river had carved a small cave.

"Could something live in there?" Breezy asked.

"Lots of things," Isaac said, crawling in, "but nothing to worry about."

"Except a skunk." Zac looked directly at his brother. Then, seeing that it was large and dry inside, he let the bird incident go and crawled in after Isaac. It was just high enough to sit. "Never dreamed we'd find so many cool things back here."

Breezy stayed outside till the boys built a fire and coaxed her in. She whimpered like a sick horse till the fire's warmth eased her heart. The fragrant pine, the dancing flames and glowing heat made the cave feel cozy. Outside the snow fell heavier, smothering the woods with more of winter.

"The fire's nice." Breezy eyes were getting sleepy.

"This is the best snow-day ever," Zac said, carving a 'Z' into the cave wall.

They munched some more, talking and laughing. When the fire died out, they left the cave, shivering until they explored some more, working their way back toward the pillar.

"Shouldn't we be near the stone thing?" Breezy looked around.

"Something's not right," Isaac said, looking at a tree with its root wrapped around a boulder, like an older brother's arm protecting a sibling. "I don't remember this." A hint of panic came through his voice. "Let's go back and find our tracks." Isaac led the weary trio, wandering about looking for anything familiar, but ultimately that sickening feeling of things gone wrong washed over them with waves of woe. After an hour of hiking, Breezy plopped onto a fallen tree.

"This isn't fun anymore. I'm getting cold."

"How'd we get lost?" Zac asked.

"We're not lost," Isaac said, "we just don't know where we are in relation to where we want to go." He zipped his coat up higher. "We're tired so things seem worse. If we just find the pillar, we'll find our way home. Come on, let's go."

Breezy whimpered as the woods darkened with the sky. It was time to be home—home drinking hot chocolate and telling stories of their day. Isaac knew their farm bordered several hundred acres of woods and fields. "Angst," he said to himself. A word he had just learned. "A feeling of deep anxiety or dread."

They entered a wide, open meadow with a rounded knoll. Stopping at a huge tree stump in the center, Isaac cleared a spot, and they plopped their weary bodies down. The stump was larger than any they had ever seen—six or seven feet across if not more. The dark gray settled in around them, pressing them down as they sat, three dark humps on the edge of the stump—cold, wet, and defeated.

"I just wanna go home," Breezy whined. "My toes are frozen."

"I'd carry you if I could," Zac said.

"Doesn't make sense." Isaac pulled off his hat, rubbing his head. "How can we be lost?" They sat in sulking silence, as the sky darkened.

"No tracks," Breezy said softly. "Why weren't there any tracks?"

"The snow covered them."

"No, not those."

"What do you mean, Breeze?"

"When we climbed out the stone pillar place, our tracks were gone."

"Our tracks going in?" Isaac leaned forward to look over at Breezy.

"Yaz. I remember now, wondering why our tracks were gone, but it passed my mind."

"I didn't even notice." Zac looked to Isaac. "What do you think it means?"

"It means... everything's all screwed up... and we're in a mess." Isaac liked challenges, but hated losing. He rubbed his head again. "No leaves, no snow, warm pillar, you see words, and now no tracks." He hated the mystery even though it could be something special. It was too big, too different, too far outside his experience and control. A stinking mystery, and he was burning brain cells with nothing to show. He pulled his hat back over his cold ears. "No tracks, huh? What next?"

"I saw more words." Zac spoke to the ground.

"When?"

"Before we had snacks."

"Same lines?" Isaac asked the questions like an officer.

"Kind of, but with stuff like, 'battles grim.'"

"Battles grim?"

"And something about 'broken fetters' and 'three ones will come.'"

"You should've told us."

Suddenly Breezy perked up and pulled her hood and headband off. "Hear that?"

"Hear what?" the boys asked.

"The music."

"Music?"

"Shhh, listen." Silence held the open meadow beneath the falling snow. Zac pulled up his wool hat. Isaac cupped his ears with gloved hands.

Breezy turned a circle. "Where is it coming from? It's... all around."

Isaac looked to Zac. "I don't hear a thing."

"You can't hear that? Don't make fun."

He listened some more. "Maybe it's the wind."

"It's music—a low flutey kind of sound." She tilted her head. "It's beautiful... the saddest, sweetest, peacefuliest music I've ever heard—like a heart lamenting."

"Peacefuliest?" Zac watched her turn a slow circle.

"Hypothermia," Isaac said out of the side of his mouth.

"I'm not hypo-nothing! I'm freezing cold but not hypo-crazy. How can't you hear that?" She cocked her head as she spoke. "Coming from... over there." She started out across the meadow.

Isaac looked up into the heavy sky. "We can't go wandering after music only you hear."

"Like, hello? What have we been doing?" Her voiced echoed off the trees circling the meadow. When Breezy set her mind or heart on something—a cause or some injustice—she took on this authority that no one with half a brain would dare stand against. The boys called it her power mode.

Zac shrugged. "Lead the way." Isaac groaned, knowing from experience not to challenge her when she shifted into power mode.

They followed Breezy marching across the meadow into the woods, her hood and headband off, hair getting wet, locked onto finding the source of the sound. The boys, hearing only silence, blindly followed as she made her way through brush and over logs. The wood became darker, the trees tighter. Like being trapped in a darkening labyrinth of doom, claustrophobic fears pressed in around them. After ten minutes, Isaac stopped.

"Come on, Breeze, this is stupid."

She twirled around, her wavy hair hung limp like a wet mop. Her face tightened. "I followed you all day. Now, I'm going this way." She shooed him away with both hands. "Go wander, go!" She turned and stumbled over a branch, catching herself just in time. Zac exhaled. She had the potential of turning hysterically angry in power mode, making her impervious to reason, but with undaunted boldness.

They trudged onward, the trees looking older, larger, with little undergrowth. Zac thought he saw something, a shadow of movement to the right. He looked hard, but all was dull gray and dark silhouettes.

"God, you gotta help us," he whispered. "You just gotta." His heart thumped hard as the darkness settled. He looked again to where he thought he saw something move. Then he squealed, "Breezy! Look! You did it."

A small yellow glow, a tiny glimmer of light, worked its way through the heavy gray.

"Told you I heard something." She shook her hair and snapped her hood up. The light led to a small cabin built into the side of a hill. The fragrance of burning wood hung in the still night air as smoke rose lazily from the center of the hill.

"I don't hear the music anymore."

"Doesn't matter." Isaac walked slowly to the door. "We'll ask to use their phone."

Breezy let the boys go first. "Looks like an old trapper kind of guy lives here."

A low wooden door stood beside a small window in a wall of hewn logs. They crowded together, looking through the window. A fireplace filled the end wall with two stuffed chairs. Someone sat on the right, smoking a long thin pipe.

"Think there's a phone here?" Zac whispered. "Looks like a hunting shack."

Isaac hesitated. "Maybe we shouldn't… looks kind of—"

"It looks a bleepity lot warmer in there than out here," Breezy said. "Creepy or not, I'm done walking."

Isaac stepped to the door. With hand raised, he paused for a moment, glancing at his brother, who gave an anxious nod.

Suddenly, a raspy growl rumbled from behind them. They

whirled about. Breezy slipped, banging her head against the window, catching herself on the ledge.

Standing in the snow was a giant lynx-like beast. It stood as tall as a tiger, staring at them as they huddled together in a mix of arms and legs. The eyes glowed from the window's light. Breezy tried to scream, but nothing came out. She ducked behind Zachary. Isaac pressed back against the door leaving Zac out front to face the beast. A snowflake came and settled right on Zachary's nose. He stood there, frozen like a rock in winter.

3 THE GRIMALKYN'S HOVEL

The giant lynx continued to growl but did not move or prepare to pounce. Then it stepped toward Zac. He pushed back into Breezy and Isaac. His foot slipped. Isaac grabbed his coat. The huge cat came right up to his chest, lifting its head just an inch or so to look Zac in the face. Its long whiskers touched his skin. Zac's eyes seemed to fill his whole face. He followed the black lines from the corners of the giant cat's eyes. They were like ancient Egyptian eyes. It had a thick mottled brown and white coat with long black tufts rising from its pointed ears. Two ruffs or beards hung down from its jaws.

Time stood still. Then, a gruff voice came from behind the giant lynx-like beast.

"Ya lookin' for someone?" A man not much taller than Zac stood with an armload of wood. Dressed in a mix of leathers and fur, his beard was thick and bushy like a lion's mane. A small hat that tied under his chin held down a mass of wiry curls. Yellow tufts of hair stuck out as if trying to escape. His eyes were peculiar as they reflected the window's light.

"Ah… we're lost," Isaac stammered. "Do you have a phone we could use?" The man stood beside the giant lynx without responding. He seemed to hold the bundle of wood without effort.

"Would ya like to come in and warm by me fire?"

"Yes, very much, thank you." Breezy quickly put a gloved hand over her mouth. Isaac gave her the 'can't-believe-you-said-that' look.

The great lynx glanced from side-to-side, and then moved toward the door. The teens shuffled out of the way, crowding the window. The big cat nudged the latch with its nose and pushed open the door. Shaking its huge fluffy paws before stepping over the high threshold, it then flicked its short stubby tail and entered the warm light. The man stood waiting for the three to follow, giving them an encouraging nod. Zac and Breezy held their breath as they stepped over the threshold into the small cabin. Isaac held the door for the undersized man.

The cabin, lit by the fire and two small lamps, looked like a trapper's shack. The walls were partially log and natural rock, with beams across the ceiling. A small wooden table with two crude benches sat off to one side. A few shelves with miscellaneous items and the large stone fireplace with its two chairs covered in furs made up the rest of the room. Strong smells of pipe smoke and animal skin lingered in the air. But it was warm—a quiet, snug kind of warm.

The man in the chair, smoking the pipe, turned to look at them. He was older, but small like the first man, with an even bushier beard of white with streaks of brown. His hair bushed out in all directions, short but thick. His skin was dark and weathered into leather-like folds, and his eyes, like the other man, were somehow different—long and thin.

The giant lynx went and sat on its haunches near the fire, dwarfing the old man while still looking intently at the three strangers. The fire's smoke and other smells all mixed into the strangeness of the cabin. The teens looked at each other, trying to sort their thoughts and feelings. The old man watched them for what seemed a very long time. The strange smells, sights and emotions soon merged into one dominate feeling—a sickening woe.

"Catch 'em in yeer traps, Garlock?" the old man asked.

"Be standin' outside, a spyin' in." The man, Garlock, stood at the open door and gave a quick whistle. He waited, and then gave another. Suddenly, a small hawk swooped in through the door forcing him to duck, bumping his head against the doorjamb. "Marrgh, flyin' with yeer eyes shut?" The hawk flew to a rafter near the fire and, after fluffing its wings, made an airy whistling call. It sounded like laughter. "Yo, real humoratin's, ya little wog."

The hawk was steel blue with rusty-colored breast and leg feathers streaked with brown. Isaac thought he knew what kind of hawk it was, but could not grab the name.

The old man continued to look at the teens. He motioned with his head for them to come near the fire and warm themselves. Zac stepped closer.

"Sorry to bother you," he said, "but we got lost and need to call our parents. Do you have a phone we could use?" He worked to control his anxious mind, trying to be polite with eyes locked on the lynx. The old man sat silent, just watching. Breezy's hands trembled. Wandering around in the cold, things going so terribly bad, and now a strange little cabin with two strange little men and a giant beast—her insides were going haywire and her head felt light.

"Would ya like some hot mulger?" Garlock asked.

Thinking they had misunderstood, but knowing he offered something hot, the boys nodded. Garlock took a blackened kettle from the hearth and poured them a drink that steamed from mugs on the small table. The drink was dark and smelled of spices and maybe milk. They still had their gloves, hats, and coats on, standing near the table, looking at the warm fire.

"Ah, thank you," Isaac said, "but we need to call our parents. If you don't have a phone, is there a neighbor who does? We'd really appreciate your help."

Again there was silence. Garlock had taken off his leather hat and coat before serving them. Although small, he looked strong and agile. His thick brindled hair, like the old man's, spread out in all directions, with his long, arched nose looking like some Roman emperor. The cabin's warmth felt good, but it was hard to fight the daunting feelings. Being inside the cabin, like at the stone pillar, did not make sense. What was happening?

"Not sure me knows yeer meanin's, heh," Garlock answered. "Where be yeer journey?"

"Home," Isaac said. "Our parents are going to be worried. Do you have a phone?"

Garlock checked with the old man still silent by the fire. "Pardons," Garlock said. "Are ya goin' be drinkin' yeer mulger before it gets a thicken?" They put the mugs to their lips looking at each other, trying to appear polite. Isaac thought to just get warmed up, and then go back out to find a house with a phone, or a road, or just something normal. There must be a road of some kind leading from this cabin.

"Hey, this stuff is good," Zac whispered.

Apprehension filled the room, but the hot drink, whatever it was, did taste good. After more awkward silence, Breezy took off her gloves and put them on the table.

"I heard music." Despite the tension, she yearned to know the source of the sad, peaceful music.

"Music?" Garlock went to the door. "Out in the wood?"

"It was beautiful."

"Yub, and ya probably found a big white stone." He placed a small beam across the door. All three looked at him with a start. He spoke sarcastically about the pillar. Why would he speak like that? Why would he fasten the door like that?

"Is the pillar close by?" Isaac asked.

"Pillar? Didn't speak a mutter 'bout a pillar. Where'd ya say ya be from?"

Isaac wondered how much he should say. "We live on Old Highway One."

Garlock narrowed his strange little eyes. He took a braided leather belt off his waist that held a long sheathed knife with a bone handle. He kept his eyes on Isaac as he hung the belt and knife on a wooden peg near the door.

The old man scratched his beard and moaned a contemplating sigh. "Do you know of the white stone?" he asked in a hushed voice clearly not wanting anyone else to hear. Zac looked up. He had been busy enjoying the hot drink. Isaac shook his head. The old man gave a little smile. "Tell me what ya know, and I'll try to help, if I can."

Again, there was silence, save for the crackle of the fire and a soft purring from the lynx as the old man scratched between its ears. Garlock sat down at the table watching the strangers. The old man waited, the fire's glow bouncing eerily off his weatherworn face.

"Is it a memorial?" Isaac asked still weary. He would cooperate enough to get directions back home.

"You've seen it, have ya?" The old man's eyes seemed to flicker as he spoke.

"Is it near by?" Isaac asked.

"You tell me."

"I can't."

"Why not?"

Isaac sighed. "We saw it, but then we got lost and ended up here."

Garlock groaned. "Let loose me beard, boy. None seen the stone since the Tarrin Wars. Ain't no stones, no matter what old Grimals say."

"Ya don't know yeer speakin's, Garlock. Keep yeerself from talkin' the fool." The old man was firm, still keeping his voice low. "Look at 'em. Ask yeerself where they be from?"

The hawk, still in the rafters, made the strange laughing sound again, like it understood the conversation. Garlock looked again at the three standing between the fireplace and the table. He saw they were different, but knew to mind his own business when strange things happened in the wood.

"Where did they get their cloth, I ask ya?" continued the old man. "How did they come through the wood? And music—is it not like I've told ya? Just dropping coins ya bargain?"

"Fuddle me whiskers," Garlock grumbled before taking a long drink.

"Please." The old man motioned them to come near. "Sit

by the fire, tell me everything."

To Zac, it seemed the good thing to do—to tell everything—to just be open and honest. They hadn't done anything wrong. Why should they hide? He moved toward the blackened fireplace made of flat stones stacked upon each other. A large black fur skin covered the floor beneath the giant lynx or whatever it was. The old man's chair angled toward the fire with the lynx at his side. Zac plopped into the other chair after taking off his coat and boots.

"We found a courtyard," he said, "with a stone pillar."

"Near the big meadow, was it?"

"It's not far from our house. When I first saw it, I read... um, I thought it was really interesting." He glanced at Isaac. "My brother thought it was a monument, a grave or something. We came back today. Then we got lost."

"You saw it this day?"

Zac nodded.

Breezy had taken off her coat and boots and sat on the fur rug pressing close to Zac's chair. She eyed the huge cat as it sat, enjoying the warmth.

"Wwe... went there this morning," she said, her voice wobbling. "It's a snow-day. We had munchies there, 'cause it was warm. Why was it warm?" The old man wagged his head. "Then we—" She suddenly stopped as the giant lynx opened its mouth into a huge fang-wielding yawn. "Ah... then we walked and walked, but stuff didn't look right. We walked for hours... then I heard the music."

Isaac still stood fully dressed. He gave Zac the look for settling in by the fire. The old man continued to study the teens. He reached and gently rubbed Zac's coat sleeve between his fingers.

"Please pardon," he said. "I be Alle-Encer and this be Garlock." Garlock gave a little nod accompanied with a grunt.

"I'm Zachary, and that's my brother, Isaac, and my friend, Breezy. You can call me Zac."

"Esteemed to meet you, Zac," he said with a nod. "Beg yeer pardon our ways. Travelers at night be rare. Travelers like you…" Alle-Encer scratched his hairy head. "Come by never."

"Can you just tell us where we are?" Isaac's voice cracked. "Our parents are going to be worried. If we could just call them."

"Call them? Are we keeping ya from calling them? How can we help ya call them?"

Frustration washed over Isaac's face. "We just need a telephone. Is there a phone somewhere?" Isaac emphasized each word. He felt stupid constantly asking for a phone.

"A telda fawn?" Alle-Encer tilted his head. "Not in these woods."

"No, he speaks of the ferns of Windlum," Garlock said. "Be far from here, lad. Them giant ferns be no place for young sproots. Me hears many a tale—"

"Garlock, that is not their quest." Alle-Encer wrinkled his brow. "What do you seek?"

Woe came over Isaac. Hope left his soul like air from a shrinking balloon. They didn't just get lost in the woods. Something else happened, and they needed to find out soon or they would be the highlight of the evening news.

Zac held his hand to his ear, pinky and thumb extended. "Telephone," he said slowly and clearly. He then tapped his finger into his left palm as if dialing. "You know, for calling friends. Ring any bells, Alexander?"

Alle-Encer shook his head. Zac glanced at Isaac.

"Electricity?" he then asked. Isaac tisked and rolled his eyes.

The old man again shook his head.

"TV?"

Again the old man shook his head. He honestly had no idea what Zac was asking.

There was a moment of eerie silence, then Breezy asked, "So where are we?"

"In the Wood of Yorne." Garlock gulped a generous slurp. "But me thinks ya not be of the Wood."

"The Wood of Yorne?" Isaac scrunched his face. "Where's that?"

Garlock guffawed, spitting his mulger and startling the little hawk. The bird seemed to scold him with a raspy cry.

"We told you what we saw," Isaac said, "so please tell us where there's a phone or road or something, anything."

"Did ya now?" the old man said looking back into the fire. "Sure ya did." He stroked the large cat's head and took a draw from his long pencil-thin pipe. He held the smoke until orange plumes wafted out from his curly mustache and beard. He turned to smile at Breezy. "The music ya heard young one has been heard before." The smoke curled out as he spoke. He blew it toward the rafters. He took another long draw from his pipe. They watched, waiting. "It comes from the stone," he said very softly, "the stone of the Prince."

"The Prince?" Breezy leaned forward.

"Marks the battle, it does—where he gave up the blood."

'And no good it done," Garlock said, "Sasson still be holdin' the power."

"Garlock!"

"Ah marrgh! All be lumpy mulger, I say. Me never be hearin' music out there. Never seen a stone of white either, and I be born and growed in Yorne."

"It's hidden. The stone has power. Evil cannot, must not, find it."

"I'm not evil."

"Can ya see what ya don't believe? If these young sprigs have seen the stone, there is purpose. Might just be our purpose, sir Garlock, to help 'em find theirs." The old man sunk a hand into his thick beard to scratch his jaw. He turned toward the fire. Its light sparkled out from his eyes as he spoke to himself.

"Where are they from?
What lies ahead?
Why have they come?
By whom are they led?"

The fire flared, then snapped as he spoke, and out flew an ember landing near his feet. He picked it up, holding it by his fingernails—they were thick, almost claw-like. He tossed the ember back into the fire. A faint smell of burnt hair rose from the rug on the floor.

"You say ya live on the side of the wood?" Alle-Encer continued to study them, especially their clothes. "And be walking from yeer home to visit the stone?"

"That's right," Isaac said.

"Walked from the edge of the wood, ya say?"

"It's not that far."

"Marrgh," Garlock growled. "Ya don't just come a walkin's." He spoke into his mug. Then noticing that all were looking at him, he spoke up. "None comes a walkin' through here, let be a handful of sproots. What weapons have ya?"

"Is this your land?" Zac asked. "We didn't mean to trespass."

Garlock let out a loud short laugh that sounded like a cough. "Hah! My land? Wouldn't that be somethin' to mix in yeer mulger? Me, ownin' the Wood." He chuckled, looking at the old man and the teens. His eyes almost shut tight. The hawk seemed to join in with a laughing whistle. Garlock looked up at the bird and snorted. He picked up his mug and chuckled again. "My land—hah!"

"One doesn't just walk through the wood of Yorne," Alle-Encer said. "Takes a young Grimal three days to walk it through. But the beasts… they move unheard, unseen till they strike." Breezy and Zac looked to Isaac who shook his head.

"Well," Isaac said, "how do explain that we just walked from our house to here? Course… I'm not sure myself."

"I cannot." The old man stared back into the fire. "It has me mind a snarled. My thoughts a tangled twist of twine." He was scratching his chin with his hand again buried inside his beard. "A mystery that burns the fragrance of fate."

"So you're saying there is no way we can walk home tonight?" Isaac said.

"This night?" Garlock barked. "Wouldn't that be a feat? I don't give ya sproots one rill before yeer fillin' the belly of a horl. It's nigh after sup and ya want to go skippin' through the wood. Hah!" He shook his hairy head. The hawk gave a long low whistle.

"You can't tell me there's bear out here." Isaac was edgy. "Fifty years ago maybe."

"Bear? What in a moss beetle's dung pile are ya munchin's?

"I-zac," Alle-Encer said, "I believe you are wise. You must know something has happened to you and yeer friends today. I believe you are no longer in yeer land. Some how you've come to us. I feel it—I know it. I believe ya did walk through the wood, yet ya did not."

Breezy looked about with nervous eyes. "What beasts?" she asked Isaac, who was still standing between the table and the fire. Isaac again shook his head.

He saw the worry on her face. His heart grew heavy, really heavy. He wished he were home in his own house—home with a good fun snow-day behind them. Why were they here in this cabin in the side of a hill with two strange men and a lynx on steroids? Why can't they just get to a stinking phone and call home? He looked up at the hawk in the rafters and sighed. It wagged its head, shrugged its wings, whistling soft and low.

4   A LATE NIGHT VISIT

"I think we should have some eat," Alle-Encer said. He looked with concern at Breezy. "I sense I must tell more than ya want to know." He gave a nod to Garlock who got up and went toward a piece of something hanging from a rafter. He sliced off chunks and put them into a black iron pot. He then added what looked like old vegetables, dried leaves and other things unknown, and then hung the pot from an iron rod above the fire.

Alle-Encer urged them to take off the rest of their wet outer clothes and set them near the fire. Isaac finally took off his backpack and coat. It was good to get out of their wet things. Snow pants and mittens, gloves and hats sat strewn about the tiny dwelling as near the fire as possible. Zac had found the chair to be wonderfully comfortable. It was certainly Garlock's and was covered with a large gray fur. It was a soft thick fur like rabbit and very long. He pulled his bare feet up under him and stared into the fire. The pot boiled and Garlock dropped in some dried leaves that offered up a rather enticing aroma.

Like a fresh breeze on a hot day, Zac felt a peace come into his heart. In spite of all the trouble and strangeness, he had joy. Everything would be okay. He could trust the old man, enjoy the fire and the food, and even touch the giant lynx—maybe. He stared into the flames some more, wondering if Isaac and Breezy felt the same. He hoped they did. It had become a long and difficult day. It hadn't been a fun snow-day like snow-days are supposed to be. Somewhere, something had gone wrong.

Or had it? Maybe not wrong. Maybe just not as planned.

He watched Breezy. She looked content sitting on the thick fur rug, holding her knees in her arms with her toes close to the fire. She stared dreamily into the flames. She was no longer concerned about the large cat just several feet away. Isaac sat at the crude table made of a solid slab of wood. He too, stared into the fire with his head propped on one hand. Zac was glad to see his brother settled down.

Hope Mom and Dad don't get too mad, he thought.

No one spoke as Garlock prepared the meal. It seemed like only a short time until he declared the 'broth be infused.' As he set the food on the table, the hawk came floating down. Garlock brought a bowl to Alle-Encer. Zac held out his hands and with a big smile nodded to Garlock. He huffed and mumbled something, then brought him a bowl.

Zac held the clay bowl with both hands. Inside was a dark stew with a big chunk of brown bread and a hand-made wooden spoon. A strong but alluring aroma filled the air. Breezy had trouble using the large wooden spoon. She watched the hawk trying to steal chunks of meat from Garlock's bowl.

"Get yeer own, ya gollywog." Garlock shooed the bird away. He had given the lynx a large bowl of stew, set between her front paws, but no bread. Isaac and Garlock sat at the table but did not speak. Garlock had taken no more than two bites when Alle-Encer reminded him of their need for drink. He grumbled something and fumbled about then gave each a clay mug of a lukewarm drink. They ate in silence.

Either the stew and bread were good, or they were really hungry. The world seemed a little brighter after eating. Zac asked Alle-Encer about the woods.

"Why is it not safe to be in the woods after dinner?"

"Horls. They narely prowl a Grimalkyn's home or pounce

in the light. But if ya give 'em a chance they'll make a meal of ya."

"What do these horls look like? And what's a grimalkyn?"

"By the horns of Morten," Garlock said. The hawk made its laughing sound again.

"We be Grimalkyns," Alle-Encer said. "Horls be large beasts of fur and claw. They, like Nusa, walk unheard, leap a hundred steps, and kill with a swipe." He put his hand on the lynx as he spoke and looked right at the big cat. The cat looked straight into his eyes. "Sorry, girl. This is Nusa, a perlin of Mersha. Befriend her and she will die for you. Betray her and she will kill you." He ran his hands along the cheekbones of the feline and then scratched behind her tufted ears. All eyes were on Nusa and the old man. "The horls are beasts, not like our valiant Nusa. They tease their prey till its life be spent and then, when the sport is gone, they eat. None but a fool travels the wood at night."

The fire crackled. Breezy looked to Zac, who looked to Isaac, who narrowed his eyes and cleared his throat.

"Have you actually seen one of these things?" Isaac asked.

"Seen one?" Garlock laughed his short rough laugh. "Yeer brother and the missy be sittin' on 'em. Trapped those last snow. Seein' 'em ain't the trouble. Killin' 'em before they eats ya be the Grimalkyn's trial."

Breezy and Zac looked down at the warm soft furs they were presently enjoying. Isaac got up from the table and touched one of the skins. A long thick fur, but soft, unlike any animal skin he had seen. No head or paws were on the skins but one still had its tail—a bushy thick tail at least five feet long. This didn't seem to be a hoax. This, unfortunately, was very real.

"So this is a horl skin?" he asked.

"Caught and tanned 'em meself."

"How big are these… horls?"

"Big enough for all of ya to ride its back, if that were somethin' ever done. Huh! Wouldn't that be a feat, ridin' a horl?" Garlock chuckled as he stretched out his arms as if holding on to something. He looked to the hawk, which bobbed its head from side-to-side.

Zac squinted in the dim light watching the hawk. He mouthed the words to Breezy, 'You see that?' Isaac had seen the hawk too and tried to ignore it.

"But you're not concerned about them during the day?" he asked.

"Oh, we be concerned, just not that concerned. They know we can see 'em and if we can see 'em, we can shoot 'em."

"With guns?" Isaac asked.

"Guns?" Garlock tilted his head. "T'was meanin' me thorne."

"Thorn?" the boys asked together.

Garlock pointed to a small bow hanging above the doorframe. It reminded Isaac of a short Mongolian bow but with a recurve that wound into a curl. The ends were flat and wide. It was made of metal. Arrows filled a fur quiver hanging beside. He wanted to look closer since he had an interest in archery and was fair with the bow, but he needed to stay on the subject of these horls.

Just as he turned back, Breezy let out a shrill scream and pointed to the window.

"What is that?!"

The dark silhouette of a giant bird's head filled the frosted glass. One black shiny eye glowed in the light. The bird was so huge that it bent its head down to peer through the window. They looked in horror as the fire's flames reflected in the large black orb.

Isaac froze, still holding the horl tail. Zac sat up in his chair. Nusa growled, hair rising on her back. The little blue hawk screeched and flew about the rafters.

"Sasson carn!" Garlock growled. "Why in Mulder's mire—"

"Shhh… look to the fire!" Alle-Encer said. "Don't let it see yeer face." He motioned to Isaac. "Sit low near me chair." Isaac could not take his eyes off the huge black bird. It moved its head, bobbing and cocking, straining to see inside. Isaac moved to the front of Alle-Encer's chair. He tried to position his long legs without infringing on Nusa who stood, eyes fixed on the window. Breezy still looked wide-eyed at the frosted glass. "Little One!" Alle-Encer snapped. Breezy jerked, then turned toward the fire. Zachary held his head low, yearning to look at the window.

"What's a Sasson carn?" he whispered. Alle-Encer slowly shook his head. Garlock had moved back against the wall and put out one of the oil lamps. The fire crackled as a loud raspy croak rattled the window. Then came a flurry of snow, and the huge bird was gone. No one moved. They listened till the fire popped out a large ember.

"Sooty scavenger." Garlock went toward the window. "Why in Mulder's mire be a Sasson carn lookin' in me window?" He stood off to one side, peering out the frosted glass.

"A carn?" Alle-Encer again dug at his beard, searching for his chin. "This day becomes a drink of savory dew."

Isaac moved away from Nusa. The big cat was still staring at the window, a soft rattle in her throat as she breathed slowly, deeply.

"What's a Sasson carn?" Zac asked again. Alle-Encer and Garlock sat waiting—waiting for something to happen. Then Nusa sat back down on her haunches still keeping her eyes on the window. Alle-Encer sighed.

"The carns," he said, his voice very low, "have served Sasson since the great war. They are his watchers, his messengers, warriors of the sky." He paused, thinking over what just happened. "One never sees 'em like that. Far off for sure, but never like this."

"Then how do you know—"

"I-zac, this be not yeer land. We know a carn when we see one." He rubbed his beard for a long time. "There is purpose… in yeer coming." He pulled on his right ear. "Garlock, they cannot stay!" Alle-Encer spoke with such urgency that it put goose bumps on all three teens.

"What ya be speakin'?" Garlock's voice squeaked a little. "Ya can't send 'em out this night. They wouldn't know a horl be on their trail till they're lookin' out through its teeth. I just be tellin' 'em they can't be walking round out there."

"Take them to…" Alle-Encer paused, then looked at Nusa and whispered into the cat's furry ear. "Nusa will guide you."

"Take 'em?" Garlock's eyes were wide. "Me? What makes ya think I be stirrin' to take these sproots anywheres?" Garlock raised his voice, which made Alle-Encer rise from his chair. He looked sternly at Garlock and instead of replying to his objections, spoke to Isaac.

"You cannot stay. Sasson now knows you're here. I do not fully understand, but trust me. A carn's presence, in this land, be danger. Follow Nusa and obey Garlock. They'll protect you in the wood. Move quickly—move quietly. Do not speak on the way. Dress now. There is little time."

The air in the room changed. All of a sudden a bad day that had gotten just about as bad as it could get, got much, much worse. None of the teens moved. They just looked at Alle-Encer. Go out in the cold again, with a grumpy Garlock and a giant lynx or perlin of Mersha whatever that was, and not even know where they were going?

Isaac stared at the window. He did not want to stay, that was for sure. Yet he saw with his own eyes the giant black bird. And the size of Nusa made him consider the talk of the horls. No. It's got to be a hoax. He grabbed his coat and called to Zac and Breezy.

"Get your stuff on, we're going home." He put on his coat and gloves. "This place is nuts. We'll go back the way we came, find a road or something—anything." He gave an awkward nod to Garlock. "Thank you for the food and letting us warm up." He put on his hat and gave Zac a stern look. "Come on, we have to get home."

Reluctant to even move toward the cold outside, they slowly gathered up their wet and yucky things. Sore and tired, Zac stood by the fire with a damp sock in each hand. Walking home now seemed horrible. Going back out into the cold, into the dark cold, with that carn thing, seemed crazy. What was happening? What had they done wrong?

5 UNSETTLING ENCOUNTER

Alle-Encer stood puzzled. Garlock put on his coat and boots and grabbed his arrows and thorne. He paused awaiting instructions from Alle-Encer who gave none. They both watched as the weary teens put on their coats and made their way to the bolted door. Alle-Encer tried to speak once again with Isaac who just shook his head.

Garlock looked through the window before lifting the beam. Nusa stood beside Alle-Encer, yellow eyes fixed on Garlock as he slowly opened the door. Frozen air rushed in, flowing across the floor, chilling the cozy room. The fire rustled in resistance. Breezy whimpered in a pony's neigh. Flakes floated softly down, but the night seemed twice as cold.

What's crazier? Zac thought. Staying here or going back into the frozen dark woods?

"Isaac, are you sure?"

"We can't stay here, Zac. We have to get home."

Garlock stepped out first. He spun around pointing his loaded thorne up to the roof. The woods lay still, resting in the quiet cold of winter's sleep. The gray had turned to softened black. They stepped out the small door and stood in the yellow light that spread out upon the snow. Their eyes, conditioned to the cabin's light, stared fearfully into the curtain of darkness that hung beyond the trees. Foreboding dread covered Isaac. This has to be a dream—freakiest, craziest, realest dream ever. We've got to get out of this.

"I can travel with ya, for a bit, if ya know yeer goin's." The short muscular man looked about. Isaac wanted his help but needed to just get away from all the weirdness.

"We can make it, thank you," he said, his voice clearly stressed.

Zac looked up at his brother who was taller by more than a foot. He deeply respected him but saw the distress in his eyes. "Isaac…?"

"Look for a glow," Isaac said. "The lights from town should reflect off the clouds." It sounded good but in every direction hung the curtain of darkness. Alle-Encer and Nusa stood in the open doorway, their shadows stretching out across the snow to where the teens stood huddled. Zachary looked beneath the little window and saw the huge tracks left by the carn. This was either a vivid, scary dream or a real, scary world.

"We came that way," Isaac said. "I don't see a road, so let's go back the way we came." He tried hard to sound confident.

Garlock gave a lingering look at Alle-Encer and Nusa. He held his thorne tight, ready for any movement in the silent wood. Zac and Breezy looked at each other and then at the warm glow coming from the cabin. What at first had seemed so strange and threatening had now become the place of longing. They turned to follow Isaac as he stepped into the darkness. Garlock came behind. His soft leather boots moved silently as he turned about, thorne string taut.

They trudged into the dark unknown, grasping for a hope of actually finding their way. No one said a word. They could not see far enough to chart any course. After ten minutes they came to a clearing.

"Is this the meadow with the huge stump?" Isaac got excited.

"Too soon," Zac said.

"Stay on the edge, lad." Garlock tried to whisper. "Don't

walk the open."

"The stump would be over there," Isaac said as he cut out into the clearing for the other side.

"Marrgh!" Garlock blew a plume of frosted air.

Isaac walked fast toward the other side of the clearing.

"Don't move yeer feets!" Garlock told Zac and Breezy as he went out after Isaac, grumbling profusely but quietly.

"This is what happens in scary movies." Breezy's voice trembled. "They split up. I always tell 'em; don't split up, but—"

Suddenly a gray flash bolted across the clearing. Isaac tumbled into the snow a dozen feet from where he had been walking.

Zac blinked several times. What had come so fast? "Isaac? Isaac!" Thumping rose into his ears. His breath came fast, his muscles twitched. Garlock shouted back to him.

"Get to that tree and don't ya move." The little man ran toward Isaac. He had taken only three steps when the gray flash came again. A huge mass landed square on top of Garlock. His arrow flew glancing off a tree. At first they thought it was a large bear, but no bear could move that fast and leap that far. As the beast held Garlock down, it turned its gaze on Zac and Breezy.

They both sunk down into the snow pressing back tight against the tree. The animal stood motionless, staring straight at them. No sound came from either Isaac or Garlock. The beast looked like a house cat but the size of a polar bear. Its tail twitched back and forth as it held one prey sizing up the others. Breezy clutched Zachary's arm, her body shaking wildly. Their skin went cold.

Zachary spoke quick and short, barely understandable. "It's all my fault—I should have stopped him—we shouldn't have come here—why didn't I stop him?" He too shook in sporadic shudders. He tried to stay quiet, but all was lost. They were all going to die in a cold wood, killed by a huge gray beast. Why didn't they listen?

The ground trembled ever so slightly. A dark bounding

flash came from the far side of the clearing and stopped near Isaac's body. The beast still pinning Garlock, gave out a wretched howling hiss. Even in the dim light they could see the hairs on its back push upward. It arched its back, tail puffed out, moving side to side. The second beast left Isaac's body and circled round toward Zac and Breezy.

Breezy gasped in short breaths, suffocating herself with fright. Zac watched the dark cat move toward them placing each foot in direct line with the other. So huge, bigger than any tiger. Its eyes did not move, locked on the trembling bodies at the tree.

They pushed themselves hard against the tree—pushing as if to get inside—to press through the bark and draw their legs and arms up into safety. Then the giant cat stopped and slunk its body to the ground.

"It's… it's…it's gonna pounce." Breezy gasped out the words.

"God help us." Zac shook and jerked. Breezy dug her face into his shoulder. She squeezed his arm tighter, struggling to breathe. Zac could feel her shaking and gasping but no longer heard her as throbbing sounds filled his ears.

The giant cat tensed, its tail twitching. Zac stared into the eyes. He watched the white mist float from the nose. In slow motion, he watched it spring. Front legs shot high into the air. The body extended full as the hind legs thrust. It soared with claws out, straight for the prey at the tree.

He watched it glide. It would strike without Breezy even seeing. All became still as the pounding faded to a solemn silence, the face of the giant cat looming in upon them. He shut his eyes and held his breath, lips and teeth clenched tight, turning to cover Breezy's head and body.

Then, as if jolted by a gunshot, there came a snarling slam of bodies, impacting and tumbling, hissing and growling like nothing heard on earth. A piercing scream came from the flailing fur and claws that tumbled right before them. Another beast had joined the fray—smaller but intensely fierce. It fastened itself onto the back of the pouncing cat, digging its fangs and claws into the neck and head of the beast. They tumbled and clawed at lightening speeds, belting into trees and brush.

It seemed long but was, in reality, over in seconds. The larger dark beast spun free, disappearing into the darkness.

Zachary breathed in spurts, pressing back against the tree. Breezy had opened her eyes to watch the screeching spectacle. The smaller cat casually licked its fur for only a moment and then walked silently toward them. Not until it was almost upon them did Zachary, through quivering lips utter the name, "Nusa?"

The giant lynx stared with her bright yellow eyes. Puffs of white mist rose from her nose and mouth. She turned toward Garlock and Isaac and then bounded into the clearing. The other giant cat had fled and Garlock was fumbling to reset an arrow into his thorne. When he saw Nusa, he ran to Isaac, hoisted him onto his small sturdy frame and carried him out of the clearing. Tears dropped on cold cheeks as they watched the strange little man and the great silent lynx bring Isaac back.

Zac stood pressed against the tree. "Is he—?"

"Taint be dead, frap-torten-da-sossel! I told 'em. Ya heard me tell 'em." Garlock set Isaac down against the tree. He stomped the snow off his clothes and flung his thick hair about. "Cursed crotters!"

"Are you okay?" Zac asked Garlock.

"Am I who?" He looked down at Isaac. "He got swiped. There be blood."

"What happened?" Isaac looked up.

"Ya didn't listen, that be what happened."

"I thought you were dead." Zac said.

"I thought we were all dead." Breezy wiped her eyes, hands twitching.

"Something knocked the wind out of me." Isaac moved his shoulders and winced.

"Them be horls," Garlock said. He brushed more snow from his leathers, stamping his feet. "Nusa kept us all from bein' hair balls."

Zachary wanted to tell of the horrible catfight, but all his cold lips could muster was, "She saved our lives." Nusa looked casually about. Isaac stood to his feet. Stuffing and shreds of cloth hung from the back of his coat.

"Ya be brone lucky, lad. Don't be fearin' the scars. Missies like 'em. Proves the tale be true."

"You guys okay?" Isaac asked.

"If alive is okay," Breezy said with a shuddering breath, "then we're okay."

Isaac wobbled, putting his hand against the tree. "Feel weak," he said. "Don't understand. Loose tigers?"

"Them be horls, lad."

Isaac squinted toward the clearing. "Just want to… get us home."

"If ya want me advice—and if ya don't—we follow Nusa." Garlock brushed snow off his chest. "The pot be startin' a boil. Not one to know much, but carns… at me hovel…"

Isaac straightened, groaning through clenched teeth. "We gotta go somewhere, some place safe."

"Safe? In this land? Hoh!" Garlock studied the tall lad. "We best get that wound salved. Horl cuts go bad."

They followed Nusa along the edge of the clearing until they neared the other side. She led them into the trees onto a small trail that meandered along a tiny brook. Breezy wanted to talk about all that had happened. She was either happy with relief or in some state of shock, but Garlock told her to 'muff it.' They were not out of danger by any means.

Zac and Breezy trailed close in the footprints of Nusa with Isaac and Garlock at the rear. Garlock held his thorne ever ready. The grace with which Nusa moved through the trees was a marvel to Zac. He tried to step like her—to copy her smooth but sudden movements. His boots made him awkward and the nylon zipping sounds from his coat defeated any stealth. It was intriguing to watch the shoulders of the giant lynx move up and down, the huge soft paws steady on the smallest of footholds.

"I smell smoke," Breezy said, quite loudly, but she wasn't hushed. Everyone but Nusa stopped to sniff the winter air. Nusa paused and looked back exhaling a warm breath that condensed to white. She then silently moved on as before. The sharp wafts of smoke grew stronger as they neared a large mound at the edge of a clearing. Nusa stopped.

Light soft flakes floated back and forth, drifting carefree through the trees. The air hung still in the quiet cold wood. Nusa walked straight toward the mound. Zachary wondered why they would climb over when they could easily walk around. Nusa went to a large boulder at the base and came to a halt. She gave a soft strange growl as the others came up in line.

"What's wrong?" Isaac whispered. Garlock turned to face the way they had just come. Zac's skin tingled. He had felt safe walking the trail with Nusa. She could defend them against any danger of this wood. Chills moved over his skin. The gray flash striking Isaac; the face of the giant cat; waiting to die at the base of the tree, and Breezy clutching his arm fighting to breathe; all came back with terror. He stepped closer toward Nusa.

They stood in silence as the lynx again gave out a soft growl. What was Nusa waiting for? Then they heard the movement of a metal latch. From the base of the mound, directly beside the boulder, an iron hinge ground out its eerie creak. A gentle female voice broke the night air.

"Nusa?" The big cat walked into the mound and disappeared. Zac squinted trying to see where she had gone. "Come, it is safe here," the gentle voice said. "Please, come in."

Zachary walked forward as one walks into a dark room. There was no high threshold like at the Grimalkyn cabin. He shuffled his feet as he walked, trying to feel for something to guide his way. "Wish I had Nusa's eyes," he said. Then a strong slender hand gently took his and led him through a passageway into a room dimly lit by a small blue flame. The rest were helped in, and he heard the door shut and the iron latch reset.

"So these are the ones," a woman said. She lit a lamp that burned bright white. Garlock went to the fireplace and began reviving the coals. Zachary had no idea regarding the time but knew it was late. He looked about the room, which rounded on the top. The woman stood from lighting the lamp. Tall and slender, she had reddish-brown hair that reached to her knees. She looked kind and moved with grace, her cheekbones high with a nose fine and slender. She wore a long fleece robe with cuffs and collar of fur.

"Your day has been long," she said. "You need warm drink and rest. Undo your garments. Set them by the fire." She poured a hot drink into tall mugs with metal handles. The aroma filled the room with thoughts of Christmas and chocolate, peppermint spice and all kinds of wonderful things. "Sit, rest." Her hair flowed like a horse's tail as she moved about the room. "I am sorry my home is small, but it keeps us close." She spoke so kind and her voice so pleasant, it was like a dream.

"Please let this be a dream," Isaac said to himself, as he stood near the fire. His back throbbed with pain. It hurt to breathe. He looked at his coat as he hung it on a peg near the mantel. Three long shreds ripped through his coat. "Mom is going kill me."

The room was larger than the Grimalkyn cabin, filling the whole underside of the mound. A doorway led into another room. Two, rather large, half-round windows filled opposite walls, each covered with a dark sheer cloth.

"This will chase the cold from your hearts." The woman handed Isaac a mug of spicy drink. It was like a hot chocolate, but had a sweet spice—a chocolate-licorice-cinnamon-peppermint sort of flavor. After she had given the others their drink, including Nusa a bowl of something warm, she brought a light to Isaac and asked, "May I look at your wound?"

"It's okay, just cut my coat."

"Then your coat bleeds." She parted the strands of cloth that were once part of his shirt. Three claws of the horl had cut into his back. "Two are scrapes," she said, "but one has torn flesh. The cold helped stay the pain."

Breezy came to look. She gasped. "Isaac, you're bleeding."

"I have seen much worse." The woman spoke with such calmness, such assurance, that it was uncanny but welcoming. She had Isaac sit on a wooden stool. Breezy stood near and watched, feeling like she belonged there, like she knew this women, like being with a beloved aunt or long-time friend of the family. She leaned in closer.

"Aiya, 'twas a tussle." Garlock sat on the ledge in front of the fire. He unlaced his high fur boots with a long sigh. "Saved our skin, she did." He put his hand on Nusa's neck. The big cat winced. "Not the first, pray the last."

"She is wounded." The woman went to a cupboard and took out a small vial with some cloth. She handed it to Breezy. "Use this to clean her wounds. Do not be afraid. She will thank you for it." It took Breezy some time to gather the courage to approach Nusa so close, and despite the fact she hated the sight of blood, she became proud of her given task. Zac knelt beside her and helped part the fur.

"She's poiky," Breezy said. She and Zac had a game of making up words. Nusa's long thick fur, like stiff grass on bare feet, was 'poiky.'

Isaac felt suddenly weak as the woman dressed his wounds. His t-shirt, under shirt, and fleece had all become dried into the blood and flesh. It was painful as she cut away some of his clothing to reveal the wound. They moved near the fire as she cleaned and wrapped his chest in cloth.

"I thought he was dead," Zachary said to the woman. "It was horrible." He still had guilt over all that happened.

"Why do you think that?" The woman gave her long hair a swing as she turned her head to face Zac.

"Think what?"

"Did he not choose to go that way—to walk the clearing?"

"Yes, but… we should have stayed at the cabin. I should've—"

"You would be in great danger." She gave Zac a lingering

look before helping Isaac with a soft knitted shirt. It went on with much less pain than his had come off. His back burned with increasing throbs. She mixed a mug of something that smelled fusty like a dry-rotted stump. "This will help. Drink it fast." He shuddered as he swallowed. It tasted like old weeds and mushrooms.

"Thank you... ma'am." He blinked a few times suppressing another shudder. "I appreciate... you helping us."

"Please call me, Mirrah. I am honored to help you."

They settled in around the fire after enjoying some bread and cheese. It was so good to be out of their wet clothes and the dark, cold woods. Mirrah's mound was safe. Isaac's pain subsided and the world, or wherever they were, seemed a little better. They did not talk much about the day but rather stared into the fire, absorbing its warmth and enjoying its simple mystery. It was good to just sit and stare, letting their hearts rest and recover.

"I'm tired." Breezy yawned with arms outstretched.

"Come this way, Brielle. You can sleep in here." Mirrah led Breezy into one of the rooms from which she later came out to say goodnight. She wore one of Mirrah's robes that trailed far behind her on the floor. The sleeves hung to her knees.

"Goodnight, Breeze." Zac got up to see her into her room. "You gonna be okay?"

"It's a nice bed, really cozy."

"Sorry about today."

"Like poop in a puddle—you didn't know. It's not your fault. But... that was horrible. I'm trying not to think about it."

"I'm just sorry you came along on this one."

"Never-lever," she said wagging her head. "Don't you ever think of leaving me out." She lowered her voice to a whisper. "I'm just glad I didn't pee my pants." They giggled together before she went into the bedroom where she and Mirrah would sleep.

Isaac and Zac would sleep on a bed spread out in front of the fire. Garlock took a large fur and settled in near the passageway to the door. Nusa lay licking her wounds by the window.

"How's your back?" Zac asked, as he crawled under a heavy horl skin.

"That drink really helped." Isaac yawned big. "What a crazy day."

They both lay beneath horl skins and watched the flames flicker in the fireplace. Zac played the day over in his mind—a long day. He worried for his mom and dad. How long would they keep looking? Maybe they will follow the trail. He wondered if Breezy would ever get to go exploring with them again. Would *they* ever get to go exploring again?

"Hey, Zac."

"Yeah?"

"How'd she know?"

"Know what?"

"What happened out there. How'd she know about me going into the open? None of us told her, did we?"

"No."

"And did you hear what she called Breezy. She used her real name. And… it's like she knew we were coming."

"You're right—like she knew."

6 BREAKFAST AT MIRRAH'S

They drifted off into a deep, heavy sleep. Isaac ran from horls, climbing a tall white pillar with black carvings. Two horls snarled close behind, clawing their way up the pillar. He desperately clung to tiny finger holds, wedging his toes into the small black incisions. The horls kept getting closer as he climbed the endless pillar of stone.

Zachary dreamt he walked barefoot with Breezy and Nusa. He and Breezy walked on each side of the big lynx, feeling the warm grass against bare toes. They crossed a green meadow as large snowflakes floated down. The day was warm and sunny and the flakes would turn into flowers as they touched the grassy meadow.

They stretched out on the sunny side of the meadow, resting their heads on the large rib cage of Nusa as she dozed in the sun. Her chest would slowly rise and fall with each long breath. Up and down—air rushing in and out of her massive lungs. The sun warmed her fur, radiating heat all through Zac's weary body.

Something tickled his nose. He opened his eyes and saw Garlock working over the fire. Zac stared up at the rounded ceiling, his head going up and down with the sound of Nusa breathing.

The great lynx slept sprawled out with the boys. A large front paw rested on Zac's chest, his head resting on hers. He studied the claws and fluffy paw. Her fur was wiry and thick, white with patches of brown and black. She breathed directly into Isaac's ear. He soon rolled the other way. Her back paw sat on the fireplace ledge, twitching and bumping Garlock as he stirred a black pot in the fire. He grumbled something about a Grimal making breakfast and a fur ball that 'don't stop a bumpin' stuff.'

Zachary breathed a big sigh as he lay there, head going up and down. He gently pushed Nusa's paw off his chest, and sat up. The cloth was drawn back from the windows. The storm passed with the night, and the sun made its way through the glistening trees. The bright morning filled the home under the mound with fresh life. Garlock gave a nod when he noticed Zac.

"Want some help?" Zac asked him quietly.

"Keep this paw out of me way." He wasn't as quiet.

Zac smiled and crawled over the fur rugs to try and move Nusa's paw. As soon as he touched it, she raised her head to look at him. He let go. The lynx sat up, stretching her jaws into a mammoth yawn. Tusk-like fangs, still tainted red, glinted in the morning light.

"Are you rested?" Mirrah came from a side room, her hair hanging loose, crimped from frequent braiding. The red-brown mane flowed behind her like a wedding veil as she walked to a marble-topped table. Small biscuits, some fruit, sliced ham and cups of juice were set out in perfect order. "Come and eat," she said softly.

Zac thanked her and went to the table. He sat alone looking out the window at the glittering snow. He did not realize how hungry and thirsty he had become. He ate and drank so fast that not until later did he realize he had burned his mouth on a piece of cooked ham.

When he finished, Mirrah came and sat across from him. She looked late thirties.

"So where are we?" Zac asked. "And why are we here?"

She smiled. "I can tell you where you are, but I cannot tell you why you have come. I was hoping you could tell me."

Zac shrugged with a goofy grin. "Not a clue."

"You are in the Wood of Yorne between Kharlome and the land of the Grimalkyns."

Zac just shrugged again with a silly face.

She studied his eyes. "From where in the kingdom do you come?"

"Kingdom?"

"The kingdom of Ariel."

"Kingdom of… Ariel?"

A moment of confusion covered Mirrah's face. She did not reply but looked intently into Zachary's eyes. He wanted to look away and normally would have. "You know Ariel," she said, her brow wrinkled. "Why do you not know his name?"

"I know who?"

Garlock came and grabbed a bun with a piece of ham. "I told Alle they don't belong here." He took an oversized bite. "Best be to send 'em back," he muffled out.

"Garlock!" Mirrah did not take her eyes off Zac.

"Just lookin' to keep us livin' be all."

Mirrah studied every inch of Zachary's face. "How do you not know the name of Ariel?"

"Sorry. Is he the king?"

"He is more than our king. He is the maker of life. Without Ariel, there would be no life, no world, no Wood of Yorne, no food, no rain nor snow."

"No horls?" Zac did not intend to provoke; he just wanted to learn about this world. They had been talking quietly, but now Isaac sat up. He had been listening from his bed. He wanted to believe they were somewhere near home, just lost in the federal land. Or maybe this was an elaborate joke—no, couldn't be. The tigers or horls were very real. Must be a dream. No… there's an explanation, somewhere.

Breezy came wandering out of her bedroom covered with the oversized robe. She plopped down next to Mirrah with a satisfied moan. She rubbed her eyes and unconsciously brushed a cheek against the soft fur collar.

"You guys sleep okay?" she asked. Then, before anyone could answer, she reached for a small bread roll and said, "I slept like a... a... I don't know, but I really slept good." She shoved the roll into her mouth almost whole and muffled out, "Truffles to boot, I'm starved."

"I see that." Zac gave her a big grin. It was good to see her feeling 'at home.' He, Garlock, and Mirrah all watched her eat.

"What?" she said after another bite. Not a single strand of her wavy locks was aligned with another. Zac just kept smiling. Isaac came and sat beside his brother.

"Anyone say grace?" He then felt awkward.

Breezy finished her roll, swallowed hard and said, "What does it matter? So we're in some totally freaked-out world where giant birds come to your windows at night and horrible cats the size of elephants attack you in the woods; we can still give thanks. Look at all this stuff. These buns are really good." She waved another warm biscuit for them all to see.

Isaac studied Mirrah in the morning's light. She looked like a certain painting, but he could not recall the artist. "We have a custom of giving thanks before we eat," he said.

"Please." Mirrah seemed anxious.

Isaac said a simple prayer of thanks for the food and for helping them escape the horls last night and Nusa leading them to this warm home and for Mirrah's wonderful hospitality. "And thank you that my back feels a whole lot better. Amen." For a moment the room was still except for Breezy chewing heartily on a piece of fruit that got shoved in after the biscuit. Zac softly chuckled.

"So your back feels better?" he asked.

"Yeah. Thanks, Mirrah. Aches a bit, but slept really good."

Mirrah smiled. She watched them as they ate. "We were speaking of Ariel," she said. "Have you—?"

"Who?" Breezy looked up.

"Ariel, the Creator."

Breezy shrugged. Isaac shook his head. "You need to help us out. Everything here is strange."

"When Ariel first created, there were no horls, no evil carns. The land was good, and all creatures lived together. They had all that was needed to enjoy life and each other. But that was long, long ago."

"So what happened?" Breezy took a drink.

"Sasson came."

"Sasson? Like in… Sasson carn?" Isaac asked, still trying to understand the giant bird. Mirrah nodded.

"Long before our time, Sasson deceived the rulers—turning them from the ways of Ariel. He has been deceiving ever since."

"He's still around?"

"Yes, he is a toreph."

"A toreph?"

"Yes." Mirrah thought he understood, but Isaac shook his head. "He is from old; he is not like us."

Zac swallowed a drink of juice or tea, he could not tell which. "So why doesn't Ariel just kick his butt and make things right?"

"He will—someday. It is said to be written on the stones of white."

Garlock listened from the hearth. "Aiya. Be clumps of rotten cheese, I say. Old Grimals been talking 'bout the stones and Ariel longer than rocks been in me fields. Ain't seen no nothin's."

"The stones exist, as does Ariel!"

Garlock turned away and pretended to busy himself with the fire. "If Ariel is, why we still under the hand of Sasson? If he cares, why we sufferin'? If he watchin's, why yeer husband…?" Garlock stopped. Mirrah looked away, and Isaac saw her pain. The room went quiet. Isaac had on his 'thinking face.'

"Do you mean a white pillar with black inscriptions?" He spoke slowly, sensing the weight of his words. Mirrah turned quick to look at him, staring deep into his blue eyes.

"What do you know of this?" she asked without breaking her stare.

"I think it's the whole reason we're here. It's the only connection I can make—before all went goofy."

She leaned closer, still studying his eyes. "You have seen a stone?"

"We saw a pillar. Everything was fine until we left the pillar."

"Pillar?"

Zac gestured with his arms out, moving them upward. "You know, a pillar."

"Yes, I know a pillar. The stone you saw was shaped as a pillar?"

"Yes," Isaac continued, "in a small courtyard. Letters, glyphs, symbols or pictographs, all etched in black."

Zac dramatically mouthed the words, 'glyphs, pictographs,' to Breezy, who just giggled. She took a bite of cheese, and in muffled speech, blurted out something that at first could not be understood. She swallowed and said the words again—words that, without her knowing, would send them on the journey of their lives.

"Zachy read them." She quickly covered her mouth with a muffled, "oops."

The room tingled with silent suspense. Mirrah turned her full attention to Zachary, her eyes wide and intense. She leaned in close and spoke in a soft, breathy whisper.

"You saw... and read... the white stone?" Her voice put goose bumps on his skin.

"Well, kind of." Zac leaned back but held her stare. "Just a little. I don't remember all the words."

"I do," Isaac said. Unlike last night, he wanted to talk this out, to uncover the mystery. He paused, recalling what he had written. He did not memorize poems like Zac, but he could remember people's words. He put on his thinking face and spoke slowly. "By the moors of Myrrh... the stonecutters... in candle light... carved the letters... on pillars white."

Mirrah jumped up from the table with a gasp. She paced back and forth in front of the window, her long hair flowing behind. She put her hands up to her mouth, uttered something, then lowered them, rubbed them together, then back to her mouth. Something major was going on. The teens watched with wonder. She stopped abruptly and turned to Garlock, "Did you know of this, Garlock of Yorne?"

"Me was... aye... well... they told of seeing a stone." He looked liked a naughty schoolboy in the principal's office. Mirrah sat back down across from the boys.

"Tell me everything. Please, I beg you! Everything you saw, everything you did."

"That's about it," Isaac said. "We went again, yesterday, and now we're here, wherever here is. Do you know where Old Highway One is? I can't figure it out. I know we're not in Kansas anymore, Toto." Zac and Breezy snickered. The room was tense, but it was such a relief to see Isaac no longer sour. They both knew, when he got mad, his thinker didn't work well. If he had time, and stayed calm, he could figure this thing out and get them home.

"So you are from Kan-sis in Toto?" Mirrah said. "I do not know of—"

Zac started laughing and almost fell off the bench. Nusa came up behind and put her head against his back.

"No, we're not from Kansas," Isaac said. "We live near the old highway, south of town, near..." He could see something was wrong. "We're not even in Minnesota, are we?" Mirrah gave a look of wish-I-could-help-but-don't-have-a-clue. He sighed, rolled his shoulders and winced.

"By the moors of Myrrh," Mirrah said. "By the moors of Myrrh, Garlock. They saw the stone of the Prince."

"Heard music, too, ma'am," Garlock muttered.

"You heard music in the wood?" Mirrah's eyes got huge.

"I heard music," Breezy said quietly. She usually would make a big boast of something like this. "It was the most beautiful music ever. It led us to Garlock's house."

"Garlock!" Mirrah gave him the look. He went back to tending the fire.

"Why don't you go see the pillar?" Isaac asked. "It shouldn't be far."

"Many have searched. The stones are hidden. They cannot be found, they are only… revealed."

"Ohhh…" all three teens said together.

"When the stones are seen, great things happen. If you have seen a stone, the Prince has beckoned you. You have been called…" Her voice trailed off.

Zac noticed Breezy's eyes began to tear. "Breeze?"

"It was so beautiful." She wiped her eyes. "So sad, yet so nice."

Mirrah put her hand on Breezy's. "You have felt the heart of the Prince."

Isaac looked out the window, his thinking face on. "You said 'one of.' There's more?"

"There are five stones hidden throughout the lands. One is the beginning—life before Sasson. One is of the wars and the kingdoms, the shaloms and their mighty deeds. The one you saw is of the Great Prince. Another speaks of what will come—the return of Ariel and the end of Sasson."

"That's four," Isaac said.

"The fifth… is yet to be written."

There was silence for a time, save the crackle of the well-tended fire. Nusa rubbed the top of her head against Zachary's back, bumping him into the table. He braced himself and laughed. He carefully turned to scratch her head. It was exciting, yet frightening, to be so close to such a large animal. He longed to befriend her.

"So, what about Nusa?" he asked rubbing the cat's large head. "Where does she come from? Is she a horl?"

Nusa drew back her head and let out a low growl. Zac pulled away. Garlock brought a black pot from the fire.

"Nusa, a horl? Hah!" He set the pot on the table, grabbed some ham and went back to the fire.

"Nusa is certainly not a horl," Mirrah said. "She is a perlin of Mersha." Mirrah looked straight at Nusa and continued. "She understands everything we say. Or better put, everything we think." She paused. "Somehow the perlins just know. Maybe the greatest gift to come from Mersha." She paused again. "And perlins do not readily share what they know."

"She can read my mind?" Breezy asked, eyes wide.

"In a way. She knows your feelings, your intentions, your attitudes. You cannot deceive a perlin."

"But horls can't do that?" Breezy stared into Nusa's eyes.

"No, the horls are cats of Bellock. They have become a serious problem."

"How many horls are out there?" Isaac asked, now that he would forever bear the scars of one. Garlock gave his usual huff when someone asked an obvious question.

"More than we would like. They were house pets of the Brones."

"Brones?" Breezy's eyes grew big again.

"Brones—the giants of Bellock."

"Giants?" All three spoke in unison.

"The horls were pets of the Brones of Bellock. During the Brone wars, whole cities were destroyed. The horls had no place to go but into the wilds. They plague the Wood and rule the plains of Mann."

"From Mulder's mire, they be," Garlock said. "Can't trap 'em fast enough. Have kits by the cord. May have to leave the Wood—wind and water pray forbid."

"So they're giant house cats?" Isaac rolled his eyes. "Wonderful. Mauled by a house cat." The teens looked at each other with bewildered faces. "So how big are these giants of Bellock?"

"The Brones are tall and strong," Mirrah said. "Great in battle, but they stay to themselves. Not many remain."

"So how tall is tall?"

"Twice my height, three times a Grimal." She smiled at Garlock.

"So how many more Nusas are out there?" Zac asked, going back to scratching Nusa's head.

"Not many. We need to help Nusa find a mate."

"Can't you take her back to Mersha to find a mate?" Breezy asked. Garlock gave his usual huff, and then realizing they could not know these things, he uttered an apology.

"We can go to Mersha," Mirrah said "but would not find perlins. The Mersans died out many cords ago. The Vogans now live among the ruins—foul beings. They would kill and eat a perlin if they could. Believe the flesh will give power to read minds." A rumble echoed in Nusa's throat. The teens exchanged more bewildered looks.

"Cords?" Isaac asked.

"Yes, many cords be twirled since the last Mersan walked the hills of blossom and bloom." Isaac shook his head. Mirrah reached inside her robe. "The question we need to answer," she withdrew a long dagger and pointed it toward the boys, "is who you three are and why you are here?" Breezy gasped and clutched Zachary's arm. Garlock drew his knife and stepped toward the table. Isaac's heart fell as he stared at the long pointed blade.

7 A KNIFE AND A POEM

Mirrah looked at them oddly then carefully handed the knife to the boys.

"Can you read this?" she asked. Breezy exhaled long and loud like a balloon. Mirrah wrinkled her brow. The knife was beautiful yet simple in design. The boys' father made custom knives, so they looked at it with special interest. The blade was about seven inches long with graceful lines that formed a tactical point—a fighting knife made for piercing. The metal had an intricate Damascus pattern with fine lines of bronze melded into the blade. The handle was of the same stone as the pillar, carved with similar inscriptions. With the light it would change from cloudy white to translucent, then clear. If viewed from the end, it became black. Isaac turned it over several times before passing it on to Zac. Nusa came and looked over Zac's shoulder. Her whiskers tickled his ear.

"Nusa." He chuckled and moved to the side.

Mirrah's eyes were locked on the boys as they handled the knife. "The script is Lorian," she said. "No one today can read it—Sasson made sure of that."

Zac held the knife for a while, looking closely at the writing. "Why do I feel like I've seen this before?" Garlock guffawed and then caught himself. Mirrah and the others looked on in silence. "This belonged to someone great, didn't it?" He looked to Mirrah for clues, but she did not say a word. Zac turned the knife around. He opened his mouth but hesitated.

"Speak your feeling," Mirrah said.

"Last one to die," Zac said barely audible. "He died of… old age—not like the others." Zac then gave a big silly grin. "Sorry, don't know why I said that." Yet he knew what he was saying was somehow true.

"What others?" Mirrah asked, eyes glowing.

"The others—the eleven."

Mirrah breathed a long sigh. She put her hand over her mouth. She was about to cry. Breezy touched Mirrah's arm.

"You okay?"

Mirrah's eyes moistened. "This is beyond wonder." She looked to Zac. The room felt frozen in time. "Can you… read it? Of course you cannot read it. But how can you know this if you do not even know the name of Ariel?" They all sat silent as she lightly wiped each eye. "This knife is old, very old," she said in almost a whisper. "It belonged to one of the eleven—the last of the mighty men—Yonnan the brother of Yannan. It has been in my family for many, many generations."

"Who were these eleven?" Isaac asked.

"The mighty men who fought beside the Prince."

"So the inscription? What does it say?"

She shook her head. Zachary looked at the black lines etched into the handle like scrimshaw. He looked for a while, thinking of the pillar, but nothing happened. He handed it back to Mirrah.

"So no one know what it says?" he asked.

"I was hoping one of you might." She passed it on to Breezy who looked at it briefly and handed it back. They sat in silence as Garlock stirred the fire sending sparks out into the room. The three were trying to take in all that had been talked about over breakfast. The sun shone off the new snow, flowing with warmth into the room. Isaac and Breezy went and sat by the fire. Zachary poured himself some drink and brought the cup to his lips. He paused a moment and set it down slowly. His eyes followed Mirrah as she carried things from the table. He cleared his throat rather loudly.

"Is there an island called... Moss?"

"Yes," she answered. "Why?"

"Well... does this make any sense?" He closed his eyes and spoke a little rhyme:

> "On the Isle of Moss,
> Near the cave of Torrin,
> Are the tombs of Dross,
> The box of Hornin."

He opened his eyes, feeling a bit foolish. Mirrah did not respond. She just stood there holding a bowl of bread as if turned to stone. Zac suddenly felt stupid for encouraging Mirrah's hope.

"I'm sorry," he said. "I just saw it... in my... mug."

Isaac came back to the table. Garlock threw another log into the fire and came near. Mirrah just stared. Garlock had his hand on his knife.

"How we know these sproots not be sent by Sasson himself? How does a carn know they be in me hovel last night? What makes ya think to be trustin' some wood mice in odd garbs? Look at 'em. They don't know a horl from a perlin." His face flushed red.

Mirrah flung her hair back and glared. "You look at them. Look at Nusa. Do you really think they are of Sasson?"

"I'm a lookin' at 'em. I'm seein' the same shiverin' mice that be standin' at me door... who go blunderin' into the wood... at night! No thorne nor blade... boltin' right into open meadow lookin' to feed starvin' horls. That be what I'm seein's. I begs yeer pardon, me lady, but just gettin' it in the open."

"So you do not think they have come by Ariel?"

"By Ariel? They can't even use a thorne or a long blade. And I'm still wonderin' if there be an Ariel. And if he be the one that sent 'em, he ought to check his stock before releasin' it. They couldn't help us out a tree-rat's hole. I put me life out for 'em last night, as did Nusa, and all we gets be a ditty that's gonna send us to the cursed Isle of Moss." He snorted as he shook his head. "Again, I beg yeer pardons. I just like it out in the air. Holdin' in smoke just makes one burn."

"Ariel's ways are not our ways." Mirrah fought to keep her composure. "He does not choose the things we would choose to show his power."

The teens sat silent as Garlock's words brought them back to reality. They were somewhere they did not belong, and they were just kids. Mirrah had made them feel they were sent somehow. Garlock brought the reality check.

"He's right," Isaac said, "we don't know anything about this world, not even how we got here. We need to get home. I need to get Zac and Breeze back. We don't belong here. We would help if... honestly, what could we do?"

Mirrah lowered her head and briefly closed her eyes, and then looked at Nusa, as if seeking help. "If Ariel has sent you, he will equip you. You need only be willing. Ariel will guide you and give whatever is needed, when it is needed." She sighed. "Surely you cannot believe you came by tossing pebbles?"

"Pebbles?"

"Ah... by chance."

"Don't know what to think." Isaac said. His back began to hurt. "We need to get home. I'm sorry you... I just don't see how..." All of a sudden, home seemed far away, like they had been gone for weeks. He had to focus to picture his room, his bed, the sofa and TV, his mother, familiar food and friends at school. "School! I have a test next week. What are we doing? Our parents are probably going crazy. I'm sorry... this isn't our world."

Mirrah swung her long thick hair in a wide circle as she turned to walk toward the window. Her arms were crossed as she stared into the clean white world of the wood. No one moved but Nusa. The giant lynx got up and went to wedge her head under Mirrah's arm. The fire popped and sparks flew about inside the fireplace. Breezy sat down on the fur rugs near the fire. She was still wrapped in her robe, but her head was down. She sniffled just a little as she wiped her eyes with one hand.

"Garlock," Mirrah turned from the window, "if you were not a trusted friend, I would think you had been sent by Sasson." She paced slowly, her face distraught. The room was very still. "Isaac," she said, "I will be honored to help you return home, but…" She paused a long time. "I believe you cannot return, until your purpose here is finished."

Zachary looked up and suddenly pointed to the window behind Mirrah. "Look!" A huge black form passed by the window. A raspy cry, rough and coarse, came from outside. For a moment no one moved. Garlock listened then laced his fur boots. He snatched up his thorne and went for the door.

"Garlock," Mirrah whispered, "you cannot. It will kill you."

"Just gonna fluff its feathers," he said, carefully raising the latch. Nusa bounded to the door and slipped out with him. The others sat silent, waiting for instruction. The last time one of these came they had to flee.

Mirrah went to the opposite window and stared into the wood. They waited. Mirrah then said softly, "It will be alright, but we need to leave." After a few more minutes of silence, Garlock and Nusa returned.

"Gone." He stamped the snow from his boots. "Hard say how long it be listenin'—tracks be all about the mound." He looked to Mirrah, his thorne in hand. "What be yeer wish?"

"We must leave," Mirrah said. "Isaac, I know you wish to return home, but now the need is your safety." She gathered things from the table. "This carn was sent to find you. Sasson wants you. He will send parlords on their worls. If we stay, we will die… or be taken to Skone Lor—his fortress." They all just stared at her. She moved like a queen in her robe and long flowing hair. "We must flee," she said again. "There is no choice now—no choice for any of us."

"Why does he want us?" Breezy asked, her eyes wide.

"I do not know. If the stone has called you…"

Isaac picked up his coat. Something strange burned in his

chest. "How much time do we have... before these parlords and horls come?"

"Not horls," Garlock snarled, "worls."

"That's what I said?"

"No, ya said—"

"Please!" Mirrah slammed a pouch onto the table. "Parlords ride worls—like horls but more powerful. We must hurry. We have maybe a rill's time. We must reach Kharlome before they reach us."

"Kharlome?" Garlock threw up his arms. "By Mulder's mire, why to be me?"

"We can find a ship there. Everyone, quickly, please."

"Ship?" Garlock wrinkled his hairy face. "Why a ship?"

"To the Isle of Moss."

"Aiya!" Garlock grumbled words no one could understand as he gathered his things. The teens stood watching.

"You are a free Grimalkyn!" Mirrah said, "no one is making you come."

"I wish I be free," he said then went back to his grumbling.

Isaac's thoughts were swimming, no, drowning. Frustration started boiling.

"What's a rill's time?" he asked.

"Oh, mighty Arnon, be we leaving or dying?" Garlock was already at the door with Nusa.

"As our meal time this morning, so is a rill." Mirrah tossed Isaac a leather pouch. "Get your things together, pack some food, talk later." The three looked at each other. This was not happening. Isaac's wound started to burn. He remembered the horls. Whatever world they were in was real—unexplainable, confusing, unwanted—but real.

"What do we do?" Zac asked.

Breezy gave them a fearful look. She had tears on her cheeks. Zac motioned for her to get her things. She turned and went into the bedroom. The fear on her face struck both boys in the gut. What were they doing? What had they gotten her into?

Zac moved fast, gathering his stuff, his mind racing. Can't

somebody help us? Why are we are always going through woods and snow? I just want to go home. A thought shot through his brain. What if we have to fight? His whole body shuddered. I'm barely a teenager. I don't want to fight.

"Here, sling this on your shoulder." Mirrah handed Zac a satchel full of food. He did not realize he had been standing, all set to go. He put it on and then suddenly turned to Isaac.

"Your backpack. Isaac, where's your backpack?"

"Must have left it at Garlock's cabin. Would have saved some pain." He arched his back, wincing. He asked Mirrah for more of the pain-killing brew. She shook her head.

"It will make you sleepy. I have dressing for your wounds. Quickly now." She then went into the bedroom and found Breezy slowly getting dressed, sniffling. Mirrah held her close. "It will be alright. I have seen us reach Kharlome. I have friends there."

Breezy sniffled loudly. "I don't want to leave. I don't want any more bad things to happen. I don't want to go out there."

Mirrah continued to hold her close. "If you trust me, then trust that we will be safe. You must get ready. We have such little time." She gave Breezy a hug and helped her get ready.

As they gathered together at the door, Mirrah took a sheathed sword off a wooden peg and handed it to Isaac. The sheath was of intricately decorated leather with small white rings. Isaac drew the blade. It was like a pirate's cutlass, but straighter. The handle was carved in the pattern of a panther or Nusa-like creature.

"It was my husband's," Mirrah said. "Even a man of peace must carry a sword." Isaac wondered if she meant her husband or him. She helped him sling the scabbard on his back. It was worn with the handle extending over the left shoulder. He groaned at first and then found a pain-free spot.

"It'll help hold your coat together," Zac said admiring the beautiful sheath.

"Keep yeer skin together, too," Garlock said. He actually smiled. "Aiya... to Kharlome then? May Ariel be walkin' with us," he growled, but they all knew, he meant every word.

8 THE TRAIL TO KHARLOME

It was hard to leave Mirrah's earth covered home. While brief, the time there had been wonderfully rich and warm. It had felt safe. It was like they had known Mirrah, Nusa, and grumpy Garlock for a long, long time, much longer than one night. And the horls... the terror of the attack was fresh, yet the dreadful fear was gone. They stepped out into the bright morning light, willing to walk the wintry woods again. But now a new dread arose—worls and parlords, whatever they were—moved somewhere in the woods. The teens ventured on. Maybe it was Mirrah. She had a strength about her, a strength of love, a love for them.

The sun was bright, the new snow white, the air crisp and clean. Nusa seemed to know the way and scouted up ahead. Mirrah took the lead, while Garlock took the rear. Mirrah had wrapped her hair with a fine cord that wound down and then back up forming a diamond pattern. She, like Garlock, wore high leather moccasins with fur linings. Her pants and jacket were like wool dyed black. She wore a dark vest of fleece into which she tucked her hair. She wrapped a thin soft fur scarf around her head and neck like an Arab kaffiyeh. A sword like Isaac's hung on her back, its handle above her left shoulder.

It was tough trudging through the snow again, legs stiff and sore. The land sparkled, as if magical. The sun's warmth poked through the trees drawing them onward. They kept a course toward the sun and eventually came to a small trail where a few deer and a fox had broken the new snow. They walked without speaking. The swoosh of nylon pants and coats sounded off in the otherwise silent wood. Garlock and Mirrah moved through the brush like deer—quiet and smooth.

After a good hour, they entered what Garlock called the 'real' wood of Yorne. Mirrah said it was an ancient wood of great history. The trees here grew huge. The land was free of brush beneath the high spreading limbs, making easier travel over rolling hills and down through sunken valleys.

Isaac stopped to look up. The trees were like nothing he had ever seen. The lowest limbs were three and four stories up. Some trees' trunks were bigger than his bedroom. "A guy could live inside these trees," he said to Zac. "Never seen a woods like this." It was mysterious yet wonderful.

"It's like we're tiny people," Breezy said, her voice low. Garlock had shushed them several times before. He did not want any 'un-be-needed jabber whilst on the trail,' but this was too amazing to keep silent. Isaac pondered the size of the trees. He had never read or heard of any trees this size on any of the continents. Angst moved his gut.

"So who are these parlords?" he quietly asked Mirrah.

"Sasson's warriors, trained killers. We must not meet them." She too, kept her voice low.

"How many will come?"

"One, maybe two."

"One or two? Will we fight them?"

"Fight them?" Mirrah sounded like she had never considered the idea. "No, you do not fight a parlord."

"Why not?"

"They are killers. In the Kal Rone revolt, a whole troop of swordsmen and two dozen archers were defeated by a single parlord." She paused. "No, we must reach Kharlome."

Isaac's heart went heavy. A wave of misery and self-pity covered his soul. Anger returned. It mixed with resentment, even spite toward this unwanted intrusion into his life. Why can't we just go home?

"We're always going uphill." Breezy sighed, slogging heavy boots through the snow.

"You are tired," Mirrah said, "but we must keep going."

Garlock uttered something about 'snuffling sproots and wallering boondas.'

Isaac stopped. He let Breezy and Zac pass before turning to face Garlock trudging up the trail. "Why are you coming with us? If you don't think we're of any good to you and your messed up world, why are you bothering yourself… and us? Don't ya know 'yeer' way home?"

Mirrah and the others stopped. Isaac's heart beat hard. Garlock stood silent in the trail. Puffs of white expelled from his bushy beard; curls of hair poked out from under his hat. Zac held his breath. Garlock either had no answer or was planning the quickest way to rid the woods of this young stranger. A chill blew down the trail. Puffs of white from Isaac's mouth met those of Garlock. The great wood waited in silence. Then, the small agile man put his head down and continued walking forward, bumping Isaac as he passed by.

Isaac stood alone, looking back down the snowy trail.

Zac walked back. "You okay?"

"No, I'm not okay. This place is nuts. This whole thing is… whatever. Zac, what are we doing? What's happening to us? I can't figure any of this. Look at this place—look at these trees—where on earth are we?"

Breezy came and stood with the boys. "It's not what we want," she said, "but it's what we got. What else can we do? We gotta go with it." A small clump of snow fell from a limb. It drifted through the air dusting Breezy's face. "Shouldn't we be thankful they're willing to help us?" She wiped her cheeks.

"And die for us," Zac said.

Isaac arched his back and winced. He stared back down the trail, shoulders drooped. Home was somewhere back that way. "I hate this place."

"Come on," Zac said, "we have to keep going, don't we?"

Isaac gave a long sigh and then shuffled up the trail behind his brother and Breezy. They stayed together as they followed the winding tracks of Mirrah and Garlock through the wood of massive trees. They stopped to look at one whose trunk looked fifteen feet in diameter. The branches spread out in colossal arches, looking magical.

As they crested a hill, the trail merged onto a small road. They turned left following the tracks. They could see they were near the edge of the wood for the road sloped down into open fields where homes sat far off in the distance. At the top of the hill, the teens stopped.

"What gives?" Zac said, his voice cracking. "We weren't walking that slow, were we?" The road was empty. Mirrah and Garlock were nowhere to be seen. A rush of panic came with a breeze. How could Mirrah have left them? Zac thought of Isaac's words to Garlock.

"You shouldn't have said—"

"Ya gonna stand there or have some eatin's?" It was Garlock's gravelly voice. They turned and saw Mirrah and Garlock sitting on a log beside a large boulder, hidden in the shadows on the other side of the road.

Zac looked down the road. "I thought those tracks were yours."

"People traveling to Kharlome," Mirrah said.

"I thought you had… left us."

"And why would ya be thinkin' that?" Garlock did not even look up.

"Come eat and rest." Mirrah brushed snow from the log. Garlock looked straight at Isaac as he came toward them. He then got up from the log to allow Isaac to sit in his spot. Isaac felt sick. He had acted foolishly, but he didn't volunteer to get stuck in this place. It wasn't his choice, that was for sure.

"I'm starving." Breezy readily sat next to Mirrah, almost falling backward off the log. Mirrah handed them some dried meat, bread and cheese. "Are we almost there?" she asked before shoving in a large chunk of cheese.

"Once we cross those open fields, over that next ridge, we

will see Kharlome. I will leave you with Garlock once we near the city. You cannot enter the city in those clothes. I will find garments. We will then wait for dusk." She looked at them with tender eyes. It was only afternoon, and they were already weary.

Nusa had appeared ever so often as they traveled. Once she passed by with a large hare in her mouth, its bright blood staining her jowls, dripping dots of red onto the blanket of white. But now she was gone.

"Will Nusa be alright in the city?" Zac asked, remembering the talk of the Vogans in Mersha.

"We will watch her close. Perlins bring a fortune as they are highly prized by rulers."

"Why?"

"What better animal to have in court than one that knows the thoughts and intentions of the heart?"

Snow fell in clumps from high up in the gigantic trees. The day was calm but for an occasional breeze. The sun still shone bright and warm, making the wintry wood feel pleasant.

"We will spend as little time as possible in Kharlome." Mirrah put things back into her bag. "The eyes of Sasson are watching."

Garlock walked up ahead to where another small road merged on the right. Zac could see that he wanted them to get moving.

"We should get going, shouldn't we?" Zac said. They got up from the log and looked down the road into the distant horizon. A long cloud of gray melded into the sky.

Mirrah sighed. "The city of Kharlome."

Garlock stood silent, waiting for them to pass. He looked about as he took up his position in the rear. Isaac said nothing in apology to the small burly man. Zac watched his brother. He once told Breezy that an apology for Isaac was like a chicken trying to lay a square egg—it was probably not going to happen and if it did, it would be painful. He told himself he would help his brother offer some kind of apology.

They had taken maybe twenty steps toward Kharlome

when suddenly Nusa came bounding up the trail that merged on the right. She ran up beside Garlock and spun about snarling with intensity. Everyone froze. Goosebumps tingled every inch of skin. Garlock crouched low with his thorne at full draw. Breezy shuffled next to Zac. The giant trees of Yorne stood still.

9 "THE HEAVENS BE A SHIFTIN'S"

"Behind those trees." Mirrah pointed to three trees across from the boulder. She held her sword firmly in both hands. Standing where the roads merged, she looked down one, then the other. Isaac jumped behind two trees that grew close together. Each tree was small for the wood, about four feet across. Zac and Breezy climbed behind a larger tree with solid root sections that extended out from the trunk like little walls. They were just high enough to hide behind. They huddled close between two sections on the backside.

Zachary peered around to see Nusa dart off into the wood. His heart pounded hard. Breezy drew her knees to her chest and put her head down. She bit her lip, breathing short, rapid breaths through her nose. A minute went by without a sound. Only falling snow from the high limbs came drifting down. Zac remembered how quickly the horls had come, struck, and then vanished.

"Do ya see anythin'?" Garlock asked Mirrah.

"No, it is hidden from me."

"Maybe ya can't see, 'cause ya already know."

Garlock had barely finished speaking when suddenly the strangest sight came bounding up the road. Atop a huge leopard-like beast rode a man with a flowing fur cape. He wore a sleeveless coat of mail made of brass colored coins that looked like large fish scales. His arms were bare, muscular with brown skin that matched his leather leggings and laced fur boots. Brass armguards with small spikes covered his forearms. Gray fur stuck out from under the armguard and from under the chest armor—a fur lining between skin and metal. His cape was brown with a leopard pattern of dark red spots inside black circles. It flowed and bounced in time with the man's long black hair as the leopard beast loped up the road.

With a zipping twang, Garlock released his arrow. The man on the giant leopard flashed his arm to the side. Zac saw the arrow glance off and disappear. By the time Garlock set another arrow, the creature was already upon him. A huge paw swiped, striking Garlock, sending his thorne and arrow into the snow near Zachary's tree. A second swipe sent Garlock tumbling toward the boulder where they had just eaten lunch.

As Mirrah stood to face the rider and beast, a second one appeared on the road that merged on her left. It too had a rider like the first but a cape of black. Its beast was black except for one red paw. It had light vertical streaks of dull gray, like a tiger's stripes, but faint. Some stripes seemed to shimmer in the sun's light. Zac peered from behind the root wall, his mouth and eyes gaping. The beast, muscular and lean, skin stretched tight flashed through the woods of white. He shuddered as he watched it come. It did not seem possible the way it came with such incredible speed. Nor did it slow as it came toward Mirrah. With a giant leap, it flew into her, knocking her backward, pinning her beneath its red paw as it slid to a stop. Her sword landed near Isaac's tree somewhere in the fresh clean snow.

The first beast pawed at Garlock who lay motionless. Like a cat with a dying mouse, it batted Garlock back and forth. The rider, still on top, taunted Garlock to stand and fight. The other man, very large, had dismounted and now stood over Mirrah with a long doubled-edged kris-style sword. He held it pointed at her throat. The black leopard continued to hold her with its huge red paw. Both beasts and riders were focused on their prey.

Zachary looked to Isaac. He saw him peering between the trees. They glanced at each other. Terror filled their eyes. Breezy kept her head buried in her arms. Zac heard her losing control. He wondered how long they could stay unnoticed. He slowly raised his head peering with one eye over the root wall. Both men had their backs to them. Zac watched the leopard's tail twitch in rhythmic pulse.

Mirrah struggled beneath the crushing red paw, fighting to draw in breath. She pushed frantically at the paw as the large man stood with sword tip at her throat. Zac looked to his brother again. Isaac sat with his back to the tree, knees up, hands over his face.

A strange fire burned in Zachary's chest. A strength, an unction, a bold zeal filled his inner gut. Without thought, he darted out from behind the tree and snatched up Garlock's thorne. He frantically felt through the snow searching for the fallen arrow. At any moment the beast pinning Mirrah could turn and see Zac on all fours. Then he saw a short line in the snow. Zac sunk in his hand and pulled out the arrow. He crawled back over the tree trunk wall. Isaac had seen him. He watched his brother set the arrow and try to draw the thorne. Zac could barely bend the metal bow. Isaac slowly shook his head.

Zac dropped to his butt. Placing his feet inside the bow, he pulled the string with both hands. Still sitting on his butt, he placed his feet and the thorne atop the root wall. He tried to aim, but it took all to just hold the string and bow. "Where do I aim?" The large man atop the leopard was still leaning over, jabbing at Garlock. Zac strained to hold the string; it cut into his bare hands. "What am I doing?" He glanced over to Isaac, struggling to hold the string.

"Tung!" Suddenly the string and arrow were gone.

Zac fell backward as the bow released. He did not see the giant leopard leap into the air, its hind legs flailing too high, collapsing down onto its shoulder and head, crushing Garlock under its weight. The rider flew headlong into the boulder and tumbled down into a dazed heap. The startled beast bolted, stumbling toward the other road, biting at its side, craning its neck, tearing at its fur. Something had pierced its side.

When the man came to his feet, he stood bewildered, watching the frenzied flailing of his beast. Zac saw the leopard spinning in a crazed circle, gnawing at its side. Snow flung in all directions. The man, tall like the other, slowly approached his beast. The huge leopard suddenly stopped, stumbled a step, then another, coughed a gargled moan and collapsed onto the snow.

The large man just watched, his sword at his side, his leopard-spotted cape hanging still. Garlock quickly rose from the snow. He turned to run, then drew his long knife and darted back toward the man. He raised his arm to thrust his knife. He looked so small approaching the large black cape. Zac was about to close his eyes when the large man spun around, knocking the knife from Garlock's hand. A second backhand sent Garlock flying onto the road. His right ear and cheek bled bright red in the fresh snow.

The man standing over Mirrah also watched the drama. Dressed like the first, except for gold-colored armor, he spoke with a deep, calm voice. A small single horn, about three inches long, protruded from the center of his forehead. The boys looked to each other and simultaneously mouthed the words, "Who are these guys?"

"Where are the strangers?" the man asked Mirrah, intense but calm. His hair, woven in small tight braids that hung down the sides of his face, was oddly identical to Mirrah's in color. A tattoo or brand of black sat high on his left cheek. His breath condensed in the air.

"They are not with us," Mirrah said.

"Where are they?"

"They wanted to go home."

"And where is their home?"

"Possibly a place called Kan-sis near Toto. I honestly do not know."

Isaac noticed that she had not lied nor had she given away

their whereabouts. Garlock, on the other hand was not faring so well. He too was being questioned. The man with the red-spotted cape had a foot on his chest. He too had a small horn, only an inch or so, right in the center of his forehead. He asked questions while looking back at his mount, now motionless in the snow. "Where are the young ones?" This man spoke in a rough hoarse voice that seemed only capable of shouting. He was angry from the tumble and Garlock's feeble ambush.

"Don't know what yer talkin' 'bout," Garlock said. The man raised his doubled-edged sword and slapped Garlock on the ear with the flat side of the blade. The cold steel against his bleeding ear made the little man groan and stiffen in the snow. Zac had made a quick peek and now sat back behind the tree. He watched Breezy. She was listening, hurting for Mirrah and Garlock.

The man raised his sword, ready to strike Garlock again as he continued to question him. "Who are they, and what purpose do they bring?"

"I told ya, I don't know yer meanin's." The sword came down harder this time. Garlock growled through his teeth and shook himself in the snow.

It was then that the black leopard began to move toward the trees behind which Isaac hid. The interrogators stopped to watch the beast move cautiously to the other side of the road. It carefully put its nose to the gap between the two trees. Isaac slunk down low. The beast sniffed and growled low. Then it thrust its right red paw through the opening around the back of the tree. Large sharp claws ripped the tree just above Isaac's head. Shreds of bark crumbled onto Isaac, dropping inside his coat, down behind his neck. He jumped away from the tree pulling out the sword from over his shoulder. The tree was large enough to hide his form.

The red paw pulled back then shot in and struck hard right where Isaac had sat. It clawed for its prey with quick, jerking movements. Isaac raised the sword high, his face contorted. Zac watched, shaking his head. Isaac swung the sword with all his might.

A scream of piercing horror filled the woods. Blood splattered across the snow. The giant leopard pulled its paw and ran. With a limping gallop it disappeared into the trees. Breezy pulled herself into a tight, quivering ball. Isaac gave his brother a quick look and stepped out from behind the tree. The sword hung loosely at his side, blood dripping from the blade. The man over Garlock swung his sword up like a batter at the plate, waiting for the pitch.

The other, seeing they had found their quarry, raised his sword to pierce Mirrah's throat. He paused, eyes narrowed, as he sized up the strange young lad. For a second of endless time their eyes locked. Isaac could not move. His hand clutched the cold sword at his side. The man held his long kris-sword just inches above Mirrah's throat, his horn, glistening in the sun. She turned her head just enough to see Isaac and utter something into the cold winter air. A silent frozen moment hung still in the ancient wood.

Then, a bolting flash of brown and white sprang from the brush. It struck the man from behind. The beast toppled the man, rolling him to the edge of the road. Together, beast and man slammed into the two trees near Isaac. Nusa had come. Snow flew as the giant lynx fought man and sword. Cries and growls echoed through the giant trees. Man and beast blurred into a fury of movements too quick to follow. As suddenly as it began, it was over.

Nusa stood to her feet, her jaws engulfing the back of the man's neck. A front paw held him down with claws clutching his leg. He desperately tried to prop himself up with his left hand as he dug for his sword in the snow. Nusa glared at the other man standing over Garlock, his sword still held high. Her breath came out in quick, steady pants, blowing hot mist into cold air—one… two… three puffs. Then, with fire in her eyes she bit down hard. Two more breaths came, and she dropped the man, face down, horn first, into the snow.

The man over Garlock stood stunned. Isaac tried to swallow, his mouth pasty dry. Rage filled the large man's face. Their eyes met in one eerie flash of time. He uttered something as he glanced at the victim beneath his feet. Garlock grimaced, his eyes shut tight. Isaac looked away. Steel pierced flesh. A gargled gasp, and the wood of Yorne fell still.

Isaac opened his eyes. The tall man had lowered his sword, but confusion covered his face. A moment passed. Then he collapsed onto his knees, eyes locked on the lad with the sword. He tried to speak something as he slowly dropped, face down into the snow.

Garlock rolled quickly away from the body. He jumped to his feet and looked for his sword.

"It is done." Mirrah came and pulled the knife of Yonnan from the fallen man's neck.

Zac was slow to move from the cover of the tree. He put his hand on Breezy. "I think it's over." She had briefly peeked when Nusa struck, but quickly hid her face back in between her knees. She looked up, her eyes red and swollen.

"What was that scream?" She crawled out from behind the tree.

Mirrah hugged Nusa. She kissed the top of her furry head. "What would we do without you?" Mirrah's hands trembled.

"Aiya," Garlock groaned, wiping the blood from his face. He stood back, eyeing the blood and bodies in the snow. He made a wide circle as he walked to Isaac and behind the tree. He picked up the bloody severed claw and gave one loud single laugh. He slapped Isaac on the back, which made Isaac cry out in pain.

"Lad, ya cut a claw from Kore. This be a prizer, boy. I'll fix it for ya to hang about yeer neck." He was grinning wide, his bushy beard spread out like a cat's whiskers. He ran about like a child on caffeine and finally handed the bloody claw to Isaac. It was black and several inches long. A tuft of red fur mixed with the blood. Garlock became very serious. He stopped to eye the two bodies and the huge dead leopard. "The heavens be a shiftin's. This never been done... ever never."

Zac handed him the thorne. Garlock turned to the dead beast lying on the road. He shook his head, "How does this be?" He slapped Zac on the shoulder, knocking him into the tree. "Ya twisted me whiskers on that one, boy."

Breezy ran to Mirrah. "I thought we were all…" She jerked with shaking spasms as Mirrah held her tight.

"It's over," Mirrah said. "We are alive, but we must go quickly. We have done a terrible thing."

"Terrible?!" Garlock huffed. "Sparklin' be the word. Do ya know who that be there in the snow?" He looked to the boys as he pointed at the man killed by Nusa. They shrugged. "That's Klonen, the parlord of Yorne. Klo… nen! By Mulder's mire! This other boon… who cares? And that claw, lad, that's a claw from Kore. This'll be the tale 'round many a fires for a ten-cord and more." Garlock turned about, waving his arms this way and that. Then he stopped. "Why be Sasson sendin' Klonen for these sproots?"

"So these are parlords… riding worls?" Isaac asked.

"They was. Ha! Aiya! Ya fight 'em, without knowin' 'em? Mighty Arnon." Garlock threw his hands up one more time.

"This looms bad." Mirrah sheathed her sword, hands still trembling. "Yes, these are parlords. Ariel has saved us, but it bodes trouble for Yorne. Sasson will kill many for this, burning homes and hovels. I do not know how this happened, but we must leave." She tossed Isaac a cloth. "Clean your sword. Leave the cloth." Isaac's hands also shook as he cleaned his sword. He gazed at the two large bodies on the snowy road. A worl, or giant leopard, lay in the road on the right. He tossed the bloodied cloth.

Garlock did a quick spinning jig. "This'll be the talk in town."

"We need to leave now." Mirrah said.

Garlock pulled his arrow from the fallen worl and cleaned it with snow. He was about to cut a claw from the dead worl when Mirrah scolded him. Isaac held out his hand with the bloody worl claw.

"Take this one," he said, "and…" There was a long pause. "And forgive me… for what I said back there."

Garlock looked at the bloody worl claw. "Ya needn't buy

me forgivin's, lad."

"I know. Just want you to have it. It'll mean more to you anyway." He smiled as Garlock took the large claw. Garlock's battered ear still bled, and his fur jacket was torn from the worl's claws. "Thank you," Isaac added, "for all you've done… for us."

A sense of shock still hung in the air as they set out for the city. It had come so suddenly and now was over. Breezy gave way to a brief shaking spasm now and then. The sun was closer to the horizon, and it was still an hour's walk to Kharlome.

"We must reach Kharlome before news of this." Mirrah began the descent out of the Wood of Yorne into the open fields outside Kharlome.

The brisk walk helped steady their hearts and calm their nerves. Isaac had been silent for quite some time before he quickened his pace to walk beside Mirrah and Nusa. Mirrah's hands were still quaking, and she often turned to look behind. Isaac stretched his stride to stay in step with the tall slender woman, his mind searching for solutions.

"May I ask you some questions?"

"Please."

"Last night, when we came to your home, it seemed you already knew what happened to us in the woods. And our names; you called Breezy by her real name."

Mirrah smiled. "I am Pharen. There are not many left. We can sometimes see and know things that are not found through the eyes and ears."

"Like intuition?"

"More. A Pharen is able to see into the whole, where time is not seen as: was, now, and will be."

"The whole?"

"The realm beyond—the complete world—the unseen real as well as this that we see. Does that bring meaning for you?"

"Actually, yes. Our eyes don't see it all. And time is tied to matter, affected by motion. You wouldn't know of Einstein would you?"

"Was he Pharen?"

Isaac chuckled. "Kind of. So you can see the future?"

"Sometimes by a glimpse, sometimes a feeling, and sometimes, a dream."

"How?"

"It is not by my will, but at Ariel's will, to be used as such."

"So you can't make it happen?"

"Some Pharens tried. They sought to control the gift, to use it for gain. They became deceivers and manipulators. Some were ensnared into serving Sasson."

"How did you see us?"

"That evening, I was reading by the fire. I saw you walking in the wood and entering Garlock's hovel. I saw you and Garlock in the meadow. I knew you were coming to my home. Ariel gave me these pictures, so I asked him who you were and what purpose you carried. He showed me only your names."

They walked on in silence, then Isaac asked, "So what purpose do you think we have?"

"I have no answer, but it is good you are willing to ask. I know Ariel has sent you. Two parlords and a worl killed in one day—never in my lifetime or my father's—only in the legends of old. Something has shifted."

"You can say that again."

"Why?"

"It means, 'I agree.' I wish I knew how we shifted from our world to this place."

"I am not sure 'place' or 'world' are the right words. I think it is something beyond the realms of what we see."

"The whole." Isaac pondered a recent discussion at school on dimensions within the atomic and subatomic, antimatter and particle anomalies. He chuckled. Could all this be happening in his own backyard? It's got to be a dream, a long dream, a very long, very real dream.

They crossed the open land of fields slowly descending. Small stone walls and stone farmhouses spread out across the fields. They occasionally heard a dog barking and wondered what they looked like considering the creatures they had seen so far. The sun was almost set in the wood behind them as the city wall came into view. Nusa no longer strayed about but walked close to Mirrah. Strange, thought Isaac, how she prefers Mirrah to Garlock, her owner. Nusa looked up at him as he considered this.

"You cannot enter the city with your clothing," Mirrah said. "Wait for me in that thicket up ahead. I am sorry; it will be cold, but we must go through the city to find a ship."

"Ship?" His stomach went nauseous. Mirrah did not answer.

When the others caught up, she pointed toward the thicket. "Wait there until I return with cloaks. Stay out of sight." Just then they heard voices coming from behind. Three men came running down the road from the wood. Mirrah gave the teens a shove. "Quickly. Behind that wall."

10   BATTLE AT THE CITY GATE

They climbed over a small stone wall and lay silent in the snow. They listened to the men shouting to Mirrah. The men came running with their mouths jabbering. With so much gasping and huffing and talking of parlords and blood, little could be understood. Mirrah told them she too had seen the dead parlords. As the men ran off, she bid the teens, farewell, promising to return as soon as she could. She walked briskly toward the city that now began to glow with a myriad of lights as the day gave way to dusk.

The air was cold as they crawled into the thicket at the edge of the field. Garlock cleared debris and snow from a grassy patch near the center. "Find dry wood," he told the boys. "It's goin' be gettin' colder." He took a pouch from his satchel and prepared for making a fire. Breezy just sat and watched. She remembered the fire in the small cave. It had been scary yet cozy. Everything had been going so well that day. How did they get lost? She thought back to their trekking about, unable to find the pillar. She remembered the absence of their tracks when leaving the pillar. Something magical had happened yesterday. Why?

All of sudden, a small fire snapped and crackled. She looked at Garlock and smiled. He was such a funny little man, or Grimalkyn, whatever that was.

"That'll keep the cold out yeer soul, missy," he said, returning her smile.

"Thank you, Garlock. You're amazing."

The boys had found some wood, but it was hard moving about the thicket and finding wood that was dry. They cleared more snow and brought some tall dead grass they had found in a gully. Breezy could only watch, mesmerized by the fire, weary from the long day. Isaac all at once realized the intense pain in his back. "Must have been running on adrenaline," he said to no one in particular.

They took the last bits of cheese and bread in their satchels and tried to enjoy their situation. They were thankful to have a fire. Sitting in the cold, waiting for someone, is always miserable.

"Where's Nusa?" Breezy said with a start. No one had noticed that she was gone until now.

"She'll be alright, missy. Don't concern yeerself. She's prob'ly getting some eatin's." They heard dogs barking and fearful whimpering. "That'd be her," he said with a grin.

The bread and cheese made them thirsty, so they scooped handfuls of snow. Zac had just filled his mouth with a handful when he heard something coming through the thicket. It was nearly dark, and their eyes had adjusted to the firelight. Garlock pulled out his knife and stepped back from the fire. Then, they saw what could only be Nusa, dragging a small goat in her mouth. She was fighting to get it through the brush and trees. She finally entered the clearing and, standing near the fire, dropped the goat.

"Oooh." Breezy squirmed backward.

"She brought it for us, Breeze," Zac said.

They watched in awe as Garlock quickly prepared the goat. Although Breezy had to hold her nose and look away most of the time, she had no problem eating once the meat was cooked. It was comical watching each other holding huge legs of goat meat, gnawing like barbarians. Nusa held her portion down on the snow between her paws and pulled at the meat, chewing loudly, making them laugh as they imitated her chomping. Garlock watched in silence; his face showed deep concern.

Isaac wiped his mouth and cleaned his hands with snow. "So is Mirrah really going to look for a ship in Kharlome?" he asked.

"That be the plan—sail to the Isle of Moss."

"What do you need there?"

"Ain't got a whisker's twitch. Ask yeer little brother."

Zac looked up, pausing mid-bite.

Isaac shook his head. "You guys are taking this too serious." His voice rose as he spoke. "We can't go off sailing somewhere 'cause of that."

"Mirrah thinks different, laddie."

Zac looked at them both and wondered. He tried to think of any other time he had ever seen letters and words like that. It was indeed highly unusual but not something for which he would charter a ship.

"Garlock," Isaac said, "why did you come with us?" He quickly added, "I mean, I'm glad, very glad, just wondering why you didn't go back home."

"Wonderin' the same…" He poked in the fire. Sparks sailed up into the darkening sky. "Just knew it be the thing to do."

"Ever been to this Isle of Moss?" Breezy asked.

"Never. They say it's from where the cursed kroaken-gaggers came. Foul creatures, should never been given life."

"Kroaken-gaggers?" they asked in unison.

"Of course, ya wouldn't know. Smelly they be. Breath will turn yeer innards out. Ya know, lizards?" They all nodded. "They're soft slimy-skinned lizards. They can stand and have the gift o' speech—only Ariel knows how they got that. When they stand, they're taller than you and me. They love flesh—foul vexations. You don't see 'em now cause they're in their holes."

"Are any around here?" Breezy asked.

"Of course, but they're all sleepin' out the cold. Snug in them holes."

"And what do their holes look like?" She looked straight at the boys.

"Some be big, in the side of a hill. When we find one, we smoke 'em out and run 'em through."

"A hole big enough for us to sit in and... say... have a fire?" Breezy held a tight gaze on the boys.

"Can be. One that size... may have a dozen sleepin' there."

The boys sat silent. Breezy gave them her meanest look. It was more like a child acting the villain in the school play. She spoke to Garlock with her eyes still on the boys.

"I think we sat and ate in one."

Garlock jerked his head back. "You're twistin' me beard." Breezy then told him how they had found the cave and built a fire, ate and talked. Garlock would erupt with laughter as she talked, struggling to restrain himself. He shook his head in bewilderment. "Yeer strange ones alright, and the hand of Ariel is right above ya." He continued to quietly laugh, looking at Nusa and shaking his head.

They huddled together about the fire, trying to stem the cold; then Breezy asked, "Shouldn't Mirrah be here by now? It feels late." Garlock's face showed that he shared the same concern. It was late. Horls would soon be roaming about the fields, and the city gates were probably closing. If she did not arrive soon they would have to seek shelter somewhere as they could not spend the night here around the fire, especially with a limited wood supply. They were all silent, contemplating. Then Isaac, whose back kept aching, stood and announced he would look for more wood.

"Stay in the thicket," Garlock said. "Don't go near the edges or into the open." Nusa got up to accompany Isaac. The sky was clear with a near full moon to light the night. He fought his way through the thick under-bush looking for anything that would burn. Then he heard faint voices back at the fire.

"Is Mirrah back?" He looked to Nusa. They stood listening since he wanted to find more wood. Then, he heard a man's voice and knew it was not Garlock's. Nusa rumbled a low growl. "We better get back." As they came closer to the fire, they saw a tall man speaking with Garlock. Nusa growled low, putting her shoulder into Isaac, causing him to stop and listen.

"Yes," the man said, "Mirrah is waiting with beds and food. We should go quickly." Isaac could faintly make out another man standing behind. It was obvious that Garlock was suspicious and reluctant to go with the man, and they couldn't fight or flee in the thicket. "Let's go. You can trust me. How do you think I found you?"

Garlock held his sword ready. "And why be ya thinkin' we know this one called Mirrah?"

Then, the man spoke to the one behind and instantly a small one-handed crossbow was aimed at Garlock's chest. The man's tone changed. "Come now, or die."

Breezy gasped and reached for Zac. Garlock did not move.

"Where is the other?" The man was gruff. Garlock did not reply. "Simple enough," he said, looking at Zac. "Tell me or she dies." He then raised his hand, ready to signal the other with the crossbow.

"He's looking for wood," Zac blurted.

"Then call him."

Zac did not know what to do. The man with the crossbow moved in closer toward Breezy. Garlock calmly sat down a little further from the fire.

"Go ahead, lad. Give a yell."

Zac gave a wimpy crackled call for Isaac. It seemed to go nowhere as if trapped in the thicket. The fire snapped loudly, and Breezy jumped. Isaac watched with Nusa at his side. He wanted to work his way to a position of ambush, but he dared not move. After ten minutes and a few more feeble calls from Zac, the man ordered them to stand and march.

"Don't bother running; my men are all about, and we wouldn't want you getting hurt." The other man followed Garlock with the crossbow aimed at his back. Isaac saw that Garlock was not carrying his thorne and quiver, so he waited.

Isaac assumed they had circled the thicket and would wait for him to emerge. Only when he looked about for Nusa did he realize she was gone. He crept toward the fire feeling for Garlock's thorne and quiver. He found them lightly covered with the dry grass. He lay motionless, listening and wondering what he should do. He fought despair, the urge to surrender. His back burned, and the resentment at being stuck in this world welled up again.

It was cold lying on the ground. The image of returning home without his brother or Breezy made his gut turn. He cursed under his breath. I'm so alone, so useless—so stupid for getting us into this. He screamed inside his mind. I hate this game. I want out. I'm done.

Self-pity came with overwhelming force. He began to hate whomever this Ariel was and his messed-up world. Any creator who brings innocent people into his battles deserves a rebellion. He had the urge to side with Sasson. Maybe he had good cause for his rebellion. Isaac wondered if they had been duped into joining the wrong side.

"This stinks." The fire burned low. He shivered. "What do I do?" He could hear the men talking outside the thicket. "Where is Mirrah?"

He decided to go out the opposite side where he had seen a stone wall. Maybe it would provide some cover. He made his way through the brush. He had slung Garlock's thorne and quiver on his back along with his sword. It hurt. Seeing no one, he hopped over the wall and followed it away from the thicket, staying low as he ran over the hard frozen ground.

He realized, as he ran, that a part of him actually found it all thrilling. The situation, tormentingly frustrating, even painful, caused something in his gut to come alive. He began to think hard as to how far it was to the city gates and if he could arrive ahead of them. He saw the road leading to the city and the numerous stone walls with little compounds spread out among the fields. The moon was now high in the sky, and he thought he saw a glimpse of the others walking down the main road. With no plan in mind other than getting as close as possible before they arrived at the city gate, he cut across open fields, jumping walls and avoiding homes.

He came around a wall overlooking a field and suddenly stopped. He gasped, holding his breath. His lungs burned. Lower down in the field were two horls. One was pulling flesh from a goat while the other snarled. Isaac pressed back against the wall and tried to breathe steady. Nerves bucking to run wild. He jumped a short wall and ran parallel to the field with the horls. "Don't need those right now."

He finally joined a small road that led to the city gates. He could see it would merge at a right angle to the main road. It hurt to run, opening his wounds. The fields had turned to walled courtyards and houses built of stone. Little alleys branched off in random directions. The cold air smelled of pig manure and straw. Dogs barked as he ran the frozen but muddy road, his winter boots clomping. He wondered about the dogs. "Don't want to… find out now," he panted.

He came around a bend and was suddenly alongside a canal that channeled water along the base of the city wall like a moat. A stone bridge just ahead, brought the main road over the canal up to the city gates. His road was lower, level with the canal. He looked ahead to a short steep embankment. It angled up to the main road and the bridge. He could see the city gates—two massive wooden doors—closed.

Footsteps on the main road were coming toward the bridge. He could not see who was coming since the road was lined with houses and walls. If it were Zac and Breezy, he had to move now to get to the bridge before them. He sprinted along the edge of the canal and came into the shadows of the bridge just as the others came up the main road. He could stand out of sight in the shadows on the lower road, yet have a clear view as they approached.

He saw only three men escorting Garlock, Zac and Breezy. His heart beat hard as he considered using the thornc. "I could try… to wound them." His stomach turned queasy at the thought of shooting someone. "I've never shot one of these… thorne things. Legs and arms are small targets." He mouthed the words as he panted. He wondered what weapons they were carrying. "Come on, decide." His heart beat so fast it made his head hurt. He slid the thorne off his shoulder, nocked an arrow and tested the string. The arrow fletching was of thin fur strips instead of feathers.

"You're good with a bow. It's just like deer hunting. Do what you have to do."

The tall man led Zac and Breezy who walked side by side. Following a ways behind came Garlock with the other two men. They walked behind him, prodding the lagging Grimalkyn with jabs and pokes.

It was happening too fast; they were almost to the bridge. Isaac drew the thorne. It was much harder than he had imagined, but it got easier as the steel unwound, like a compound bow at full draw. He dared not aim at the tall man since Breezy and Zac were right behind. Garlock blocked the view of one of the men behind him, so he took aim at the man behind Garlock's right. He could hear them talking—hear his own breathing—his pulse thumping loud in his ears. He aimed for the man's thighs. He held steady as the tall man walked up the bridge toward the gates. His target was now only thirty feet away. He suddenly realized he had no plan after the first shot.

This whole thing is crazy. I'm fifteen and aiming at someone I don't even know. He no longer whispered but spoke the words in his mind.

They were almost past the angle for him to shoot, when something fast came out of the shadows behind them. It tackled the man behind Garlock's left and dragged him down the embankment off the other side. The tall man in front did not even notice as he, Zac, and Breezy continued to the gate. The other guard behind Garlock stopped and slung his small crossbow into position. Isaac knew it could only be Nusa, and if the other side was like this one, there was no room for her to hide.

He let the arrow fly.

Only when he opened his eyes did he realize he had shot blind. He saw his arrow, deep in the guard's hamstring. The man dropped backward to the ground with a cry of pain, accidentally firing his crossbow. The bolt thumped into the gate just beside the tall man's head.

"You fool," he shouted, whirling around to then stand stunned. Isaac nocked another arrow and ran out of the shadows up the embankment onto the main road. Garlock reclaimed his sword from the wounded guard.

Now in plain sight, Isaac aimed at the tall man standing at the gate.

"Shoot 'em!" Garlock yelled.

Seeing Isaac hesitate the tall man grabbed Breezy, holding her as a shield.

"Open the gate!" he yelled.

"Shoot!" Garlock yelled again.

The large gate on the right creaked open and the tall man pulled Breezy inside. Zac was left standing alone, dazed at what had just happened.

"Come on," Isaac called.

"Breezy!" Zac yelled, looking for her through the open gate.

"Run!" Isaac knew a hundred men could come out that gate any moment.

Suddenly the tall man reached out and grabbed Zachary by his coat. Zac pulled away falling to the ground. Isaac released his arrow more out of terror than thought. It pierced the tall man's right hand, pinning it to the wooden gate. A cry of agony and rage filled the crisp night air. Zachary scrambled to his feet and ran back over the stone bridge. He passed the fallen guard then spun back and scooped up the crossbow. He took a few more running steps then turned back and jerked a small quiver of bolts off the man's belt.

Garlock, Isaac, and Zac then ran back down the main road. Small alleyways branched off to the left and right. They heard the twang of crossbows followed by zings and metal bolts striking the cobblestones as they ran.

"This way," Zac called out, turning to the right. Isaac looked back at the city gate. No one pursued them. They followed Zac to the right down a small alley that ran parallel to the city wall. It crossed over the same canal that flowed toward the city gate. Nusa joined them as they ran over a little stone bridge. The alley eventually met the city wall again but half a mile up from the gate. The wall was filled with windows. Random lights shone out from the wall. Garlock said that people lived inside the wall.

"Why is no one chasing us?" Isaac asked in panting breaths.

"Horls," Garlock said bent over, hands on his thighs, breathing hard. "Where ya takin' us, lad?"

"I'm not sure," Zac said. "But I think… we go this way."

"What do you mean, think?" Isaac asked rather rudely.

"We should go this way… that's all."

Clutching their sides, gasping, they slowed to a walk. Garlock saw a young woman looking out from a small window in the wall two stories up. "What's this?" he whispered. They slipped into the shadows to watch. The woman looked about the alleys and courtyards below, then up at the moon shining bright. They fought to quiet their panting. Some dogs barked. The woman continued to search the alleys below.

Then, without saying anything, Zachary stepped out of the shadows and into the moon's full light. Isaac grabbed at his coat sleeve, but Zac jerked his arm away. The woman saw him.

"Zac," Isaac whispered sternly. Nusa suddenly gave an eerie low-pitched call that echoed off the city wall. Garlock groaned, wagging his head.

11 "LET'S GO DIE IN GLORY"

"Who are you?" the young woman called in hushed voice.

"Who are *you*?" Zac asked in the same manner.

"Are you in need of help?" She leaned further out the window. Nusa responded with another groaning call. The woman waited, and then was gone.

"We need to move," Garlock said from the shadows.

Suddenly a large knotted rope dropped from the window in the wall. The woman looked out again. Long, black hair hung from her head.

"May we come up?" Zachary called trying to keep his voice low.

"We?"

"Three of us." He motioned for the others to show themselves. Garlock was reluctant to expose his position to an unknown. Nusa suddenly bounded toward the knotted rope and digging in her claws climbed it like a frightened cat up a tree.

"Hoh," Garlock said, "put that in yeer mulger." They followed Nusa up the rope where they were met by a girl Isaac's height and age. She helped them into the room one by one and closed the small wooden doors over the window. The room was small and simple, tiny actually.

The girl's hair was a thick, black mane of crimped spirals reaching out and down to her lower back. Dressed in a long robe like Mirrah's, her facial features and light bronze skin, stunningly beautiful, seemed to glow in the fire's light. She went to stand beside Nusa scratching between the big lynx's tufted ears.

"I am Eryn of Myrrh." She looked directly at Isaac. He did not respond but only stared. Her dark eyes, intense and intriguing, held his gaze.

"I'm Zac, and this is Garlock. And that's my brother, Isaac of La La land." Zac was still breathing hard.

"Garlock of Yorne?"

"Yes, me lady Eryn. You've done grown." He gave a slight bow. "Not seen ya since ya be a green sprig."

"Is your uncle well?"

"He be well, miss."

Turning back to Isaac, she asked, "La La land? It must be far."

"No, it's, I mean, yes," Isaac stumbled over the words. "We're not... we're strangers... we're... I'm not from La La land." He gave Zac the look. "We're from... well it wouldn't matter, you wouldn't know. We come from a different place... dimension... vortex... I actually don't have a clue right now." Eryn tilted her head.

"Ya seen Mirrah?" Garlock asked.

"Mirrah?"

"Be travelin' with her. She went to buy cloaks and that be the last."

Garlock went on to tell of the teens coming from the wood, the carns, the horls, Klonen and Kore's claw, the thicket, and the battle at the city gate. Eryn listened with wonder.

"Carns... parlords... Klonen..." Eryn said the words slowly, especially the name, Klonen. She stood and walked about the tiny room, deep in thought. "Was the horn cut?"

"Pardon?"

"The other? Did he have his horn?" She looked very intense as she asked this question. The boys shrugged.

"Be not that one, miss." Garlock spoke gently. "It be the young one, the small horned."

"Garr," she said with a huff while studying the boys' clothes. "Mirrah brought you here… to Kharlome. Why?" She tossed her long thick hair to one side and looked hard at the boys. "Who are you? Why would Sasson want you?" Isaac was about to ask her why they were being hunted when she suddenly turned on Garlock. "Why do you lie to me, Garlock of Yorne? Maybe in a thousand moons with an army of Pharens, maybe then, but Klonen and Garr—and his worl—in one day? Why do you speak such jawble?" She eyed the boys again.

"Miss Eryn, me speaks the truth."

"He's telling the truth," Isaac said.

"And who are you to make such claim. The claw of Kore and live to tell? Do I look like a blind boonda?" She grabbed a knife that hung near the fire then suddenly stopped. A light rapping came from the door. She listened. No one moved. It came again. Eryn stepped to the wooden door. "Proclaim yourself?"

"It's me, Sherrabella."

Eryn opened the door slowly and just enough to let a young girl through. She was a little shorter than Zac and looked to be about his age. She wore plain loose fitted clothing, thin and patched. Her face was smudged a little. Her hair, streaked in blonde, yellow and light brown, was pulled into a loose ponytail. She stepped back when she saw the two boys.

"What brings you?" Eryn asked.

"Mirrah's in trouble," the girl blurted. Then lowering her voice to a whisper. "She's being held… in the corlord's palace." She stepped forward, away from the door. "My lord was called. The whole town is crowing about two dead parlords and a worl." Her light blue eyes grew large as she spoke. "They're saying Mirrah was involved."

"Those drogs on the road." Garlock rubbed his hairy head.

"And there's talk of a girl, in strange clothes." The young girl risked a quick look at Isaac and Zac. "Just came to tell you 'bout Mirrah. I must go, the steward may call me." They lightly touched foreheads, and then Eryn gave her a quick hug and quietly bolted the door after she left.

"A servant girl to Heebrin, advisor to Barthowl, the corlord of Kharlome. She puts herself at great risk to bring this news. She has a brave, kind heart."

"Does ya believe me now?" Garlock raised his brows. Eryn did not reply. Garlock scratched his beard. "Now what're we gonna do? Should've stayed in me hovel, me should have."

Eryn sat, her tone softer as she asked again why Mirrah had brought them to Kharlome. Garlock sighed a long exaggerated groan.

"To find a ship, miss Eryn, for the Isle of Moss." He went on to tell her about the knife of Yonnan and Zachary's poem in the tea. Eryn studied Zac in silence for a long, long time before she asked if he could remember the poem. He thought for a moment.

"On the Isle of Moss
Near the cave of Torrin,
In the tombs of Dross;
The box of Hornin."

Eryn put her hand lightly over her mouth. Zac got goose bumps. Something big was going on. He had a part, yet hadn't a clue why. His belly stirred; it felt good.

"They knew we be waitin' in the thicket," Garlock said, "and they knew of the sproots."

Eryn did not respond. She ran both hands through her thick hair. "The Isle of Moss. The knife of Yonnan. The girl makes three." Then, she suddenly jumped to her feet. "Forgive me. You must be hungry and thirsty. Your day has been long and you are battle worn."

"Ah, thanks," Isaac said, "but we really need to find Brielle."

"And Mirrah," both Zac and Garlock said together.

"Mirrah is strong. We must trust. Undo your...   those

garments. I will make some meal."

The 'meal' was good—some kind of oatmeal with chewy raisin-like things and some little crunchies. They were either hungry or it was genuinely good. The fragrance and flavor of the warm drink was soothing. When Isaac asked for cold water, Eryn told him it was not good for his 'inner workings,' so he drank mug after mug of warm drinks and hot tea.

The events of the day replayed in his mind. He wished he had not let the second arrow fly, pinning the man's hand to the gate. It could make things worse.

"How did you come to my window?" Eryn asked, as she sat on the floor, cross-legged on a sheepskin rug, holding a mug with both hands.

"Why'd you throw down the rope?" Zac asked. He thought she looked Italian or maybe Egyptian.

"Before you came, as I prepared for bed, I saw someone beneath my window, a boy in need of help."

Zac chuckled. "I just felt we were to run this way. I wasn't sure, but it seemed right."

"The hand of Ariel." She looked toward the window.

"Are you a Pharen?" Isaac asked. The girl looked long at him. Her eyes drew him in. They were dark, maybe dark blue. No, they have purple in them. Is that possible? Isaac found himself mesmerized. She's so... What did I ask?

"I'll go into the city," Eryn said moving quickly toward a side room. "I'll learn what I can." She soon came out dressed in a black loose fitting cloth wrapped tight about her ankles and wrists—a long, red cloth sash wrapped about her waist. She looked like a Japanese ninja with really long hair. She wore a sword on her back like Isaac and Mirrah. Her hair was wound into a long ponytail. She put on a short hooded cloak that hid her sword. She then strapped a long knife to her right thigh.

"Wow, you look cool," Zac said.

"I am not cold. Bolt the door behind me. I will tap thrice then once."

After she left, Isaac stood gaping. "Is she real?"

Garlock tended to the small fireplace, stoking it with charcoal. Zac curled up on the soft, short couch. Isaac grabbed a pillow and lay on a large sheepskin rug near the fire. No horl skins. He wondered why as he gazed into the glowing flames.

The next thing he knew, he was running about a dirty village made of stone walls, stone homes, and frozen mud roads. A man with an arrow stuck in his hand chased him, yelling strange and garbled things. Breezy was just out of sight, always turning a corner leaving whatever street he was on. No matter how hard he ran, the man was behind him yelling, and Breezy always disappeared around the next corner. Then, he saw her step inside a huge door. He ran up to it and began knocking. He would knock three times, then once, but each time she would call out: "Who is there? Is anybody there?"

Eryn kept knocking on the door, calling to the boys and Garlock. Finally Isaac woke and undid the bolt. He rubbed his eyes, "Sorry about that." He looked to Nusa who had woken him. Garlock was snoring near the fire, and Zac was near comatose on the couch.

Eryn dropped a bag of something on the floor. "Wake them. We need to act now." Isaac didn't even want to think about what she was going to propose. "Mirrah and your friend are indeed in Barthowl's palace. If we go tonight, I can maybe arrange for them to escape and for us to leave the city before dawn." She looked at him, enthusiastically awaiting his response. He stretched his jaws wide and gave an uncontrolled yawn. Although that was certainly not the answer he wanted to give, it was the most honest.

"Say what?" He scratched his head, trying to flatten some unruly hair.

"They are in the palace, not the prison. I believe we can overpower those guarding the doors and hallways. I have already arranged for a boat to leave at a moments notice."

Overpower? Isaac sighed. I'm already overpowered. Who is this girl? He was about to tell her she was too young to be talking like this.

"Well?" she asked.

"You're serious, aren't you?"

"Serious? You think we are tossing pebbles?"

"Pebbles? Sorry, it's just that my adventure, danger, near death punch card is full and I'd like to cash it in on the free burger and fries meal."

Eryn stared at him, completely bewildered.

"Okay, I'll keep the card. Should I wake them up?"

Garlock awoke with a start when Nusa nudged his head. Zachary only moaned and rolled over. Isaac shivered, as the room had grown cold. He figured it was well after midnight. They must have slept for a few hours at least. He thought of his broken watch he had left at home, wondering if time was the same here. Would his watch be moving faster or slower? He knew that neither Zac nor Breezy wore a watch, and he had not seen anything yet that looked like a clock. What he did know, was that it was late, and he was not in any condition to be 'overpowering' anybody. He winced as he bent over to awaken Zac.

"Let me get you something." Eryn went to a corner kitchen area. As they slowly awoke, she gave them all a strong brewed tea. "This will give you strength and clear your heads." They drank while talking quietly about how to best enter and exit the royal palace. Isaac couldn't believe they were actually holding such a conversation.

"I take it," he asked, "that we cannot hold some kind of meeting with this guy? Negotiate or something?"

"Isaac of La La," Eryn said, "Barthowl will probably sell or kill Mirrah in the city square tomorrow. Your friend Breezy will be sent to Sasson and will never be seen again." Isaac's eyes got big. "If we don't act tonight, while the guards are unprepared, we will lose our only chance." She pulled two dark cloaks from the bag on the floor and handed them to the boys. "Can you use that weapon?" she asked Zac, pointing to the one-handed crossbow and quiver of bolts.

"I think so."

"Put on the cloaks, follow me, and pray that Ariel walks with us." Zac rubbed sleep from his eyes, but he felt chipper. Isaac too, perked up as they pulled the cloaks over their coats. He handed Garlock the thorne and quiver.

"Ya did well, sir Isaac," he said very solemn. "Ya saved our smelly skins, ya did." The Grimal smiled and slung the thorne and quiver over his shoulder, and drinking down the last of the tea. "Well, we haven't come here to gab and sip brew. Let's go die in glory." The boys looked at each other, eyebrows raised high.

"It means," Eryn said, giving Garlock that same look Mirrah gives, "let us put our plan to action."

"We have a plan?" Isaac asked.

"Yes, follow me."

12 A LATE NIGHT RESCUE

They went single file down small corridors and narrow stairs that seemed to meander in every possible direction but straight. "How does she find her way home?" Isaac whispered. Then they opened a metal gate and walked into a large city square. It was cobblestone with shops lining every side. Most were closed down and quiet except for a pub of some kind at the far end. The boys could see why Eryn wanted to travel at this time of night. They stayed to the edge of the square, moving through the shadows.

They left the square and walked a narrow stone street that followed a small canal of clear water. Zac watched silvery fish facing into the current of the stream. The moonlight danced on the ripples and flashed off their slender bodies. It was all rather beautiful. He turned and saw a small boy sleeping in a corner, curled up, shivering on the cold stones. He reached out to call for Eryn, but they were already moving on ahead. He glanced back at the boy as he ran to catch them.

The street merged into another, and then another, crossed another little canal, up stairs and down. It was like the corridors inside the city wall. They occasionally saw dark forms sleeping on steps or narrow alleyways. Strong smells, mostly unpleasant, clung to the walls in the dark alleys and damp stone streets. Three men seemed to be pounding someone in a corner street. Zac shivered. He tried to stay brave.

"I see why the plan is to follow her," he whispered to Isaac. "Don't want to get lost in this part of town."

Finally, they saw a lighted palace at the far end of a wide smooth-stoned street that had an oval shaped pool running full length down the center. The street was lined with large stone statues of men with long crimped hair hanging down to their shoulders and funny beards of the same. They had small round hats that tapered to the top, reminding Isaac of the Assyrian kings of ancient history. More than thirty of them lined both sides of the street, standing twenty feet tall and each distinct yet similar. They held a long staff tucked under the left arm and set in the open left hand. Colorful banners hung from the staves that leaned out over the road. Together they formed a beautiful vaulted canopy above the road and icy pool.

"It must look neat in the sunlight," Zachary said.

"I believe Mirrah and Breezy are on the right side, near the back," Eryn whispered. "We will get close, then find a way in."

"You believe?" Isaac's tone seemed rude. "Hardly a plan."

They made their way down the right side of the street staying beneath the statues and their shadows. As they came closer, they could see steps leading up through massive pillars into the royal palace. It was four stories high and looked to have several hundred rooms. Only a few lights shone in windows here and there. Guard activity was minimal, which seemed encouraging, if that were possible.

Zac's heart pumped, and the adrenaline surged. It's too much for one day. He worried for Breezy.

They made their way around the palace toward the back corner. There were dozens of large arch-topped windows with plated glass.

"How can we find them in this huge place?" Isaac grumbled. He was losing faith in 'the plan.'

"They are maybe on the second floor, in a bedroom," Eryn said.

Maybe? Bedroom? Isaac grumbled under his breath. I thought this was a rescue mission. They're probably in plush beds with flannel sheets and down pillows. He shivered, huddling near some bushes. "How do you know where they are?"

"Sherrabella's cousin told us. She works in the palace."

"Whatever."

"I plan to find them quickly," Eryn said, "but if you do not hear from me in one loc, make your way to the port and find a ship called, The Silver Blade. Hide yourselves there. If I do not return with Mirrah and Breezy before sunrise, you must sail on without us. Captain Boar knows your destination. Keep ready."

"Sail on without them? Who's captain Boar? And what the devil is a loc?" Isaac got downright nasty.

"Yes, you must." With that, Eryn ran across the garden toward a row of arched windows near the ground. She went along reaching up to test each window until she found one that swung out. She pulled herself up and inside, leaving the window slightly ajar. They waited in silence, watching for any movement in the other windows.

"So what the hoola is a loc?" Isaac asked.

"A loc be…" Garlock scanned the palace for any sigh of Eryn.

"Be what?"

"Ai, there's ah… twenty locs to a day and its night, so each a tenth."

"You mean a twentieth."

"If I meant a twentieth, me would've said such. What be a twentieth, and who's tellin' who?"

"Okay, but you don't have to be a lumpy-grumpy."

"Lumpy what? And who be 'okay'?"

"Okay means, yes, or it's good."

"Why not just say, yes?"

"Okay, enough… just tell me what's a loc?"

"Ya speak like ya got a bat in yeer beard, boy."

"What is that supposed to mean?"

"It means," Zac joined the strained conversation, "that you

are not being very nice. You're really crabby."

"Whatever. Are you going to tell me or not?"

"Tell ya what?" Now Garlock spoke harshly.

Zac quickly answered before Isaac could make things worse. "Please tell us how you measure time. Like, what's a loc?"

"Oh. Well, there's ten parts to a night—a loc."

Isaac muttered some calculations. "Sixty times twenty four... divided by twenty... ah... seventy two minute hours. That helps. And during the day it's called what?"

"A loc." Garlock looked at him, tilting his head as if wondering how this boy ever got as far as he did. Zac just shook his head. He would have laughed if it weren't so cold and his heart wasn't beating so fast.

Garlock just sighed. "Two locs be a twill. And then there's a fifth—bein' a fifth of a loc."

"So about fifteen minutes. Then what's a rill?" Isaac thought back to Mirrah's home.

"A rill be a loc and a half." Garlock kept looking intently toward the palace. Isaac was about to ask why it was called a rill, then figured, why bother? It was getting really cold standing in the snow. He wondered how much more he could take.

"In the window," Zac pointed, "looks like Eryn." She had passed by a second floor window. Suddenly, she got slammed back against the window and they could see her wrestling. A man, much bigger than she, had his arm around her neck, pushing her head against the window. They watched the black silhouettes struggling behind the glass.

Eryn tugged and jerked at the arm around her neck, jostling back and forth. The boys and Garlock just stood, watching her being choked to death, their mouths gaping, like children at a shadow-puppet play in the park.

Garlock had his thorne ready, but the window was closed, and Eryn was in front. She struggled frantically, trying to reach her knife on her thigh, but it was pinned to the windowsill.

Garlock ran from the shadows. He searched for some way

to climb the wall to reach Eryn. He jumped for a ledge when the window high above suddenly flung wide open. A solid, heavy thud hit just beside the little Grimalkyn. As a cloud of flurries billowed out and upward, they saw a dark body lay motionless in the snow. Garlock looked up at the window. Eryn leaned out with both hands on the sill, gasping in breaths of night air. The puffs of breath floated casually off, unaware they could have been the last.

"Did you see that?" Zac was giddy. "She flipped him right over—right out the window."

"Yeah, I saw that."

Nusa approached the man on the ground. Eryn called quietly for them to wait. She then lowered a rope of bed linens knotted together.

"That's original." Isaac ran from the shadows. An ornery, cynical exhaustion pressed on him. You're running on mega stress, he told himself. And with a lack of sleep. This may be a dream, but focus like it's real. If a dream—no loss. If it's real…

Nusa was again the first up the cloth rope. The boys wished she had waited, the cloth shredding with her claws and weight. Zachary climbed up next, and then Isaac, who groaned with every pull.

"We have to stop meeting like this," he said to Eryn through clenched teeth. She pulled him through the window without reply. With everyone inside, they faintly saw they were in a bedroom with lavish décor and carved furniture. Nusa made her way into the hallway.

"She will find them," Eryn whispered. They stayed together behind Nusa walking slowly down the hall. The ceiling must have been fifteen feet high. Several doors over nine feet tall with arches at the top lined the hall.

"Tall people," Zac whispered.

The boys tried to move unheard, but winter boots and snow gear are not the best choice for stealth operations. They walked like buff robots, arms held outward and legs apart. The whiff… whiff… whiff… of snow pants and coats echoed in the halls.

Nusa broke into a trot as they turned into a central hall. They had been walking on a woven runner, so when the great lynx cut the corner, she slipped on the polished stone floor. Extended her claws, she clinked and scraped the stone.

"Nusa, draw in your claws," Eryn scolded.

They heard muffled talking somewhere behind them, but Nusa did not seem concerned so they walked on—whiff... whiff... whiff... At the end of the central hall was a large window where corridors led off to the right and left. Nusa paused at the right corridor. Eryn poked her head around the corner. Two tall men stood outside a set of double doors halfway down on the left.

"Good job, Nusa."

Garlock took a look and asked, "So what's yeer plan, miss?"

"We need to overpower them, but it must be with silence."

Overpower them? Isaac shook his head. Got to find her a new word.

Oil lamps hung from the walls offering dim light in the hallway and corridor. It was enough light to see the men were holding long spears with an additional crescent-moon shaped blade. No other doors were in the corridor, so Eryn suggested rushing them. Isaac envisioned this beautiful girl rushing down the narrow hall with her blade swinging, long black hair flying out behind her. Then a flash of the crescent-moon blade slicing through the air, and it's all over.

A strange feeling came over him. The orneriness briefly lifted. He suddenly had deep concern—a bond with Eryn and Garlock. They've put their lives at risk, when none of this would have happened if he had not wandered into their world. There has to be a better plan.

"Draw them out and ambush them," he whispered to Eryn.

"Ambush? How?"

"Give them something to investigate and then 'overpower' them."

"Like what?"

Zac suddenly jumped out into the hall. His heavy boots thumped the floor. "Like this," he said as he waved at the guards. "Hey, monkey butts." He then ran straight across the main hall into the other corridor. The guards stood dumbstruck; then one bolted off in pursuit. The floor shook with his weight as he ran. When he came out the corridor, Eryn did a leg sweep, bringing the man down with a clang and a mighty thud. Garlock knocked the man's head with the pommel of his knife. The big guard lay still—thoroughly 'overpowered.'

The other man, seeing his enemy was but a girl and a Grimalkyn, came charging down the corridor. He raised his halberd preparing to slice and dice. Eryn and Garlock backed out into the main hall. They wanted to draw him out for Nusa. When he came into the hall, he looked to his left and saw Isaac and Nusa. He swung his halberd at Isaac's head. Like an ax into a stump, the crescent blade sunk into the wall right where Isaac stood. Isaac jerked back, but the spear point grazed his forehead. His eyes were wide as he caught the eyes of the tall dark guard.

With a jerk, the blade was free, but Nusa had pounced. The guard went down with a thunderous clang, landing atop the first guard. Nusa held him by the face. She kept twisting as the guard fought with one hand, reaching for his knife with the other. Garlock stepped on the man's hand just as he drew the knife. Eryn held her sword by the blade tip. She swung it underhand, golf swing style. The handle clunked the guard aside the head. A dull thump, like smacking a pumpkin, echoed down the hall. Isaac cringed. Nusa released her grip.

Isaac touched his own forehead. Something sticky dripped above his right eye. Zac came and surveyed the two guards spread out on the hallway floor.

"That, Miss Eryn, is an ambush."

"I like it, Sir Zac." Eryn then saw Isaac touching his forehead. "Are you cut?"

"Just another flesh wound," he sighed. "Don't trouble yourself for me."

"If you wish."

He groaned with teeth clenched tight. The cut stung.

Eryn ran to the double doors and found them locked. Nusa clawed at the threshold. She gave out a purring whine and Eryn tapped three times then once. Soon Mirrah was behind the door.

"It's locked," she whispered.

"Let me see," Zac pushed his way through. Having played around with lock picking techniques, he bent down to look. It was a wide, rectangle slot. "Probably quite simple," he said.

"We don't have time, Zac." Isaac looked back at the hallway and the guards on the floor. The 'overpowering' had not exactly been 'with silence.' Garlock came up and grasped the door latch. He twisted with all his might until the handle snapped. The door was still locked and now without a handle.

"Nice work, Sasquatch," Isaac said.

They could hear Breezy talking with Mirrah. They had found them but were now separated by a simple lock. Eryn put her lips to the crack between the doors. "Can you make a rope?"

"Eryn?" Mirrah asked.

"Yes, it is I. Can you make a rope and open your window?"

"We will try." They could hear bare feet running back across the floor. Zac knew if he had time and some stiff wire, he could open the lock. The large doors were solid wood so breaking in would wake the whole palace. Then Isaac noticed the hinges; the pins were on the outside. The lock was meant to keep people in, not out.

"Give me your knife, Garlock." With a little prying of the knife, the pins went up and out. He had trouble reaching the highest hinge but after it gave way, the door was loose enough for them to pry it open from the hinged side. It was extremely heavy and remained connected to the lock. It opened in such a cockeyed manner that he stood, balancing it, knowing it could fall at any moment. He asked for help to break it free.

"No time." Eryn squeezed through the opening. He struggled to balance it as the others went through. Mirrah had already tied sheets and bedding together into a rope as Garlock opened the window. The room was plush with one large bed.

They slid the bed near the window and tied the cloth rope to a bedpost. Down below were gardens and frozen pools like on the other side. Breezy was the first one down, hesitating in the windowsill.

"Do I have to?" she whined.

"You stay, you die," Eryn said.

"We must leave here, Breezy." Mirrah helped her out the window. "There is no choice today." Zac then followed her down.

Isaac was still afraid to let go of the door. It must weigh two hundred pounds, he thought. "Where is Nusa?" he called in a whisper.

"She will find her own way." Mirrah climbed out over the window ledge. "I hope." When only Eryn and Isaac were left, Eryn called for him to let go of the door and climb down.

"It will fall," he said. "You go."

"No, let go the door and climb down."

"You're wasting time, go."

She glared at him. He could see her lips drawn tight. With one graceful leap, she stood in the windowsill, holding the linen rope waiting for him to let go of the door. He balanced it best he could and gingerly walked away toward the window.

"Told you it would stay," she said.

"Don't get snooty, just get moving."

Isaac started to follow her down when he heard the metal in the lock snap with a high pitch ting. He waited for the inevitable crash. Nothing happened immediately, and then it came down, thundering through the palace like an explosion.

"Told ya," he said as he dropped off from the end of the bed-sheet rope. She didn't care enough to respond but gave orders to enter the shrubs and run back toward the city. As they ran, she told Mirrah of the boat in the harbor.

"Take the strangers," she said to Mirrah. "Garlock and I will stay behind to stop any pursuers."

"What about Nusa?" Zac asked. "We can't leave her here."

"We will find Nusa, now go!"

Mirrah led through the snowy gardens, staying out of the

moonlight. Isaac thought of the long road leading to the palace. Surely they would be stopped somewhere on that road if not at the arch where the palace road entered the city. It had been warm inside the palace, so Breezy had trouble adjusting to the cold and stress. She shook uncontrollably, her teeth chattering like a chipmunk.

Lights came on inside the palace as they made their way down the road, staying behind the giant stone figures. "Winter boots weren't made for running," Isaac grumbled. Why are there no guards on the grounds? he thought. He touched his forehead as he ran. The blood had formed a crust over the cut. He probably had blood down his face and into his shirt. "The fun here never stops," he said as he ran bringing up the rear.

They came to the palace gate—an arch of huge stonework leading into the city. It was quiet but for the pubs here and there. They ran into an alley and waited, listening to each other's heavy breathing, with poor Brielle still shivering, but only in spurts.

"We wait but a fifth," Mirrah said breathing hard. "If they do not come, we will go to the ship." Isaac still had his thoughts on why no one pursued them. The waiting seemed long and stretched their nerves. Isaac grew restless. Mirrah finally said with a sigh, "We need to go."

"We can wait longer," Zac said, "it's still dark."

"We should go. Pray they meet us at the harbor."

Mirrah and Breezy had dressed quickly before leaving the room. They finished lacing their boots and tucking things in as they waited. Mirrah of course did not have her sword. Zac wondered about the ancient knife of Yonnan, whether it had been taken from her.

They moved single file through back streets and alleys. Some places stunk so bad, that Breezy gagged. She said the stench was absolutely horrid, which she shortened to 'abhorrid.' Isaac tried to correct her with 'abhor,' but she insisted the smells were 'abhorrid.'

It was hard not to stumble in the dark streets. The boys had so many questions for Breezy, but no one spoke as they ran on and on. They changed directions so many times, they wondered if Mirrah was lost. A woman screamed somewhere behind a stone wall. Breezy whimpered, running close behind Mirrah. Then they caught the smell of fish and salt water, drying seaweed, and other ocean smells.

The streets angled downward, and soon they were on an open wooden boardwalk that followed the coastline in both directions. Random piers led out from the boardwalk to which hundreds of small boats where moored. Other boats anchored in the open water with several small ships farther out. Lights bobbed up and down all along the coast so that it looked like Christmas.

"Do you know which pier?" Isaac asked.

"No, I do not."

"Oh, boy."

13 THE SILVER BLADE

They stood looking at the long boardwalk and the vast harbor beyond. To walk it all would take hours. "Did she tell you anything about where it would be?" Isaac asked.

"Yes, on the pier by the Red House and Spoon. I thought I knew where it was, but in the dark… It has been a long time."

"House and Spoon?" all three asked in unison.

"A place to eat and sleep. Do you not have these?"

Some fishermen prepared their boats and nets, but Mirrah was hesitant to ask them, anxious about being noticed or leaving a trail.

"Ariel please help us," she whispered. "Which way should we go?" Suddenly they heard commotion coming from the alley down which they had come. Mirrah didn't know which way to run.

"Get out of sight," Isaac said moving toward a wooden stall behind them. The boardwalk was slippery from the sea mist and cold. Trying to hide, without appearing as such, they stood in the darkness of the stall. Breezy muffled a gasp when she saw what could only be Nusa. The lynx immediately turned left, slipping on the wet, icy boards. She spun around to position herself on the other side of where the alley entered the boardwalk. She looked straight across at Isaac and the others.

In an instant, Isaac knew what she was doing. Pulling out his sword, he crept forward, crouching low near a pile of fishing nets. He was directly across from Nusa; the others hid in the shadows a few yards behind.

Zachary watched his brother. A swirl of emotion suddenly swept over him. Joy upon seeing Nusa, dread of what approached, stress and strain from the last two days, and weariness dragging a deep despair. It sucked the hope out from his soul. He grabbed Breezy's arm, slinking back into the flimsy wall of the market stall. He fought the urge to panic, to give up, but without hope…

Eryn came running onto the boardwalk and turned left. She ran like an Olympic athlete making her victory lap. Then came little Garlock, running with short but powerful strides. He briefly slid onto the boardwalk looking right and then left. He did not even see Isaac or the others in the shadows. He ran past Nusa after Eryn.

Isaac watched Nusa drop into a crouching position and knew that the time had come. It sounded like a dozen footsteps were charging down the alleyway, boots clomping on the cobblestones. Suddenly, he grabbed a handful of fishing net and ran across the opening toward Nusa. Mirrah, seeing what he was doing, stepped forward and pulled the net taut. As soon as she pulled, a horde of tall men in black leathers and spears with crescent-moon blades, ran headlong into the net. Isaac and Mirrah held tight, but the guards' momentum jerked them both onto the boardwalk.

The first four men were in a pile on the pier, with spears, arms and legs tangled hopelessly in the net. The fifth man tried to leap over the pile but caught his boot and fell headlong rolling on the boardwalk. He tried to regain his footing as he tumbled. When he was finally upright, it was just in time to slide off the boardwalk onto the rocks and water below.

Two more guards came to a running stop right before the flailing mess in the net. The one nearest Isaac saw him there on the icy planks. He raised his spear. Nusa sprang. They tumbled backward falling behind the other guard. This other guard held his spear, ready to pin Mirrah to the boardwalk. He looked away when Nusa struck. Mirrah reached up and grabbed the spear, but he jerked it free, cutting her left shoulder. He held it high and aimed. Mirrah lay trapped on the icy boardwalk.

Isaac had left his sword at the pile of nets. He watched the guard prepare to strike Mirrah. Isaac shut his eyes and prayed. A cry of pain filled the air, but it was not Mirrah. He opened his eyes. The guard had dropped his spear and now frantically clutched at his right buttock. Sunken deep into the muscle was a small but painful bolt from a crossbow. Mirrah saw Zachary's white teeth shining in the moonlight.

Hearing more footsteps in the alleyway, she yelled to them. "Run to Eryn and do not look back." Getting up, she grabbed the guard's spear and held him back. She picked up her husband's sword and tossed it to Isaac.

Zac and Breezy still stood in the shadows. "Run!" Mirrah shouted. They made their way around the still flailing pile of guards in the net. They ran passed Isaac and Nusa but stopped when they heard Mirrah's muffled cry. Turning back they saw her, face down on the boardwalk. Someone had grabbed her foot and now another guard stood poised, spear ready.

Breezy scooped up an egg shaped rock and stretched her long thin arm way behind her. Bringing her left leg up high like a pitcher throwing a fastball, she hurled the stone. There was a dull thud followed by the rock dropping on the planks. The guard stood frozen over Mirrah for just a moment, wobbled a little, then collapsed into a heap. Mirrah struggled free and joined them as they ran. They slipped and slid past Garlock who had his thorne aimed at two guards in pursuit.

Eryn stood waiting. They clamored into a large rowboat with a burly looking man at the oars. A pile of supplies covered with sailcloth sat near the back. Nusa positioned herself at the bow. She looked like Washington about to cross the Potomac. Garlock came running and jumped aboard.

"Won't be any more troublin' from those drogs."

They rowed out toward a ship anchored near the mouth of the harbor. They could faintly see fishermen gathering on the boardwalk watching the palace guards untangle themselves. As they rowed out, they saw one man walking down the pier from where they had come.

"Will anyone come after us?" Breezy asked, her voice quaking.

"We will be safe, once out to sea." Eryn kept her eyes on the harbor.

Garlock turned to Isaac. "Ya did well, laddie, brone well."

"We all did well. It's good to have you two back." Isaac sighed and smiled at Mirrah and Breezy. He was exhausted. His back burned. The cut on his forehead throbbed. I feel horrible—even 'abhorrid.' But he also felt good—a full, exciting, satisfied good, stirring somewhere inside. And the orneriness was gone. He looked about the harbor with its ships and bobbing lights. Is this real? How can this be real?

Mirrah put her arm around Breezy and held her tight. "You all risked your lives for us. How did you know where we were?"

"A little friend of mine," Eryn said. "She risked her life, as well. Her lord is a hard man. I hope she is safe."

Garlock spoke to Mirrah. "They knew to find us in the thicket, me lady."

"Yes," Mirrah said, "those men from the wood. They made a ruckus and pointed me out when I entered the city. I was taken to the palace along with them. I told Barthowl I had also seen the dead parlords in the wood, but nothing more. They released me, so I went to the market and bought three cloaks. Right before I reached the thicket, I was overtaken by six men. They had been hiding in wait for me."

"Like they knew where you were going?" Isaac asked. He had been thinking about their escape from the palace.

"Yes, but how?"

"Those men from the wood—they must have seen us enter the thicket." Isaac was deep in thought. He looked back at the pier. It was dark, but he could still see the tall form of a lone man standing, watching.

He thought to suggest they change course for a different

ship, to throw off whoever stood watching. They approached a large 18th century style vessel, like something from a pirate movie. He looked back at the man on the pier, now a small black silhouette. "Who are you?"

The sea air was miserably damp and cold. Zac, who sat in the back of the boat, rested his head on the pile of supplies covered with sailcloth. Although his heart still beat hard, the gentle rocking soothed his soul. His head throbbed with weariness. It had been a long, long day. He was too tired to think things through. He knew Isaac would be analyzing all that had happened. He could see the parlords riding their mighty worls, capes flapping with the loping beasts.

Suddenly, he sat up. Only Isaac noticed. Zac then put his head back down on the sailcloth, eyes open, as if listening. Then straightened up quickly again.

"What's under here?" he asked. No one heard him, so he called out again. "Hey guys, what's under here?"

"Supplies, food." Eryn said, tired and lost in thought.

"What kind of food?"

Eryn sighed. "Dried meat, flour, fruits."

"That's it?" Zac put his ear back down on the covered boxes.

To Isaac's surprise, they rowed past the large ship and then angled around behind it, making their way toward the mouth of the harbor. They were going out into the open sea, using the large vessel as a shield from the pier. Isaac watched Eryn at the bow. Maybe she does know what she's doing. Wonder how old she is…?

He could see the silhouette of a smaller ship out at sea. The waves grew rough as they left the harbor. Breezy held Mirrah's arm, breathing fast through her nose as the boat rose and fell with the waves. As they neared the smaller ship, the moon painted its name bright and clear. "The Silver Blade." Isaac watched it roll upon the waves. He said the ship looked like a 15th century caravel—a small, fast ship with triangular sails.

They struggled to climb the rope ladder, but soon everyone was on board. The crew looked to be about a dozen men. A short stocky man, bald with bright red sideburns and no left ear, came and gave the three a sturdy look-over. Eryn introduced him as captain Boar. The men had almost finished hauling the supplies on board when someone gave out a call from the rowboat below.

"Milady," a crewman called, "take a look-see, pleasin." Eryn peered over the rails. In the rowboat, stood a crewman holding the sailcloth he had just pulled off the last of the supplies. Huddled at the end of the boat was a girl sobbing uncontrollably. She was on her knees with her face pressed almost to the boat's hull with hands over her head. She looked as if awaiting a beating.

"Show yourself," Eryn called down. The girl slowly lifted her head and looked up awkwardly toward Eryn, her face bruised and dirty. "Sherrabella?" The girl tried to speak but burst into sobs. The crew hoisted her up in the cargo net with the rest of the supplies.

They brought her into the cabin and sat her by the charcoal brazier with some hot drink. She sat twitching from the cold and trauma. Breezy put a fleece robe around her shoulders. Eryn had given the command to set sail, knowing, without having to ask, what had happened to Sherrabella.

It took some time before she could speak, and even then the story came out in broken sobs. She had returned, after seeing Eryn, to an angry master. He beat her and accused her of all sorts of things. In a rage, he locked her out in the cold. She ran back to Eryn's, but no one answered, so she went about trying to find a warm place.

"That's when I saw you going to the harbor," she said, calming down. "I wanted to call to you, but I was so afraid... so ashamed."

Eryn was seated across from Sherrabella and gently put her hands on the young girl's cheeks, drawing her close. She let their foreheads touch. "Don't you ever hesitate to call for me, especially if you feel ashamed." She spoke softly. Sherrabella took a long shuddering breath, and with an equally long sigh, she finally calmed.

"I saw you talk with the boatman, but you ran and were gone. I hid until I could climb under the sailcloth." Mirrah brought a bowl of hot water for the young girl's frozen toes and fingers.

"Sherrabella," Eryn said with tears on her cheeks. "You are now my sister. I will die before I let this happen again." The girl lowered her head. Breezy sniffled and put an arm around Sherrabella.

Once the ship got underway, with introductions and cabin arrangements complete, the sky began to lighten. They had a simple meal together after which Eryn tended to Isaac's head and Mirrah's shoulder. After some chatting about the events of the night, especially Isaac's sudden idea to net the guards, the three crawled into their bunks and did not wake until the sun was a glowing ball of red dropping in the distant west.

Eryn and Mirrah were sitting at a wooden table inside the main cabin. Isaac was the first to awake. He shuffled to the table in thick wool socks, wearing his shredded coat. Through the cabin's west window he saw the sun dropping into the horizon. The ship rose with the swells making hanging lanterns sway. A charcoal brazier of glowing coals sat near the table.

"I'm becoming nocturnal," he said with a yawn. He sat and patted his rumpled hair, helping himself to some dried figs and dark bread, things he would never have eaten three days ago. Mirrah slid a clay mug to him.

"For your wounds," she said, then giving her ever-so-pleasant smile.

Eryn smirked as she raised her mug to her lips. "You slept like... a kroak in the winter." Her dark eyes reflected the evening light.

Isaac watched her drink. Warm light flooded the cabin as the sun neared the edge of the sea. Soft, yellow rays painted Eryn's face. While girls were not really his thing, Isaac found himself captivated. He had never known or even been near a girl like her. His cheeks got suddenly warm as he sipped the hot tea.

Eryn bit into a small purple fruit, her lips turning purplish-red. He thought about the night as he watched her eat. She arranged for a ship while coordinating a rescue mission all in a moment's planning and all after midnight. He remembered how ornery he had been. Seeing her now in the evening light, he scolded himself for acting so stupid. Without thinking, he blurted out, "I was quite a jerk last night."

"A jork?" Eryn put the fruit down. "I hope not." She chuckled.

"Lack of sleep I suppose and… a lot of weird things going on."

'True, but a jork?"

"A jerk—rude and ornery idiot who thinks he knows everything—why are you laughing?"

Eryn smirked with a girlish giggle, trying to cover her mouth. "Rude and ornery I understand," she said, "but jorky idiot is new to me." She continued to laugh, turning away towards Mirrah.

"A jork," Mirrah explained, "is a large, fat, lazy beast that loves to sleep in its own… excrement."

"Oh." He smiled at Eryn. She laughed again, looking away.

Mirrah leaned forward. "Isaac, you were in Barthowl's palace. Sasson's power lingers there. It seeks your weakness. For you to be rude and ornery… he was searching your heart."

"The power lingers?"

Mirrah urged him to drink the tea. "Sasson's power is heavy in Kharlome. Death, pain and suffering emanates from the air itself. We Pharens feel the war inside. Remember in my home, when Garlock proposed that you were servants of Sasson? Moments later we saw the carn. His power reached us there. You must not always assume your feelings are your own."

Isaac took a drink and sat back, studying the two Pharens. They both had their long hair loose. Mirrah's hung straight and even. Eryn's kinky spirals lay full and thick down her back. Mirrah's eyes held such kindness, yet such strength. Eryn's eyes pulled at him. Her fine features drew his gaze more than he wished. He longed to know her age. What if she's older? She looks sixteen… maybe. But the girl last night—the way she took charge. Never had he seen or known a girl like Eryn. She continued to smile at him, as she had liked the 'jorky idiot' confession. A flood of silly thoughts rushed through his head. His face grew warm again.

"Well that's certainly something to think about," he said, "the feelings thing." He stared down into his mug.

He learned that Mirrah and her husband had raised Eryn since she was a child. She had lost both her parents in one night, a tragedy that neither seemed willing to discuss.

Isaac thought more about the rescue as he sipped the healing tea. "I have a question. The rescue last night—if that were in a movie, we'd think it was a trap, allowed to happen, like part of a greater plan. Know what I mean?"

"Movie?" they both asked.

"Yeah, wasn't it almost too easy? Where were all the guards?"

"Oh," Eryn said. "Barthowl does not need many guards. What we did last night…" She turned to Mirrah and smiled. "Has anyone done that before?"

"Last night," Mirrah said, "breaking into Barthowl's palace and striking guards… not in my lifetime. People kill and rob each other but no one attacks the corlord."

Isaac watched Eryn's eyes light up.

"As for a greater plan," Mirrah continued, "we have wondered if he let us go. Barthowl may be under orders from Sasson to learn the reason you three have come. We cannot know, but we best be careful. Now, drink that brew."

Zac came to the table with a huge yawn. He studied Isaac's blood crusted forehead. "So it wasn't all a dream?" he said as he sat. The salve Eryn applied seemed to have pulled the cut together.

Sherrabella came with a washbasin of hot water for the boys. She wore some of Eryn's clothes with sleeves and legs rolled up to make them wearable. Zac fought hard not to laugh. She was a lovely girl. His heart ached as he looked at her bruised face. She set the water and towels at the end of the table and gave a slight bow.

"Thank you," he said. It was awkward having someone bow to him. When she left he asked Eryn, "Is she always going to be a servant girl?"

"She was born a servant."

"Does she have to stay a servant? Is it a law?"

Eryn and Mirrah both pondered the new thought. Not only was attacking the corlord's palace something new, but a servant changing their role… Mirrah only moved her lips, but the boys knew what she said. "The heavens are shifting."

Breezy came in from being out on the deck. "You lazy bones finally crawl out of your crypt?" She carried a jubilant smile. "The sunset was funderful."

"Fun-what?"

"Fantastically fun and wonderful. Did you see it?"

"Sunset?" Zac looked about. "Isn't it—?"

"This ship is so cool." Breezy grabbed a ripe purple plum hidden beneath a piece of dark bread. Both boys watched her take a bite. It was the last plum. She giggled a mischievous victory laugh. "You guys have to come explore with me."

"In a bit," Isaac said. He touched his forehead. His back radiated a dull ache, but the sharp pain was gone. Again the events replayed in his mind, and again he searched for answers. He would not stop seeking an explanation for this world or how they had been plunged, rather painfully, into it. The boys ate and then washed up with the hot water.

The ship turned south as the evening went on, and the air became warmer. They did explore the ship with Breezy; carrying lanterns made it all the more fun. Some parts were amazing; others down right stunk. Some of the crew seemed fearful of them. The teens strange clothes mixed with tales of carns, dead parlords, and a worl claw, made for hushed talks and murmuring glances.

One crewman, a gangly man, named Ferro, seemed particularly offended by their presence. Breezy heard him grumble about having strangers on board, especially women, and a stowaway, especially a girl, as being bad luck for any ship.

She decided to pay it no-never-mind and enjoy the adventure.

They all ended up around the table that evening, talking, laughing, and eating, except for Sherrabella. She would sit by, quietly watching for someone to be in need of more drink or food, tending to the water kettle or the charcoal brazier.

Finally Zac asked, "Can I invite her to sit with us?"

"You can try," Eryn said.

Zac made room between him and Breezy on the bench and called to Sherrabella. She looked at him and quickly dropped her head without moving from her spot by the water kettle.

"Breezy," Zac said, "tomorrow we're going to turn that girl back into a girl." He and Breezy then did some complex funky handshake and with big smiles lightly bonked their foreheads together and giggled. Sherrabella watched with eyes wide and mouth ajar. Nusa got up from a corner near a window. The big cat stretched and went out on deck.

"How long is our journey?" Isaac asked. Strange emotions filled his soul. It was exciting, yet it was totally crazy. They were on a ship when they needed to get back home. Grimalkyns, horls, parlords and worls—the images flashed through his mind. He was on a continual search for a thread, something to connect the dots.

"We will stop for supplies in two days time," Eryn said. "After that we hope to reach the isle in about fourteen, if the weather is good."

"Fourteen?" The teens were stunned.

Isaac tried to hide his shock and dismay. "The cursed Isle of Moss, I presume?" He looked at Garlock, who sat by the brazier with a long, wavy, pencil-thin pipe. Garlock looked up with a snort, then smiled just a tad.

"Yes," Eryn said, very solemn, "the Isle of Moss… land of the kroaken-gaggers." Mirrah reached over and touched her hand.

"Ariel is with us. He knows what awaits."

It was after midnight when they climbed back into their bunks. The wind was steady, and the sea rocked the ship like a baby's cradle. Isaac wondered how long it would last. He kept replaying the escape. Did Barthowl let them go? Is this a trap? He touched his head. That guard didn't think so. He sure seemed bent on taking my head. He closed his eyes and listened to the creaks and groans as the air turned yet warmer. "Fourteen days." He sighed long and slow. He let the gentle sway ease his mind. As he drifted into sleep, a dark tall form stood at the end of a distant pier, watching, waiting.

"Who are you?"

14 "ARIEL IS SPEAKING"

The weather did stay nice for the next two days, and on the third, they anchored outside a small port called Wensly's Ale. The three stayed on board with Nusa, as Mirrah, Eryn, Garlock and some of the crew went ashore for supplies. It was late in the day when they came back with casks and wooden boxes. Once everything was hoisted aboard, they weighed anchor and sailed out into the open sea.

Both Mirrah and Garlock had purchased new swords. Nothing fancy they said.

"But it'll open a kroak's belly be the sure." Garlock swung the blade up into the imaginary beast before him.

Over the next few days, Zac and Breezy made Sherrabella their special project. Breezy braided Sherrabella's hair into cute braids and taught her how to write her name, which led to teaching her the alphabet and reading simple words, then sentences. She learned quickly, which helped her gain self-esteem. They treated her as an equal and would not allow her to wait on them, although she would still wait on the others, which they allowed as she wanted to earn her keep.

Zac and Breezy had this game of treating her like royalty if she ever waited on them. They would call her 'highness,' 'princess,' and 'your ladyship.' It was hard for her at first, but soon she began to laugh and relax around them. It was fun seeing her come alive and blossom with self-respect.

Eryn taught Zac the Pharrian writing system, which was simplified from middle Pharrian. He learned so quick that she taught him some of the middle Pharrian symbols, a monosyllabic system with each stroke or symbol representing a full syllable. Zac found it pure joy to sound out whatever Eryn wrote. He most often did not know the meaning, but could pronounce the sounds.

The boys and Breezy enjoyed learning to fence. Eryn and Mirrah took turns teaching them how to parry, lunge, and to anticipate their opponent's moves. They would spend hours on deck learning different techniques with different weapons. They set up an old barrel, and Eryn taught them how to throw a long knife underhand, like a softball throw. Mirrah showed them how to throw overhand, adjusting the spin for different length knives. Isaac found Mirrah's husband's sword to be the most versatile. It was useful in close combat and yet could be thrown with accuracy. He grew to appreciate its design and craftsmanship.

His back had healed much faster than he thought possible. Mirrah's tea and dressing wraps had near magical effects. He listened in as she taught Eryn the ingredients and methods of preparation, but to Isaac, little was familiar.

Garlock helped Isaac learn the ways of the thorne. They would shoot from awkward positions moving about the ship. He had Isaac lie on his back and shoot across his chest, or on his stomach, propped on elbows. He even hung him upside down from a yardarm and tossing him the thorne and arrow, he yelled, "There's a kroak behind ya. Kill 'em or die." Isaac had to spin himself around, draw the bow while spinning in the sea air and release before he rotated past the target. At first arrows ended up in places they did not belong, some going overboard. But he learned fast, it all being very thrilling.

Breezy had taken a particular liking to a weapon called the felkin. It worked like a slingshot but was worn on the left hand as a fingerless glove. A piece of soft leather slipped over the palm and thumb on which the two rubber straps and a pouch were attached. Pulled back like a slingshot, using a steel ball, it could nearly explode a melon, as Breezy accidentally learned on the first try.

She soon became very proficient. She could take a steel ball from a pouch at her waist, load it, pull the sling back to her right ear and fire three shots before Zac could spell 'Mississippi' forwards, then backwards. Isaac said it was just under five seconds. When not in use, she would fasten the rubber straps to a leather armband on her forearm so the felkin could be easily worn and ready within seconds.

They all developed a great respect for Mirrah, Eryn and Garlock. Breezy and Sherrabella became inseparable. Sherrabella, or Bella as she became known, showed Breezy how to sew, and they made their own wardrobe accessories from any loose cloth on board.

Nusa would occasionally go into running fits, darting about the deck over rails, bounding up stairs, and clawing furiously into the mast, which brought a stern scolding from captain Boar. At night, they all gathered around the table enjoying great conversation as each shared things from their different worlds. Zac loved to sit in a large window seat with Nusa, while Breezy and Bella sat side-by-side sewing. Garlock had a small pipe flute that he would pull out from somewhere in his vest. He played many fascinating tunes, sometimes late into the night.

One evening, Isaac asked Mirrah about her husband. He had wanted to ask ever since she handed him the sword.

"He was kind, strong and brave, always learning. Amazed at what a person could do if they did not give up. He was leader of the Pharens of Yorne—a great, noble man."

"May I ask what happened?"

"He was betrayed," she said, looking away.

"By Grimals it be," Garlock said with a growl. "Grims not worthy a life. Ashamed it makes me. They called for help then bound him—sold him to Sasson—foul dung beetles."

"He often helped the Grimalkyns of Yorne," Mirrah said.

"He taught them the ways of Ariel, to live free of Sasson's power."

"Helped us Grimals greatly, he did. Taught Alle-Encer many things— things that stopped us beatin' each other."

"But you are Pharens," Isaac said. "Didn't you see what was going to happen?"

"I think he did. But he had promised his help."

"He knew?" Breezy looked up from her sewing, "and went anyway?"

Mirrah looked off as into a distant place. The ship groaned as it slowly swayed.

"How long ago?" Isaac asked.

"Three rings have past."

"Could he still be alive?"

"No, I have heard nothing. But at times I feel—"

"Better he be dead," Garlock said. "Sorry me lady, but three rings in the belly of Skone Lor be too long for any man or beast. Unless he forsook the Pharen way and swore allegiance to Sasson, mighty Arnon forbid."

"Garlock…" Mirrah gave the kindest, sternest, disapproving look possible. No one spoke for some time as the ship creaked and groaned with every sway, gently back and forth. Eryn had been strangely quiet during the conversation— her eyes and thoughts somewhere else.

They awoke to a dark and drizzly day. The wind came in gusts and put everyone at odds with the ship's motion. All but the crew got scrambled innards, with lots of lying around inside the cabin. Garlock seemed the least effected by the jostling ship, so he sat smoking his long pipe telling fantastic tales.

"Did me tell the time Alle and me be surrounded by kroaks?" he spoke from one side of his mouth as he lit his pipe. Isaac and Zac sat in the window with Nusa while Breezy put Bella's hair into French braids. "We was walkin' the wood, near the river's fork. The land is low and kroaks be likin' it there. But we need be checkin' the traps. Been a bad season for trappin's." He let a large plume of blue smoke float up out of his open mouth, the aroma sharp and strong but pleasant.

"We be walkin' a trail that flanked the river through boggy land. Bugs be flyin' bout, and we had our thornes in hand. One tic the trail be clear, the next, a kroak be standin' right there, makin' me eyeballs burn. Before we could draw a thorne, we heard two more hissing behind us. The one be taller than sir Isaac. Yellow skin be on its belly, black with spots be on its back. Red beady eyes lookin' down. The foul beast worked its tongue, be formin' words me tells ya."

"'Aim da arrow, die da slowly,' croaked the foul bag of slime.

'Let us pass,' ordered Alle-Encer, 'or the wrath of Ariel you will face.' The kroak only laughed a coughing, smelly belch of mockery.

'Me care none for Ariel, me want but yar flesh.' Kroaks have no teeth, ya know. No, ya don't know. They gulp ya up into their mouths, suffocatin' ya with the foul breath." Mirrah stepped into the cabin. She listened for two seconds.

"Garlock! What are you speaking?"

"Just a tale, me lady. Just tellin' 'em a tale." She gave a stern look as she went into a room off the main cabin.

"As I was sayin's, they haven't teeth to kill or chew, so they swallow ya whole." Mirrah poked her head out of the room and called to Breezy and Bella. "Come girls, there is no worth in these tales." They got up and went into the room with Mirrah who shut the door.

"Can't a Grimal tell a tale 'round here? Be tellin' the truth, ya know." The boys nodded. "So we stood there with this foul slime skin in front and two the likes behind. They knew we could open their bellies if given the chance, so they hoped to talk us into dying.

'Put down da arrow, us let yoose run, what say?' The fool beast tried a trick us into making a run for it. We knew to run be death for the sure. If we moved a muscle the two behind would have our heads inside their foul toothless gaps before we could take a breath. We was sweatin' a wantin' to what to do.

'I command you in Ariel's name to let us pass,' Alle-Encer be sayin's.

'Give us yar flesh and yoose can pass,' laughed the kroaken-gagger. The two behind gave up evil coughs thinkin' they were laughin's. Slimy spit sprayed the back of me neck. Was wishin' to grab me long knife and open the yellow belly, but Alle gave one last word.

'Let us pass now or die,' he warned. He then whispered to me the name of a Grimal dance. It be one where yeer standin' side-by-side with yeer partner. Ya spin away quick turnin' 'round about. Me knew his meanin' so waited his word.

The kroak coughed another foul laugh, be mockin' Alle-Encer. The two behind hissed and coughed.

'Shall we dance, my friend?' Alle said, to which we whirled about, drawing our long knifes. The two behind struck, mouths gapped wide. But we be not there." Garlock chuckled. "I ran me blade up the soft belly, a green one he be, and jerked it all about. Saw the innards—"

"Okay," Zac said covering his ears, "got the picture."

"Go on," Isaac said, "just spare the gory stuff."

"Well as be sayin's, after me taught that green kroak the ways of Garlock of Yorne, me spun round to render the yellow belly the same, but the talkin' coward be gone. Them two behind us now floppin' there gaspin' and coughin's, blood be—"

"Yes, got that part, thank you very much." Zac blinked wide eyes.

"Sorry, lad, but ya needs to know. Be ready or ya die. No foolin' with them beasts."

Isaac gripped the handle of his sword. The leather wrapping stuck to his palm as he squeezed it tight. "We'll try to be ready," he said.

"Ain't no trying, lad. Ain't no choice. Ya ready yeerself or ya die."

Isaac looked over at Zac. His heart went heavy. Garlock's words hung in his ears. 'Ain't no choice.' An image of home suddenly filled his mind. He saw his mother standing on the front porch. She was saying something, calling to him.

"Ready yourself, Isaac. There's no choice... ready yourself."

The weather stayed nasty for several more days, although the air warmed, even getting hot at times. They shed their winter pants and coats, running around in stocking feet and jeans. Slowly they adjusted to the rolling of the ship, their appetites returning. One of the crew caught a large marlin that became quite the event as it took several hours to bring it aboard. As the cook grilled the marlin steaks, the sky cleared, so they dined on the deck, watching the sun and sky work a wonder just for them. The images of home lessened. Feelings of having always lived in this world, with these friends, rose in their hearts. A friendship of trust grew among them like none they had ever known.

One day Zac was exercising Nusa by swinging a fur ball on a rope when a crewman called out, "The Isle of Moss... the Isle of Moss." Everyone came on deck and looked into the horizon. A mountain of green rose from the sea with smaller mountains spreading out to the sides. It was evening when they lowered anchor near a beach of reddish brown sand.

"We will go ashore at first light," Eryn said with authority. "May Ariel help us find what we came for and quickly. The less time we spend here..."

"The better," Garlock muttered under his beard.

That evening, Mirrah brought out a sack and dumped its contents on the cabin floor.

"Your curious boots will not do where we are going." She lifted up a leather lace-up boot. Three pair of high lace-up moccasin style boots spread out across the floor. Breezy giggled with delight as she pulled hers on. She tucked her dirty jeans inside, tightened the lacing, and danced around the cabin like a joyful princess in full regalia. They were nice boots and fit them all well. Isaac stood with hands on hips. His jeans tucked in like Breezy, his flannel shirt hung open with a t-shirt underneath. He felt like a pirate of sorts. It was good, but it seemed to make home drift further into the endless horizon.

Mirrah then took out a small bundle of cloth and unwrapped it. Everyone came over to see. Inside the cloth was a knife similar in design to the knife of Yonnan. It was sheathed in a dark brown leather scabbard. Scrimshawed into the bone handle was a Perlin on a rocky ledge overlooking a valley and a mountain range beyond.

She unsheathed the knife and skillfully twirled it about, flipping it overhand to underhand. "This knife is good in combat," she said. "It is good for throwing, has a firm grip, very good for... for peeling fruit." She smiled as she slipped it back into its sheath. Then with both hands she held it out to Zachary. "Please accept this gift in honor of saving my life on the pier." Zac took the knife from her hands and turned it over several times, smiling intensely.

"Seriously?" he said. "Wow, thanks, Mirrah. It's awesome." He handed it to Isaac who was joined by Breezy. They were still admiring the knife when Garlock came into the room carrying a shinny new thorne and a handful of arrows. He held them out to Isaac who was more than a foot taller than Garlock.

"And these, laddie, be for you. For bravin' the fires of danger. Fightin' when most be a runnin's." He handed the thorne and arrows to Isaac with both hands extended, his face very solemn. "And I means what I be a sayin's."

Isaac stood speechless. His face flushed red.

"Thank you, Garlock. Sorry for the stuff I said to you."

"Wouldn't know what stuffs yeer meanin's," Garlock said beaming. "Tomorrow, we'll make a nest for them arrows," by which he meant a quiver.

Mirrah then took something out of her pocket and handed it to Breezy. "We have only known you for a short time, but we feel you are a sister. We would like you to have this, a symbol of our new friendship." She handed Breezy a fine gold chain with a small smooth stone. The stone's color was like the pillar—crystal white, translucent and sometimes clear, then from the side, it became black. When held just right, a blue-green glow emanated from somewhere inside. It was a real puzzle as they all handled it, seeing black then clear, searching for the occasional magic blue-green.

Mirrah then revealed a gold chain about her neck, pulling a similar stone out for Breezy to see. Breezy turned it over and then exclaimed: "I see writing—inside."

"Lorian, which I cannot read."

"How'd it get inside?"

"No one knows, a mystery from the past."

Eryn lifted a stone from beneath her clothing. "We are sisters," she said embracing Breezy. "For as long as there is night and day, cold and warm, good times and bad, we are sisters." Warmth filled Breezy's heart. She cried and smiled at the same time. It was like Christmas, but much more special.

Eryn showed how her stone also had symbols of Lorian script written mysteriously inside. "Wish I knew its meaning. If only we could read the sacred script." She fondled the stone for a while before dropping it back inside her clothing. Breezy kept looking for writing inside her stone, but only saw the occasional blue-green glow. She tucked the gem beneath her shirt like Mirrah and Eryn and wiped her eyes. Deep inside, something changed.

Later that evening after dinner, Mirrah pulled the knife of Yonnan from inside her sash. She placed it on the table. Zac looked with surprise.

"I thought you lost it to Barthowl."

Mirrah smiled and shook her head. "I kept it hidden and prayed they would not ask." They all studied the knife again as Mirrah repeated the poem Zac had spoken at her home. "Cave of Torrin… tombs of Dross… box of Hornin…"

"Do you know any of these names or places?" Isaac asked.

"Torrin was a mighty leader in Sasson's army. He was banished to the Isle of Moss for conspiring to build his own kingdom. His tomb or cave must be somewhere on the island. Dross and Hornin…" She shook her head looking to Eryn.

"We will know when the time is right," Eryn said.

"Can I ask you something?" Isaac rolled an arrow between his fingers. "I've been wondering this for a long time." Both women nodded, their hair hung like veils, eyes twinkling as if light came from within. Isaac sighted down the arrow. "You all dropped everything when we came. You left your homes, put your lives in danger, paid out whatever it takes to get a ship, crew, and supplies, sailed to an island you seem to dread, and all of it seems to be on a little ditty with strange names that my little brother could have just pulled from the air." He stuck the sharp arrow point into the table. "Why? Why would you do that? Isn't that a bit bizarre?"

Mirrah's eyes misted as she listened. The cabin swayed with a gust and leveled. "Ariel speaks softly," she said. "Those who are listening, eager to serve, will quickly obey. Those with dull ears say it is the wind or tossing pebbles." Isaac pulled the arrow tip from the table and let it drop, sticking into the wood floor.

"Why doesn't he speak loud enough so everyone can hear? Make it plain?"

"If he is loud, people obey out of fear, not love—with reluctance instead of eagerness. We seek to act on his slightest whisper."

Eryn swung her hair to one side. "I follow your thoughts, Isaac. You feel he is just your little brother. But I believe, that he, like you and Breezy, are not here by tossing pebbles. Zachary's knowledge of that knife… the parlords…" She leaned back, her eyes lit up. "Although you think we acted foolishly, my heart is stirred, your words encourage us."

Mirrah tenderly touched Breezy's hair. "Ariel is speaking. We must not doubt. If we do not act on what he shows us, he will find someone who will."

Isaac sat silent. He fought the idea that they could be part of a grander scheme—that there was actual order in all this running and chaos.

"Why us?" he asked. "Why does Ariel need us? We're just kids."

"He does not need any of us," Mirrah said, "but he invites us… to work with him… to fight along side him… to die for him."

"Die?" Isaac thrust the arrow hard into the floor. "We're a little young for that."

Mirrah's eyes looked with love. The ship groaned with a sway then leveled.

"Not all death is of the body."

15   THE ISLE OF MOSS

The next day grew warm and muggy. During breakfast, Eryn and Mirrah, with their long braids tucked into cloth sashes wrapped around their waists, suggested that Breezy and Bella stay on the ship.

"I know you think it's dangerous," Breezy said, "and I'm a little scared—no, a lot scared." Her voice rose. She flopped her hands down at her sides. "But I don't think I just accidentally fell through the time-space-warp thingy-ma-jig that blopped us here. I'm here for some reason, too."

Mirrah chuckled at her antics, pulling a long knife from her sash, a knife just like Eryn's. "I knew you would want to come." She handed it to Breezy. "A gift, for saving my life with a stone." Breezy squealed with joy.

"Thank you, Mirrah!" She immediately displayed the knife to the boys.

"Eryn will show you how to strap it to your leg. And you better take this." She handed Breezy the felkin with its pouch of steel balls."

Eryn gave everyone a satchel with miscellaneous items. After lowering the rowboat they climbed down the rope ladder. Nusa was lowered down clinging to a rope. She, like most felines, was more fond of climbing up than down. Bella stayed behind with tears in her light blue eyes. A large crewman rowed them ashore, riding the surf up onto the beach.

"No wondering about the name," Isaac said, as they walked the brown sand. Trees lined the beach and where the sand ended, moss, thick moss, began. It was dark green, light green, reddish green, blue green and very green green. It was in the trees, on the branches, about the trunks, covering every piece of ground and rock.

"Looks like the day after a green snowstorm." Breezy slowly put on her felkin and armguard, her brow wrinkled.

It was awkward to be on solid ground, or terra firma, as Isaac called it. Zac said it was because they now had sea legs. Breezy and Zac wanted to play in the surf before searching for whatever they had come to find.

"Where do we go from here?" Isaac looked about the beach and mossy wood beyond.

Eryn adjusted her sword. "We need to find something that leads through the trees." They had sailed the length of the island, and the captain said this beach was the landing point on his charts, albeit the charts were very old. "No one has been here for a great time," Eryn said, looking about, "a long, great time."

Garlock stood looking into the trees and moss. "Best we don't just go a walkin' in there. Could be crawlin' with kroaks."

"Why don't we go through that archway?" Breezy pointed down the beach. "I bet there's a road or something there."

"What archway?" the group asked.

"The huge one on the edge of the trees down there." She pointed again. Zac came up beside her and squinted. "Breeze?"

"Right there! You can't see that?" All but Nusa were straining and shielding their eyes to find whatever she was seeing.

"Breeze, not a good time to be fooling," Zac whispered. She did not answer but started walking stoutly down the beach toward whatever she saw. Mirrah shrugged and walked behind her. Eryn continued looking about.

Not until they were nearly beneath it did they see what Breezy had seen. Just inside the edge of the trees, stood a massive stone archway covered mostly with thick moss. It looked like some ancient temple lost in the jungles of South America. Beneath the arch was the remnant of a narrow stone-paved road with small wagon ruts worn into the stone.

"Now do you see it?" Breezy stood directly under the arch, arms spread wide with a silly grin. "How did you guys not see this—it's huge?" Mirrah came up and wrapped her arms around Breezy, almost smothering her.

"My Brielle."

"We gonna be huggin' or hikin'?" Garlock led the way into the green forest of moss and trees. The leaves overhead formed a canopy of rubbery green. Although they covered the sky, sunlight diffused its way through, casting a green glow upon the already green mossy ground. Even their skin reflected tints of green. Moss hung like curtains from vines and branches. Strange noises echoed in the trees high above.

Nusa stayed close, not like in the Wood of Yorne. Garlock was in the lead, followed by Mirrah and Zac. Eryn took up the rear. Isaac saw Garlock ready his thorne and so did the same. Zac had his hand on his knife with his crossbow slung over his back. He was told not to load his crossbow when walking single file since the firing mechanism was not reliable.

Large bugs zoomed about causing Breezy alarm. She loaded her felkin and took aim at ones that came too close. Nusa would snap at whatever flew within range. Off to the side of the road sat a large cone shaped pile of black jelly almost two feet high.

"What is that?" Zac asked. "Looks like jelly."

"Moss beetle dung pile," Garlock said out of the side of his mouth. "Stay away. Take a moon's passing to get yeer nose clear. Dumb things, eat bongly moss. Makes their dung stink so high the clouds cry. Protects 'em though. Nothin' goes near."

Zac saw several more piles as they walked. "So not something to spread on your morning toast." Everyone chuckled, especially Garlock.

Then, he was suddenly silenced.

Without warning a giant brown lizard flashed from the left and plunged its mouth over Garlock's head. It jerked him off the road and into the forest. It had come on its hind legs, but now ran on all fours. Garlock, with head and shoulders smothered inside the beast's huge mouth, flailed about furiously. His arms and legs stuck out like a bug being eaten by a lizard. As quick as it had come it vanished into the forest of green.

Nusa sprang. As the lizard scurried over the moss, she leapt high, claws extended. With a chilling growl she landed on the slimy beast. It could not run under her weight and thrashed about, jerking Garlock side-to-side. At first, no one moved. Then Eryn dashed off into the spongy moss. Like a football player running through tires, she lifted her legs high, fighting to run.

The teens stood frozen, peering through the trees, watching the battle. The giant salamander, its skin brown and smooth, covered in a film of slime to which moss and twigs stuck, lashed about as Nusa, riding its back, kept trying to bite into the neck but would shake her jowls and snarl. She kept the beast from running, but not from smothering Garlock, his head still inside the monster's mouth.

He kept reaching for his knife but the creature's writhing tossed him like a dog with a rag doll. Eryn ran with sword drawn. Nusa finally sunk fangs deep into the neck. The slimy beast opened its mouth and shrieked a piercing scream. With a cough, it spit Garlock out onto the moss. He jumped to his feet gasping. He shook his head. Foamy slime flung out in all directions.

Eryn finally arrived but did not know where to strike. Nusa held her bite. Garlock drew his sword from over his shoulder. Holding it high with point down, he thrust it into the monster's head. The point sunk, going through into the spongy ground. The beast shrieked and squealed like a tortured pig. It jerked about with Nusa riding rodeo, claws and jaw set deep.

Garlock put one knee over its mouth and gave his sword a violent twist. The tail thrashed about then twitched and quivered to a stop. Eryn stood, still holding her sword high, eyes wide.

Nusa leapt from the dead beast and shook her jowls. Garlock stepped back and whipped his head hard, flinging more slime from off his beard and hair. He bent over and coughed, stamping his feet wildly, shuddering like he had swallowed absolute horridness.

"Aurgh!" he screamed, "I hate them cursed beasts. May them all meet the sword and be cut for bait." He tried to brush the frothy slime from his chest and shoulders. He shook himself again and then shuddered some more. Nusa, still trying to clean the bitter taste from her mouth, shook her head, flicking her tongue. Garlock pulled his sword from the dead beast and wiped it on a moss-covered tree. They walked together over the spongy ground with eyes alert.

When Garlock stepped onto the road, he looked straight at the boys. Breathing heavy, he said, "That me lads... is a kroaken-gagger... any questions?" Both boys shook their heads, eyes wide with terror. Breezy clung to Mirrah's arm. She had held her so tight that Mirrah was rendered useless during the attack.

Garlock continued spitting and cursing as Eryn now took the lead and put him at the rear. Breezy and the boys were reluctant to travel on. It had come so fast, how could they protect themselves? The group walked on much slower. The teens bunched together, almost tripping themselves. Everyone looked about, straining, peering, listening.

Without any more attacks, they came to an intersection with a small square post in the center. The stone post stood maybe four feet high with carved writing. Leading off to the left and right were similar moss roads as well as one straight ahead. Eryn and Mirrah studied the writing on the post. It made Zac remember the first day he had seen the stone pillar. He had liked it there, inside the courtyard. The winsome longing returned.

"Can you read it?" Isaac asked the women.

They shook their heads.

Zac looked at the carvings. They were not beautiful like the ones on the stone pillar. In fact they made him feel uneasy, what he called the 'hoobie-joobies.'

"Do you see anything?" Mirrah asked Zac. He looked again at the post and shrugged.

"No, but I'd go this way." He nodded to the right.

"Why?" Eryn asked.

"I don't know why. Same reason I went to your window, I guess."

They looked off each direction and finally took Zac's road to the right. After ten minutes of following the mossy road, Zac suddenly felt a dreadful doubt. They were going to their death or worse. What was he doing? Why did he think he knew which way to go? Why did Mirrah think he would know? I'm just a kid—I'm just me. "But this is the way," he whispered. "I don't know why... but this is the way."

They walked on in silence as the battle waged inside Zac's head. Suddenly Breezy let out a shrilling scream. In the middle of the road stood two large kroaken-gaggers. They were salamanders in every aspect except their monstrous size, for standing erect, they looked to be eight feet tall.

Eryn and Mirrah, who had been walking side-by-side, froze. The kroaks had appeared like an illusion. Their large mouths were slightly open releasing a low guttural gurgling as their heads swayed back and forth.

Suddenly Isaac spun around drawing his thorne as he turned. Behind Garlock, in the rear, was a third kroak, huge, bright green, its mouth gaping wide. It was arched back about to thrust its jaws over Garlock's unsuspecting head. Garlock's hand was on his thorne string, his vision locked on the two kroaks up ahead. He did not even see Isaac aiming directly above him. Isaac released his arrow just as the kroak went to engulf Garlock. Instead of hitting its chest, his arrow went straight into the monster's head as it came down upon Garlock. Jerking backwards, then stumbling sideways down the road, it dropped to all fours scurrying off into the mossy terrain.

By the time Garlock looked behind and back again, the two kroaks at the front were gone. Isaac looked down. He had already loaded his thorne with another arrow. His hands shook as adrenaline continued to flood his arteries.

No one spoke. Nusa had not moved. She could not anticipate these beasts, nor did she want to do battle with them. Her usual quiet confidence was gone. She, like the others, seemed shaken. The sounds from high above had gone still. The forest seemed to hold its breath. The group waited.

Then Garlock loosed a thunderous cry. "Hah!" he boomed. "Put that in yeer slimy mulger, ya soft bellied booglies! Ya be messin' with the wrong foe! Ya be but fool-bound fiends, ya be." Then raising his thorne overhead and shaking it wildly, he called out again, "Ya be messin' with Isaac of Kan-sis, our Isaac the Mighty. Hah!"

"Garlock," Eryn scolded, "stop telling the world we are here." Garlock beamed at Isaac.

"Taught him, I did. Ho, Isaac. Ya shot two toes above me head. Aiya!" He went on chuckling and did a little jig. "Be Isaac the Mighty, hah!" Isaac, still breathing a bit heavy, smiled at Garlock's antics. But he felt strange. How did he know to turn around? And how did he load his thorne so fast? He watched Garlock dance about. This isn't over, he thought. We shouldn't celebrate till it's over. Mirrah held her gaze on Isaac as they all breathed a sigh and continued down the mossy road.

Garlock shouldered his thorne and drew his sword, saying it provided better 'head smotherin' protection.' Eryn and Mirrah held swords ready. Breezy walked close between Isaac and Zac, her hand on her felkin. Shrieks and cries came again from high up in the trees. The air grew sticky and hot as they went deeper into the forest, away from the ocean breeze. Apprehension hung heavy as they pondered how quickly the kroaks had come and gone. They moved ahead slowly, looking all about. Isaac asked why Nusa could not detect the kroaks.

"They smell like the moss they be crawlin' in," Garlock

said. "Nusa can't sniff 'em out."

"Look, up ahead," Breezy said, "another archway. Looks like a city gate." Everyone stopped to look.

"Do I need glasses?" Zac strained to see where she was pointing.

"Up there, through those trees."

Once again, no one could see to which she was pointing. They went on ahead and finally caught a glimpse of a stone archway and a crumbling city wall. They walked with caution as the road angled to the left heading straight for the archway.

Two large iron gates sat inside the arch. It stood as part of a walled compound built into the base of a high cliff. The cliff seemed hundreds of feet high with long hanging vines. It was so straight it looked like it had been sliced with a knife. As they neared they saw the gates were ten feet tall. The wall of mortared stones had rusted iron spikes jutting outward from the top.

"To keep the kroaks out," Garlock said.

"Look at that!" Eryn pointed at the arch. Written on the stone arch above the doors were inscriptions like on the post at the intersection. Underneath hung a metal sign written in a different script. "That's middle Pharrian!" She studied the metal sign for a moment. "It says 'The Cave of Torrin!'" She turned to face the group. She glowed with excitement. "We found it."

Zac pointed to the writing on the stone arch. "What language is that?" He got the same feeling as from the stone post.

"Tornic," Eryn said, "the language of Torrin's kingdom. This is where Torrin lived out his banishment. The cliff must have a cave—the cave of Torrin."

Eryn hurriedly went up to the huge iron doors. One was partially opened. Sand covered the archway floor. She looked inside and stepped through. Mirrah was looking up at the inscriptions. She hesitated but finally stepped in after Eryn.

Zac peeked into the compound. Ancient buildings of mud and stone lined the walls and cliff. "I don't like this place," he whispered. "Gives me the creepies."

Garlock and Nusa kept watch outside. They looked for anything moving in the forest. The air was hot without a breeze. Beetles buzzed loudly in the trees. Isaac stepped through and noticed a worn trail in the sand leading into the compound.

"Something still lives here," he said.

The cliff sunk inward behind the buildings. From where they stood, it seemed to be a massive cave. Mirrah and Isaac moved in slow. Crumbled buildings—ancient homes—filled the walled compound. Eryn moved toward the cave at the rear. She peeked into what appeared to be a simple home of some kind with two windows and a door of unusual height. Suddenly she backed away and turning toward the archway, put two fingers to her mouth and frantically motioned for Isaac and Mirrah to go back. They went back out without a sound and moved a good distance from the gates before Eryn spoke.

"Kroaken-gaggers," she said breathing hard. "Six, seven, no, a hoard, sleeping. The place could be full of them."

Isaac looked at the sun shining into the compound. "Warm with ready-made shelters. No digging required. It's Beverly Hills for upper class kroaks."

"Back to the ship, I say." Garlock pulled at some crusted slime stuck in his beard.

"But we need to get to that cave," Eryn said. "How do we overpower that many kroaks?"

Isaac looked about. "Overpower? Say the poem again."

"On the Isle of Moss," Mirrah whispered, "near the cave of Torrin. In the tombs of Dross…"

"Near, not in. I don't think we need to get ourselves covered in kroak slime just yet." It was awkward taking his brother's poem seriously let alone literally. "We need to find the tombs of Dross, near the cave of Torrin."

They looked around as Garlock and Nusa stood guard. Zac said to push the gate shut and lock the kroaks in. Isaac said the sand around the gate was too thick.

"What if we take that trail?" Breezy pointed toward the cliff wall. A small path of stone and moss wound toward the cliff. The indentation was barely visible. They saw no other possibilities, so Eryn led them single file down the path. The sky was open as fewer trees grew near the compound. The land looked to have been cultivated at one time.

As they followed Eryn, Isaac asked Mirrah how they knew middle Pharrian.

"Can all Pharens read it?"

"No, not many. It is forbidden. No one Eryn's age. And she knows more than most sages. Reads every piece she can find."

Eryn looked back as she walked. "The Pharens go back a long time," she said. Mirrah let Isaac pass and walk with Eryn. "Some of the eleven, like Yonnan, were Pharens—recorders for the Lorians."

"But you can't read the knife of Yonnan?"

"Sasson made sure no one would ever read Lorian script— the script of the white stones."

"So why was that iron sign written in middle Pharrian?"

"After Torrin, this became an island for undesirables— criminals and rebels, the insane and diseased. They were sent here to die in the mouths of kroaken-gaggers. Many Pharens were sent here as well. Pharens love to read and write. Legend says that Yonnan, last of the eleven, was sent here to die, but instead he became a father to the outcasts. He tended the sick and established order, building defenses against the kroaks. Sasson was said to be on his way to kill him personally when Yonnan finally died of old age."

Just as Eryn finished speaking, they came to a clearing at the base of the towering cliff. The crumbled remains of another small compound spread out over the sandy ground. A small stone archway was all that remained of its protective wall. No iron gates, no spikes, just a wall of crumbled stone. Small dwellings, mostly rubble, sat tucked beneath the cliff.

Eryn looked up at the writing on the archway and shook her head. It was Tornic, carved into the stone. She and Isaac stepped through the archway. They held their weapons ready, but it looked like an archeological dig site with buildings and walls only partially standing, giving no place for large kroaks to hide. Stone rubble lay scattered over the sand.

As the others came in and looked about, Eryn walked back to stare up at the capstone's inscription. Unlike the other arch, this one barely stood. Isaac walked out with her. He noticed two rusted rings where an iron sign must have hung.

"Well?" he asked.

"It is Tornic; I cannot read it."

Isaac looked around the rubble in the archway. He pushed some rocks aside and dug something out of the sand. He stood holding a heavy metal sign. An inscription of curved lines was cut through the metal.

"How about this one?"

"Isaac! You surprise me… but… it does not fit."

"What does it say?"

"Just one word."

"Yeah?"

"Manure."

"Manure?" He set the heavy iron plate down against a rock. "Sure you read it right?"

She gave him a stern look of annoyance. She stared at the metal plate. "It could also mean trash or garbage—that sort of thing." Isaac watched her as she tried to make sense of the iron sign. Her black kinky hair glistened in the sun. Her skin and eyes seemed to glow. He pushed back the feelings stirring inside.

"Was it a dumpsite?" he asked.

"Maybe, but clearly people lived here. Could I be mistaken? No, I am not mistaken."

"No… never," Isaac said. She gave another annoyed look. He wanted to kick his own butt. He thought about the sign and the ruins of the small compound. Its wall had been crude in construction. He wondered how many kroaks it actually kept out. He tried to picture their meager existence. "Maybe it's lost in translation. Could it be something like a degrading term for the unwanted trash of society?"

"Oh, I suppose," Eryn looked again at the sign.

Isaac then dropped his head back. "I am so stupid! 'Tombs of dross.' The dross of society, the rejects lived here. If they had tombs or graves…" He suddenly got very excited, more than ever since entering this peculiar world. He ran into the ruins and told everyone to look for what might be graves or tombs. He went on about the box of Hornin being in the tombs of dross. "A cemetery, burial grounds, anything like that." He ran around in circles, so excited, he actually went nowhere.

Eryn stood watching. A tingly joy swelled up inside. She shook her head and smiled. "Interesting boy." She then ran in after Isaac, into the ruins of the ancient compound called, 'Manure.'

16 THE TOMBS OF DROSS

Mirrah, having gone toward the cliff at the far end from the compound, motioned for Isaac. "I may have found that of which you speak," she said quietly as he came near. The others came through the rubble and walkways of the ruins to see what Mirrah had found. Dug into the side of the cliff were nine small holes. The openings were about three feet wide and evenly spaced.

"Could they be tombs?" Mirrah whispered.

"Kroak dens, be the like." Garlock pulled his thorne string taut.

"They're man-made," Isaac said.

"They're creepy and forbidding," Breezy whispered.

"Foreboding," Isaac said as he knelt down near an opening and studied the sandy ground. He cautiously poked his head into one of the holes. He jerked back and coughed. Garlock prepared to fire. Isaac held up his hand. Taking a deep breath, he again looked inside. After a moment of listening, he asked, "Do we have any flashlights—I mean lamps?"

Eryn took out a small oil lamp the size of a medicine bottle. Attached to the side was a piece of spring steel with a flint end that, when bent back, would strike a rough piece of metal near the wick of the lamp. Taking off the cover off the lamp wick, she flicked the spring several times and blew gently. Soon there was a flame. She knelt down beside Isaac at the opening.

"I don't think there's any kroaks," he whispered, "just reeks." Eryn looked inside with the lamp and then crawled in. "You just got to be first."

Mirrah took a similar lamp from her satchel and, after lighting it, cautiously looked into the next hole with Garlock standing at the ready. Kroaken-gagger tracks were everywhere in the ruins but nothing near the holes.

"Come, look!" Eryn poked her head out. Isaac and Mirrah crawled in. Garlock kept guard with Nusa while Zac and Breezy stood waiting. Inside the air was pungent and musty while the floor was cool, damp sand.

"No wonder the kroaks don't come in," Isaac said, trying not to breathe. The cave was circular, no bigger than his bedroom and just high enough to stand. Along the walls, from floor to ceiling, cut right into the sandstone, were square holes about two feet wide, extending back six or seven feet. Each square opening held either a stone box or the decayed remains of a skeleton. Inscriptions were carved into the walls and the stone boxes. Eryn was ecstatically trying to read whatever came into the lamplight.

"Catacombs with sarcophagi," Isaac said.

"No, they are tombs. Some have coffins." Eryn was exuberant, even giddy. "These are middle Pharrian. 'Morpheon, Tellapo, Ronnan…'" She scurried about on her knees dusting off the inscriptions and pronouncing the names of ancients. Isaac watched as Mirrah joined in the hunt for Hornin's tomb.

Both women read out loud whatever inscriptions they could find. Some names, some epitaphs, some too eroded with time, but all seemed to be middle Pharrian. Isaac sat near the opening trying to grab some fresh air. He watched the two crawling on hands and knees, their little lamps casting shadows across the dusty bones.

"I don't think it would be in here," Isaac said. Eryn continued reading off names then suddenly stopped and put the lamp toward his face.

"Why?"

"Cause you can read these. Yonnan's knife is in Lorian. Wouldn't Hornin's tomb be the same?"

"No, maybe, I do not know. Why are you just sitting there? Help us look." Eryn's voice rose to almost a squeak. "Some of these have dates—up to the last purge."

Mirrah thought about what Isaac said. Everything was in middle Pharrian. She crawled out and breathed long breaths of fresh air. Isaac followed her out.

"May I see the knife?" he asked. Mirrah reached inside her sash and handed him the knife of Yonnan. "If these lines correspond to the poem, the last few inscriptions, if…well, these may be the name of Hornin." He traced the last two inscriptions from the knife into the sand. "What if we split up and look for these symbols? If we don't find anything, we try another set. His name is on here, right?"

Mirrah studied the lines in the sand. "There is one more lamp in Garlock's pouch."

Eryn crawled out and flopped against the cliff wall. She brushed spider webs from her hair. The wind of euphoria had already passed. She sat discouraged.

Isaac suggested they split into pairs and look for a tomb with the Lorian script. Nusa was to stand guard. Breezy and Mirrah would start on the left, Zac and Garlock take the middle and Isaac and Eryn the far right. "It stinks a bit," Isaac told Zac and Breezy. "Just crawl out if you need air." With a few big breaths they split up and crawled into the tombs of Dross.

After only one minute Breezy crawled out shouting "Mirrah says to come here. This one's all ancient stuff."

Everyone crawled in and started searching for anything that resembled the last characters on the knife handle. They were constantly asking Mirrah to show them the knife. Many of these sarcophagi were crumbling and the name could no longer be seen. After a good half hour, they became discouraged, especially Eryn.

"I am going to the next tomb," she said.

She and Isaac crawled into the next cave, which also had many names in the ancient script. "I know you're excited," Isaac said, "but you need to take your time. We've come a long way. We'll find it." The others came in to join them, and after another half hour of smelly, dirty searching, they crawled out and sat against the cliff wall.

A small stream of water fell somewhere from high up the cliff face. It came down just inside the compound wall to the right of the caves. Breezy found it mesmerizing to watch the water drop from high above.

"Three seconds," she said to Zac, taking out a small water flask inside her satchel. "Makes me thirsty. Wish we could go swimming."

Eryn got up to crawl into the next tomb, so they all crawled in after. They searched each name as they did the previous with the same result.

"We have missed something," Eryn said with a huff. "In the tombs of Dross, the box of Hornin." She mused a bit and then asked Mirrah, "Did you miss something that night— something said?"

"No. We just need to ask Ariel for help." She looked up at the ceiling as if to the sky. "Ariel," she prayed, "you brought us these friends, you brought us together, you brought us here, please help us fulfill our purpose."

"I am going to the next," Eryn said. The others did the same. This tomb, like the first, was all in middle Pharrian. After ten minutes, Eryn became very discouraged. She was about to crawl out when Breezy called with great excitement. Eryn came over and looked. She dusted out the inscriptions and softly mouthed the words 'Hornin of...'

"Is this it?" Breezy asked. She was shifting all about, waiting to spin a twirl of celebration.

"More light," Eryn called. They all huddled around the hole in the second row near the floor. Their combined light fully illuminated the side of the tomb wall. Inside was a stone box on which were written two scripts—one like the knife handle, the other apparently middle Pharrian.

"Well?" Breezy asked still going from one foot to the other.

"Hornin of… somewhere." Eryn lightly rubbed the stone. "This script looks like the knife. Help me pull it out."

Eryn and Isaac tried to grasp the sides of the sarcophagus, or stone coffin, but the space between the coffin and the square opening was only enough to wedge a flat hand. It was to be pushed in and not pulled back out. A lid of stone sat heavy on top leaving nothing to grip and pull.

"Help me push the lid." Isaac tried to push the stone lid towards the back. It did not budge.

"Step aside." Garlock took a few steps back and then gave a firm stout kick. He had intended to kick the lid loose, but instead he punched a hole in the end of the stone coffin. "Moldy mulger."

Eryn chastised him for careless destruction of ancient artifacts, but it did enable them to grasp the lid and slide it out. Landing on the sandy floor with a heavy thud it broke into several pieces. Then, with a chorus of grunts and groans, they pulled the sarcophagus out. It slipped from Eryn's grasp and partially crumbled into itself.

Garlock mumbled something about careless destruction of artifacts. A collection of bones and rubble now lay on the tomb floor. A skull seemed to stare straight up at Breezy. She wanted to scream and run but could not think of missing out. Eryn and Isaac lifted the broken stone pieces off the dry skeletal remains. Remnants of cloth lay scattered amongst the bones. Eryn carefully moved things around.

"Nothing but bones," she said. She had been on her knees and now sat back. She let out a huge sigh. Isaac picked up the skull and looked inside. He sought to find her something.

Mirrah stood staring down at the bones. "We do not know what we are looking for. We may have found it and do not even know."

"Maybe there is another box of Hornin," Breezy said very quietly. No one answered.

Isaac sat with his back against the wall. He stared at the box and Eryn as the lamps flickered out ripples of yellow light.

"Let me see your lamp." Isaac held Eryn's lamp over the remains, searching the bones for a clue. He rubbed the sides looking for any other inscriptions. He checked the back of the box. He was about to suggest they flip it over when he looked back into the hole from which it had come. He shoved the torch in, illuminating the square hole. Its sides bore the chisel marks made centuries before. He then put his head and shoulders in. It was almost comical—his upper body fully inside the square hole—his butt and legs dangling out with his toes kicking the bones of Hornin.

"Oh yeah, baby," came this muffled call from inside the hole. He squirmed back out. "Can't reach it." He brushed spider web off his face. Eryn grabbed the lamp and looked into the hole. Something black filled the back end of the cubicle. She crawled in like Isaac had done, but she too could not get a hold on whatever was there. She frantically kicked and groaned, trying to grasp whatever lay tucked inside the tomb.

"Zacman," Isaac said, "crawl in there and see if you can get a grip on that thing and I'll drag you out."

"I heard Breezy say she would go in there." Zac bent over to look into the tomb. Breezy gave him a swat.

"Just get a grip on it, and I'll drag you out."

Zac took a few breaths then coughed. He looked into the hole again. "Indiana Zac and the search for the big black thing at the end of the small dark tomb." He wiggled in up past his knees. Isaac pushed his feet. A little later, Zac yelled a slightly panicked call to drag him out. Isaac pulled him by his ankles while Eryn held his body. Zac came out holding a black metal box. They tried to lift him out over the bones of Hornin, but Isaac tripped and lost his grip. Zac's lower body dropped into the coffin. He kicked wildly with his feet fumbling among the bones. Eryn helped him stand and step out of the box. He shook himself and spat.

"Okay, that was fun!" he said with more spitting.

"Really?" Eryn asked.

"Ironic humor," Isaac said.

"I do not understand."

"It was creepy," Zac said.

"Try a kroak's throat," Garlock said, "and you'd say that tomb be cozy."

Eryn looked at both boys and shook her head.

The air was thick with anticipation as they took the black metal box out into the daylight. No one spoke as Eryn set it on a flat stone of rubble. Nusa came near to sniff the ancient relic.

"It has a lock," Eryn said breathing hard, desperate to open the box. Was this what they had come to find or just some ordinary burial items? Zac took out his knife and began cleaning away the rust from the lock. When he pried at a piece of rust the whole lock and hinge simply dropped off into the sand.

"Well done." Isaac slapped his brother on the shoulder. Eryn was already lifting the lid. She forced it open only part way when it too snapped off at the hinges. Lifting the lid completely off they all stared at what looked like another box made of brass. Eryn carefully lifted this box out and, kneeling down, she set it on her thighs. Three symbols in middle Pharrian were carved in a triangle on the top of the box. Eryn wiped them with her fingers.

"That's *So!*" Zac shouted so loud it made them all jump. "The number three, right?"

"That is right," Eryn said. "And the others?"

"That one looks like *Faln*. I remember it because it means 'for certain,' and Fall is for certain." He bubbled with excitement, making his crawl into the tomb hole worth it all.

"It is *Faln* and you 'certainly' amaze me."

"Had a good teacher."

Eryn studied the symbols. *So* was on top. *Faln* was in the lower right.

"It can also mean certainty as in..." she spoke slowly, "as in destiny or the end of something. Sometimes it means... death." She gave Mirrah a lingering glance.

"And the other?" Isaac asked.

"*Tur...* to come carrying something, like to arrive at someone's house bringing something large. I have also seen it used as to hug or embrace." She looked again at Mirrah. Isaac watched Eryn's eyes as she mouthed the words, lightly touching the brass box. Her eyes were apprehensive.

"Three will certainly bring something?" Eryn said.

"Three bring destiny," Mirrah said.

Isaac watched them both, knowing there was more. He studied Eryn's face as she continued to touch the symbols, moving only her lips. Why had she not opened the box?

"What is it?" he asked.

Eryn cleared her throat. "It is written in a triangle," she paused. "It can be read either way—three bring destiny—or destiny will bring three." Eryn looked up at Mirrah. She then looked at the three teens. Isaac and Zac were covered in dirt. "It could also mean..." she trailed off, slowly tracing the carved lines with her slender fingers.

Isaac looked hard at both women, his face very firm. "*So— Tur—Faln*. Three bring destiny—three embrace death." He spoke the words without emotion—just stating a fact.

"No!" Eryn stopped him. "It means... it can mean a lot of things."

She tried to open the box. It was in two parts. A top cover fit tight over a bottom box. It took a while to separate the halves using knives to break the sides free. Eryn finally got the top half to slide up and off. Inside was something wrapped in old dried leather.

"Could there be jewels?" Breezy asked.

Eryn tried to lift it out. It seemed stuck inside. Isaac pushed the black iron box off the flat stone. He took the brass box from Eryn and flipped it over with a smack on the stone. He then lifted off the brass box. Eryn scolded him and then looked at what lie on the stone. A large book wrapped with a leather cover sat on the stone. The bottom cover wrapped over up onto the top. It tapered into a strap that was then tucked through a loop in the top cover. The same triangle of symbols was carved into the leather cover. Isaac said the book was a foot square and at least five inches thick.

The strap, snugly stuck in the loop and the leather, which

though old and cracked, was still somewhat pliable. Eryn tenderly worked the strap loose and slowly unwrapped the leather cover. She opened the large book near the center. It seemed to creak and groan as if awakened from the dead. As pages met the light of day, Eryn gave out a long quivering gasp.

"Mirrah!" Eryn's voice quivered. The pages were filled with what looked like two different languages. One seemed to be the script like the knife of Yonnan, and the other, written every other line, was middle Pharrian.

Mirrah dropped to her knees beside Eryn and studied the open pages. Tears filled her eyes. She quickly wiped them to look again at the thick yellow pages written with two distinct scripts. She finally put her hands on her knees and with sobs of joy poured out praises to Ariel.

Breezy looked frightened and put an arm around Mirrah. Eryn slowly turned the stiff yellow pages. Some were thick and almost rigid, crackling as she moved them left to right. The boys and Garlock just stood there feeling awkward.

Isaac studied the pages with Eryn. The edges were rough and uncut. "It's Lorian with middle Pharrian written interlinear, right?" he said. "And the five stone pillars are written in Lorian script." Eryn looked up at him; tears poured down her face as she nodded. Isaac exhaled and looked up at the cliff overhead. "Finally, we're getting somewhere." Whatever these pillars contained, this book was possibly the last key to learning their knowledge.

After more awkwardness of tears and crying, Eryn looked up at the teens. "Do you know what you have done?" Eryn wiped her eyes. "This is… is… beyond the wonderful. Now I can—" she broke into a full blown sob.

"Now you can learn the Lorian script and read the pillars," Isaac said, "provided you can find them."

Eryn nodded. "This book and the stones will bring the end of Sasson."

Breezy started to cry. Zac's eyes welled with tears. He looked at his brother and smiled. Mirrah got up and hugged Breezy, then Zac and finally Isaac. Garlock turned away, rubbing his eyes, muttering about sand and dust.

Eryn tenderly let the pages rest and stood before Isaac. Her beautiful eyes were red and swollen, her face dirty from the tomb. She reached out and held his hands in hers, looking deeply into his eyes.

"Thank you," she said. "Ariel is with you. He brought you here. He will bring you home again." Still holding Isaac's hand, she wiped her nose. "From Pharens long dead and the living... we thank you."

She then hugged Breezy and Zac and repeated her gratitude. She kept shaking her head. "I cannot believe what we have found. Ariel has led us. This is more than fantastic, more than wonderful, this is—"

"Funderful," Zac said. Breezy laughed, wiping her eyes. A joy, beyond what they had ever known, filled each heart. For the teens, they had endured hardships never imagined, faced dangers they hoped to soon forget and made friendships they would always remember. They were part of something special in a world not their own. No clue why. Unsure as to how it fit together, but now certain, it was not by 'tossing pebbles.' This could not have happened without them.

They watched as Eryn and Mirrah briefly studied more of the pages. Garlock suggested that 'being they found whats they come for, they ought to be movin' on.' Eryn reluctantly put the book back into the brass box. "It has records, histories, ancient secrets," she said as she unwrapped her sash belt and skillfully tied it around the box to be carried at her side.

"Very carryable," Breezy said smiling at Zac.

He nodded, "Carryable indeed."

"Can we go home now?" Isaac asked. A sadness came. It surprised him.

"I believe so," Mirrah said. "Your purpose was great. No wonder Sasson wanted you stopped."

"I'll bet me own beard he won't be dancin' happy when he learns a this." Garlock said. "Best we be gettin' off this mossy rock."

"We should put Hornin's bones back," Isaac said looking

into the cave. Eryn flashed a smile, and they both went back inside.

"I will never forget you," she said as they collected the bones and laid them back inside the square hole. He followed her movements. Floods of emotion surged inside. He had never known a girl like Eryn. None of his friends would ever believe him even if he had a picture. He reached into the broken coffin at the same time as Eryn. They bonked heads. She giggled. Isaac's heart ached. So much had happened, and so fast. It would be a relief for it to be a dream, yet so sad.

"Ariel sent you," Eryn said softly. "I believe I will miss you."

Isaac almost told her what he really felt, that she was amazing and beautiful, and how he wished he could take her to school for just one day. He knew he would never, ever forget her.

"We aren't home yet," he said as he put the last bone in place. "It ain't over till the fat lady sings."

"Huh?"

"Nothing."

They crawled out, and Eryn slung the brass box on her side as they all prepared to leave the tombs of Dross. Their main concern was the napping kroaks inside Torrin's compound.

"They're most certainly done napping," Isaac said. "Could be dozens running around."

Garlock held his sword upward. "Hold yer swords and knives unsheathed," he ordered. "Walk in pairs, stayin' close. Those bein' on the left, watch left, on the right, watch right." Eryn and Isaac followed Nusa. Mirrah and Breezy followed them, with Garlock and Zac in the rear. Everyone held a sword or knife in hand. "Stay together—stay alert," Garlock barked, "and we'll be back before the aft-noon's mulger."

They left the ruins of Dross and saw nothing while walking the path to Torrin's compound. They quietly passed the large Torrin archway turning onto the road. It was hard for Garlock and Zac to turn their backs on the kroak napping grounds. After every five steps, Garlock would glance back. They reached the stone post intersection seeing nothing but moss entrenched forest and heard nothing other than the strange cries high up in the trees.

"Maybe we frightened them off," Isaac said, "when Garlock killed that one."

"And you another," Eryn said.

Isaac thought again how he had turned without knowing why. This world was different. He was different. He thought back to the night in the wood of Yorne—the horl's sudden attack. Kroaks, like horls, came without warning.

They quickened their pace, moving in silence, ever looking, ever listening. The moss on the road was not thick like in the trees. It was like walking a thin foam mattress, squishy yet firm. The large bugs pestered more than in the morning, some downright frightening as they dove at faces and circled overhead. It was pointless trying to hit them, but being a natural reflex, they slashed and swung with a greater chance of someone getting injured by a bug-swatting sword than by any harm the bugs could bring. The air became hot and sticky even in the shaded forest.

"I'm really thirsty," Breezy said, "but I don't want to look away, or put my knife down." A whiff of ocean breeze drifted through the forest.

"We are almost there," Mirrah said. "You can drink your water on the beach." They heard the distant sound of waves, and soon they felt the ocean air working its way through the humid forest. When they saw the archway with the beautiful azure waters behind, they all breathed a joyful sigh of relief.

"We made it," Eryn said.

Isaac exhaled. "That was not fun." They approached the archway with weapons still ready, Garlock still glancing behind.

"Does Sasson still banish people here?" Zac asked.

"No," Mirrah said, "he has not banished anyone here in my life time."

They walked through the archway onto the beach and breathed the fresh sea air. Isaac squinted, scanning the sea. Then with a heavy sigh, "I think he just did."

17 BANISHED

"Where's the ship?" Breezy dropped her knife.

"Where's the longboat?" Eryn looked up and down the beach. The ship and longboat were nowhere in sight. The oarsman was to anchor beyond the surf, out of danger and await their return.

"Maybe he went back to the ship." Zac peeked through between Eryn and Isaac. "But where's the ship?" They all stood beyond the archway looking dumfounded out into the open sea.

"I have known captain Boar since I was young," Eryn said. "He would not do this—not without a fight."

"Look." Breezy pointed down the beach near where they had first landed. Four or five kroaks scurried about the beach. They scampered around the base of a large tree like hounds having treed a coon. Garlock unslung his thorne, nocked an arrow and aimed.

"You can't shoot that far," Isaac said, "let alone hit anything." Garlock's arrow soared over the sand. Isaac lost sight of it and was about to say, 'told ya so' when a kroak suddenly leapt into the air, spun about madly and dashed off into the trees. "No way. I would've—" He didn't finish before Garlock, who had already nocked a second arrow, let the string twang. A kroak looked their way and stood upright to get a better view. No sooner had it stood than Garlock's arrow pierced its chest. It stumbled backward a few steps before collapsing on its side in the brown-red sand. Isaac looked at Garlock astonished. "How did you do that?"

"Ya goin' catch bugs or shoot?" Garlock said putting a third arrow to the string. "Ya need to know yeer enemy—to anticipates 'em."

"Look," Breezy said, "in the tree. Someone's in that tree." They all started jogging down the beach toward a large tree that seemed to have someone or something in the lower branches. The remaining kroaks had run off into the forest after Garlock's display of skill. Nusa suddenly bounded on up ahead, covering large spans of sand in each leap. Coming to the tree, she slowly approached the dead kroak, made a wide circle and then tried to climb up the tree. The mossy bark peeled away beneath her claws. She stood stretched out against the trunk making a comical meowish groan.

Eryn, first to reach the tree, stood looking up for a moment as if unable to believe her eyes. As the others came near, they saw, hanging on a limb with toes just touching a limb beneath, was a terrified Sherrabella.

"Sherrabella," Eryn cried, "what are you doing up there?" Sherrabella hung by her armpits and chin, afraid to put her weight onto the branch beneath. Her whole body shook as she cried.

"How'd she get up there?" Zac asked.

"How do we get her down?" Isaac studied the moss-covered trunk.

"Don't you let go, Bella," Breezy called. "We'll get you down."

Isaac stood against the tree. "Take off the book, Eryn, and climb up my back." Eryn handed the brass box to Breezy, and as Garlock and Mirrah helped her up onto Isaac's back, she talked soothingly to Bella. Isaac had forgotten about his back wounds. As Eryn scrambled up, he groaned, wondering what he had been thinking.

"Hang on for me. Do not let go." Eryn climbed, stood on the lower limb and put her arms around Bella. "I will lower you to Isaac and Mirrah, tally?" Garlock kept an eye out for kroaks as Eryn lowered her down while balancing on the limb. Nusa gave out low meows as if crying for Bella. Eryn slipped and almost fell once, then twice, but managed to lower Bella with one hand. She then swung from the branch and dropped fluidly onto the sand.

They quickly walked to where the beach was wide, giving room between the forest and waves. It took some time for Bella to calm down enough for them to get the story. The gangly crewman, Ferro, persuaded the others that they were on a doomed mission. If they sailed on with the strangers, it would bring death to them and their families. Captain Boar tried to stop him but was put on shore with Sherrabella.

"The captain shoved me... up... the tree," Bella said between sobs. "Right... before the..." She broke down into a full out cry again. They eventually pieced together the story of how the captain gave his life to save her from the kroaks. Garlock kicked a cloud of sand toward the spot where the ship had been anchored.

"I knew that drog, Ferro, be spoilin' mulger. If I finds 'em, I'll drop in the salty brew."

"So we're marooned." Isaac looked off into the horizon of blue. No one answered. It was mid-afternoon. He wondered what night would be like and what they could do to prepare. Breezy sat with Bella, holding her close. Mirrah looked up and down the beach.

"We could travel back to the tombs," she said, "prepare to spend the night there." Breezy and Zac groaned.

"Sleep with the dead?" Breezy said.

"Probably don't snore." Zac tried to ease her fear.

"It would be a safe place." Eryn slung the book over her shoulder.

"But not the walkin' there, missy," Garlock said shaking his head. "Best not stack our cakes too high."

"It would be safe," Isaac said, "but getting there and

back…"

"And what would we do there?" Zac asked.

"We need to find a safe place, near the sea." Isaac continued looking up and down the beach. Driftwood lay scattered about but not enough to build a protective fire and keep it going all night. And that would be only one night. "We need a safe place till we find a way off. What if we checkout the coast or those other roads?"

Garlock muttered curses at Ferro under his breath. Breezy said she did not want to go back into 'bug land.' They were all hot, sweaty, and hungry. No one moved.

"How often do ships come this way?" Isaac asked.

"It is not a shipping route." Eryn stared off into the sea. "Nor a stopping point. It is an isle of… banishment." Isaac watched her. She looked about ready to break down and cry. It had been a fear-filled morning for everyone. Finding this book was Eryn's whole world. Being banished to a forsaken isle defeated everything. Book or no book, they could not sit here and wait to die in the mouths of slimy kroaks.

"We need to find food, water and shelter," he said with authority. It made him think back to the night of wandering lost in the woods. He had tried to lead, but in fear. "Some of you stay here, it seems safe on the beach. Whoever wants, can come with me."

Mirrah suggested that she and Eryn stay with Breezy, Bella and Zac. Nusa could accompany Isaac and Garlock. Eryn handed Isaac a small ivory tube. She took a similar one from her satchel and putting it to her lips, blew out a brief shrill whistle. It faintly echoed off the cliffs at Torrin's cave.

"If help is needed," she said.

Nusa led the way as Isaac, choosing to carry his thorne, and Garlock wielding his sword, walked back up the beach to the stone archway. They looked back at the huddle on the beach before entering the kroak-infested forest of moss.

"Let's try the road to the left," Isaac said. "We'll have to play it by ear."

"Play with our ears?"

"Just see what we find."

"Why didn't ya just say that?"

"Well… it's…." Nusa looked back at them and Isaac swore she shook her head.

They came to the stone post without seeing or hearing anything except the bugs and the cries from whatever roamed above. They turned left, opposite the way they had taken to the Cave of Torrin. The road slowly climbed up and back toward the sea. After about fifteen minutes or a fifth, they could see an opening and small cliffs up ahead. Nusa continued leading the way but stayed close.

Suddenly Isaac whirled around—thorne drawn—then paused. Garlock turned to look back down the road. For a brief second nothing happened. Then Isaac whispered, "Ready your thorne."

"Why in Mulder's mire—"

"Heeeeeeh," came a loud breathy hiss. Nusa gave out a snarling roar. Isaac and Garlock turned back around to see Nusa face to face with a lizard on all fours. It was over twice her size, easily fifteen feet long. Unlike the kroaks, it had leathery skin with folds like a komodo dragon. Saliva dripped from it gaping jaws as it gave another throaty, gargling hiss.

But Isaac only watched it briefly. He turned back and again told Garlock to ready his thorne. He had not finished speaking when three kroaks came out of the trees. One on the road, standing upright, was a greenish-brown with tints of yellow on its belly. Two others slithered on the mossy floor, one on each side. They were reddish-brown with stripes of green. He noticed them only slightly as he let his arrow fly. It pierced the chest of the upright kroak just as the reddish-brown near Garlock rose upright and lunged for his hairy head. Garlock swung his sword with both hands cutting off a portion of its lower jaw. It screeched a horrid hiss that filled the forest air just as Nusa cut a swath across the large lizard's nose.

Isaac had set a second arrow for the other reddish brown, but it was already in retreat. He spun about to see Nusa leap aside as the large lizard snapped for her leg. She rose up over its head. Standing on her hind feet, she sliced her claws into the eye of the beast, fanning with both paws before leaping backward. It all happened in a flash of movement. The lizard scooted backward then whirled about and disappeared into the moss and trees. A foul odor filled the hot humid air.

Isaac held his thorne at ready, turning side-to-side. Garlock looked at the severed jaw lying on the moss-covered road. He panted in quick short breaths.

"Does ya right, ya... ya... slimy... foul... big mouthed piece of... rotten flesh."

They scanned the trees, and then Isaac slowly lowered his thorne. The kroak he had shot was nowhere in sight, but as he looked, he saw his arrow protruding from a tree. It had gone clean through the kroak and lodged into the mossy bark.

"Look at that," he said pointing, "went right through."

"How'd ya know they be?" Garlock asked.

"Felt they were behind us, but when I turned to shoot they weren't there... yet. How does that happen?"

"Ya got me, unless ya be a Pharen."

With his knife and some effort, Isaac pulled his arrow from the tree and they continued up the small road.

"So what kind of lizard was that?" Isaac asked, watching Nusa for any signs of wounding.

"Tanglin' me beard. A bull kroak, me guessin's. Best we don't see more of his likes."

After a few minutes walk, the road came to an abrupt end. A small trail through the trees led to an opening up ahead.

"Road construction must have gone over budget," Isaac said. "Safe to go through there?"

Garlock laughed. "Safe as any place on this cursed, mossed-up rock."

They cautiously worked through the trail, thick moss squishing, sometimes oozing beneath their feet. It led to an open rocky ledge overlooking the forest and ocean far below. They walked upward onto a high point of level open rock. A large fire pit with a crude stone table sat on the open rock. A large block of stone seemed to serve as a chair. Both the table and chair were too large, twice the normal size, but could be nothing other than a table and chair.

Beyond the fire pit, they saw a small cave opening into a rock wall on the right. It had a simple gate of iron bars and wire, an obvious protection against kroaks and other such beasts. The most striking sight was the skeletal remains of what looked to be a giant human. The upper skeleton sat piled upright beside the small iron gate.

"Look at the size of these bones." Isaac stood over the remains. "They're two or three times a normal man. What was this?"

"A Brone," Garlock said. "Didn't know Brones be sent here."

"Brone?"

"Brones of Bellock. The ones who gave us them lovely horls."

The leg bones extended out from the rock wall while the upper skeleton and skull lay piled against the wall.

"It's like he died sitting against the wall," Isaac said.

"Prob'ly watchin' the sunset."

The view from the top of the ledge was spectacular. To the left was the forest extending to the massive cliff at the cave of Torrin. To the right was the vast open sea. Ahead to the west, far down below, was the small harbor and beach where Zac and the girls were awaiting their return.

"Look at that!" Isaac shouted pointing to the beach. As soon as he called out they heard the faint shrill of Eryn's whistle. Nusa looked intently at the beach, growling, her hackles rising.

"Argh," Garlock kicked the rocky ground. "Smarmy beasts won't give a rest."

On the beach far below, Zac and the girls, stood waist deep in the surf. Waves knocked them about as seven or eight kroaks scurried back and forth along the beach. Some stood upright, running toward them as the waters receded then backing up as waves rolled in. Others, on all fours, frantically tried to reach their prey. Isaac could see Eryn holding the book high under her arm, the bone whistle to her lips.

"Best we run," Garlock hollered into the open air.

"Wait a sec," Isaac ran to the cave. He peeked inside and quickly tested the iron gate. "This'll work," he said joining Garlock and Nusa as they ran past the giant table and chair toward the mossy trail.

Garlock did surprisingly well in matching Isaac's long stride, his legs short but quick. Nusa would lunge ahead then wait for them to catch up. It seemed a lot further running back. Finally they came through the stone archway onto the beach.

Both had readied their thornes and Garlock let an arrow fly while still on the run. Isaac ran on and then stopped to aim. His arrow hit a kroak in the tail. It wasn't the one he had aimed for, but was glad it found something for his effort. He was greatly impressed at the thorne's ability to send the arrow over such a great distance. They ran together behind Nusa.

Garlock was able to load and shoot while running. Two kroaks, seeing new prey approach, stood and faced them. Garlock shot. His arrow pierced the soft chest. Isaac stopped to aim at the other kroak. He was about to shoot when he remembered Garlock's advice. He lowered his aim toward the kroak's feet.

The kroak dropped to all fours just as Isaac released. His arrow zipped into the giant salamander's skull. The beast shivered in the sand before rolling onto its side, vainly trying to reach the arrow with its front claws. It slowly clawed at the arrow protruding from its skull as they ran past. It looked to be in slow motion, using up its last drops of life, trying to dislodge the projectile. By the time they reached Zac and the girls, the other kroaks had fled into the trees.

"Thank you, Ariel," Mirrah called out over the surf as they waded through the rolling waves.

"Good they do not like the sea." Eryn held the book high, helping Bella walk ashore.

They told of the attack, and Isaac finished by telling them about the Brone skeleton and the cave. "It looks safe. I think we should make it our camp for the night."

As they walked back up the beach toward the archway, Isaac went to pull his arrow from the dead kroak's skull. He stopped short as he saw how large the lizard was up close. Sand stuck to its slime, and blood still oozed from its head. His stomach tightened. Garlock watched him and then came over. The small burly man put his sandaled foot with its claw-like toenails firmly on the dead beast's head and jerked the arrow out.

"You clean it." He handed Isaac the arrow, blood still dripping, as he swaggered on up the beach.

18   THE GROTTO

Bella, being quite shaken by her second kroak attack, stayed close to Zac and Breezy as they made their way through the forest of kroaks, bugs, and moss. They did not see any kroaks in the forest save one that ran across the road far ahead. It chased a small rodent and seemed oblivious to their presence. Isaac thought about the recent kroak attack—the large one in front and the three from behind. Can they organize?

The sun neared the western sea as they lifted the gridiron gate from the cave mouth. The late afternoon light shone straight into the cave, illuminating a small living space larger than the tombs but not any higher. Isaac called it a grotto. A sand floor with nothing but the rotted remains of a human-sized bed, it was dry and the air clean.

"Well done, Isaac," Mirrah said as they crawled inside. She stood and lightly bumped her head on the ceiling.

Isaac looked about the grotto. "That's not a giant's bed." Eryn tried to light her lamp, but the wick had gotten wet. Garlock came in and lit his lamp. The room was large enough for all of them to sleep on the sand floor. It seemed to be a natural cave that someone had enlarged with hammer and chisel. They hauled out the remains of the bed and a few other miscellaneous items too rusted to identify, and finished by sweeping the floor with a branch.

Garlock handed his lamp to Isaac, "Burn out the spiders in them holes. Some be big enough to eat, but we ain't that hungry... yet." Isaac took the lamp and found that to which Garlock referred. Numerous small holes the size of his thumb dotted the cave ceiling. He held the flame up to one and blew to direct the heat into the hole. Immediately a spider like creature shot out and scurried down the cave wall. He jumped back, almost dropping the lamp. He watched it scutter into another hole.

"I meant for ya to kill 'em." Garlock had lingered to watch Isaac, knowing full well what would happen. Isaac took a blunt tipped arrow from his quiver, shoved it into the hole where the spider had crawled. He heard a popping crunch and ooze dripped from the hole. He looked back at Garlock silhouetted by the afternoon sun. Garlock chuckled and went out to work on the gridiron gate.

The sun was setting when Zac, Breezy and Bella came yelling they had found water on the north side of the outcropping. Everyone went to see and drink. They found a steady flow of water that came winding down the rock, channeled from somewhere above and flowed into a small pool chiseled in the rock.

"Somebody knew what they were doing," Mirrah said. "Thank you Ariel and to whomever made this pool."

They drank and washed, then went back to build a fire. As they sat around the fire drying clothes and watching the sun nestle down behind the sea's vast horizon, they talked of the irony of such a beautiful view on such a cursed island.

"I think Garlock's right," Isaac said, "the Brone died watching the sunset."

They all were hungry so the conversation turned to food. Garlock offered to get one of the dead kroaks for dinner but was quickly booed. Not only was it too dangerous to enter the forest, but the thought of eating one of the slimy beasts was more than they could stomach.

"It's getting dark." Eryn gathered her things. "May not be

safe even by the fire."

Mirrah motioned for the girls to follow suit. "And it has been a very, very long day," she said with a yawn.

They all went inside and fastened the iron grid to the cave's opening. It felt safe inside, a bit eerie at first, but safe. They lit only one lamp, not knowing how long they would be living on the mossy isle of banishment. After they had all settled onto the sandy floor and watched the last bit of light fade from the evening sky, they talked about the day and made plans for tomorrow.

"Thanks for finding this cave, guys," Breezy said. "Sleeping in the tombs or on the beach... way too hoobie-joobie." She shook herself in a dramatic shudder.

"Thank you, Ariel," Mirrah said, "for watching over us today and providing this cave and fresh water."

"If he be watchin'..." Garlock honestly tried to be respectful. "Just getting it in the opens—why'd he let the ship and crew sail? We done obeyed, came and found the book, puttin' our flesh to harm, if ya follow me sayin's."

"Ariel does not make someone—man, Grimalkyn, or Pharen—do something against their will. The frightening of the crew was most certainly Sasson's doing. If they chose to listen and sail away, that was their choice. Ariel will not use his power to force them into doing his will."

"Then how we to get our land back from Sasson's wretched hand?"

"By letting Ariel work through us."

"We tried that and here we be—abandoned."

"He still knows where we are." Mirrah's voice dropped a bit as thoughts of their predicament and her trust in Ariel engaged for battle. Isaac's stomach growled. They had finished their water and snacks back at the ruins of Dross. He too questioned whether this Ariel was really watching. They found the book. They cooperated—no—plunged in headfirst, without knowing what was going on. Shouldn't it be time to go home?

Eryn had taken out the book and opened to the first page.

"'The histories of the Lorians, Pharens, and Saffarians.' What are Saffarians?" she asked Mirrah. Mirrah shook her head. Eryn read more.

"'Hidden by veil, the pillars and power,
Hidden from evils that destroy and…'"

She paused with her fingers to her lips, breathing short, shuddered breaths. A distant voice echoed from within…'a very old glyph. See the tail like of a serpentine.' She sat in silence for a long time, twirling a lock of her hair. "I have not read these words since…" She sighed and read more.

"'Be three that will come, three that will see,
Guided and led, to guide and to lead.
The times they will turn, the true to be tried,
Hearts will be tested, yet love will abide.'"

An awe of some kind filled the room, a silence of deep wonder. Eryn looked long at the teens, and then began pouring over the pages, muttering in the language of the long dead Pharens. Her face reflected the soft lamplight, her black twisty hair hung loose. She would utter little 'aha's and 'hmm's or softly gasp ever so often. Nusa lay near the mouth of the cave. The teens and Bella had snuggled together into the sand with extra clothes and whatnot for pillows.

"Why do you call him, Ariel?" Breezy asked Mirrah.

"*Ah* in Lorian was a word for the creator of everything. *Ra* means all powerful. *El*… love and goodness. *Ah-Ra-El*—all powerful creator, full of love and goodness—Ariel."

"Oh, okay. I like that."

"Why do you say, 'okay'?"

"Ho!" Eryn exclaimed, "Here is something about Hornin." Everyone sat up to listen as Eryn read. She translated as she read, so would sometimes pause and mutter. "Ahh… 'Hornin of Lore, son of Mardok, son of…' yes, yes, lots of names. Lore? Mirrah, he was from the ancient cliff city. A Lorian?

Ahh… 'being blessed with learning the divine language of the stones.'"

"A Lorian?" Mirrah became lost in thought.

"What is a Lorian?" Isaac asked.

Mirrah did not answer, so Eryn looked up from the book. "The Lorians were the great ones, the ones who kept the land free. They were mighty men and women with powers like no one today. They could see like Pharens, shoot like Grimalkyns, heal like Mirrah, and fight like… well, like parlords. Lorian princes rode on seraphs. Do you have seraphs? Seraphs are giant birds of greatness. The Lorians fought Sasson and kept the land free."

"Where are they now?"

"Gone—murdered."

"Well that doesn't make sense." Isaac said rather sharply. "If they were so great why are they all dead?"

Mirrah took a handful of sand and sprinkled it out around her. A breeze blew through the grotto and spread some of the dust. "They were divided." She stared at the sandy floor as if in mourning. "Under the Great Prince, they had pushed Sasson back to Skone Lor. They formed the white stones and held the land free for many rones. Battles still waged, but life was good. Sasson stood restrained."

"So what happened?" Zac asked.

"And what's a rone?" Isaac had his skeptical thinking face on.

"A rone is the reign of a shalom, a Lorian prince. The shaloms would all elect one prince to rule. United, the land stood free."

"So what happened?" Zac asked again.

"Sasson is crafty. His power is deceit, and he knows the heart of man. He finds our weakness and aims with deadly skill. All great men have weakness. He sowed seeds of discord and waited. The Lorians eventually fought each other, and Sasson took them one by one."

She continued to stare at the sand as the air fell still. "They have been silenced, yet from the dust their voices whisper."

She paused again. "My father saw one—when he was a boy—high overhead—a Lorian prince upon a mighty seraph—riding the shoulders of the wings. I had always hoped I would see one someday. I have heard rumor that one still lives—a shalom even, somewhere hiding, waiting." Another breeze came and swirled through the grotto. Eryn's lamp flickered as she held it over the book. A wonder held the room as Eryn read on.

"Hornin had three children," she said, "two sons and a girl—adopted. The girl was adopted."

"Huh," Breezy chuckled.

"He sent them away!" She looked up with alarm. "When Loria fell, he sent them... to Yorne... to find the stone... to hide themselves there. Why would he...?" She looked up again, her face perplexed. She tilted the book toward the light and read more. "Their names were Isaroc, Zakorin, and Brealina, who was affectionately called Alina, which means..." Eryn abruptly stopped and looked up at the teens all huddled together. Her mouth hung open.

"Well?" Breezy asked.

Eryn just stared.

"Well?"

"It means... small wind or—"

"No way." Isaac sat up. A chill ran down his back.

"Isaac?"

"That's a bunch of bunk." He got to his knees. "You're just making that up. I can't believe you would... you think you can toy with us—play with our minds?" He stood and walked toward the opening. His stomach growled. He stepped over Nusa, undid the iron gate, and looked back. "You think we're puppets—you pull our strings and we dance? What next?" He crawled out grumbling about being played for a fool and fighting battles not their own.

"Isaac," Mirrah called after him, "it is not safe." He reached back inside and grabbed his sword that leaned near the opening. Nusa got up and followed him out.

No one spoke inside the grotto. Zac shrugged and watched Eryn drop her head. Her hair hid her face as she softly cried.

Zac looked to the opening, worried for Isaac, thinking about what Eryn had just read. It did seem oddly strange.

Isaac sat down on a boulder looking out over the ocean. A wind came up from the sea and parted his growing bangs. Nusa came out and sat beside him. They both looked up at the stars spreading out over the vast dark sea. Isaac's emotions seemed out of control. The similarity of those names could not possibly be real. It's a dream or some game. I feel manipulated. What's next?

"She tells the truth," came a low, soft female voice. He looked back thinking Mirrah had come behind him. No one there. He looked over his left.

"You can trust her: trust her heart." The voice was definitely a woman's, low like a tenor. It was not Mirrah and certainly not Breezy or Bella. He kept looking all about. Nusa nudged him, pressing her head against his shoulder.

"Did you hear someone?" he asked the giant lynx.

"Do what you know is right," came the voice again. He looked over at Nusa. She nudged him again. A soft purr resonated from her throat. She then looked into his eyes.

"I wish I knew your purpose," came the voice. "I wish I could do more." Nusa then got up and went back toward the cave, standing guard outside. Isaac looked at her, bewildered. He listened hard, looking all about but did not hear the voice again.

Inside the grotto all was silent, except for Eryn's short petite sniffles.

"May I read more?" she softly asked.

"Please," Zachary said.

"He says," she sniffed rather loudly, "that he was entrusted with this book—the last copy of the divine script." She paused for a long minute. "He was betrayed by one of his friends—no one is named. He escaped death and was banished... here. Somehow—'by the hand of Ariel' he says—he was able to save the book from discovery. He lived in a small cave atop a...

rocky knoll." She looked up. Nusa came back inside with Isaac close behind.

"Sorry," he said as he lay back down on the sand.

Zac watched in amazement. Isaac humbly apologizing— it was like a solar eclipse. You made sure to watch cause you knew it would be a long time before you saw another.

Eryn continued with her reading. "He was befriended, protected by one Soren of Aden." She looked toward the opening. "That is in Bellock."

"The Brones of Bellock kind of Bellock?" Zac asked, sitting up.

The light flickered a little as the ocean breeze swirled into the grotto. "Says he spent his days on the rocky knoll transcribing the Lorian script."

Zac bolted upright. "He lived here! And the giant outside is Soren of… that place in Bellock." Everyone looked toward the opening. Zac was giddy. "Is that cool or what?"

"Cool?" Eryn tilted her head then went back to reading. "A band of Pharens swore to secretly teach their children the forbidden script." She paused for a long time, her eyes somewhere else. She sighed and cleared her throat. "That would have followed the Sacron purge over a hundred cords ago."

"A hundred cords?" Breezy asked.

"A long time, is it not?"

"No, what's a cord?"

"Five rings."

"Five rings?"

"Yes."

Mirrah chuckled. "A ring is from one springtime to another. As in the words of Barley Ma-gundy: 'From spring to spring, the blossoms bring, the pure in heart, another ring.' A cord is five rings."

"Oh, we call them, years." Breezy lay with her head propped on her elbow. She rubbed her eyes with the other hand and yawned. "Five hundred years. That's a long time to keep a secret."

Eryn closed the book and caressed the heavy leather cover, tenderly tucking the strap through the loop. "In the face of death, they kept the language alive. This book is not yet fifty cords." Eryn flung her long black hair to one side. "His banishment here was the perfect place for him to write. And now, as middle Pharrian goes the way of the Lorian script, here we are, in Hornin's cave, with his book." She again lightly brushed the leather cover. "I shall translate it into the Pharrian of today."

Isaac watched her fondle the book, feeling like an absolute idiot. "But not in this same grotto, I hope."

Eryn looked up and smiled. "I better save the oil." She put the book back into the brass box. The grotto grew quiet except for Nusa snoring as Eryn put out her lamp.

The teens and Bella snuggled into the sand as Garlock took out his long thin flute and began to play. The tune rose and swung low, sad and slow, pensive, reflective. Sleep drifted in with the warm ocean breeze. The old Grimalkyn melody brought Breezy back to that night in the snowy cold wood. She thought she could almost hear the music again. It pulled at her heart. She remembered trudging through the snowy wood, yearning to know the maker of the mystical sounds.

So much had happened since that night. She thought about how different things had become. How different she had become. She knew she was changing, not sure just how, but she knew. She wondered if they would ever see their home again. How would she ever say goodbye to Sherrabella, the closet friend she's ever had—and Mirrah and Eryn? She wondered what lay ahead for her and the boys—for all of them.

She thought about the huge doors into Torrin's compound, the tombs with bones and the book in the brass box. She shuddered when she remembered the kroaks. She saw them chasing Garlock into the ocean, playing with him like dolphins would a ball. Then, she too was standing in the waves as kroaks swam about her feet like sharks. She wanted to run, but they were everywhere. She tried to scream when suddenly the waves pulled back, leaving her all alone on a dry sandy beach. A man stood off in the distance, looking straight at her. He drew her gaze, but not that he was handsome; it was more than that. He had a presence of power and wonder, yet warmth and wholeness. A kindness came from his eyes. She felt it.

"Who are you?" she asked.

"I know where you are. Don't be afraid."

She wanted to ask questions, but nothing would come to mind. She looked at him awhile longer; then he was gone. The waves came back around her feet, up to her knees, and panic filled her heart. She kicked at the kroaks, but they were not there, only waves washed back and forth—gentle waves—back and forth. The light reflecting off the waves became brighter and brighter until she heard someone calling her name.

"Breezy, Breezy." She opened her eyes, and she was back in the cave, on the sandy floor. Bella knelt in the opening, light shining all around her. "You need to wake," Bella said. "You need to get up."

Breezy raised her head and blinked into the brightness. "Looks like morning came and went." A huge yawn morphed into a silly smile. Bella giggled.

"You slept long but now must eat."

"Eat? What do we have?"

The guys had found some moss rats, large opossum looking things that made for good target practice. Zac was telling everyone how he had killed one with his crossbow when Breezy came stumbling out of the cave into the sunlight. Rested and looking forward to a new day, her stomach growled with extreme hunger. Her eyes narrowed when she saw the rats impaled on sticks cooking over the smoky fire. She instantly felt like she just stepped off the puke-a-whirl at the fair.

"Please tell me that's not breakfast."

"It's not," Zac said, "it's lunch."

Mirrah had found some leafy greens and herbs in a small plot on top of the cave's rocky mound. "Ariel has led us here, he knows what we need. If Hornin and a Brone could live here, so can we."

Breezy managed to eat when things were prepared and looked a little more appetizing. "I wish I could say it tastes like chicken," she said, "but it tastes like moss. Not complaining," she quickly added, "just getting it out in the open." She smiled at Garlock who gave a wink.

"I like it," Sherrabella said sweetly. "If it goes down and stays down, it's good." Everyone laughed. She smiled and joined in their laughter. It was not laughter from good times, but of good friends enduring hard times.

"He saw 'em come before they came," Garlock said to Mirrah and Eryn, filling his mouth full of moss-rat meat. "Isaac the mighty done saw the kroaks before they jumped us, like a Pharen he was."

Both Mirrah and Eryn stopped eating and looked intently at Isaac who just shrugged. He had not told them yesterday when giving the account of the attack. Garlock had not said anything, thinking it was Isaac's story to tell. But today he could not let it pass. The women waited for him to explain. Isaac swallowed and cleared his throat.

"I just knew there were some behind us and turned to shoot, but they weren't there."

"He told me to ready me thorne, but I just stood there watchin' the moss grow over me toes."

"Then they appeared just like I had... seen them."

"You can see the future?" Zac perked up. "Sweet."

"I think it's like you reading the pillar and the knife. It just happens when it's needed."

Mirrah and Eryn looked at each other with angelic smiles. "You have no idea," Mirrah said, "the wisdom in your words."

"I dreamed something last night." Breezy stared into the fire, her thoughts far away. "It was something important, but now it's gone. How come I can't remember?"

"You will if you need to." Mirrah held a piece of meat for Nusa. They talked on of building a raft or a signal fire, of exploring and setting traps, of kroaks and salt water.

"The currents around the island will take you far out to sea," Eryn said. "Captain Boar explained to me why this was a choice for banishment. Even with sails you could not find land by chance. We would need charts and a stable swift craft, otherwise we would drift aimlessly, drifting to a slow, miserable death."

They agreed to explore the more open rocky ground around their lookout ledge. They talked of giving the Brone a burial or leaving him to continue watching the sunset. Isaac propped his skull on a stick against the rock wall. "For a better view," he said. They tried to follow the channeled water coming down from the rocks above, but it became too much trouble for such little purpose. They found more small garden plots, with herbs still growing after so many years. The day ended like the first, sitting around the fire, watching the sunset, but this time they had rat meat with herbs.

"What more could anyone need?" Isaac gestured toward the setting sun with a blackened rat leg in his hand.

"We need Ariel's help," Mirrah said. "I am thankful, but we must leave this island. We must fulfill our purpose."

"He knows where we are." Eryn slowly roasted a rat over the fire.

"That's it!" Breezy shouted, making Bella jump. "I remember my dream. I saw a man, a lovely man. He said he knew where we were. And we weren't to be afraid." She went on to tell about the water, the kroaks, and the more than handsome man. She ended by asking, "Who was he?"

"I think you have seen the Prince," Mirrah said.

"The Prince?"

"Yes, and you are his messenger. We must not worry. We can trust."

Eryn stared at the roasting rat, oily juices dripping, sizzling on the coals. "We can trust... but for how long?"

19 A DREAM AND A SHIP

The next day was like the previous, as was the next and the next. They found ways to make life more comfortable. Bella taught them how to make sleeping mats from tall dry grass. They learned where and when the kroaks tended to roam and hunt. Mirrah continued to seek out different herbs and eatable plants. She found purple berries and a plot of white roots that resembled potatoes. They rationed firewood, traveling further each day to find more. The days ran together. No one except Bella looked forward to meals as the moss-rat became almost unbearable. She told of the times that she was forced to eat scraps or go hungry. For her, meat, even moss-rat, was always something special.

Many boat plans were suggested, ideas and chances for rescue discussed. The more they talked, the more they realized why this island was chosen for banishment. Since no one was banished here anymore, there was no reason to expect a passing ship of any kind.

"It'll take a miracle," Zac said one night as they sat around the fire. No one answered as the sparks snapped and rose up into the darkening sky. Even Mirrah began to doubt if they would ever leave the Isle of Moss.

They had to continually explore new areas to find food.

One day, Isaac and Garlock hiked over a ridge far above the rocky knoll and found a beautiful pool of light blue water. It was a difficult hike but through mostly open country. That day became infamous as they excitedly made the hike to swim and bathe.

The pool had a small waterfall with a ledge where they could jump and dive. Mirrah and Eryn stayed where they could touch. Breezy taught Bella how to dog paddle and eventually they climbed the rock ledge and together plunged into the refreshing cool water. Garlock stood atop the ledge and declared that he was 'never so vigorated.' That day therefore, became know as 'Vigor day.' It was evening by the time they hiked down with everyone feeling wholly refreshed and thoroughly invigorated.

Garlock had seen fish in the pool and said he would seek out material to construct a net. The following day, he and Isaac came proudly to the evening fire bearing a string of twelve good-sized fish. With great eagerness, they sat roasting the fish around the fire that night.

Breezy picked a bone from a fillet with her long thin fingers. "These are absolutely, fantastically delectable," she said with a cheek full of fish. "They don't taste even a teeny weeny like moss." Like yesterday's vigor day, it was a life giving time that had come none too soon. They all knew things were still glum, but as Garlock said, 'Ya best enjoy the good when it comes.'

When he finished eating, Isaac began cleaning an arrow, rubbing it with sand in his palm. "Found it in a shriveled up kroak—lime green one. Had to be the first one I shot—the one fixing to have a Grimalkyn stew." He smiled at Garlock.

"And you pulled it out?" Breezy said with a scrunched face.

"Can't waste them. This arrow might save your life someday."

"I shot an arrow into the air," Zac mimed shooting an arrow. "It fell to earth, I knew not where." He put his hand above his eyes, looking. Bella watched him intently, mouthing the words after he spoke them. "I breathed a song into the air.

Long, long afterward in a kroak, I found the arrow still unbroke." Isaac smiled. Breezy giggled. Zac then looked out to the sea, his voice softer. "And the song, from beginning to end, I found again in the heart of a friend."

The next few days grew increasingly difficult as they caught only a few more fish, and the moss-rats became sparse. Dark eyes and weary faces stared into the evening fires. A few outbursts of frustration occurred over trivial things, and Mirrah wondered how long could they survive. Eryn continued to study the ancient book but only during the day to save the oil.

"I'm still hungry," Breezy whined one evening, massaging her tummy.

"Everyone's hungry, Breeze." Isaac gave a long sigh and watched the sun disappear to end another day. He scratched a mark outside the cave entrance. He had kept track of their days on the 'cursed' isle. He sat in silence for a while, then without anyone listening, he softly uttered, "I think it's Christmas Eve."

That evening, as Garlock played his flute inside the cave, it was especially sad and mellow. It was as if his soul were crying through the little reed whistle. It made Bella softly cry as she lay next to Breezy on her grass mat in the sand.

"It'll be okay, Bell," Breezy said softly, stroking Bella's hair. She wondered though. Were they ever going to get off this island? She listened to Garlock's mournful flute as she lay there in the cave, staring into the darkness. She thought back to the day they had found the pool—Vigor day. It had been so much fun, and now she was so lonely, so hungry. It had been such a warm sunny day, perfect for the cool blue water. She remembered the fun they had swimming and splashing about. She saw it all again in her mind as Garlock sat on the rocks by the pool playing his mournful tune.

She splashed again with Bella as the boys climbed the rock and jumped from the ledge. Suddenly Zac was hollering from atop the ledge and pointing into the pool, but she could not hear what he was saying. He became sepia-colored like an old silent movie, pointing and mouthing something but without sound.

Then Bella screamed and disappeared under the water. Breezy saw a large snake like monster with a top fin the length of its body coil around Bella. She watched in horror as it wrapped itself around her. It was taking Bella down into the pool, deeper and deeper. Breezy peered into the beautiful blue water. Bella's eyes stared back, wide with terror, her arms outstretched as the monster took her further and further down. Breezy began to shake.

"Bella!" she tried to scream. "Beeellaaa," but nothing came out her mouth.

Then, she was awake, inside the cave. She could hear the others breathing, her own heart pounding as she tried to see in the darkness, to see if Bella still lay beside her. She reached over and touched Bella's soft hair. Bella softly moaned and turned.

For quite some time, Breezy lay in the dark, staring at the ceiling. Then, she found herself alone on the rocky knoll looking out over the vast blue. She saw a ship far out at sea. It was coming from the west and would pass the island into the east. She watched its sails buffer and ripple in the wind. A red and purple flag flapped in rhythm from the mast. She could see the pilot at the helm as crewmen went about the ship. Every detail came vivid and clear.

Sitting in the center of the ship near the main mast was an older Grimalkyn in a fur-covered chair. A long thin pipe that gave out wisps of green tinted smoke, hung from bearded lips on a weatherworn face beneath a thick white beard with streaks of brown. The old Grimal sat content by the fireplace, his feet propped on a keg. Breezy watched him draw the smoke, hold it in and let out rings of greenish white. He looked familiar sitting by the flat-stone fireplace. It's strange to have a fireplace on the deck of a ship. Why would someone...?

That's Alle-Encer! She sat upright. She was back in the cave, and the darkness had begun to fade. She sat there listening to all the breathing. It reminded her of the other dream. She checked to see if Bella was still by her side. What should I do? She wanted to run out and see if a ship was passing by. That would be stupid. It's still dark. What would I do anyway?

She sat there in the darkness, unable to lie back down. With a groaning sigh, she crept quietly over the sand floor, trying to find a path through the bodies. Nusa lifted her head slightly to watch as Breezy undid the vine rope securing the iron grid. A faint fire smell drifted from the coals in the fire pit. The rocks were cool and damp on her bare feet. Stars still lingered in the morning sky as she walked the rocky knoll out to the northern point. She strained to see if anything could possibly be seen out on the mass of dark gray.

"This is stupid," she said, looking behind her. "Who knows what's crawling around out here?" She looked again—there was nothing to be seen. She thought of the dream and the ship. "Just another crazy dream." Her words seemed to go out from her mouth a foot or two and then vaporize in the cool morning air. "God... Ariel... can I call you, Ariel? We need your help, please do something."

She turned to walk back into the cave but decided to stir the fire back to life. She was often the last one up, so she could at least surprise the others by having the fire ready. Then, she remembered there was no food to cook. Her heart sank as she thought now of her hunger.

The coals breathed a flame to life as she stirred them with a charred stick. She put a few of the small sticks on the flame and watched it grow. What would we do without fire? It gives life; it takes life. She thought back on the dream. It was so real, so vivid. It got her out of bed.

The fire continued to grow, and she wondered if she had started it too early. The others may sleep another half hour. Shouldn't waste the wood. She watched it for a while thinking about the dream in the pool, hoping it had zero meaning. She thought about going back to bed, but the sky was getting lighter. And I'm hungry. I'll just lie there and think about food.

A little smoke swirled over into her eyes, so she got up and walked over the rocks. The sand and small stones were sticking to her feet, and she started to feel ornery.

"I'm tired of this game," she said out loud. "I want to go home." Her heart turned heavy, but she fought the urge to cry. Why fight it? I've put up with more crap than anybody at school would ever believe.

She walked to look at the ocean again. A tear ran down each cheek. One streamed into the corner of her mouth, and she liked the salty taste. Wish we had salt to put on our food. Wish we had food. She wiped her eyes with her right hand but suddenly stopped, slowly lowering her hand. Blinking to get the last tears out, she quickly rubbed her eyes and then gave out a lung-bursting scream.

"Shiiiiiiip! Ship, ship, ship, ship, ship!" She jumped up and down, pointing with both hands into the western sky. Far in the faint horizon, just like in her dream, came a ship passing by on the north.

"Guys, get up! Get up, get up! There's a ship." She kept jumping up and down, waiting for someone to acknowledge her discovery when she thought of the fire. She ran back to grab a flaming stick when the others all came piling out.

"There's a ship out there," she said to them. "We need to signal the ship." With the stick she ran to the edge of the knoll, waving the little flame back and forth until it quickly vanished into glowing embers. It made her cry.

When the others realized there was an actual ship, they rapidly argued about whether to signal or not.

"It could be a Sasson ship," Garlock said. "Why else would it pass this way?" Hard words flashed back and forth as they wrestled with what action to take.

"Alle-Encer is on that ship," Breezy said. No one responded, thinking she had become the first to crack. "I saw the ship in my dream. Alle-Encer is on that ship."

Mirrah suddenly gave orders. "Garlock, build up the fire. Isaac, gather anything that will burn. Use the oil in the lamps if you have to."

No one moved.

"Now!" she yelled. They had never seen Mirrah like this.

Within seconds, they all looked like kroaks running about trying to catch bumblebees.

"I came out," Breezy said to Mirrah, "cause I saw the ship in my dream. I saw Alle-Encer on the ship, sitting by the fire. It can't be coincidence," she sobbed. "It just can't be."

Garlock, Eryn and the boys frantically tried to work the small fire into a blaze. They scooped up anything that would burn.

"But why would they send a boat ashore," Isaac said, fanning the fire with a leafy branch, "just because they see a fire?"

"We can only try what we can try," Mirrah answered.

The ship came into view as it made its way across the northern horizon toward the east. They could not see the sails or flag, but it was similar in design as the ship they had hired.

"The flag is red and purple," Breezy said to Mirrah, "and it's got a branch with three leaves, and they're yellow." She spoke matter-of-factly. "How do we get them to see us?"

"We ask Ariel to tell them." Mirrah watch the ship, then looked back at the fire.

"Maybe we should go down to the beach," Zac said. "There's nothing left to burn up here."

"It would take too long." Isaac came to look. The sun broke the horizon, dispelling the light from their fire. "We need to make smoke."

"They will have a crystal." Eryn joined them on the rocky outlook. "If we stay here, they may see us."

Garlock went to work up smoke.

"Wave something bright," Mirrah ordered. "Whatever you have." The boys took off their shirts and waved them in the sky. Mirrah and Eryn took off their red sashes. Breezy and Bella waved their arms, jumping and yelling.

The ship continued on its course, coming nearer as it passed their knoll but made no sign of having sighted them.

"Why would they risk coming ashore?" Isaac paused to give his arms a rest.

"Because Alle-Encer is on that ship," Breezy said, teetering on hysterical. "He's looking for us, that's why!"

Only Zac and Mirrah continued waving as the ship drifted on. Whoever would be looking would be looking backwards now. The sun peeked over the cave, warming them as they watched the ship sail away.

Zac darted off, running back into the cave. He came out with Isaac's sword. He almost tripped over the Brone's leg bone as he ran. He rubbed the sword frantically with his shirt as he clamored onto the top of the cave. He tried directing the sun's morning rays back toward the disappearing ship. He bent the sword to focus it into a beam. He thought he saw it hit the water near the boat, and then he saw it hit the side of the ship.

"Come on, God, give us a break," he said to himself. The others came up on the rock hill that formed the cave. They could look northeast from up there and would call out whenever they thought they saw his reflected beam touch the ship. Although it was encouraging, it was not enough. The ship neither slowed nor altered course.

Zac lowered the shiny blade.

"Good try, Zac," Isaac said. "Need a flare." He thought of trying to make something with the oil and a t-shirt, but there was no tube and the sky brightened with every moment. It would just waste the oil. He sat down on the hard rock and watched the ship. Breezy gasped out whimpering cries, sniffling loudly. Bella went to hold her. Breezy pushed her away.

"You stupid ship," she hollered at the sea. "I hate you. Why did you wake me up? Why did you even come this way? I hope you sail into a hurricane, you stupid… stupid bundle of junk." She flopped down on the rock, and Bella was at first afraid to touch her. Mirrah gave Bella a nod, and she knelt down beside Breezy.

Sadness filled the morning as they watched the ship sail on. They had used up all their wood. Garlock walked off with Nusa to hunt moss-rat without inviting the boys.

"He must not go alone," Mirrah told the boys. So putting on their shoes and shirts, they took up their weapons and followed his trail.

Breezy cried for a long time atop the hill. She finally turned to Bella and took her hand. "I'm sorry, Bella. Please forgive me."

"You don't need to say that."

"Yes I do. I pushed you away. I'm sorry."

"But I know your heart's thought. You weren't mad at me."

"Oh Bell, you are the best friend, ever."

"You are my only friend… ever." They leaned their heads together like girls do. Then, it became Bella's turn to let out a scream. "Aheee! Breezy, look!"

The ship had completely come about and was sailing sharply toward the island. The women came running to see what had happened. The ship then turned to angle away from the island, and Breezy almost broke down again.

"Their tacking to sail into the wind," Eryn said. "They are working their way back to the bay." They watched in silence as the ship came back around the north point toward the bay.

"Gather your things." Mirrah ran down the rock. "I will leave a message for the men." It was the first time Breezy had heard her refer to the boys as men. She also realized they were going to travel through the forest by themselves. Mirrah took a burnt stick, and on a large flat rock near the fire, wrote: 'ship returned, gone to beach.'

"I will call them as we go," Eryn said, referring to her bone whistle. They quickly gathered up everything and headed toward the mossy trail. Breezy looked back at the blackened fire pit, the cave and the lonely Brone skeleton propped against the wall.

"Sorry to leave you all alone," she said, "but the food was bland… and too mossy." Bella heard her and giggled. Mirrah was behind them and chuckled to herself. Such pure hearts, she thought. No wonder Sasson hates them.

As they entered the mossy forest, Eryn blew three short blasts on her whistle. It was the non-danger signal to rally. She knew Isaac had the other whistle, so she waited for the signal of acknowledgment. Only buzzing bugs and birds high above gave a response.

They stayed close, walking the moss road into the forest. The sun's rays had not yet reached through the trees. A dark, green haze hung in the tension filled air. Breezy called it the mist of gloomy green. They knew the kroaks were most active in the morning, so they held their weapons ready, jumping at the slightest sound.

When they finally reached the post intersection, Eryn gave another round of three short blasts. Once again they listened for Isaac to answer. She called again, blowing harder. The high shrill cut the damp air, but no response came.

"Where are you, Isaac of Kan-sis?"

They decided to start down the road toward the beach and trust the boys would follow. They walked holding their swords upward above their heads. Breezy held her felkin ready, heart pounding. Her stomach stirred, but it wasn't from hunger. Something was wrong. Bella shrieked as a kroak ran across the road up ahead.

"Isn't this the time you should be seeing future kind of stuff?" Breezy said to Mirrah.

"Ariel is with us. Keep alert."

They were halfway to the beach when Eryn blew again on the whistle. They had not been able to leave a message at the intersection and were uneasy leaving Garlock and the boys. They listened and then walked on, hearts beating way too fast. The air grew tense as bugs zoomed in and out. Breezy bobbed her head as a large winged beetle buzzed past. She was about to say something when they all stopped mid-step. A distant whistle came through the mist of gloomy green. It was not the signal to acknowledge. It was one long blast—the signal for help.

20 THE CAVE GORRON

All four stood and listened.

"Maybe Isaac forgot the signal," Breezy said. They continued listening, but nothing more came. Eryn blew the signal of acknowledgement.

They ran back down the forest road toward the intersection. Sometimes the moss would shift on the stones causing someone to nearly stumble. Eryn's twisty thick hair floated out behind her, the brass box bouncing at her side. Mirrah had loosely tied her locks into her cloth belt. They had not had the time to twist or braid it, as was their custom. Breezy and Bella fought to keep pace. Panic teased their minds as Eryn zoomed out ahead. Breezy fought the urged to cry out.

They stopped at the stone post, painfully catching their breath. Eryn blew three short calls.

"How do we find them?" She looked about.

"Which way... do we go?" Breezy panted, bent over with head raised. The gloomy mist swirled all around them. Eryn blew her whistle again, and again no response.

Then, something came running down the road straight ahead. They had never traveled that road leading out from the post. Mirrah and Eryn readied their swords. Breezy pulled back her felkin, her heart pounding up into her ears.

Suddenly, Nusa bounded full speed around a bend, her claws flinging moss high into the air behind her. As soon as she saw them, she slid to a turning stop and ran the other way.

"Stay close!" Eryn darted after Nusa. All Breezy could think, was that they were going deeper into the forest, further from the beach, further from the ship. It's hard to run in the wrong direction, especially on an empty stomach. A thousand thoughts filled her mind. Where are the boys? How will they find them? Why does Eryn have to run so fast?

She thought she would die of side pain when they finally turned a corner and stopped. The path led directly into a large, dark cave. Over the cave mouth hung twisty vines that grew from high above. Nusa paused in the opening. Eryn called everyone to follow and ran to the cave, ducking through the vines into the darkness.

Breezy groaned as she and Bella passed through. The vines left slime on their hair and skin. The black rock inside was moist with green slimy icicles hanging from cracks that dripped from the ceiling.

"Ohhhh, God," Breezy whispered. Bella reached out and took her hand.

"Stay close girls," Mirrah said over her shoulder.

"Sure, like we're going... to wander off and..." Breezy did not bother to finish. Goose bumps covered her skin as she huffed and puffed, venturing deeper into the cave of dark, damp, cold.

More vines of slime hung from the ceiling. They stuck to their skin as they walked deeper into the darkness. Eryn had her lamp lit and was trying to light Mirrah's. The floor was smooth with sand. Two rails of rusted iron ran beneath their feet.

"For mining," Mirrah whispered. "Do you see Nusa?"

Eryn jogged ahead. "Up here. Hurry!"

Bella squeezed Breezy's hand so tight it hurt. Breezy looked back over her shoulder. Part of her did not want to look. She was learning to face danger, especially if it came from behind. She saw the cave opening disappear as they turned a corner.

The water that dripped from the ceiling felt soapy. Breezy tried to wipe it off. Mirrah looked back. "Minerals in the water," she said. "It is good for the skin."

Finally Nusa's large yellow eyes glowed back at them. She stood near a fork in the cave. Random beams of dim light came down from high above. The trail to the left was a massive fissure or crack in the mountain. Rays of light streaked through the rock and vines. It looked like a cathedral with high vaulted ceilings. The iron rails on the ground split off in both directions. To the right they led into a small square cave of total darkness.

"Please go left," Breezy whispered as Bella squeezed her hand.

Nusa continued to stand on the side to the left. A rattling purr resounded in her throat. She pawed the sand at the base of a rock wall.

"What is it, Nusa?" Eryn stepped over the iron rails to where Nusa pawed. At the base of the rock wall was a small tunnel. "What is it, girl?" she whispered, looking at the tunnel. It was about two feet in diameter. Nusa continued to purr. Eryn got down on the sand and hesitantly extended her lamp into the tunnel. Two bright eyes reflected back at her, she jumped to her feet, sword ready. Nusa looked into the hole and gave a low rumbling purr.

"Nusa?" A muffled voice came from inside the tunnel. "Is it safe?"

"That's Zac!" Breezy shouted.

"Breezy?"

"Zac, what are you doing?"

A frightened boy came crawling out, face dirty and looking haggard. He had been crying and now fought the urge as feelings ran wild.

"Where are the others?" Mirrah asked.

Zac gasped out the words. "It took them... that way." He pointed down the cavern to their left.

"What took them?"

He put his arms out wide and shook his head. "A giant ape

like thing… really, really big… gross, ugly." He shivered a little. Mirrah pulled him close.

"It took Garlock and Isaac?"

Zac nodded, glancing at Breezy, fighting the urge to cry.

They tried to ask what happened, but Zac broke into a cautious run, jogging down the fissure to the left. He followed the iron rails, moving in and out of the shafts of light. Light and dark played upon them as they followed. The opening above became an ever-lowering ceiling of dripping vines. With only two lamps, Breezy and Bella felt surrounded by darkness. They turned a sharp corner and saw a dim light coming from a cavern up ahead. The iron rails continued on into more dim damp cold.

"In there." Zac pointed to the cavern. Light diffused down from an opening high above. Piles of bones lined the entrance, some with rotting flesh. A putrid smell of smoke and acrid sweat mixed with the rotting flesh and drifted out from the dim lit cavern. Breezy's stomach tried to launch a protest as her head and eyes spun in opposite directions.

"Kroak bones," Eryn whispered.

They dropped down and watched from the cavern entrance. Huddled near a small fire was a large ape-like being busily working with something. Neither Garlock nor Isaac were anywhere in sight. The creature reached out its large oversized hand and hung something on a wooden peg stuck in the cavern wall. As the beast withdrew its hand, Breezy and Bella gasped. Hanging upside down by one leg, lashed to the peg a dozen feet off the ground, dangled Isaac. He wiggled about trying to undo the lashing around his arms and chest. He tried bending to reach the vines about his leg. He looked like an insect struggling in a spider's sticky web.

The beast continued to fiddle with something near the fire as it sat on its haunches. Thick plates of skin, like armor, grew in sections on its back, shoulders and thighs, while rust colored bristles filled in the gaps. Just sitting, head down, it was over seven feet high.

"Ohhhh, mercy," Breezy moaned.

"What do we do?" Zac looked to Eryn and Mirrah.

"Cave gorron," Mirrah said the words slowly. "Heard many tales. Never have seen one." She paused. "This is not good."

"We have to do something." Zac loaded his crossbow.

"We need a plan," Eryn said. "We need to—" As she spoke, the beast held Garlock up with its left hand. It had one thumb and three fingers, large and thick, covered with bristles and scars. In its right hand was a thin, sharpened stick.

"It's going skewer him like a hotdog." Zac dashed into the cavern and ran toward the beast. He fired the crossbow as he ran. It struck the beast in the back of the neck.

The gorron roared out a hoarse cry. It spun toward the opening almost dropping Garlock into the fire. It pawed at the back of its head with its clumsy fingers. Zac dove and rolled behind a pile of kroak bones. He sat up to reload. Nusa stood right beside him. Eryn and Mirrah watched from the cavern's opening.

The beast thrashed about trying to pull the tiny bolt from the base of its neck. The more it tried the deeper it went. Standing to its full height, almost filling the cavern, it looked to be fifteen feet tall.

"You need real fingers, ya butt-head." Zac dashed across the cavern floor diving behind another pile of bones. The horrid stench made his stomach tighten. Nusa came to his side, growling.

Garlock struggled free from the dried vines wrapped around his arms and chest. He stood and ran toward Isaac. Taking out his long knife, he tossed it up just as the gorron reached down and scooped him up. It held him in its massive left hand while still scratching for the bolt with the other. It turned in circles trying to find the back of its neck.

Isaac had caught the knife and cut at the cords about his arms. Zac saw what Garlock had been running toward. A thorne lay just outside the fire ring. "But Garlock has the arrows." He looked back at Mirrah and Eryn. They were hiding behind a pile of bones on the other side. He looked to Isaac hanging upside down. His quiver was still on his back, wrapped up with his arms. Though upside down, three arrows were still inside.

Zac stepped out from behind a boulder and waited. When the beast saw him, it gave out a horrid roar and reached over the fire with its right hand. Zac fired, aiming for an eye. His bolt hit near the Adam's apple. The cave gorron dug at it like a cat stung by a bee. It dropped Garlock onto the rocks, right near the fire.

The huge beast flung a small boulder at Zac. It smashed like thunder inside the cavern walls. The gorron raged about trying to find the tiny bolts in its neck. Garlock tried to rise to his feet but fell. Zac saw him and ran toward the thorne that lay in the sand. He picked up the thorne and called out, "Isaac, an arrow." He could not pull back a thorne, but hoped to shoot like he had in the parlords' attack. As soon as he called out, the gorron grabbed for him. With all his strength, he flung the thorne up toward Isaac, then rolled to the fire.

The gorron's hand came down over Zac, its large bristled fingers and thumb opened wide. Zac pulled a burning stick from the fire. He shoved it into the black leathery palm. A cry of rage shook the cavern walls. Large yellow eyes, bewildered, stared at the singed hand, then at the menace lying in the sand. It hissed and spit at Zac, showing its tusks stained with red. A mouth of large floppy lips dripped with froth. The nose, an open oblong hole, sat beneath a ridge of dark bone that ran from the nose up over the forehead, over the crown to the back of the neck—a short sharp mohawk of bone.

The beast raised its huge fist to pummel the source of pain, to pound it into the sand. Zac propped the burning stick upward. Lying on his back, he stared up, defenseless. He watched the black hairy fist rise high up into the cavern ceiling. It would fall like a hammer, crushing the life out from him. A scream echoed through the foul chamber. It was Breezy.

Zac turned his head. He saw Breezy, eyes wide with terror. He closed his eyes and waited.

But the fist did not fall. Instead the cavern filled with a thundering roar. Zac opened his eyes. The beast stumbled backward over some rocks and into a pile of bones. Zachary sat up. The gorron thrashed about in the rotting bones, bellowing out screams of agony. Zac looked back in time to see Isaac cut the vines and plummet to the cavern floor; the thorne still in his hand. He landed on his side, gasping, trying to breathe, his lungs shocked by the fall.

Zac looked back at the wailing beast. It shook its head madly, mauling its own eye, standing, stumbling, falling. Eryn had come and now helped Isaac to his feet. "Good shot," she said. Mirrah called for Zac to run. She had Garlock by the arm. It took Zac a second to realize it was over. He wasn't dead or going to die. He ran to help Mirrah with Garlock. Isaac doubled-over as Eryn pulled at his arm. Breezy and Bella were at the opening, jumping and waving, calling to them like cheerleaders at the game.

As they ran, the gorron continued to scream, sending horrid echoes through the darkness. In the chaos, Eryn's lamp got left behind, so Mirrah led the way. Nusa ran ahead calling back for them with high-pitched groans of urgency. Isaac got his breath back and helped carry Garlock.

When they finally broke through the vine-covered opening, they paused to catch their breath. The fresh forest air was a gift of new life. They huddled, bent over, heaving and panting.

"A ship… in the bay," Eryn said. "We must keep moving."

"Find me thorne and sword, lad," Garlock said. Zac ran over to where the gorron had ambushed them. When he found the sword and thorne he started to tell the girls what had happened, but realized it could wait. They ran on.

When they passed the stone post, they could still hear the painful wail echoing from within the mountain. Zac looked back with pity.

Garlock started to hobble on his own. "The ship came back, ya say?"

"It turned back and may still be in the bay," Eryn answered. "We must hurry!"

They had run only a short ways from the intersection when Bella screamed. Everyone froze as kroaks by the dozens came out from behind trees and rocks. The forest and road ahead were suddenly filled with kroaks of all colors and size. Some stood, some crawled, the cowardly lurked behind trees. In all directions, the mossy forest produced kroaks. Nusa growled long and low. Mirrah uttered cries to Ariel. Eryn clutched the book at her side.

From Isaac, life drained. This was too much. A tear pooled in his eye. I hate this game. I've played long enough—whoever you are—this is too much. "You've gone too far!" he said out loud, surprising himself.

It startled the kroaken-gaggers. They bobbed about croaking and gargling. They sounded like a frog-croaking fest in a Florida swamp. Breezy and Bella clung to Mirrah. The others formed a circle. Nusa's hackles stiffened. Kroaks scurried and bobbed all around them, moving closer, croaking louder, wagging their heads back and forth.

"Ariel, help us," Mirrah's voice went weak. Bella pushed her face into Mirrah's side. Breezy fought the fear, trying to aim her felkin, rapidly shifting from left to right. The kroaks moved closer, tormenting the tiny circle. No one spoke. There was nothing to say. The struggle was over. They would stand as long as they could. Eryn's hand tenderly went down over the box at her side.

Isaac heard her whimper. He clenched his jaw tight, breathing hard and fast through his nose. He stared out at the sea of kroaks. He was spent. He had not even begun to process the gorron ordeal. The boy inside wanted to turn and run. But run where?

The kroaks were hesitant, as if mustering courage. They bounced like wild natives, croaking and coughing, their slimy tails swiping back and forth. They slowly edged closer, louder. Isaac's thorne was in full draw, aimed at the nearest, largest kroak.

Suddenly his focus shifted. Back behind the encroaching ring, sat the leathery-skinned lizard. Perched on a large mossy boulder, it sat, eye scarred shut from Nusa's claw.

"I wonder." Isaac altered his aim and let the string slide.

His thorne lunged, recoiling smoothly in his grip. The arrow sped through the trees of mossy green. The large lizard jerked violently, opening its mouth into a wide yawn. A moment passed. Then a horrid, agonizing scream filled the humid air. Isaac's arrow had found its mark. It struck deep into the lizard's eye.

The forest of moss went eerily silent. As quickly as they had come, the kroaks were gone. The huddled group held their breath, too stunned to move.

"Hah!" Garlock shouted. "Put that in yeer mulger. What be good for a gorron be good for a bull kroak. Isaac, me lad! Hah!"

"Was aiming for the chest… but that works. Shall we?" He put another arrow to the string, leaving his quiver empty. His whole body shook. He glanced at Eryn. She watched in shock, wondering.

They ran as fast as they could, staying tight together, looking all about, ready for anything. The stone archway to the beach finally came into view just as Garlock slowed to a feeble limp. They stumbled out onto the beach not knowing what would be in the harbor—their ship of hope or a ship of doom.

21 GRAY-SAIL

A small hawk flew past as they stepped into the open. It sailed down the beach where two men held a long boat ready to launch into the waves. A little man with a bushy white beard stood watching. Emerging slowly, they saw the hawk swoop past the man, looping back and alighting upon his shoulder. Nusa shot out in a blur of brown and white. The teens had never seen her move so fast. She went straight toward the little man, galloping over the black sand. She ran right passed him. Sand flung as she dug to turn about and run tight circles around the white-bearded man.

"Alle-Encer?" Garlock's gravelly voice cracked. "How can this be?"

With a scream and a shout, Breezy dashed off to follow Nusa as the others jogged behind. Isaac stayed back with Garlock as they both hobbled along, Garlock grimacing with every step.

"Ya made me proud," Garlock said.

"Made me sore." Isaac's chest, back, and hip had tightened with pain.

"Be a lifetime's worth, huh?" They watched the celebration up ahead. Nusa raced up and down the beach. She ran back to Isaac and Garlock, did a loop and bolted back to the others.

As Garlock limped up to Alle-Encer, the older Grimal wore a huge grin. "Trouble keepin' steps with the young sproots?"

Garlock groaned. "You enjoyin' yeer sunshine cruise?" They embraced, briefly touching foreheads. The grand reunion, although joyous, was kept short. To leave the isle was foremost on everyone's mind.

"And besides," Breezy said, climbing into the long boat, "I'm really hungry."

They all talked at once as the men rowed them out to the ship—so much to tell, so much to hear. The joy of seeing Alle-Encer quickly washed away the morning's terrors. Aboard the ship, they enjoyed a splendid feast, as common food had now become a delicacy.

"This is so good," Breezy said, mouth stuffed full. She thought back over the morning: the dream, the ship, the despair and then the horrid cave gorron and the kroaks. Maybe that was all a dream, and this is real.

After breakfast, Zac and Isaac sat silent. With worn, dazed eyes they watched Alle-Encer's little hawk move about the table politely picking scraps from plates. It seemed to enjoy taunting Garlock, trying to grab choice pieces straight from his plate. Garlock would give it an evil eye and grab his knife. Once the bird managed to steal a piece of meat right from his fork. It quickly flew off to escape Garlock's slash. Landing on the windowsill, it snickered in a whistling fashion as it tore the meat between its talons.

The boys sat listening to all the talk between Mirrah, Eryn, Garlock and Alle-Encer, as Breezy and Bella went out to walk the deck. Many of the morning's events were passed over lightly. They spoke quietly of the parlords, the tombs, and especially the book.

"I followed yeer tracks in the morning," Alle-Encer said. "Saw ya met some horls. Was hoping to give young Isaac his bag." He had already given the backpack to Isaac earlier that day. They had gotten a kick out of the stale crackers and candy wrappers, which then brought memories of home.

"Tercel told me of the carn at Mirrah's and yeer trip to Kharlome." He tossed the hawk a piece of meat. "I went to Kharlome and learned what had happened on the wharf and that you had gone to sea, on The Silver Blade, I was told. For a twelfth-night and seven, I sat by the fire wondering. Then, in a dream, I saw meself aboard a ship called the Fare Whether. Didn't know if such a ship be. When I went to Kharlome and found it true, it be hoisting sails. Tercel didn't like the idea, but we boarded, none to knowing where we were bound. Tested me strength, but here we are, together on the Fare Whether." His thick, white beard bobbled up and down as he spoke. The hawk had watched him retell the events, nodding when he told of boarding the Fare Whether.

"Silver Blade," Garlock growled out the name. "I'd like to put me long blade to the likes of that seaman, Ferro." He picked up his knife.

"The Silver Blade..." Alle-Encer slapped his knee. "Found off the coasts of Hether Dawn. Sacked and burned by Rue pirates."

"Survivors?" Mirrah asked.

"Be Rues, milady." Alle-Encer shook his head.

"Hah!" Garlock snorted. "Ya drink what ya brew. They brewed sour mulger, now they be drinkin' it."

"So where are we sailing?" Isaac asked. "Or do I want to know?" He managed a weary smile. Mirrah looked at him and Zac like a mother would her children.

"To take you home," she said. Both boys gave little response. Zac just stared, chewing on a piece of salted ham, his face bruised and scratched from the tussle with the gorron. Isaac gave a slight nod. Home... could they really get back home?

"We have arranged with the captain," Eryn said, "to put us ashore at Hether Dawn. From there we can board a ship to Kharlome."

The rest of the day was spent tending wounds, washing clothes and eating lots of food. That evening on the upper deck they all sat with mugs of mulger and other spiced drinks, watching the sun and sky mix together another masterpiece of beauty. The sea was calm and everyone, except Isaac and Zac, shared details of the dramatic morning. It already seemed distant.

Even Bella joined in, describing Zachary's attack on the cave gorron with vivid detail. He was a hero like no other. Her blue eyes sparkled as she spoke of his courage and speed. Eryn told of Isaac's skill with the thorne—shooting the cave gorron while upside-down—scattering an army of kroaks with just one arrow. She smiled at him.

"One arrow, one army."

He gave a quick, polite nod. Tercel, the hawk, gave a long, low whistle.

"So why'd ya turn the ship 'bout?" Garlock asked Alle-Encer. "Ya looked to be sailing on."

"That we were, being already off course. A storm pushed us near the Isle of Moss. I had been seeking hard to know Ariel's way. Having sailed past a twelfth-night, I gave doubt a cozy chair by me own heart's fire." He took a slow draw from his long pipe. Breezy remembered her dream. "Last night I dreamt," he continued, as greenish white smoke drifted up over his stubby nose. "I saw the young ones high on a rock, waving a lantern back and forth. Its light flashed across me eyes." He took another draw from his pipe. The spicy smoke blew about on the high deck. "When I awoke and walked the deck to greet the day, there be a light flashing in me eyes."

Everyone turned to Breezy and then to Zac. He gave no expression. He thought back to the early morning, polishing and trying to bend the sword. He chuckled inwardly. Big doors swing on little hinges. "Thanks for not sleeping in," he finally said with a smirk.

"I sent Tercel to see if it was like I dreamed. It took some convincing though, to get the captain to turn about and let me go ashore. Cost me a few stones."

"To Alle-Encer," Mirrah said, lifting her mug, "we are forever in your debt." Everyone joined in the toast. Isaac commented about familiar customs in an unfamiliar world.

"And to Tercel," Zac said, to which the hawk lifted out its wings, looked into the sky and screeched his ear-piercing call.

The stars awoke as the ship swayed lazily into the night. Although exhausted, no one wanted to go below and sleep. The conversations slowed, and Garlock took out his flute. The melody was new—alive, but not lively, full, and with depth. It sang of adventure, of trust, of doubt and worry, mixed with joy and contentment. The sounds floated off the back of the high deck up over the vast expanse of blue-gray sea. Heaviness turned to ease, weariness to rest.

"I think today was Christmas," Isaac said softly to his brother. "If I figured right."

"Really?"

Bella and Breezy brought up a large woolen blanket, wrapped themselves together, and fell fast asleep on the deck. Nusa lay beside them, almost smothering Bella. Garlock lowered the flute as the night turned cool.

"Thanks," Isaac said, barely audible. "Thanks for teaching me to shoot… upside down." Garlock chuckled once. A twinkle flickered in his eyes.

"Ya both made me proud, brone, mighty proud."

The sun was up before anyone stirred, as weeks on the island had worn them thin. The quest for food, avoiding kroaks, and the nights in the grotto had taken their toll. Isaac and Garlock awoke sore from the gorron encounter. No one seemed eager to talk about the events of that day. Breezy wanted to ask how the gorron ambushed them, how Zac got into the tunnel, but she knew it'd be best to wait.

That morning over breakfast, which turned into lunch, Zac started feeling better. He sat with Garlock tossing nuts into a brass pot.

"So why didn't we hear any talking kroaks?" Everyone stopped to listen. "You said they talk." Garlock fiddled with a nut and gave it a toss as if he didn't hear. "Well?" Zac asked again.

"Ho, laddie, me just makin' a tale worth bein' told." He tossed another nut and smiled. "Didn't know ya was hopin' to sit and jabber with 'em." Zac frowned at first, and then broke into a good laugh that was joined by the others. They ate and laughed some more as the troubles and toils of the mossy isle drifted off into the sea.

Later, when Alle-Encer went to nap and Tercel perched near the window, Zac asked Garlock about the strange hawk. "So is it the same when Alle-Encer says Tercel talks to him? Is he just making a tale worth bein' told?"

"Ho, no, laddie. Tercel's a talker alright." Zac gave Garlock the look. "I be speakin' honest. He knows and he talks, but only Alle understands."

"Actually understands us and talks?"

"Say somethin' disagreeable 'bout Alle-Encer, and see what comes back to ya."

Zac looked over at Tercel. The hawk shrugged up its wings, and gave a little screeching laugh. Zac widened his eyes, then squinted, wondering hard if he was being played.

The next two days passed with no one doing anything that wasn't fun or restful. Scrapes and cuts were mended, as were clothes and wounded souls. An east wind blew strong from behind, moving them quickly without rough seas.

On the fifth day at sea they woke to a northwest wind. By late afternoon, the sky turned dark and the air cool. A ship was spotted to the northwest on a course that would bring them close. The crewmen were anxious, not able to identify its markings but they muttered among themselves, saying it bore a gray sail.

"Should we be worried?" Breezy asked Mirrah. They stood on the upper deck watching the distant ship steadily come into view. Isaac and Alle-Encer were below, napping in the cabin.

"The captain says there are no markings, only a gray sail." Mirrah sighed heavily.

"Pirates?" Zac asked.

Garlock rubbed his beard. "If they be Rue pirates, we best

be sayin' prayers."

"Rue pirates?"

"The Rues," Mirrah said, "or pirates of regret, never leave survivors."

"You mean like…" Zac looked at Breezy and Bella.

"They have taken slaves," Mirrah said. "But usually, all are… given rest."

"Be workin' a vengeance," Garlock said, "repayin' some blood." He snarled, shaking his head.

Silence reigned as they watched the mystery ship draw near. It soon became clear that it was making for their ship. Mirrah became increasingly uneasy. The captain came up the stairway to the upper deck. Several crewmen with crossbows came with him.

"They're aiming for us," the captain said, "and they're not pirates." He whistled as he spoke, missing his two front teeth. He was almost Mirrah's height, an average build. It was clear he was shaken by the impending encounter. His left ear was completely gone.

Zac saw Breezy staring. "Sliced by a pirate's sword," he whispered, "just before they knocked out his teeth."

The captain shifted his weight. He was clearly uneasy. "It looks like… well… 'tis quite certain… it be a gray sail—a Sasson runner."

Mirrah's countenance fell.

"What business have you with Sasson?" The captain's face strained. "I'm not losing my ship and crew."

Eryn stepped forward to face the captain. "What are you saying?"

"I'm saying we'll have to put you over the rail." Eryn reached for her knife, but three crewmen raised loaded crossbows. Garlock growled and cursed under his breath.

"Surely you wouldn't." Mirrah put her arms around the girls.

"We've done enough, bringing you off the isle."

"To dump us in the sea?"

"I'm not giving chase to a Sasson runner." He turned and

shouted, "Throw 'em over." The men with crossbows stepped aside as four large crewmen came up onto the upper deck.

"At least put us in a boat," Mirrah said.

"And why should I do that?"

"Because you are a captain and a man."

He looked at Zac and the girls. Garlock breathed heavy through his nose. Eryn watched for a chance to turn the tables.

"Put 'em in a boat... cursed be the day." He turned to descend down the ladder steps to the main deck but froze.

"You touch them and you die." It was Isaac. The large crewmen turned around to see the lad, the one they had been hearing about, aiming his thorne up at the captain's throat. Nusa stood beside him snarling.

"You've only one arrow, boy."

"You've only one life, sir."

"You all will die."

"If that's how you want it." He heard men coming up behind him. Nusa turned to face them. "Tell them to hold still." Isaac held his thorne steady at the man's throat. Garlock was shifting back and forth, trying to see the action through the crewmen on the upper deck. For a moment, no one moved.

Then, that which makes legends—happened.

Isaac looked up into the darkening sky, aimed his thorne straight up, paused briefly, then released his last arrow.

"What in Morten's mulger?!" Garlock moaned.

A rough, piercing cry echoed through the air as a large dark form filled the sky. Flying directly out beyond the ship, with an arrow in its chest, was a giant, dark gray hawk. It swooped low as it tried to grasp the arrow with its long hooked beak. Flapping erratically, it flew out a hundred yards and looped back just above the waves. It floated on the sea breeze, following up the ship's wake, straight for the high deck. It rose, talons thrust forward. Suddenly it shot straight for Mirrah and the girls.

Breezy and Bella screamed. Mirrah turned and pulled them down. Eryn and Zac ducked behind the railings. The carn passed over, knocking Garlock into the crewmen. Its dark wings swept the high deck, propelling them all into a pile before slamming its talons into the chest of the awestruck captain.

Carn and captain tumbled down onto the main deck directly in front of Isaac. He jumped back and watched the colossal raptor gasp for breath, its wings flopping with feeble attempts to thrust it back into its domain. The talons, meant for Mirrah and the girls, closed tightly about the captain's chest. The man lay there, wide-eyed, unable to move.

The bird lay partly on its side, partly on its chest. The right wing went up and over the side rail. Bright red blood seeped as the arrow pressed deep, the black-feathered chest heaving. The large, hooked beak strained toward Isaac's feet as an eye glared up to him. He stood, watching his reflection in the glossy, black orb. Then the beak opened, gasping, tongue fluttering, as if trying to speak. A long, airy, gargled breath met the moist sea air.

"Hhhooo aarrhhh yooohh?" Hushed and low, it resonated through the ship, sending chills that ran deep and cold. A shadowy face appeared within the hawk's black eye—faint, but real. Then the eye clouded white and slowly turned to stone.

22 INTO THE WIND

The men on the upper deck got to their feet to face Mirrah and Eryn holding crossbows. No one spoke. The ship creaked and rolled. A sail whipped and snapped with a crack.

"That's a carn!" Garlock peered down at the hawk, its huge wings covering deck and rail. "The boy's killed a carn." The crewmen behind Isaac retreated to the far side of the ship. Like cornered kittens hiding from a dog, they huddled. The sight of a dead carn on their ship was beyond their mind's eye.

Isaac pried the talons off the captain's chest and helped him stand. Stains of red spread out across the man's white shirt.

"You need Mirrah," Isaac said. The captain stared at the carn, not hearing a word. "Mirrah, take him to the cabin. Garlock, help me get this thing off the ship." Mirrah handed her crossbow to Zac and took the girls and the captain into the cabin.

Eryn motioned for the crewmen on high deck to move away. They gave no resistance, moving to one side, away from the stairs leading down to the dead carn. Eryn looked out to the Sasson ship. Standing like a goddess, her hair drifted up into the rising wind as the sky turned dark.

Garlock stood still. Like a boy seeing his first gorilla, he just stared from a distance. Isaac went to pull the arrow from its chest. Garlock took one step forward.

"Sometimes… be best… to leave things be," he said with staggered words.

"Grab the talons." Isaac called to him. "Let's roll it over the side." It was easier said than done, as they wrestled the huge feathery beast over the rail. Nusa growled, and they turned to see the crewmen lower the longboat.

"Ya cowards!" Garlock shouted. The bird splashed into the rising waves just as the longboat dropped and the crewmen quickly descended over the side. "By the beard of Arnon, how we goin' sail this keg?"

Alle-Encer came sleepily out of the cabin. "Where's the crew?" he asked, rubbing his eyes.

"Ya missed it!" Garlock threw his hands into the air. "Be sleepin' like a kroak, and ya missed it."

"Alle-Encer," Eryn shouted down, "to the helm! We are hunted by a Sasson vessel. Get the wind into our sails." He stood there, not sure of what he just heard. "Now!"

He scampered up the ladder to a small deck, near the bow. It was higher than the high deck and only large enough for two men. He spun the wheel and caught the wind that now came in forceful gusts of biting cold. The dark sky became ugly green.

"Looks like tornado weather," Zac shouted into the wind. "What's your plan?" He followed Eryn down to the main deck. They stood with Garlock and Isaac.

"Even if we could sail this thing," Isaac said, "could we outrun that ship?"

"I am not a sailor, but we must try." Eryn acted strong, but Isaac saw her eyes. This was more serious than anything they had encountered. Anger surged, not for himself, but for Eryn, for Mirrah, for Bella.

"Do you people ever have a normal day?" Isaac said.

"We did before you kroaks came." Garlock wiped his hands of carn blood.

He enjoys this, Isaac thought. Like he's found a missing part of himself. He would rather die in this than grow old smoking a long pipe by the fire.

"Well, I'm tired of fighting," Isaac said. "I'm tired of running." He looked down at his feet; blood stained the deck where he stood.

"If we quit now," Eryn shouted as she lashed down a loose rope, "We have only delayed our deaths. We have purpose… and it is more than surviving." She held back her swirling hair. Garlock tightened ropes on the port side, pulling sails tighter.

"I don't want this fight," Isaac yelled to her.

"In your world, you have a choice?" Eryn braced herself as the ship lunged. "Here we must take what comes." She looked at his tall thin frame balancing on the rolling deck. He had lost weight. He looked so weary. How much more could he take?

Isaac strained to look into the wind. The gray-sail ship sped closer. Zac stood beside him. Their hair was long and whipped about with the wind. Sea spray flew across the deck, as the gusts became billows. Eryn gathered her hair and tied it tight with a small red string. She flung the long ponytail behind her just as a wave came splashing over the rails, soaking their feet.

She walked over the slippery deck to Isaac. They stood eye to eye. The wind and the rocking pushed and pulled them in unison. "You cannot quit now," she said. "We need your help. And…"

"And what?"

"I cannot swim."

"Call the captain!" Alle-Encer shouted. The pursuing ship was close enough now where they could see its crewmen. A dozen men in black uniforms lined the deck. They stood waiting with weapons ready. "We need the wind of heaven," Alle-Encer called. Zac went to find the captain.

Isaac and Eryn still stood facing each other. "What can I do?" he said, not sure if it was a question or a statement.

"Be strong with me." She squeezed his hands in hers. Then, in two leaping strides, she was up on the high deck.

Isaac ran to the port side to see the ship within a hundred yards. Three men at the bow were holding grappling hooks. A forward sail, gray and worn, bore three faint markings—a long-tailed S, then a single lighting bolt S, and another long-tailed S.

A feeling of dread, a presence of evil, like a liquid fear, washed over him. This was more than a physical battle. He thought of the carn. How did he know? Something had guided him.

"I don't know what's going on," he looked up into the dark green sky, his face battered by the wind, "but we need your help. If you are God here, as Ariel, please don't leave us now." He watched the gray-sail ship slowly close the gap. "I don't know where we are or what's happened, but please help."

Zac and Mirrah came out with the captain. He looked weak and sore. Alle-Encer called to him. "How do we catch more wind?" The captain looked at the storm and then the sails and shook his head.

"This wind will bust her riggings," he shouted, coughing up blood. Another wave came splashing onto the deck. A rope snapped loose and Nusa instantly leapt and caught it in her mouth, digging her claws into the wooden deck, as Isaac pulled to tie it down.

The sails bucked. The ship rose, rocking as another wave, higher, came washing over the rails. It knocked Zac and the captain off their feet. The ship rolled again, they slid toward Isaac.

"We have to drop sails," the captain said, as Isaac helped him up. "This storm will shatter the mast."

"We have to outrun that ship," Isaac shouted.

The captain shook his head. "This storm... is just beginning." He kept coughing blood as Mirrah came to help him. She eyed the crewmen on the Sasson ship. It was angling toward them as the waves became monstrous. The men aboard the gray-sail stood expressionless, riding the waves without concern. They held fast the rail, waiting; their faces void of life.

A cloud of fog filled the rolling sea between them. A wall of wave struck the bow. It thrust the Fare Whether upward sending all but Alle-Encer stumbling back toward the cabin.

"Take him inside," Isaac shouted to Mirrah. "Zac, get a sword and be ready to cut their lines."

Garlock ran about the ship trying to be a one-man crew. "The winds be killin' her." He grabbed the rail alongside Isaac.

The fog grew thick, a heavy, wet cloud of cold. The Sasson ship was almost upon them, fading in and out as the fog and darkness pressed in.

Eryn jumped from the high deck. "Loose the sails!" she called, frantically untying the ropes. "Hurry." They watched her for a moment, and then everyone began undoing ropes to let the sails flap freely in the wind. They crossed to the starboard and did the same. The ship suddenly slowed. They looked for the gray-sail but saw only the fog of darkness and cold.

"They'll ram us!" Garlock grabbed the railing, bracing himself for a collision.

"Or pass by." Eryn got the words out just as a wave crashed over the rail knocking them all off their feet. They flailed about like fish on the slippery deck. Eryn helped Zac to his feet as another came washing over. The waters pulled at him as if trying to tear him from her grasp. They slipped and grabbed, struggling to stay aright.

The fog grew so dense they could not see the bow of their own ship. The sails flapped madly in the wind. Ropes cracked like whips. Garlock braced himself again, expecting the Sasson ship to strike them portside. Alle-Encer, old as he was, held the wheel firm, steering into the waves as best he could.

"Help me with the anchors," Eryn shouted. It took all three of them to lower the two iron anchors. Zac stood at the portside, waiting to cut any grappling hooks that came aboard. He strained to see the ship but saw only darkness.

Suddenly a blast of wind rammed their ship pushing it over portside. It leaned so low the yardarms touched the waves. They all slid across the deck, pilling onto the rail near Zac. They clung to the rail staring into the dark churning sea. Zac thought the ship would come up over him, dumping him as it capsized, trapping him beneath as it sunk. He clutched the rail, staring into the dark waves of death.

The wind held them there, shoving the ship, rocking it closer and closer toward its death. Zac hugged the wet rail, his whole body shaking. The ship seemed to balance on its side, tipping and bobbing at the mercy of the sea. Water splashed up and over, pulling at them, pounding and beating.

Finally the ship rolled back, briefly leveling enough for them to stand. But it was teasing. Another gale hit and shoved them again. Alle-Encer bashed about in the pilot's deck. Nusa looked pathetic, her stiff fur blotched and matted with salt water. She would try and shake, but the wind flung the rain with a vengeance.

There was no sign of the gray-sail ship. The sky poured black rain mixed with dread and darkness. Waves surged over the deck, greedily grasping for any loose victim as the winds shook the ship, rattling the riggings and shredding the sails.

"The book!" Eryn ran to the cabin. Isaac tried to follow over the rolling wet deck. He was thinking hard.

"My pack," he shouted as he came through the cabin door. "There's a trash bag in my pack." He thought of the irony—a two-cent bag to save a priceless book. Together they put the book inside the trash bag, wrapping it tight with string. The ship rolled about so hard, they held the center post to keep themselves upright. Isaac shoved the book into his pack and slung it over his shoulder. He looked about, thinking what to take when the ship goes down.

They went back out on deck. Zac still faithfully waited to cut any grappling hooks. He looked extremely weary; hair matted flat, eyes filling with terror. Garlock had given up on sails and rigging. Alle-Encer kept trying to steer the drifting ship. Without sails, it was pointless. Only then did Isaac think of Mirrah and the girls. He had not seen them in the cabin as they were in a side room.

He and Eryn made their way to Zac and Garlock on portside when suddenly everything jolted and spun. A thundering crack echoed deep inside the ship. They were flung across the deck slamming into the starboard rail. The ship leaned to the starboard and stuck. It pulsated back and forth with the waves. The timbers beneath buckled and shattered with explosive booms. A huge wave flooded the deck. It pulled Zac and Garlock down onto the starboard rail.

"We've run aground!" Garlock shouted over the pounding and cracking. A rope snapped out from a sail and lashed his head. "We'll be ripped about like horl's prey. Look!" He pointed to the cabin door. Mirrah was trying to climb out. The deck slanted so much that she had to pull herself up by grasping the doorjamb.

Isaac looked about, searching how to get her and the girls out of the cabin. The ship lunged as a wave struck the hull. They were now more in the water than on the deck. He partly swum, partly walked the rail toward the cabin. He grabbed the stairs that led to the high deck and climbed upward toward the cabin door. The ship listed further on its side. "They'll drown in there." The windows were either under the sea or at the portside, high in the foggy sky. If they could not climb up as Mirrah had done...? Rope, he needed rope.

"Get some rope," he shouted back to Eryn and Garlock. "Rope some timbers together. Rope yourselves together." His eyes met Eryn's. For the first time he saw real fear in her eyes. He saw Zac, terrified, waist deep in the surging sea, standing on the side rail, hand propped against the slanted deck.

Isaac glanced up at Mirrah. With great dismay, she looked to him. The rain pelted his skin, stinging like beads of ice. He struggled to find some way to reach her and the girls. He looked back at Eryn. She wasn't moving. They were all watching him, shielding their eyes from the rain. He looked at the pilot's deck for Alle-Encer.

"Alle-Encer!" The elderly Grimal was gone. Broken timbers and debris sloshed about in the waves. Isaac clung to the stairs, looking for a rope—anything to climb the deck and reach Mirrah. Frustration boiled. Why aren't they making a raft? Just tie something together. Mirrah get something to help the girls out of the cabin. Somebody do something!

The shipped lunged. It came down with a jarring crash. The railing under Zac, Eryn and Garlock, shattered. They plunged into the dark water as broken railing sloshed about with the debris.

"Zaaaac!" Isaac shouted. The cold, wet wind blew his voice

back into his face. "Zac!" he shouted again. He thought he saw something in the swirling debris, but the wind aimed the rain at his eyes. With a lunge, he dropped into the churning waves of blackness. He heard Mirrah's faint call as he swam, fighting the waters, searching for anything alive.

He rose upward with a surge, pausing only a moment before dropping down to see a wall of water all around. He heard a call and knew it was Zac. It sounded too far away. Anger fueled his arms and legs as he fought the rolling waves. He tried to yell for Zac, but the water rushed in, smothering his call. He coughed and spit, fighting the urge to cry.

Suddenly he was eight, playing by the river with Zac and Breezy. 'I promise I'll watch them,' he told his mother. But while he tossed rocks at frogs and chased a snake, Zac and Breezy crawled into a hole under the bridge. Isaac called and called, finally running back to the house in tears, bawling that they had drowned. His mother came, running with panic. Zac and Breezy crawled out the hole, thinking it all a game. 'When you take charge of someone, you keep that charge,' his mother scolded. He vowed he would never let it happen again.

He heard another call. It sounded like Eryn, but it was behind him. The sky was so dark, the rain so heavy, the waves so high. Why do they conspire against me?

The weight of the book on his back was too heavy. To swim with clothes, his sword and the backpack, in waves and rain, became too much. He looked back to the ship; it was gone. The fog buried everything. I've lost them. He did not know which way was which. He tried to fight the feelings that raged inside.

In the end, a heavy sadness came and settled. It was more than despair, more than self-pity, pity for having lived such a short life. It was more than the agony of losing his brother and Breezy. It was death. Why fight it? Was it not stupid to keep struggling, futile to prolong the inevitable. He thrashed in the waves, kicking to stay afloat. A smart boy would stop wasting good energy on such a pointless goal. His heart turned heavy.

It was all so heavy. Death pushed him down. He let his arms drop, his legs hung still. Sinking down into the darkness, he looked up at the last of life. He saw his mother running, her long braid swaying as she ran, calling his name, calling for Zac and Breezy.

Umpf! Something hard bumped his side. Round and solid, it rose with the waves. He held tight, resting his head on his arm. He closed his eyes, and cried on the inside. Horls bounded through a meadow, a parlord in a wood, held his sword high, an arrow pierced a hand, pinning it to a city gate. Then, he was on The Silver Blade— throwing knives and shooting upside-down. Memories came in waves as he rode the swells. An ugly gorron screamed in pain, a misty forest full of kroaks faded in and out. He saw Eryn's dark eyes… "One arrow, one army."

Upward he rose with a wave and dropped. He was not cold. The wind and rain were cold, but in the water he was warm.

He saw a Brone, lean and tall, bald with a full beard staring out into the setting sun. The giant's clothes were tattered and crudely mended, his body thin, as he sat beside a small cave, leaning back against the rock as his fire slowly died with the sun's last light. He was a good Brone. He enjoyed a good view.

Isaac drifted with the wind, riding the surge of the waves. He tried to look about. The rain stung. He closed his eyes again and saw a light, a small light inside a cave. Someone sat at a wooden table, writing in a book, a large book, as an oil lamp flickered. The man kept writing, muttering to himself, writing… writing… writing.

23 WASHED ASHORE

Zachary looked up at Eryn. She knelt on all fours, coughing and vomiting seawater. Garlock staggered up the rocky beach, collapsing into a soggy heap. Zac made his way over the smooth stones. Gentle waves rolled casually over his feet. How could the storm have come and gone so fast. He came and stood knee deep next to Eryn, her face just above the waves, her long hair flowing back and forth with the sea.

"You okay?" His voice croaked. His throat burned. She bobbed her head up and coughed. Zac stood, wanting to help somehow. He then stumbled his way to the shore. In the horizon, the sun glowed beneath a band of dark sky. A calm breeze blew warm. Zac shivered.

He sat down next to Garlock, watching Eryn stagger to the shore, his mind numb. He tried to focus his thoughts. They had all gone under when the rail broke. He thought they would never find the surface and breathe. The ship had broken apart where they had stood watching Isaac. The whole side gave way into an undertow that pulled them down and out from the ship. When they finally surfaced, there were timbers and debris floating all about.

Eryn had thrashed wildly in the waves. She tried to run in the water, attempting to reach a large fragment of the ship's hull. It floated timber-side up, which made a crude, partially submerged raft. Zac remembered fighting the waves trying to help Eryn even though he knew she would pull him under. He had swum towards her with all his strength when his arm struck a large square beam. He swam with the beam, toward Eryn. She kept going under spitting and coughing until he reached her. With one hand on the beam, he grabbed her arm and pulled her up. She held tight as he kicked toward the floating fragment of the ship.

Garlock had joined them. He too had found a piece of wood from the ship. The rain came hard and the waves seemed monstrous. They wedged themselves between the rib-timbers with the ship's planking underneath, fighting to hold on. Every other wave sent someone sliding off.

Eryn had been terrified. She kept calling for Isaac. The rain, wind, and darkness made it impossible to see the ship. The fog was so thick they could not see the waves coming. They would suddenly start rising, tilting upward then plunge down into darkness.

Zac now watched the sun set, shivering as he sat on the rocky beach. It was strange to see the sun peeking through after such darkness. He wondered how long they had fought with the sea. Garlock rolled over onto his back and gave a long, painful groan.

"Does me look like a fish? Marrgh, never again—be I live three hundred rings."

Eryn dropped beside Zac. "Thank you," her voice raw and painful. She coughed and cleared her throat. She looked a mess. "You saved my life. I will never—" She coughed again. Zachary did not answer. He watched the red sun melt into the orange and yellow sky.

Garlock looked about. "So where the waves done brought us? Not the Isle of Moss, me hopes." Large rocks, sand and black pebbles were beneath them. Deciduous trees and palms lined the beach behind them. Large rock outcroppings extended into the sea on both sides.

"I do not know," Eryn said, her voice cracking. She tried to swallow but had nothing.

"Any way to make a fire?" Zac asked, shivering even more.

"Me fire kit was on the ship." Garlock rose slowly, sore in every joint and muscle. "But we can try. Let's go poke about."

Zac looked out into the sea before getting up. A great heaviness came over him as he thought about Isaac and the others. Eryn put her hand on his shoulder.

"We trust." She winced as she spoke. "We have to trust." She took his hand. For a moment, the shivering stopped. A strange kind of peace entered his heart. It drove the anxious pain away, bringing a sense of gratitude. He and Garlock and Eryn were alive—cold and miserable, but alive. He scolded himself. How can you be thankful when the others could be...? He stopped the thought. The peace and gratitude returned. He breathed a long, slow sigh.

"Thank you."

Isaac watched the sun breakout beneath the dark band of sky. He had clung to the round beam for several hours. Probably a mast or yard arm, he figured. The sea and wind had finally calmed. It had been hell, riding up and down in the pelting rain.

He could now see a long coastline in the distance. At first he had kicked hard, but then realized he was slowly drifting toward it. It'll probably be dark by the time I get there. Hope I don't pass by in the dark. A panic of despair came back as he saw himself drifting past into an endless black sea.

It was twilight when he touched the jagged reef beneath. He kicked to catch a small wave that carried him toward the shore. He could just make out the trees lining the beach as he felt his way over the rocks. Sand and pebbles swirled around his feet pushing from behind then pulling as the wave sunk back into the sea.

His legs wobbled as he walked up the beach. He flopped onto a sandy patch and tried to roll over onto his back. "The book." He sat up and took off his pack. It was heavy with water dripping from every seam. He considered opening his pack to inspect the book. "Let stuff dry." He groaned as he lay back down and gazed up into the sky. The sand was warm.

His body still rose and dropped with the waves. He thought of Zac and the others. Pain filled his heart. He pleaded that this be only a dream. A flash of home passed through his mind. Life there is so simple. Go to school, avoid the jerks, do your homework. Just stay out of trouble and life is good. What did I do to deserve this? I'm a good kid. Why am I being punished?

Anger swelled again. He knew it would not help. On the isle he had let the 'why's and 'how's go. But there's got to be a key, something to get home. "It's a Rubik's cube… in real life." As he spoke the words, he realized how alone he was.

He sat up and looked down the darkening beach. His head felt woozy. "Sloggy," he said. "I feel sloggy. Breezy would like that one. I'll have to…" The pain returned, trying to take his heart. "I'll have to remember it… when I see her again."

He walked the beach, soaked and shivering. He had no idea where he was going, or where he would spend the night. I'm walking in the dark on a strange beach… He reached up and grabbed the handle of his sword. With the backpack in his left hand, he drew the sword. He swung it left then right. The taunting fears backed away. "Should wash the blade," he said. "Saltwater could make it rust."

He looked up into a large tree. Sleeping in a tree perplexed him. "How do you keep from falling out?" He pictured tying himself around a limb. "No rope." It took courage to speak out loud, alone on a dark beach. He swung his sword some more. He liked the feel, the balance and grace as he twirled it about.

The sleek blade moved through the air as he parried, feinting left, then lunged. He imagined kroaks dressed in pirates' garb, wielding swords and cutlasses. "Ya slimy kroaks," he said, imitating Garlock. "Give me yeer best." He slashed the blade through a large fern, spun about and sliced off the leaf of a leaning palm. He paused, surveying his handiwork.

"Should stay on the beach." He turned back toward the beach looking for some kind of shelter. He wished he could start a fire. He pictured Garlock using his fire kit. The little Grimalkyn was fast once he found a bird's nest or dry fluff. Isaac considered the idea of making a fire. It just made him sad. His wet clothes hung so heavy and cold. A fire would feel so good, would feel safe. He could cook something... if he had something. Fire—the gift of the gods. He had used his matches that snowy day in the cave, wishing more than once he had brought a lighter.

The sky darkened, offering no stars or moon. It too, hung heavy, as if trying to press him down, to smother him under its darkness. He squeezed his sword. "I can do this." His stomach answered with an aching growl.

Suddenly he stopped.

"Smoke." He sniffed, turning about. "Over there." He walked quickly but warily down the beach. The sharp smell grew stronger. His blood raced. He thought back to the cave gorron and the smoky cavern. The horror spiked his nerves.

He pushed himself onward—slow and careful, feeling for his footing, trying to move in silence. He slung the pack on his back and climbed over a ridge of rock. The gentle waves would occasionally catch somewhere beneath and shoot their spray upward with a muffled kaloosh. A salty mist would follow. As he came over the ridge, he saw a fire on the beach far ahead. It was in the open, in the middle of a large beach. "Can't sneak up on that." He sat low, watching the small glow, listening to the waves strike the rock. Kaloosh... kaloosh...

A single form sat by the fire. "If no one else comes..." He whispered now. "I'll walk the tree line to get closer. I can handle one." As soon as he spoke, a large animal passed near the fire. It reminded him of Nusa. He thought back to the shipwreck. Where was Nusa? Was she in the cabin with Mirrah? He had not thought of her until now. Memories of the wreck came flowing over him—the girls trapped in the cabin.

He climbed down off the ridge and made his way over the stony beach toward the trees. It was hard to walk without making the round rocks shift and move. The beach here seemed to be all rounded pebbles and stones. He saw the animal get up and leave the fire, moving into the darkness. Isaac stopped and held his breath. He listened. Kaloosh... kaloosh...

"What have I got to loose... ah... it's called life... whatever." A few stars broke through a hole in the sky. He walked slowly toward the trees. He was almost to the tree line when a large dark form came out of the blackness.

He flashed his sword and stood his ground, his heart pumping hard. The dark form just stood there, a large beast walking on all fours. Something overhead fluttered like wings then disappeared. The beast shifted its weight and vanished. Isaac blinked his eyes, straining to see into the dark. He tried to steady his lungs, to hear through thudding ears.

"Ho, hey-ho!" came a voice from the beach. "Sir Isaac, is that you?"

Isaac stood frozen. His heart beat so fast it made his hands and arms shake. "Who are you?" he called out.

"I asked first. Be you, Isaac, the mighty?"

A gush of childish joy washed up through his soul. "I am Isaac," he called back, his voice crackled. "Not mighty—just Isaac." Tears blurred his vision as he ran over the pebbled beach toward the yellow flames.

The black form came in alongside him, and he heard the short quick breaths of Nusa, jogging gracefully, lightly bumping him. Warm tears dropped down his cheeks. Joy glowed inside.

Alle-Encer stood in the firelight wearing what could only be Grimalkyn underwear. Tercel the hawk, sat on his left shoulder. Isaac wanted to hug the old Grimal, shake his hand or something to show his joy. Alle-Encer just stood there, smiling as Nusa ran tight circles around the fire. Rocks shot out knocking like billiard balls. Isaac wiped his eyes and tried to catch his breath.

"Wow, am I glad to see you."

"As are we. Thank Ariel" Tercel bobbed his head and

whistled loud. Alle-Encer gestured for Isaac to sit. The smell of cooked meat mingled with the smoke. Small bones sat charred in the coals. Isaac's stomach growled.

"Me pardons," Alle-Encer said. "She caught a coot. We just ate the last bits."

Isaac sighed. "Doesn't matter. I'm just glad to see you."

Alle-Encer's clothes were spread out on the beach and propped near the fire.

"Take off yeer wet things, I'll snare up more wood."

Although his stomach ached, it was good drying by the fire. They shared stories of what happened that day. Alle-Encer had been thrown from the pilot's deck. No one saw as they all watched Isaac trying to reach Mirrah. Nusa went in after the old Grimal, keeping him afloat until they found a broad plank from the ship.

"I tried to call out, but the sea filled me throat." He smiled.

Isaac lightly chuckled. Joy and anxious worry played tug-of-war at his heart. He looked out over the sea.

"We trust," Alle-Encer said. "My soul tells me they are safe."

They listened to the waves washing the pebbles, rolling them up and down the beach. The kaloosh at the rock point could still be heard. Isaac wiggled out a spot to lie down in the rocks. Alle-Encer took a burning twig from the fire. He held it out and watched the flame.

"Wish I had me pipe," he said.

"Wish we had water." Isaac's throat burned from the seawater. More stars made their way into the black ceiling. Isaac shivered. It would be a while before his clothes were dry. Nusa came and stretched out beside him, her fur soft and warm against his bare back.

"Thanks, girl." He rubbed her head. "So, where are we?"

Alle-Encer put more wood on the fire. "I ponder… Hether Dawn. Come morn we'll find a road and make our way to a city."

"Sasson people around here?"

"Sasson drogs be everywhere."

"What about horls?"

"If this be Hether Dawn, there'll be no horls. It's an island kingdom. Horls don't swim."

They watched more stars breakthrough. The moon was nowhere to be seen. Alle-Encer tossed some driftwood onto the fire. Sparks rose high then drifted with the breeze.

"The dead carn on the deck," he said rather solemn, "may I ask how that be?"

Isaac thought back. "I just saw it—through the clouds, circling overhead. I knew if I shot… One of those things you do without really thinking, I guess."

"Not one I'd be doing."

They sat listening to the waves and crackling fire for a time. Isaac recalled the shadowy face in the eye of the dying carn. Alle-Encer held Tercel on his arm and stroked his head and back.

"Ya don't know, do ya?"

"Know what?" Isaac asked.

"To just threaten a carn be death—death to yeer family, yeer friends, yeer livestock—death by fire. They burn yeer hovels with all inside. Ya watch before ya hang." The fire popped, and a spark landed on Isaac's leg. He flicked it off before it burned his skin. Alle-Encer noticed with interest.

"No carns been killed for a long, long time. Not since Lorians walked the land—rather, flew the skies—be better said."

Isaac remembered the talk of Lorians while in the grotto. He lay back and watched the darkness overhead finally give way to stars. He told himself to get up and gather wood for the night, but the fire's warmth and Nusa's fur held him down. His whole body ached. What a day. The words of Longfellow's poem came to mind.

"Not enjoyment and not sorrow, is our destined end or way…" He could hear Zac walking through the house reciting the lines over and over. This particular stanza had struck a chord with him. He spoke the words slowly, letting them drift off with the ocean breeze. He opened his mouth to recite the last line when Allen-Encer spoke into the darkness.

"But to act that each tomorrow, finds us further than today."

Isaac chuckled. "Zac taught you, too, huh?"

"Zachary? That be an old Grimal rhyme from the Tollin days. How be it ya know its lines?"

Isaac bolted upright, startling Nusa. "Old Grimalkyn rhyme? What are you talking about? That's Longfellow's *Psalm of Life*."

"Longfellow? Those be the words of Barley Ma-gundy. Who be Longfellow?"

Isaac waited for a smirk or a wink. Alle-Encer had a way of catching him. The bushy old Grimalkyn just sat staring, his strange eyes glowing in the fire's light.

"You're teasing me, aren't you?"

Alle-Encer shook his head. "Barley be the golden balladeer of mulger hones. He put song in the soul of Grimals. Barley could 'weave words into webs of wonder.'"

"Come on, don't mess with me; it's been a hard day."

"Isaac," the little man leaned toward the fire, his furry face glowing in the yellow light, "I speaks but truth."

"But that's impossible. How can two people in two worlds write the same lines?"

"You've heard these lines before?"

"Yes. My little brother learning Longfellow."

"Twisting…" Alle-Encer dug his claw-like fingernails into his beard. "A real beard twister."

Isaac lay back down with a long sigh. He pondered the possibilities of such a thing happening. How can it be? But then how did he walk out of a marble courtyard and end up here, shipwrecked on a beach with a giant lynx that understands thought and a bushy little man who communicates with a hawk? He wished Zac were here. He could recite the poem and see if any other lines matched. This whole world is weird. It's been a long day, a very, very long day. Barley Ma-gundy?

Zac watched Garlock search out some fine grass, a few downy feathers and some dry twigs. He showed Zac the rock he would use to strike against his knife. Eryn had gathered driftwood, and they soon had a small fire smoking and crackling. They, too, shed their outer clothes to dry by the fire. And they, too, were hungry and very thirsty. Plans for the morning, where they were, and concerns for the others filled their conversation.

Zac yawned. "So, is this my bed?" he said, shifting some sand that filled a dip between two spots of rocky ground. They had settled between the water and the trees, closer to the latter than they wanted, but the beach was small.

Eryn gathered some dry grass and bound it into a small bundle. She knelt down next to Zac and tenderly tucked it under his head.

"Thanks," he said. She smiled, a beautiful smile, even though she looked a mess. Garlock had gathered a large pile of driftwood. Zac stared into the flames and thought of Isaac and Breezy. Another wave of darkened worry came. He fought the urge to let it turn to dismay. He thought about trust. As Eryn snuggled in near the fire he said a little prayer. "God, Ariel— you know who you are—please take care of them."

The fire snapped, sending sparks dancing upward into the night sky. A large ember popped out landing near Garlock's feet. He picked it up with his claw-like fingernails and tossed it back. The singed hair reminded Zac of Alle-Encer's questioning poem.

"Where are they from?

What lies ahead?

Why have they come?

By whom are they led?" Garlock and Eryn listened with wonder. "Strange I should remember that," he said. The fire popped again. "Just plain strange."

24 TRAPPED

Breezy watched Mirrah. The tall slender woman struggled to hold herself upright in the cabin doorway. Breezy tried to work her way up to Mirrah, grasping and slipping her way up the slanted floor. The ship rocked with violent jerks as wave after wave slammed the upright hull. Grounded on the reef, the ship sat on its side, rolling up then back with every pounding wave.

Breezy looked back at Sherrabella. The servant girl, who had become her best friend, stood waist deep in seawater. The ocean poured into the cabin. The floor, so slanted and slippery, seemed impossible to climb.

Bella stared up at her—bright blue eyes, shocked with terror. Breezy yelled to her to start climbing. Then the horrid dream came flooding back into her mind. She again saw the serpent wrapping around Bella, dragging her down, deeper and deeper.

"I'll come get you, Bella," Breezy shouted over the cracking and groaning ship. She looked about the room for something she could use.

"Use this." Mirrah tossed Breezy her long cloth belt. Breezy slipped as she caught it, sliding down and under the water. She came up right next to Bella, spitting the salty sea with a vengeance. Rage rushed through her limbs. She stood trapped in a stupid sinking ship with no stupid way out. The water pounded and pulled at her, slamming her into Bella. She fought hard to just stand. How could they climb up to Mirrah at the doorway?

Panic tried to grip her soul. She wanted to scream, but the horrid dream kept flashing. She tensed her jaw and looked around the contorted cabin. "It ain't over 'till it's over," she said through tight angry lips. "Grab this." She gave Bella one end of Mirrah's cloth belt. She tied the other end around her waist and took out her knife. She thrust the blade into the wall and pulled herself up the slippery, slopping floor.

The cabin shook as another wave slammed into the floundering ship. Bella slipped and screamed, then went under. She pulled Breezy down. Breezy thrust her knife into the wooded floor and held with all her strength. Objects sloshed about inside the cabin. A small wooden chest bumped her forehead. Its metal corner drew blood.

"Stouch!" she cried out, spitting water. It was her word for 'stop it' and 'ouch.' "Stupid, dumb, stupid thing." It made her hold even tighter. Bella was back on her feet, trying to follow Breezy up the wall, using her nails to grip the wooden planking. Breezy tried to get back to her feet but kept slipping on the wet floor.

Mirrah watched them then looked outside to Isaac. She searched for something that she could use to help the girls. The ship lunged with a booming crack and Mirrah screamed. Breezy heard Isaac yelling for Zac. Her cold, wet skin tingled. More water flooded the cabin. She held her knife with both hands as she now lay in the water on the slanted floor. Her head was just above the surface. Bella stood, neck just above the water, eyes wild. Breezy so wanted to cry, to cry for Bella, for herself, for Isaac and Zac.

"God, are you watching what's going on here?" She tried to be respectful, but He didn't seem to be keeping his side of the bargain. Not sure just what that bargain was, but thought it meant help in times like this. "You're making me wonder if you care," she said again. She hoped to make God angry, just a little or at least enough to get some help.

Then, she saw Mirrah pull her long braid out from beneath her vest. She sat down in the slanted doorway, knees hanging outside. She hung upside down and tossed her long braid to Breezy. At first it seemed like a joke. Breezy wondered if this were a dream like her other dreams. She thought of the pain for Mirrah, to pull themselves up by her hair.

"No," she called to Mirrah, "I won't." Breezy looked back. Bella's eyes were wide, wide like a horse in terror, her head bent back, fighting to keep her mouth above the sloshing sea.

Mirrah dropped her arms back over her head. She wrapped her long fingers tightly around her braid. "Climb, Brielle!" Breezy could not take her eyes off Bella. The horror of the dream came stronger. She sheathed her knife, reached up and clutching Mirrah's thick braid, pulled. Mirrah gave a muffled cry, and Breezy wept inside. She pulled hard but did not have the strength to drag herself and Bella up the slippery floor.

Mirrah pulled her own braid. Breezy could not see her face but she knew. She thought of when her mother would brush her hair and how any little tangle made her cry.

"This is crazy." Breezy said, struggling toward the door. "I am so sorry, Mirrah."

"Pull, Brielle!" Mirrah shouted again.

Another wave rocked the ship, jolting Mirrah's hold. Bella screamed. Breezy tightened her grip. The ship rocked back the other way, and Breezy scrambled as quick as she could. Clasping Mirrah's wrist, a surge of life came through. She clamored up over Mirrah, into the doorway.

"I'm so sorry."

"Get in the door and pull Bella."

Soon all three huddled in the doorway looking out onto the demolished deck. No one was in sight. Planking and debris sloshed about in the waters around the ship. A trail of wreckage drifted off into the dark mist. Shredded sails played tag with the wind.

"The captain," Mirrah gasped. "He is in that room."

"We can't go back there," Breezy said.

"We cannot leave him."

Breezy looked back into the calamity that was once a peaceful cabin. Debris floated about banging and bumping with the surge and flow.

"He was gonna throw us overboard." Breezy yelled over the rumbling wind and waves.

"He came back for us on the island."

Breezy saw a rope in the waves that washed over the mangled deck. "Hold the belt." She slid out the doorway, grabbing the rope, she hauled in as much as she could, and cut it off.

"Tie this around me." She dropped back into the cabin, slipping and swimming to the side room. The door was open, but the captain was gone. The window, smashed by the sea, sat under water as debris rushed in and out with every violent surge.

"He's gone!" she yelled back, then pushed into the water as Mirrah and Bella pulled.

"Maybe out the window," Bella said. "Maybe swam—he is a pilot of the sea."

"There is nothing more we can do," Mirrah said.

Using the rope and cloth belt, they made their way out and up the stairs to the upper deck. On the inclined deck they lay huddled together, feet against the taffrail, shivering in the wind, as the rain and spray battered their open bodies.

"So this… is how… we d-die?" Breezy shook with violent jerks as an icy dread seeped into her heart. Her lips quivered. "It's… n-not fair. I didn't… d-do anything. Why… is this happ-ppening? G-God, I thought you c-cared."

Mirrah had no answer. "Ariel, we need you," she said, her voice broken. "Please—help us."

Sherrabella shook so hard, her elbow bruised Breezy's rib. They lay on the deck, side-by-side, shivering with jerking spasms, like three fresh-caught fish, breathing their last, waiting to die.

Breezy could hear Isaac giving one of his speeches on

hypothermia. 'A condition in which the body core is below 95 degrees as a result of exposure to cold.' She laughed just once, as the words seemed to stream into her mind. How can I remember that? 'Apathy, poor judgment, drowsiness and coma.' Again the words flowed into her mind. Being near death must heighten your memory, she thought.

The wind seemed anxious, bent on drawing out their very life. With each shiver and spasm, their heat and hope got swept away, absorbed into the gusts and gales that carried their life out over the dark sea to be dropped aimlessly into the waves.

"We have to l-leave here," Breezy suddenly shouted into the wind.

"This is the s-safest place, out of the w-water," Mirrah said. Her slender body shook in short jerks.

"No! We'll die! Have to get out... of the wind and rain."

"No, we are safe here, out of the water."

The 'poor judgment' part of Isaac's speech kept repeating as Breezy got up. She went down the slanted stairs to the main deck. It was nearly under water as the ship settled further into the reef, splintering apart as wave after wave slammed into the stranded boat.

"Do not go into the cabin," Mirrah said, clutching Bella on the mangled stairs.

"We gotta find shelter." Breezy shielded her eyes. The rain stung as she looked up to Mirrah. Water surged up over her knees as wreckage sloshed about in the churning sea. A large chest floated near the center mast. She remembered it being tied to the deck. It held ropes and pins for rigging or shrouds and cleats as Isaac so willingly explained. It now partially floated, jerking about in the water, anchored by one rope fastened to its brass handle.

They stood, soaked and dripping. Their hair, matted flat, stuck to their faces. The ship gave up something with every wave, cracking and snapping as shredded sails with loose rigging lashed about. The wind and rain were so cold, the sky thick, dense, and dark.

Despair came hard and heavy—pressing into their souls.

Hopelessness unknown, unnatural, descended on them, suffocating any lingering, smoldering hope. Breezy looked to Mirrah. The brave Pharen woman with her hope, faith, and trust, was sinking with the ship.

A large wave struck. With full force, it slammed the exposed hull. Bella slipped from the stairs onto the deck and slid down into the waves. The surge washed her up the deck for just a moment, arms held upward. Breezy saw the face of terror. Then the water sucked her out into the endless sea.

"Beeellaaa!" Breezy yelled, "swim to us! Dog paddle!"

"She will drown." Mirrah's face turned ashen-white.

Breezy looked for the rope, but it was gone. She thought of the chest floating near the mast. It was full of ropes... but the waves... they kept coming, washing over the deck, surging through the ship, ripping away its innards, dragging their victims into the rolling darkness.

"Bella, come back!" Breezy called again, eyeing the chest of ropes. They could see her bobbing in the waves twenty feet from the ship. Her arms and hands flailed aimlessly.

"You have to save her," Mirrah said. "I cannot swim."

"You can't swim?" Breezy looked out at poor Bella trying to grab for anything to stay afloat. As a wave rode up onto the deck, Breezy dove. She swam toward the chest as the wave surged. The force seemed bent on dragging her out. It pulled at her arms, pushed on her back. Like schoolyard bullies, it jerked and tugged, taunting her to 'come out and play.'

She fought the surge and reached the chest, cutting it free. She struggled putting her knife back into the sheath, scanning the waters for Bella. She tried to open the chest, bouncing back and forth in the waves. She screamed with rage, coughing as water filled her mouth. She pushed off to launch the chest toward Bella, to swim it out to her...

"Owww! Her ankle jerked backward. Under the water something held her foot tight. She kicked and pulled, hugging the chest of ropes. Mirrah watched from the mangled stairs, her eyes wrought with horror.

Then it came—a wave like none of the others. It struck the

upturned hull with explosive force, washing high over the ship. Mirrah, ripped from the stairs, tumbled with the wave out into the sea. Breezy clutched the chest handle with both hands, fingers wrapped tight as the water poured over, covering her in darkness, panic screaming through every nerve and cell.

The wave pulled at her; it wanted the chest, it wanted her flesh. It ripped and tugged as she fought beneath the surge. Pinned by her ankle, shoulders stretched by the chest, she held her breath till lungs burned. The tug of war between ship and sea would take her to her grave, a cold, wet grave of lonely, pointless death.

The wave did not relent. It held her down beneath its weight, jerking and pulling till the ship gave up its guest. Suddenly, her ankle broke free and she washed out with the flow, holding the brass handle with one hand she swam with the other. She tried to call for Mirrah and Bella. Her muffled, coughing cry blew off with a gust of salty spray. She strained to find them, to see them, to hear them. She looked back as the ship faded into the foggy mist. Bobbing about, she drifted in the stream of debris, another victim claimed by the sea.

Panic pulsed through her body. She fought to be tough like the boys—to be a tomboy instead of a skinny, clumsy girl. She pushed up bravery, telling it to stand and fight, but it too, sank, drowning in the waves.

"Why is this happening?" she bawled out the words. She tried to call for Mirrah and Bella, but her voice came out so weak, so useless. She pulled herself up on the chest as high as she could, squinting, straining to see through the rain. Waves, wreckage, darkness and dread, was all she could see.

"Oh God, please help." Painful cries gushed from deep within. "I thought you were with us. Are you on coffee break?" She let herself sob. "Where are you?"

She realized she was not shaking anymore. The water was warm, warmer than she expected. A piece of sailcloth suddenly wrapped around her arm. It frightened her and she almost lost the chest as she fought to shake off the heavy cloth. A thought came to drape it over her head. She pulled it up and over. It formed a little canopy that shielded the rain and wind. She felt warmer.

"I need to stay strong." It sounded good to hear her voice inside the canopy. "No matter what comes... have to hold on." The images of Bella struggling in the waves would mix with the horrid dream. Isaac's cry for Zac, echoed in her mind. Mirrah's hopeless face... She clenched her jaw and held the chest tight. "I'm not giving in." Like holding onto hope, she knew she must not let go.

Thoughts of Zac and Isaac, Mirrah, Bella and Eryn came in and swirled around inside her mind. She rose and dropped with the waves. The dream of Alle-Encer, Garlock and the kroaks, their time on the island, all came in vivid color as she floated, endlessly rising up and down beneath her tent of cloth.

Hours passed, her hand became locked to the chest. She remembered the handsome man on the beach. 'I know where you are, do not be afraid.' Hope filled her heart. She could almost hear his voice. No... she could hear his voice. He was calling to her, shouting to her.

"Ah, there one, there one." It echoed out over the waves. Something splashed in the water and the chest jerked just a little. Panic flushed her heart. Sharks? Another splash and again the chest jerked. Then it moved. She was being pulled through the water. She tried to let go, but her hand was frozen.

"Aha, you snare it," came the voice again.

She lifted the sailcloth off her head with a gasp. Right beside her, rising up out of the sea, was a huge wall of brown. Then, the chest started to lift out of the water. It pulled her arm upward till her hand came free and the sailcloth slid off her head.

"Ho, looky looky."

Breezy looked up to find the voices. A small ship rose above her. Skinny-armed men were pointing down at her as others pulled the rope that had hooked the chest. They were collecting items from the sea, throwing grappling hooks to snag whatever came by. She tread water, staring up at them. Are they real, she wondered? Have I slipped into a coma?

A large rope dropped into the waves in front of her. She tried to grab hold, but her strength was gone. She wrapped her arms and legs around, but it slid through as the men on board pulled.

Her feet caught something underneath and she rose quickly up out of the water. Standing on a large knot tied into the end of the rope, her face pressed into the rough fibers. The rope smelled like moss-rat—musty and damp. She spun as they pulled her up out of the sea, squinting into the sun's rays. It shone out beneath a heavy layer of dark cloud. Even though it would set in minutes, she felt its warmth. A peace came, working its way down her whole body—like standing under a warm shower, a shower of serenity. She breathed a sigh and briefly forgot about where she was.

"Hi-oh, carfo, carfo." The deck was lined with small, wiry men, all eager to help the young girl over the rail onto the deck. Breezy looked and felt like a drowned moss-rat. A circle of bronze haired men, with small beady eyes formed around her. She just stood there dripping a small puddle into existence beneath her feet.

"Get towo, get towo." A short mouse-eyed man excitedly gave orders. Three men stumbled over each other in response. Breezy gazed at the scrawny men. They were skin stretched tight over muscle. All had strange bronze-colored hair, smooth skin and brown beady eyes. One of them reached out and pinched Breezy's arm.

"Stouch!" She jerked her arm. "That hurt." Silence held the men for about three seconds; then they all burst into laughter, slapping each other, pushing and hacking. Breezy squinted one eye and cocked her head. A stockier man saw her expression, pointed and started a whole new set of antics. They seemed to enjoy slapping each other, bouncing on one foot and pointing at the wet young maiden.

Three men came running up, each handing her a large rough cloth. She understood and began to dry herself. They all stood silent, watching intently.

"A little privacy here." Breezy turned to face the last of the setting sun. Feeling awkward, but strangely happy, a surge of joy, strange joy, went through her. She chuckled just a little. I'm soaking wet, surrounded by a bunch of corny sailors, bound for who knows where. Should be terrified—really—but I feel happy. I must be losing my mind. Is this how it feels? It's not bad, really.

She finished drying herself and turned to hand the towel back. A second man gave another, so she wrapped it around her wet head. She shifted her weight onto one hip. Her right knee was sore. The sailors did not move. Only their eyelids blinked as if in unison. "I'm done." She put her hand on her hip. With the towel around her head, the gawking sailors all about, and the setting sun's glow on her face, she looked like a fashion star holding a glamour pose at a photo shoot.

"Peese forro me." The short little boss-man motioned her. The scruffy sailors parted, and Breezy 'forrowed' the little man. They went to a cellar-like door that led down a steep ladder into a small room below. She took a big breath and grabbed hope, that mysterious hope that came in the dark turbulent sea.

They walked a very narrow passage that smelled like sweat and old bacon. They stopped at a doorway only five feet high. The little boss-man pushed it open and gave a polite little smile and nod. Breezy went in as the door closed behind.

It was dark and the air stale. A small round window let in the last glimmer of sun. She stood waiting for her eyes to adjust, when suddenly the room filled with a scream. Breezy slammed back against the door and drew her knife. Her heart raced wildly. She strained to see in the dimness. Two dark shapes formed inside the room, coming closer with every breath. Breezy crouched low. With her jaw set tight she squeezed the handle of her long blade.

25 BOUND FOR HETHER DAWN

"Breezy? It's Breezy!" Bella squealed with delight. "Mirrah, it's Breezy!"

As her eyes adjusted, Breezy saw Mirrah and Bella standing beside two crude bunks. Soon they were all hugging and crying, telling excited accounts of survival at sea. The ugliness somehow turned glorious as they each retold how they hung on and were finally rescued.

"I clung to Mirrah so tight, my hands cramped shut." Bella told how she and Mirrah had hung hand in hand over a large cask. With no way to hold the cask, they held hands. "Like sacks on a donkey," Bella said.

"It was hard and painful," Mirrah said, "but we are safe." Although weary, hope had come back into her gentle eyes.

"So who are these guys?" Breezy sat on a wooden bunk.

"Boondas—sea faring people. They have no country. The sea is their home."

"What will they do with us?"

"Take us to the nearest port—Hether Dawn."

"They seem nice."

"Things are not always what they seem."

"What do you mean?"

"We must be careful."

They talked more of what had happened and what to do when they reached Hether Dawn. There was a light tap at the door.

"Hung-gwee? Ladies hung-gwee?"

They went up on the deck where the men were sitting in a large circle. A black charcoal brazier sat in the middle with light blue flames rising from the coals. A few lanterns swung back and forth with the ship, illuminating the cool dusk air. The men quickly made room for the women to sit. Breezy noticed that many of them had gold of some kind—rings and bracelets, earrings and necklaces, even armbands. Much of it looked like women's jewelry. Strange, she thought.

A brown bread with very salty meat was passed to the girls. The men ate with vigor, crumbs tumbling out as they talked and laughed, smacking their lips with every bite. They all drank from one large bronze vase with handles on each side. Breezy watched the reddish liquid drip from their lips. When it was passed to her, she was so thirsty she actually brought it to her mouth. A whiff made her think otherwise.

"Smells like rotten pickles," she said, handing it to Bella. The Boondas snickered and chomped their food with even more vigor. They watched the girls intently, speaking a rapid chattery language with funny clicks and pops from down inside their throats. Sometimes they spoke in hushed tones. They would quickly smile when they noticed one of the girls watching them.

"What are they saying?" Breezy asked the boss-man.

"Tey tink you very pretty," he said with a smile that had more gaps than teeth. Breezy felt a chill and nudged closer to Bella.

"How long to Hether Dawn?" she asked Mirrah, her stomach feeling queasy. It was not from the food.

"Hever Don toe-marro," the boss-man answered quickly. He seemed excited, too excited. "You not worry. Take gooood care you. Eat, eat."

The men all raised their bread and loudly smacked their lips. "Eat, eat," they said in unison. Laughing and nearly choking, they slapped each other, striking any bare arms and legs. Breezy scooted even closer to Bella, who scooted close to Mirrah.

When they finished eating, they were free to roam about the ship. It was a simple ship, rather small with two triangular sails. Breezy wondered why there were no fishing nets. Mirrah got the boss-man to boil them some water to drink. Breezy was so thirsty she burned her mouth. The sky was dark and the air cool, so they went below into their little cabin. As there were only two beds, Breezy and Bella shared the upper bunk. Although exhausted, sleep would not come. The traumatic events of the day played over and over in Breezy's mind long into the night.

She was swimming again in the waves—swimming with all her might. Boats full of lip smacking Boondas and howling kroaks chased her over the waves. She would scream, but water filled her mouth. Something grabbed her leg, and she awoke with a start. Her throat was dry with thirst. She lay listening to the groans and creaks as the ship rolled with the wind and waves. She worried for Zachary and Isaac. Where could they be? She thought she heard someone talking outside the door, but soon she was back in the water—swimming after Bella with a 'towo' around her head.

Zac awoke while it was dark with the eastern sky giving a hint of light. He thought for sure he had heard something moving in the trees. He rubbed his hip. The sand had shifted, exposing a rough rock. The fire smoldered with red pulsating glows as the ocean breeze caressed the coals. He listened, hearing mostly Garlock's heavy breathing. Then he heard it again. Something moved about in the trees. He turned his head, careful not to make a sound, straining to see through the darkness.

"Where's Eryn?" he whispered out loud, then scolded himself for having spoken. She was gone. The noise came again. He squinted to where a faint rustling came from the brush below the trees. He held his breath and listened. Images raced through his mind—kidnappers, pirates, horls. He tried to focus. Where's a knife, a sword?

The rustling stopped. He held his breath again. Garlock snorted. The coals popped as a breeze rolled over them. Then a flurry of sounds came from the brush. A grunt and a piercing squeal cut through the air. Zac sat up. He strained to see into the dark. Then came more squealing and finally a muffled groan.

Garlock was up, looking all around. "What in Morten's mulger…?"

Eryn came out from the trees, holding a small pig-like animal. "Carabid," she said. Blood dripped from her long knife. "Can only find them just before dawn." She plopped it next to Garlock. "I killed it—you clean it."

Garlock flopped back onto the sand and groaned. "Aiya, I still be sleepin' and not a tissel-bit hungry." His stomach produced a mighty growl just as he spoke.

"Truth makes her voice heard," Eryn said. She went to wash in the waves. "Even if by a Grimal's belly."

Zac just sat, trying to clear his head. "Beats the alarm clock." He chuckled at the words from his mouth. He was sore, hungry, very thirsty, and separated from his brother and home. Should be terrified. He looked at the creature by the fire. It had a pig's head and feet, but a back like an armadillo. He dropped back onto the sand as thoughts of yesterday romped in his head. He thought of Isaac and Breezy, wondering where they might be, trying not to think the worst.

The east glowed red by the time Garlock had prepared and cooked the carabid. It actually tasted good but made them even thirstier. Garlock tossed the carcass into the fire, and they were soon walking the beach. They searched for signs of the others and anything useful from the wreckage. Coming to a high cliff that extended far out into the surf, they were forced to turn away from the sea and hike into the trees. Zac stopped and looked back over the rolling waves. Eryn came and stood beside him.

"He is alive," she said. "I know it. And besides, he has the book."

Isaac and Alle-Encer awoke to find Nusa dragging a small goat over the rocky beach. It had a collar with a small bell. They looked at each other and knew what the other was thinking.

"She takes from only those who have plenty." Alle-Encer gave a mischievous grin. He showed Isaac how to clean and skin the animal. He explained the best cuts and the uses for various parts. Isaac wanted to search the beach, but Alle-Encer insisted they eat first. "The gulls will leave us nothing." They ate till their stomachs hurt.

Isaac sat back and enjoyed feeding Tercel who liked the meat raw, especially the organs. The bird was small like a goshawk or merlin. It sat on his left shoulder eating from his hand. Sometimes the hawk nipped his fingers as it eagerly snatched the morsels. It hurt but he chuckled. He felt alive. The smell of smoke and the crackling fire, the washing waves on the stones, the gulls that squawked overhead and Nusa tearing the goat flesh from between her paws, all made him feel like he was fully alive, inside life, not just sampling it from the outside. A real kind of life was all around him.

They cooked some thin strips and wrapped them in large leaves. These were for the journey ahead, wherever that may be. Isaac took the book out of the plastic bag.

"Amazing. This thing is still dry."

Alle-Encer thoughtfully scratched his beard. "Ariel be watching."

Isaac let everything dry before putting it back into his pack. They all craved water as they left their little camp, the gulls swooping in as soon as Nusa left. They walked the beaches until the sun was hot, finding no signs of the others. Alle-Encer suggested they seek the city, most likely Hether Dawn, and search there. Isaac looked one last time out over the sea. Alle-Encer reached up and touched his shoulder.

"When nothing can be done, lad, we trust."

Isaac nodded, and they walked till they found a trail leading through the trees. Tercel had flown off after breakfast and had not yet returned.

Soon they were on a road that took them through a small fishing village. People stopped to watch Nusa as they passed by. Alle-Encer asked directions from an older man who muttered a few things and pointed.

"Are we safe here?" Isaac asked.

"If we stay out of danger." Alle-Encer winked. Isaac shook his head and smiled. He liked Alle-Encer. He had a strong confidence, a humble assurance.

After an hour, or closer to a lock, they came to a spring beside the road. Alle-Encer had bought some fruit and nuts along the way, so they stopped to rest. Isaac drank so much water his stomach hurt. "That's good water." He wiped his arm across his mouth.

Alle-Encer looked off down the road for a moment. Isaac wondered if he was concerned for Tercel who had still not returned. Alle-Encer then looked at the spring of water seeping from the ground.

"From springs flow life, from life spring flows. In the spring of life, life grows, 'til all springs to life beneath your toes." Alle-Encer gave a winsome smile.

"Barley Ma-gundy?"

"No, Alle-Encer of Yorne—fresh as the water itself."

"You just made that up?"

"The best kind."

They chuckled and continued on their way. Isaac marveled at how good he felt. He had to remind himself that his brother and friends might be dead or in serious trouble. It was like he needed to worry for them, that it was wrong to feel good inside. He remembered Alle-Encer's words: 'When nothing can be done, we trust.' Maybe I'm just trusting, he thought.

"So where are we?"

"Hether Dawn."

"I thought we were walking to Hether Dawn?"

"We're in the land of Hether Dawn, walking to the city of Hether Dawn."

"Big city like Kharlome?"

"Much bigger."

"Corlords?"

"No corlords. No rulers like Barthowl. Ruled by a king."

"Under Sasson?"

"Not sure."

"Could a king protect us?"

"Maybe. No, could not, and most prob'ly would not. But maybe."

"So what are we hoping to do?"

"To find the others."

Just then, Tercel came dropping out of the sky, cutting sharply upward and gracefully landing on Alle-Encer's shoulder. The little hawk bobbed its head, whispering whistle sounds into Alle-Encer's ear. Isaac figured he was being played for a fool, that it was meant to be a joke on him. Then Alle-Encer exclaimed: "They're safe. Your brother, Garlock, and Eryn are safe." Isaac knew Alle-Encer would never joke about something like that. From that day on, he never doubted the little hawk.

"Where?"

"They are in a forest, walking toward the city. I believe we will join them today."

Joy like he had never known rushed through his soul. He did not realize how heavy the burden had been. "Any sign of Breezy?" Tercel shook his head and gave a low whistle.

Breezy awoke to see Mirrah and Bella putting on their outer clothes. She rubbed her eyes and sat up.

"Did we wake you?" Bella asked, her voice so sweet.

"Bella, you are too nice. No, you didn't wake me." The sunlight glowed through the little round window. She took a big breath. "So today, we go to Hether Dawn?"

"Yes, and pray all goes well." Mirrah braided her hair.

"Have you seen anything, you know, future stuff?"

"I have not seen anything since we left my home. I am beginning to wonder if I am still a Pharen." She smiled, but

Breezy knew her concern.

"It'll be alright." Breezy hopped down from the bunk. "We just need to trust."

Their clothes were still damp and rather clammy. Breezy mused how she would have complained without ceasing if she were back home wearing smelly damp clothes. A gentle knock sounded on the door.

"Ladies sleep done? Hever Don come." They opened to see a young Boonda bow as he backed away from the door. He motioned for them to follow him to the deck.

The sun warmed the sky over the harbor of Hether Dawn. Ships and small boats seemed to bob about everywhere. Gulls squawked and darted through the menagerie of sails and ships. They skimmed over the water, circling near fisherman who sorted fish on docks and piers.

Breezy smiled. What a beautiful day. She stretched her arms out wide. Even her damp clothes did not feel as bad. How was yesterday so nasty, and today… so brand new? Today is going to be a turning point. She could feel it. After today, everything would be different. She sniffed the air.

"I smell pancakes." She turned to Bella and Mirrah as they all stood watching the activity of the morning harbor. She realized how hungry she was—hungry for familiar food. The smell took her thoughts back to the morning at the boys' house. It was so exciting, a snow day, an expedition to the pillar. Having breakfast together, talking about all they would do that day. That day was a turning point, that's for sure.

She watched a small boat with one sail glide past their little ship. I really should face reality. Huh! Reality. As if there is such a thing. Wouldn't know it if it hit me in the head.

The pancake aroma filled the air, and soon a man came out with a huge platter of yellow pancakes. He set them on a barrel with a small pitcher beside. The bronze haired Boondas came by and, taking several pancakes, poured a white substance from the pitcher, folded the cakes in half, and shoved them in their mouths whole.

They motioned, with their cheeks bulging like chipmunks in

autumn, for the women to come help themselves. The sweet milky substance on the pancakes tasted good, even helping Mirrah let her tensions slide. It was indeed, a beautiful day. They were not drifting helplessly in the rolling sea, but were in Hether Dawn where they would find the others and take a ship to Kharlome, where they would... Breezy tilted her head and stopped her chewing. Where they would... do what?

She was sitting on the chest from the Fare Whether when some men shouted from the pier, and the ship turned to drift in slowly. Breezy stood to watch them throw the ropes and draw the ship alongside a large wooden pier.

"Hever Don, beauties." It was the little boss-man. He had come up behind them and now excitedly pointed to the vast harbor and city beyond. "Bling you safe to Hever Don."

"Yes, thank you," Mirrah said. She reached inside her clothing and handed the man three small shining stones. He smiled with exuberance and bowed slightly.

"Take you meet flends." He then climbed over the side down a rope to the pier. They were lowered over the side and were greeted by a group of similar looking men. "My flends, tey help you."

"Thank you," Mirrah said. Breezy heard the concern in her voice.

The men stepped aside forming a line down the pier. They gestured for the women to go ahead. Mirrah led the way followed by Breezy and Bella. As soon as they began walking, a lasso of rope seemed to come out of nowhere. It dropped and tightened over each of them. Their arms were suddenly bound to their sides. Before they could scream, a stinky, knotted rag got pushed into their mouths. Strong arms held them tight. A dark sack came down, and everything went black.

26 HETHER DAWN

Breezy fought like a wild cat, but it was hopeless. A man on each side held her arms, pulling her forward down the pier. She heard Bella whimpering behind and Mirrah scuffling up ahead fighting with her captors. Breezy's heart sank. She cried but no tears came. Yesterday's agony and all the weariness came back into her heart. Despair took hold. She went limp. How can this be happening? Why doesn't Mirrah see these things? Why do bad things keep coming? Her legs didn't want to move. She shuffled, and the men jerked her arms.

They left the pier and walked onto dirt and gravel, finally stopping when someone bound their hands behind them. A strong, fishy smoke filled the air. The hoods were taken off and they saw they were in a small room with loose plank siding. Morning light shone through the cracks creating beams of gray smoky light.

Breezy could still hear the gulls and sounds from the harbor. Two captors stood on each side, gripping the upper arms tightly. The rag inside her mouth tasted of rotten fish. It was tied behind her head, pulling her hair. She wanted to scream but would not take a breath. She shook herself, stamping her feet, but it made them grip even harder, hurting her long skinny arms.

A short fat man came in and looked them over carefully, poking his finger into Breezy side. She kicked and squirmed. The fat man giggled like a little girl. His hair looked like he had just crawled out of bed and had not seen a comb in years. He made the men turn the girls around slowly. As they turned, they saw the boss-man from the ship. He was smiling and even gave a little bow. He and the fat man talked rapidly, arguing fiercely back and forth. Finally, the fat man counted out stones for the boss-man. When the boss-man tucked the stones away, he looked at them and bowed.

"Soddy ladies. Must sell de catch-ed fish." He bowed, smiled and was gone. Breezy tried to spit but all she mustered was an angry hiss.

Eryn, Zac and Garlock walked single file through a dense forest. They were on some sort of trail, but it was not easy. It was somewhat open and airy, a pleasant forest compared to the Isle of Moss. Songbirds whistled in the trees. Zac looked up as he walked, watching birds fly about among the leaves. He pushed a branch aside and let it fling back slapping Garlock in the face.

Garlock growled. "Do that again and I be—"

"Forgiving you each and every time." Eryn finished his sentence speaking quite firmly for a young girl to an older Grimalkyn.

"Sorry, Garlock," Zac said. "Didn't mean to."

"Aiya, this forest be growin' as we walk. Me thinks there be no end."

"We have not even walked a twill," Eryn's words were harsh. "Thought a Grimal like you could walk all day."

"I've traveled more in one day than you in yeer whole spriggin' life. Ya be a child. Think ya can tell me what is?"

"I think—" She spun around to face Garlock, grabbing the sword on her back, her teeth clenched tight. She paused, snorted through her nose and turned back around.

"Whoa," Zac said very quietly. He envisioned himself trying to break up a fight. The image did not look pretty.

They walked on in silence. Zac was careful to not let even a twig lash back on Garlock. Thirst filled his mind more than anything else. Finally, Eryn stopped and stood still. Through the trees they saw a donkey pulling a cart over a dusty road. Fine clouds of red dust rose from behind the cart and beneath the plodding beast. An old woman sat hunched over holding a red cord to the donkey. Eryn ran out to the road.

"Is this the way to the city?" she asked the old woman. Zac and Garlock came out of the forest and joined her walking alongside the cart. The woman looked at them a moment before looking back down the road. "We were shipwrecked and washed ashore. Can you please tell us if this is the way to the city?"

"Which way do ya tink ya should go?" the woman said in a crotchety old voice. It sounded more squeak and squawk than human.

"Well, I do not know; that is why I am asking."

"Which way dos ya supposes?" The woman gave an ugly near toothless smile, one tooth on the top, two up from the bottom. Her long, gray black hair hung down as she sat hunched, cranking her neck to look at Eryn.

"I would suppose," Eryn said, with an obvious sigh, "that it is this way."

"Den why ya need of askings me?"

"Well, I want to make sure before walking all day."

"So ya tinks if I tell ya, it'll be a sure?"

"Well, I assume you live here and know the way."

"Dat I do, but why dat make ya sure?"

"I assumed you would tell me the truth."

"Yaaa, but all dat assuminating, what good be me answer? Still can't be knowing for a sure."

"No, but it would help."

"How be dat? Trust an old hoagfish ya never done seen before? Trust her above yar own supposings?" Eryn did not reply as they walked slowly beside the cart. Dust rose into little swirls around their feet. "If ya gots dat kind of doubt," the old woman's voice squawked, "ya best not be going anywheres."

Zac stepped close to Eryn. "Maybe we should ask someone else."

"This is the way." Eryn stepped into a full walking pace, passing the slow, plodding donkey. When they walked a ways ahead of the old woman, Eryn looked back and chuckled. "Thank you," she whispered.

The sun got warm as they walked the dusty road. Zac thought his throat would dry shut. His tongue kept getting stuck to the roof of his mouth. He thought he heard water trickling somewhere. I'm so thirsty, I'm hearing mirages, he said to himself. Can you hear a mirage? Then something he never had happen, happened.

"I smell water." He sniffed the air. Walking to the forest side of the road, he pushed through the grass. "This way," he called back. Eryn and Garlock just stood watching. He went into the forest, so they followed. He had gone maybe twenty or thirty feet when he found a small stream flowing quietly through the trees. He turned to call them, but they already stood behind him.

"By Mulder's mire, I never..." Garlock dropped to all fours.

"Thank you." Eryn touched his head before kneeling down to drink.

They sat and drank by the little stream until they saw the old woman pass by in her cart. They could see the road, but were out of sight among the trees and grass. Birds sang as the stream burbled and plunked through the small rocks and pools.

Suddenly, a band of horsemen came thundering down the road. Dust rose high as they galloped toward the city. Nine riders, dressed in bright yellow and purple uniforms, rode in pairs with one in the lead. A long wagon trailed behind, pulled by two hefty horses, their hooves the size of dinner plates. They came fast with dust that billowed a lengthy cloud, smothering the old woman and her donkey. She hacked and coughed as they ran her off the road. When the dust settled she was plodding on as before.

"Who were they?" Zac asked.

"I do not know." Eryn watched with concern.

"Could they be looking for us?"

"I hope not."

They walked out onto the road coming up to the old woman again.

"Who were those horsemen?" Eryn asked her.

"Did ya get lost?" The woman did not even look over at Eryn.

"We stopped to drink from a small stream."

"De stream in de trees?"

"Yes."

"Ya didn't?"

"Why?" Eryn looked intensely at the old woman.

"Why da ya tink?"

"Poisoned?"

"Is dat what ya tink?"

"It tasted sweet, like good water."

"Den it must be." The old woman let out a hideous rasping laugh. She sounded like she would choke to death, but she flashed her three-toothed grin. "Den... it must... beeee." She hacked and coughed again barely able to get the words out.

"Let us move on," Eryn said with disgust, shaking her head and walking as rapidly as possible. Zac wondered if it really was bad water. No, the old woman was just playing tricks on them. It had tasted good, and nothing seemed unusual. He chuckled to himself. "Hoagfish, huh... that fits."

They came to a high point where they could see all around. Several miles ahead they saw a huge city in a large open valley surrounded on three sides by hills. To the north of the city was the sea.

"Hether Dawn, I believe," Eryn said. "We were nearing when the storm hit."

"Are we safe here?" Zac wiped his brow.

"I hope so." She took the string out of her braid and gave her hair a shake. She fluffed it out letting it fall all about her shoulders and back. "Can you make it?" she asked Zac.

"Still thirsty. It's so hot and dry."

They stood looking over the valley with the city below. It was like a small kingdom as the valley extended for many miles to the south. Eryn looked back down the road. Zac knew what she was thinking. Lines of red dirt formed at the corners of her nose and mouth. Rings around her eyes made her look rather funny. I must look the same, he thought. Their clothes were covered in fine dust.

"Do you think we'll find them?" he asked. Eryn just stood scanning the landscape. A gust blew dust up into their eyes. She turned and let the wind play with her hair.

"We must find them," she said. "He has the book."

"Den, it must beeee," Garlock said, imitating the voice of the old woman. He sounded so like her it made Eryn and Zac spin around. Then they all broke into a long, dry laugh. Garlock imitated the woman's raspy laugh so well that Zac had to put his hands on his knees to hold himself up. He looked back expecting the old woman to come plodding up the road. He laughed until he cried. It washed the dust from his eyes.

Isaac and Alle-Encer saw the city of Hether Dawn up ahead. They were following a caravan of carts and mules, loaded with produce to sell in the city.

"Tell me about Eryn," Isaac said, as they walked along. Tercel gave a low whistle.

"What do you want to know?"

"Like how old is she?"

"Eryn be... let me ponder... she's twirled three cords I believe."

"Fifteen?"

"I ponder such."

"And she lives alone?"

"Her mam and pap be murdered. 'Twas parlords of Yorne, one whose blood just be spilt, thanks to you and yeer kin."

"One of those dudes killed her parents?"

"Klonen, who rode Kore, whose claw you liberated." Isaac thought back to that terrifying day. It already seemed like months ago. "The other be an old parlord. You'll know him—

his horn's but a nub, cut by a Lorian blade."

Isaac remembered Eryn's questions that night in Kharlome, asking if the horn was cut. Something stirred inside. He suddenly knew he would meet this de-horned parlord.

"You three have rippled the air," Alle-Encer said. "Don't know how, but change has certainly come." Isaac looked down, the dust swirling as they walked. He thought of the symbols on the book. *So—Tur—Faln.* Three bring destiny—three embrace death.

"So why were they killed—Eryn's parents, I mean?"

"For teaching her Pharrian, the old Pharrian. I remember it well. Taken in winter, they were. Dragged behind worls—pulled through the wood—house abalzing." His eyes seemed to drift off. "Eryn be but a cord—bright and lively. Always talking, always learning, always reading. Loved the scrolls and books, specially them old ones."

Alle-Encer watched the traveling dust cloud drift off with the wind as the caravan of merchants moved toward the city. Nusa followed near the trees and fields that edged the road. Alle-Encer became lost in thought.

"So what happened?"

"Oye. They be dragged through the wood at night. Been a cold winter, the horls being hungry and all. Tied 'em each to an oak—facing the other."

"What about Eryn?"

"Tied up tight like her mam and pap—tight so the horls would have to pull, tearing the flesh—"

"I get it. But she was only five?"

"Mirrah saw it—the way Pharens see. Her and Tesoro, they ran through the wood, at night mind you—horls all about and hungry. Not sure where, just following their thoughts. Saved Eryn, they did. Fought four horls to reach her. Saved her like a jewel from thieves."

"Fifteen… raised by Mirrah…"

"A real jewel, eh?" Alle-Encer gave his mischievous smile.

They walked in silence as Isaac thought of Eryn and Zac. It was such a relief to know they were alive and on their way to the city. His thoughts turned to Breezy. The image of the girls trapped inside the sinking cabin came back in full color. He tried to have hope—to trust, but he was tired. It can be hard to hope when you're tired.

27 SOLD

Breezy, Mirrah, and Bella were led up a stairway behind a large platform like an outdoor theater. A man came and undid the smelly rags and the lasso about their arms, leaving their hands bound. Breezy started scolding him for treating them such. He slapped her face. It stung horribly. She had never been slapped in her whole life. A flush of tears filled her eyes, but she made no sound, her lips tight. She would have slapped him back if her hands were not bound. In a way she was glad they were, yet it was horrible losing freedom.

They heard lots of shouting and catcalls. Numbers were yelled back and forth until the dreaded words rang loud and clear—'sold.'

"We're being sold," Breezy whispered to Mirrah.

"I am so sorry, Breezy. Please forgive me."

"But we still trust, right?" She waited for Mirrah's enduring words.

"Yes… of course."

But Breezy knew, for Mirrah, it was gone. Her skin tingled, feeling the fearful dread come like cold, damp wind.

"Well, I still trust," she said loudly. "These… these… moss beetles aren't going to have their way without a fight, I'll tell ya that." The man came near and raised his hand. Breezy cowered, but no slap came.

"You best shut them lovely lips or things go bad," he said, his voice rough and hoarse. He was bearded, looking and smelling like he had not bathed his entire life. It reminded her of the cave gorron and the putrid cavern. She pictured Zac running, hiding behind the horrid piles of bones and yuck. He was so brave that day. *I wish I could be brave.*

Suddenly she was thrust out onto the stage. A large crowd was gathered in the square. Some wore beautiful garments that flowed with vibrant colors, while others were dirty and in need of combs. They cheered as Breezy came out. She looked back with hopes that Mirrah and Bella would be brought out too. Her face still stung from the smelly man's slap.

The crowd was so noisy the auctioneer could not get a base price. She heard seventy stones shouted out by a nice looking man with a long flowing hat. He had a tiny little beard that reminded her of a musketeer. *What will he do with me?*

"Seventy-five," another man shouted from the back. He was tall, an older gentleman with long white hair, but kind looking. The crowd cheered and whistled.

"Eighty," shouted the musketeer-looking man. The crowd gasped at the price. Breezy sensed the excitement. *At least they appreciate quality here. Get a grip! You're being sold at a slave market.*

"Does I hear eighty-five?" the auctioneer barked out over the crowd. Breezy's knees went suddenly weak. This was real and happening too fast. *I'm going to be separated from Mirrah and Bella. I'm going to be sold as a slave to someone I do not know in a land I.... How can this be happening? Things like this don't happen. I'm not even thirteen. Or am I? What day is it? Did I miss my birthday?*

"Eighty-five," a new voice called from the crowd. The people turned and a hush fell over the audience. A very nice looking young man, dressed in dark blue silky clothing walked toward the stage to examine the young specimen. The crowd parted as he walked, keeping their distance. Two tall men in black, muscular with long knives on their belts, followed close behind like bodyguards. His silky shirt fluttered as he walked. It reflected light making him look like an angel.

As he came near, he took a quick step and leapt up onto the stage. The crowd cheered with admiration. He walked up to Breezy and looked her in the eyes. He tilted his head just a little, and Breezy knew it was her 'freakish' eyes. She looked away. He was very handsome with dark eyes and brows. She wanted to look at him again but held her head down. She could feel his eyes examining her.

"Does I hear ninety?" the rough voice barked. "Ninety? Anyone for ninety?"

Silence held the crowd as the man took out something and gave it to the auctioneer, not even taking his eyes off Breezy. Then he turned and hopped off the stage. One of the muscular men in black walked over to the steps at the end of the platform. He waited for Breezy. She stood there, stunned. The auctioneer gave her a shove toward the steps, where she nearly stumbled as she went down off the stage.

As soon as she stepped off the last step, the muscular man slipped a noose made of fine, white leather around her neck. The other end looped around his wrist. I'm a dog on a leash, she thought. He led her through the crowd to the man in blue silk. He did not introduce himself. They just stood there waiting for the next item.

Mirrah came out next. When the crowd saw her long braid, hushed talk filled the square. It seemed no one would bid on a Pharen. Breezy almost asked her new owner why. She marveled at her lack of fear. I must be in shock. It's going to hit me soon.

The auctioneer tried hard to establish a price for Mirrah. One man offered twenty stones. Even Breezy knew that he was not serious. Finally, the man in silk spoke to the bodyguard on his right. That man went up to the stage and looked Mirrah over. She stood, head down. Breezy clenched her teeth, breathing hard through her nose.

The man offered the auctioneer something, and Mirrah was led down the steps toward Breezy. When Breezy realized they were possibly going to be together, she could not hold back.

"Mirrah, we are still—" As soon as she spoke the leash jerked tight. It hurt and Breezy turned to give the muscular bodyguard a firm kick. She swung her foot back but stopped. The man looked at her expressionless.

No leash went on Mirrah's neck; she just stood next to the other bodyguard in black. He held her by the arm.

Bella came last, crying a face full of tears, her hair a mess, her clothes ragged. The crowd jeered and the price of ten stones got offered right away. The auctioneer was mean to her as he turned her around for the people to see. Breezy boiled, a groaning pain knotting in her stomach.

"Fifteen stones," someone shouted.

"Fifteen, does I hear twenty?"

Breezy turned to the handsome man in silk.

"I don't know who you are but—" Again the noose jerked. Breezy jerked back. "But I think this is stupid!" The noose pulled tight, choking her. She spun and kicked the bodyguard holding the leash. She caught his left shin and he winced and looked confused. She turned back to the man in silk. He too, seemed confused.

"She is... my sis...ter." Her words came out in breathy rasps. The tall man in silk just watched, his dark eyes startled.

"Sold for fifteen." Breezy spun around to see Bella being pulled off the stage.

"You bunch of thugs," she tried to shout as she fought against the noose like a stubborn dog's first day on the leash. It hurt, but a zeal for Bella rose from deep inside, coming from her soul.

"You bunch of... you... stupid jerks." She tried hard to scream the words, but the noose pulled tighter. She kicked, willing to die before she saw Bella sold into slavery again. Her cry came out in a harsh whisper, but it was loud enough for the crowd to hear. The square had gone silent, watching Breezy challenge her new owner, watching with stunned interest.

She continued to struggle, cutting off all her air. She was strangling herself and didn't care. She heard Mirrah crying and pleading. The man in silk just watched. Then the bodyguard holding the leash, slapped her face. It stung like the first, but it made her belly burn. She turned and lunged toward him, planting her shoulder straight into his gut. He stepped backward, but his heel caught the cobblestone. Suddenly, they both toppled down. Breezy landed on his chest with a thud.

The man's head clunked hard upon the stone. He lay still, just staring up into the open sky. Breezy knew she was in trouble, but a burning rage filled her soul. The undaunted boldness of power mode came full force. She rolled over onto the dirty pavement and sat up, trying to stand with hands bound. As she pushed, she touched the man's knife. She looked at her new owner who still just stood wide-eyed. If they weren't going to move, she would. Staying down, she pulled the knife out, hiding it behind her. Quickly but carefully, she cut at the ropes.

The man holding Mirrah looked to the man in silk. Breezy worked the knife. They thought she was just sitting, waiting for her guard to stand her up. When the rope gave way, she swung the knife up, slicing the leash still in his hand.

Before they realized it, she stood, knife in hand, threatening the man in silk. The severed leash hung like a necktie. No one moved. Breezy thought of the parlord facing Isaac. They've never been challenged.

"Let her go, you doofus, you pile of… of… buffalo dung." Breezy waved and poked the knife at the man holding Mirrah. Mirrah shook her head at Breezy. The man in silk gave no command.

"Now!" Breezy shouted. Her voiced echoed through the square. The man slowly let loose his grip on Mirrah, but the woman did not move. She continued shaking her head.

"Mirrah, come over here," Breezy ordered, then pleaded. "Please?" Mirrah just stood. The crowd was strangely silent as they watched the drama, like this young girl had them frozen in time. Breezy looked about for Bella, but she was gone. "Bella!" she cried. "Bellaaaa!"

A balding Grimalkyn came up to look closely at Mirrah. He

was dirty looking. His bushy yellow-white beard had streaks of red and held scraps from his morning breakfast and maybe even yesterday's lunch. He pointed his hand at Mirrah and looked at the handsome man in silk.

"Does Ya Sovereigncy know who she be?" he said, with a frog-like voice. "Does ya know, Yeer Essence?" The handsome man did not respond but looked closely at Mirrah then back to the dirty Grimalkyn. He did not seem concerned over Breezy standing with the knife.

"She be the wife of Bain Sarro, the Sasson drog." The crowd that now pressed in close gave out muffled gasps. "She be Mirrah of Myrrh, Yeer Essence. I knows it like me own head."

The crowd murmured loudly as poor Breezy stood there with the knife, now bewildered like the rest. The man she had knocked down sat up, dazed. He got to his feet as Breezy pushed back against the crowd—trapped inside a tight ring of gawkers.

"Are you Bain Sarro's wife?" The man in silk finally spoke. His voice was calm and resonant. He spoke as a gentleman.

"I am Mirrah of Myrrh but am not such said wife."

"Aiyo, Yeer Highness," the bald Grimalkyn pointed his dirty fingers at Mirrah. "She knows him as he used to be— Tesoro of Yorne."

Mirrah glared at the bald Grimal, trying to recall who he may be. The dirty Grimal looked away then slunk into the crowd. The handsome man studied Mirrah.

"Is this true?" he asked.

"My husband is dead."

He then turned his attention to Breezy, still standing with the bodyguard's knife.

"This wild one is yours?" he asked Mirrah.

"Yes, Your Highness—please show mercy." Mirrah's voice quivered. "She is from another land."

"I reasoned such." He motioned with his head for Breezy to hand the knife back. "Come." He turned and the crowd spread.

"Mirrah?" Breezy's shoulders slumped.

"Come, Brielle."

"But what about Bella?"

"Come!"

Breezy handed the knife back to her keeper. She took the leather leash off her neck and handed that to him as well. He followed her out the square, rubbing the back of his head, thoroughly confused.

The crowd parted as the man in silk led his new acquisitions out of the public square. A small horse-drawn carriage waited just beyond. Two black horses with untrimmed manes stood patiently in front of a boxy carriage. The man who had held Mirrah, opened the door as the man in silk motioned for Mirrah and Breezy to step up inside.

They sat together, facing the man in silk, jostling over the stone streets. Breezy heard the bodyguards calling for people to clear the way. The snap from a whip would crack the air, as the men would give a shout. She churned inside, her pulse still pumping wildly. The stomach knot faded, but the ache for Bella grew painful.

On a balcony overlooking the auction square, stood a very large man with long rusty-red hair, his face drawn and gaunt. A dark nub of horn protruded from his forehead, a wide up-side-down triangle. He wore a sleeveless chest plate of chain mail that looked like fish scales and had armguards of brass—the armor of a parlord. He silently watched as Breezy and Mirrah climbed into the carriage.

"Mirrah of Myrrh… and the girl…" He rested his hand atop the long knife at his belt. "Finally… fate befriends me."

The carriage left the bustling city, climbing a large hill that overlooked the harbor and the vast kingdom below. They neared a large palace of pinkish-blue stone. The morning sun glazed the palace walls, rays reflecting golden beauty from the stone. Glossy black stone trimmed the numerous windows and doors. Large spires rose high with banners casually waving to the warming sun.

No one spoke inside the carriage. The handsome man in silk watched them both for a very long, very awkward time. Breezy churned with questions, confusing thoughts filled her head. She dared not open her mouth, feeling really dumb now, riding together in a civilized manner. I am *never* opening my mouth again.

She thought of the time at school when she had spoken out against her friends. They were mistreating the homely girl— Beatrice Mole. Why name your kid, Beatrice? I mean, really. And Mole? Change your name or something. They had joined in with Mandy Morgon, the official school jerk and were pushing and teasing Beatrice. Breezy stuck her finger in Mandy's face and told her to back off or meet the wrath of Brielle.

Why did I say that? All I got was pummeled. I've got to learn to keep my mouth shut.

The handsome man finally spoke. "Explain yourself," he said to Mirrah, who gave a simple nod. "Who are you, and why were you being sold?"

"We were shipwrecked, Your Highness. Picked up by Boondas. I am Mirrah of Myrrh, wife of..." She struggled to finish.

"Wife of Bain Sarro."

"No, Your Highness. My husband was Tesoro, the Pharen leader of Yorne. He is no more." The handsome man laid his head back, watching Mirrah. He then stared at Breezy, eyeing her clothes for a long, long time.

The carriage stopped outside a large set of doors. As they stepped out after the handsome man in silk, he extended his hand to Mirrah. Were it not that he had purchased them and put a leash about her neck, Breezy would have thought him a very nice, good-looking gentleman.

They walked into a large marble hall lined with banners and drapes. The marble floor and walls were polished smooth, echoing their footsteps. Large round columns extended high into a vaulted ceiling like in a large cathedral. Light streamed in through windows high above. White silky curtains waved about with the morning breeze, as fragrance, like Christmas, wafted through the halls. Colorful birds in small wicker cages that hung near the high windows sang various songs as they hopped about inside their airy prisons. Guardsmen with long halberds stood at attention near the columns. They wore uniforms of bright yellow and purple. Breezy and Mirrah walked on in silence, following the man in silk, listening to their footsteps and pondering their fate.

28 KIDNAPPED

Isaac and Alle-Encer walked the dusty road toward the outskirts of the city. Nusa kept to a grove just off the road, her short nose at the base of a large tree. She looked up at Isaac.

"What's up, girl?" he asked, joining the giant lynx in the grove, knowing instantly what she wanted. Alle-Encer watched him kneel behind the tree. After a few minutes, he and Nusa came out of the trees as Tercel flew to Alle-Encer's shoulder. Isaac adjusted the pack on his back and scratched between Nusa's tufted ears. Alle-Encer nodded, as Tercel perched on the old Grimal's shoulder, chirping a garbled squawk.

"What do you think?" Isaac asked. Alle-Encer looked off toward the city.

"Trust no future, however pleasant."

Small roads merged as they neared the city. Sellers lined the streets with all kinds of produce. Alle-Encer bought some fruit that grew in bunches like grapes but large like golf balls and were covered with a thin brown skin. Inside was a white jelly with a pit like a hickory nut. Nusa watched Isaac closely as he pealed away the thin outer skin to eat the sweet and juicy fruit. He offered her one, but she dropped it from her mouth, licking her chops.

Stone and wood buildings lined the streets. Alleys and

narrow paths went off in random directions. The air was thick with noise, smoke, and pungent smells. Round pancake breads fried in large kettles of smoking oil. Boiled eggs sat steaming in wicker baskets. Alle-Encer stopped and bought some steamed buns—white gooey bread with minced meat inside.

"Is she safe?" Isaac asked, tossing the lynx a white bun. People stared and pointed at the giant cat, jostling to keep out of her way.

Alle-Encer gave his usual unconcerned look. "Best not stay too long. Best keep moving." They came to a large city square with sellers scattered throughout. Little booths and stalls sold goods of all kinds.

"So how do we find them?" Isaac swallowed the last of the gooey buns. "They could be anywhere."

"Where would yeer brother be?"

"Where would Garlock be?"

"Garlock will follow Eryn and yeer brother. Eryn will go to a high place." Alle-Encer then spoke to Tercel who lunged upward from off his shoulder and sailed out over the crowd. He looped back climbing upward in a widening circle.

They passed a meat-seller who had bright red-butchered meat. Blood drained from the stone table on which the cuts were displayed. Flies buzzed and crawled about the warm flesh. Nusa purred loudly as Alle-Encer bought a large slab and half a liver. The butcher leaned out to watch Nusa tear the flesh from between her fluffy paws and gulp it down.

"Be a fine beast ya got there." He wiped his hands on his blood-soaked apron, his face red and bulging. "She'd call a fine price ya knows." Nusa growled. The man stepped backward, saying no more. They quickly walked on.

Isaac saw Grimalkyns among the buyers and sellers. They looked surprisingly similar to Alle-Encer and Garlock—same bushy beards and heads of thick hair. Their agile stature and walk, mannerisms and speech, all resembled his two Grimalkyn friends. He stopped to survey the tumult of the square.

"Where are you, Zachary?"

Zac looked at all the people milling about the markets, some so dirty, it was painful to pass them, their stench overpowering. Some were well dressed in fancy, frilly outfits, even capes with elaborate folds and cording. Women with various hats and long gloves up to their elbows strolled about.

Some streets were narrow and so crowded they had to squeeze through the bustling bodies. Different languages were heard at different stalls and vendors. Neither Eryn nor Garlock had ever been to Hether Dawn. They wandered aimlessly through the busy streets without plan or direction. Finally, Garlock saw a Grimalkyn hone—a place for Grimalkyns to sit, talk and drink spiced mulger.

Eryn was not delighted, but Zac thought it wonderful. Garlock did the honors of ordering as they sat around low tables barely two feet off the pine needle-covered floor. Their stools were half the table height causing Eryn to sit sideways at the table.

The mulger smelled good. Zac thought back to the night in Garlock's hovel—the apprehension and excitement blending with the cozy quaint cabin and the fire. It seemed so long ago. He remembered his sense of adventure, his eagerness to experience the uniqueness of the Grimalkyn cabin. Yes, he had been afraid, but it hadn't squelched his love for the adventure.

"This mulger will do, eh sprig?" Garlock raised his mug to Zac who raised his in return with a smile. It went down smooth with a spicy bite.

"If one is starving," Eryn said, looking away. She seemed edgy. She had become increasingly so as they neared the city. Garlock made a clicking sound and a short girl came with some oranges. She was a Grimalkyn, no taller than a ten-year-old, but clearly a young woman. Zac watched her move about—small and muscular with an athletic grace.

She'd whip my butt in a fight, he thought.

The oranges made him realize his hunger. "Could we get some bread or—?"

"We best proceed." Eryn stood abruptly. She stared out the entrance of the hone. "We need to keep searching." Garlock made a low growl and downed the last of his mulger. Zac wanted to sit and rest, to eat something solid. His skin itched from the salt water in his clothes. They stepped out the mulger hone just as a small hawk flew low over the streets and stone buildings. Zac watched it cruise slowly out over the fluid crowd.

"Tercel?" He turned to ask Eryn and Garlock, but they were already walking down the street to his right. He hurried to catch up with them. They stopped to watch a man in the center of a small crowd who juggled four long daggers, spinning them up into the air. Each toss seemed effortless, catching the handle, flinging the knife. The sun glanced off their shiny blades sending sparkling light into the crowd. He caught and tossed, rotating left as he flung the glistening blades. When he had turned full circle he suddenly let them drop one by one blade first into a log at his feet. The long knives twanged in sequence coming down side-by-side only inches apart. The crowd approved. Zac wished he had some coins to toss into the wooden bowl that thumped with tarnished disks of brass.

Eryn urged them on, impatiently trying to keep them on course, wherever that was. They stopped and bought some small red berries, a little smaller than cherries. They were tart but fun to eat.

"So just where we be a goin'?" Garlock asked with a mouthful. Eryn stopped and turned to face him.

"If you want to lead, then lead." She stood there, eyes narrowed, her face dirty and tired. She breathed heavy with shoulders drooped. Garlock spit a glob of red seeds and juice.

"Where think yeer brother be?" Garlock asked Zac.

"Could still be on the ship, I don't know." Zac had red lines around his mouth. He tried to focus.

"No," Eryn said, "he is here in the city, somewhere. I feel it. I wish I could see something. Why can I not see?" Zac knew she meant her Pharen gift.

"I wish you could too," he said quietly. He popped some berries into his mouth. It was hard to see Eryn so stressed and worried, scanning the crowd with eyes so weary.

He saw two large black hawks circling high above the city. His skin prickled. He thought of Tercel and wondered if the black hawks would dive on a small bird like him. He wondered again if it had been Tercel flying through the city, looking for them perhaps. The hawks rode the high currents in large interloping circles, slowly scanning the city below. Suddenly, a burly hand grabbed his shoulder, as something sharp and cold pressed his neck.

"Ya moves, ya bleeds," a frog-like voice spoke in his ear.

Zac turned, but a sharp point pricked his under chin. His heart sped as he looked for Garlock and Eryn. He saw them at the end of the square, walking through the crowd unaware.

"Izz way," the voice said, as the knife went to his lower back. Zac spit the berries onto the stone pavement. The knifepoint poked hard into his back. The voice shuffled him through the crowd into a small alley. Three rough looking Grimalkyns waited with ropes. A rag went over his face. He tried to fight, but his eyes blurred, his gut turning woozy. His legs went weak, and his head swung about in wide looping circles like a ball on a rope. "How'd my head... get... way out... way out... way... out...?"

"Zac?" Eryn called, looking back into the crowd. "Zachary!"

Garlock hopped up onto a stone wall at the edge of a stream that ran through the city square. Although he stood on his toes, he could not really see over the crowd.

"Mighty Arnon, where he be?"

"Zachary!" Eryn shouted again, not wanting to draw attention, but something was wrong.

They ran back through the crowd to where the knife juggler had performed. He now tossed swords and flaming sticks. Eryn's heart pumped fast. "Evil taints the air," she whispered. A small, brown speckled hawk with bluish wings swooped over their heads, and then dove straight for Garlock. The Grimalkyn ducked as the hawk shot back up into the sky, whistling a piercing cry.

"Ya bangety ball of fluff!" Garlock shouted into the sky.

The bird swooped back down with diving speed, then suddenly opened its wings and landed on Eryn's shoulder. She winced as the hawk flapped a time or two, talons clutching her flesh a bit too tight.

"Tercel! Oh, thank Ariel." The hawk responded with a piercing whistle. Eryn winced again putting a finger to her ear. "Have you seen Zac?" she asked the little hawk. "We have lost him." Tercel made a low whistle and wildly shook his head side-to-side. "Is Alle-Encer near?" Tercel bobbed vigorously and whistled high short peeps. "Find Zachary." Eryn tilted her head away from the bird. "Please, Tercel, go find Zac." He jumped from her shoulder and flapped his small quick wings. They watched as he circled above the square.

The strain of the weeks past seemed to come all at once upon Eryn. A shade of dismal gray settled over her beautiful face. They hurried through the square looking in alleys and shops, waiting for Tercel to return. Finally, the little hawk zoomed overhead, landing onto Eryn's shoulder.

"Did you see him?" she asked. Tercel wagged his head side-to-side with a long low whistle. Eryn sighed heavy. "Oh, Ariel, we need your help." Just then, Isaac came running through the crowded square, panting heavily.

"Isaac!" Eryn threw her arms around him, smothering his face with her hair.

Garlock whacked him on the side. "Isaac me lad, have ya seen Alle-Encer? Is he with ya?"

"He's coming… with Nusa." Isaac pointed back through the square. "Man, am I glad… to see you guys." He looked around. "Where's Zac?"

"We just," Eryn's eyes moistened, "lost him."

"Vanished like smoke from me long pipe."

"Something is wrong," Eryn said. "He was here."

Isaac clenched his fists. He spun around looking through the crowd. "Zaaaaac!" he shouted into the mass of bodies. People stopped to stare. "Zachary! Where are you?"

Eryn turned to the hawk. "You can find him. Go." Tercel

launched once again from her shoulder.

"He was with you?" Isaac spoke harshly. "How'd you lose him?" Eryn's eyes filled with tears.

Garlock put his hand up on Isaac's shoulder. "He be here, and then he be gone. Me thinks he be nabbed."

Isaac, still catching his breath, tried to push the anger back. Can't think when I'm mad. He looked at Eryn. A wet line ran down beneath each eye. Her face was dirty, her hair a mess, her eyes worn and weary.

"The fun just doesn't end here, does it?" he said. Eryn studied his face, confused. He saw his reflection in her dark eyes. "So where'd you last see him?"

"I will show you." Eryn grabbed his hand and led him through the crowd. They went to where Zac had stood watching the black hawks.

Isaac looked around, dread pounding at his heart. He tried to think, to stay calm. An old voice came. Like you're some Sherlock Holmes, yeah right. Like you're going to find some stupid clue. Give up. He fought to work against the voice. "I can find him. Can't believe he's gone... again." He did not realize he spoke out loud.

"We will find him." Eryn touched his arm.

Isaac looked at something several feet away. On one of the large smooth stones that formed the pavement was a reddish smudge. It was a line with a slight barb on one end. It could easily have been a simple foot smudge or it could be an arrow pointing to an alley at the edge of the square.

"Could Zac have done that?" Isaac pointed to the reddish arrow.

"It's bungleberry juice," Garlock said. "He and me be eatin' 'em."

They went over to the alley leading out of the market square. A dozen yards into the alley they saw scattered bungleberry berries and more red smudges. Two reddish lines, like something being dragged, streaked the cobblestones. "Look!" Isaac pointed to a wooden doorway with two faint marks of red. He and Eryn drew their swords as Garlock pushed on the door.

It opened with a groan—a small heavy door on iron hinges. Smoke drifted out as the fresh air rushed in. Like Garlock's hovel, a foot high board ran across the bottom of the doorway. Isaac figured it was to keep the rats out. They stepped over the threshold, careful to remain silent. Onions and fried pork fat seemed to permeate the stale air. It was surprisingly dark for early morning. A small oil lamp burned on the far side. A crude ladder led up to a loft. Meats and braided garlic hung randomly about, as a fire smoldered in a blackened fireplace. Dirty wooden plates and clay mugs filled a wooden table.

"Hello?" Isaac called softly. The room was silent. Eryn looked at him funny.

"Who is, Hello?"

"Alle-Encer," Isaac said.

"In here?"

"No. He won't know where we are." Isaac looked back to the door.

"Tercel be tellin' 'em," Garlock whispered.

Eryn then held up her hand. "Listen." Muffled voices came from behind a set of low doors across the dirty room. They inched closer and Garlock gasped.

"Grimals," he tired to whisper. "Grims from Yorne." They could hear the familiar accent as someone counted along with the faint sound of stones clinking together. An argument suddenly broke out, and then a low, steady voice said something about an agreed price and cutting throats in one swipe. Eryn's skin tingled as she listened, her hands quaking. Isaac watched and wondered, squeezing tighter the handle of his sword.

29   A GRIMALKYN BRAWL

"You okay?" Isaac whispered.

"That voice…"

"Is Zac in there?" He pressed his ear to the door.

"Let's find out." Garlock put both hands on the wooden doors. Eryn and Isaac held swords ready. There were no handles, but a high threshold stood on their side of the doors. "Tsa, nat, sarn," Garlock counted in some old Grimalkyn dialect. Isaac held his breath. Garlock slammed into the doors.

Wham! Nothing happened. He charged again.

"Be bolted!"

Shouting came from the other side. Shuffling, banging, then a door slammed.

Isaac yelled as he thrust his shoulder into the door. It responded with a rattle and gave him pain. Fury raged as he looked around the room. He grabbed the wooden table and called for Garlock. They picked up the table and ran it forward like a battering ram into a castle gate. Plates and mugs flew about, smashing into the wooden doors. In all the commotion, Isaac never considered that he could be mistaken.

"Again!" he shouted. They stepped back and rammed the table forward, but again, the doors only rattled.

Suddenly, a frog-like voice came from behind. "What ya be

doin' ya wogs?" Four rough Grimalkyns stood in the doorway to the alley—their long knives drawn as they spread out into the room.

"Come to rob us, they 'ave," said one with reddish hair streaked brown. Their beards were fully braided, thick and dirty. Isaac realized how awkward it must look, holding a table with plates, mugs and utensils scattered all over the floor. He glanced to Garlock and Eryn, hoping they would have some way to get out of this.

"We are looking for someone," Eryn said. "We think he is behind those doors."

"Aren't no one bein' behind them doors," the frog-voiced Grimalkyn said. His head nearly bald, but his beard was thick, yellow and white with streaks of red.

"Let us look, and we'll pay you for your stuff." Isaac set the table down.

"Oh, ya be payin's. That's assured."

"Let us see who's behind those doors, and we'll leave." Isaac's blood pumped red. He knew his brother was around here somewhere.

"Ya not be seein' nobody," the Grimalkyn's face turned ugly. "But ya be a payin' plenty." He gave a nod to the others and they moved in. Isaac felt he was in an old western movie.

This is where I pull out my six-shooter and drop 'em all to the dirty floor, he thought.

"We do not mean harm," Eryn said. "We are just looking for a lost friend. Let us pay for the damage and be on our way." The Grimals did not answer. They just kept coming forward in a line, blocking the only way out.

These aren't dumb kroaks, Isaac thought. This is serious. He noticed a knife hanging on the belt of the balding Grimalkyn. It looked just like the knife Mirrah had given Zac on the Fare Whether. He reached around to a ledge and grabbed the small oil lamp.

"That's my brother's knife, you swine." He hurled the lamp. The Grimal ducked as it smashed on the wall behind. Flames spread out and up the wall.

"Ya cloddy Vogan," yelled the balding Grimalkyn. He raised his arm and flung his long knife. Isaac twisted his torso just as the blade brushed against his chest and stuck with a twang in the wall. The others charged forward, their blades sliced back and forth. Garlock put one hand on the table and leapt across to stand beside Isaac. Eryn backed away toward the bolted door.

"Grab the table," Isaac said, lifting the table to his chest. Using it like a shield they rushed into the Grimalkyns. Two of them stumbled backward falling beneath the table. The red-haired Grimal faced Eryn's flashing sword. She backed him into the fireplace. The balding one with Zac's knife turned and ran.

"Yeer mothers be drogs," he cursed as he leapt over the threshold into the alley. The two under the table scurried to their feet and followed him out the door. The red-haired one stood helpless against the three. He flashed his long knife back and forth from Eryn to Isaac to Garlock.

"Put out the fire," Isaac told Garlock. He then stepped toward the trapped Grimalkyn. "Where's my brother?"

"Ya comes near, and I'll mince yeer innards."

Isaac's face turned fierce. He gripped his sword tight. His arm tensed. All the pain and rage were about to get plunged into this filthy, bearded being. Eryn watched him. He looked older than he should. The Grimalkyn pressed back against the fireplace.

"Tell me where my brother is." Isaac spoke through clenched teeth, his sword aimed at the little man's belly. Eryn knocked his sword aside and pressed hers into the dirty beard.

"Drop your knife," she said. It thumped on the floor. "Did you take a young boy from the square?"

"Don't be knowin'—"

Isaac pushed Eryn aside. "You lying dog." Every muscle tightened.

"Isaac, stop!" Eryn pushed him back, pressing her blade harder into the Grimal's neck. "Did you sell him?"

"I told ya—"

"Don't lie to me. Who bought him?"

"Let me kill him." Isaac stepped closer. Eryn pushed him away with her hip.

"Aiya." Garlock came over. "End the drog's life." He walked up quickly with his knife drawn, ready to plunge it into the cornered Grimalkyn.

"Let him speak," Eryn said, "then do what you like."

"Grimals don't squawk. Just stick 'em."

Isaac drew his arm back, his face tight and red. "Foul drog, taking my brother—"

The Grimal's eyes got wide. "Hold yeer blade!" He looked side-to-side, sweat beaded on his brow. "Sold 'em, we did… to a parlord."

Eryn stepped back. "Parlord?"

The Grimal nodded. "Be that one, Armadon."

Eryn lowered her sword.

"Who's Armadon?" Isaac asked. Eryn suddenly pressed into the Grimalkyn, her blade tight under his chin.

"Where? Tell me now!" She pushed her blade harder. Isaac stepped back and watched. A fury now possessed her soul. "Talk or I'll drain every drop of your vile blood."

"The harbor, maybe?"

"Why?"

"By the beard of Arnon, be all Spikel's doin's." His voice rose to a squeak.

Garlock came back in. "Spikel of Yorne? Marrgh!" He looked the dirty Grimal in the face. "Ya be Elgin of Yorne, be ya not?" The terrified Grimal's bushy eyebrows rose an inch. Garlock poked the man's belly with his knife. "Be facin' Garlock of Yorne, ya pile of moss beetle's…" He flung his hand toward the door. "That hairless drog… Spikel?" The Grimalkyn nodded.

"Elgin…" Eryn again lowered her sword. "Spikel…" She backed away, and then walked to the door in silence. Garlock poked the Grimal one more time, saying something in Grimalkyn with a very nasty tone, then followed Eryn. He looked back and shook his head as he stepped into the alley.

Isaac stood there, still guarding the prisoner, totally confused. Finally he left, backing away toward the door.

"What was that all about and who's Armadon?" he asked, squinting in the sunlight. "Why did you guys leave me?"

What's a guy?" Garlock looked around the alley.

"Why'd you walk? Who's that Grimal? And who has Zac?"

"Elgin and Spikel be of the ones that sold Mirrah's love. Give a nod, miss Eryn, and I'll drain 'em dry." Garlock skillfully twirled his knife about, spitting the name of Spikel. Without a word, Eryn sheathed her sword and walked the alley toward the square, her shoulders slumped.

"And who's Armadon?"

Garlock touched the butt of his knife to the center of his forehead, then flipping his knife around, sliced downward. "The one that done her mam and pap."

A chill crept up Isaac's back.

They followed Eryn into the square. She turned a corner and plopped down onto a stone step, the entrance into a rug shop. She buried her head into her hands. Muffled sobs mixed with the clamor of the market square. Isaac and Garlock stood watching, trying not to look as awkward as they felt. Isaac thumped his hand against his knife, tapping his foot. He looked around, scanning the mulling crowd.

"We need to find Zac. We need to move now."

"Were ya gonna split that Grimal's carcass?" Garlock asked, unconcerned over Eryn's behavior and the need to find Zac.

"I don't know." Isaac, although irritated, spoke quietly, trying not to disturb Eryn. "Why? Were you?"

"I be but foolin'—to make him squawk." Garlock made no effort to be quiet.

"I'm not sure what I was doing. Not sure what we're doing now."

Eryn kept crying into her hands. He realized it was the first time he had seen her this way. He dropped the pack off his shoulders and sat down beside her. Three times he tried to put his arm around her and pulled it back. I wish Breezy were here; she'd know what to do. He lifted his arm one more time as

Eryn wiped her eyes and looked up.

"I am so sorry," she whispered.

"We need to go after Zac."

She shook her head. "He is gone…"

"No, we can find him."

Eryn wagged her head, muttering Zachary's name.

"I'll go find him." Isaac stood, drawing his sword. "You stay with Eryn."

Garlock shook his head. "No, lad. We stay togethers."

Isaac groaned, his jaws tight. Eryn looked up and wiped the tears on her face. They mixed with the road dust into dirty smudges. She looked at the dusty pack. He plopped back down

"The book's okay," he said. "Actually survived the water. Not sure how—was a real…" He suddenly saw all they had gone through, from the cold night of wandering the wood to the dank, smelly gorron cave. The battle with the parlords, the kroaks, the shipwreck, everything, in detail, came racing back through his mind.

He saw that something wanted them stopped—stopped dead. Yet each trial, each threat had actually strengthened them. As long as they faced the challenge and stood their ground, they had a good chance of surviving. Everything he endured had pushed him to his breaking point, yet he survived—survived and came out stronger. That which was trying to kill him, actually strengthened him.

He saw purpose, if he chose, a crucial purpose for this world and for themselves, and perhaps their own world. Something or someone was helping, was leading, they only needed to follow… to stay strong… to trust.

"Isaac?" Eryn said softly. "Are you… oh-kay?"

He blinked. "I just… saw it."

"Saw what?"

"I saw it… clearly. Our purpose… our destiny." He tried to explain, but it was more feeling than thought. It had been so clear, so real. He looked her in the eyes. "It's going to be okay, if we don't give up."

"Oh-kay." Eryn tried to smile. "I like this word, 'oh-kay.'"

A shrill whistle broke the noisy air above the market. Tercel came swooping down, buzzing Garlock's head. He flinched, cursing in Grimal.

Isaac stood. "Alle-Encer must be near." Eryn put out her hand for him to pull her up. It was so unlike her that he just stared at her hand. She gave his leg a swat and again held out her hand. As he pulled her up, she scooped up the backpack and slung it over her shoulders.

"Alle-Encer." Isaac pointed into the crowd. The elderly Grimalkyn walked casually through the busy shoppers, beggars, and performers, with Nusa close at his side. It was comical watching people fan out as the giant lynx came through the crowd.

Alle-Encer stretched out his arms and embraced Eryn, touching his forehead to hers. Nusa made funny purring sounds and rubbed her head into Eryn's side.

"Why you all standing about?" he asked. Tercel drifted down to alight on Alle-Encer's shoulder.

"Didn't he tell ya?" Garlock looked at Tercel with a scowl.

"Told me ya lost Zac."

"We thinks Armadon's a taken 'em."

Alle-Encer stiffened. Nusa rumbled her throat as Tercel flapped and let out a squawk.

"Armadon?" Alle-Encer's wrinkled face, wrinkled more. "Are you sure?"

"Elgin of Yorne, say it so. He be with Spikel."

"Spikel of Limsten?"

"Be. They nabbed the boy for pay."

"Armadon... here in Hether Dawn..." He looked around. "Any Grimal caves? I'm a starving."

"We need to find my brother."

"Need to find some eat." Alle-Encer peered about looking for a Grimal hone.

Isaac groaned as they moved through the crowd. He fought to stay calm. Despite seeing it all 'clearly,' angst and worry still pursued him, taunting his heart and mind like a gang of thugs. Where was his brother? He tried to keep the feelings of destiny, the purpose and trust. A battle raged as he walked in silence.

Alle-Encer stopped as they came by a little café with small round tables, open to the street, without door or windows—a Grimal hone.

"Have ya all eaten?" he asked.

"We have," Eryn said.

"Good, let's get some eat." Alle-Encer walked into the hone and went to a table at the rear. Grimalkyns shuffled about, scrambling to exit, as Nusa made her way through the tables. The owner rose in protest. Nusa looked him straight in the eye and growled, her head equal to his. He stepped back and asked what they 'be liken to devour?'

They sat around a low table on small stools. Alle-Encer ordered various drinks, steamed breads, and fruity cakes. They talked in hushed tones of all that had taken place since the shipwreck. They concluded that if Armadon was truly in Hether Dawn, he had come on the Sasson vessel.

Eryn had put the pack between her feet. She reached down to touch it. Isaac watched her. She seemed troubled. It started when she heard the voice behind the wooden doors—the voice of this one called Armadon. He watched her fidget with the straps on his pack. He took a bite of fruity cake and forced it down with a warm brown drink.

"So how do we get Zac, and find the girls?" he asked. "Elgin said the harbor."

"Elgin be a liar," Garlock growled, "a bad liar."

"So that means…?"

"Means we don't know puddins."

"Pooshhh," Alle-Encer whispered. It was the Grimal way of saying 'shhh.' "First we need to learn more, to see more. Tercel will scout the city. We'll need weapons."

"We need to get moving," Isaac said. He took a drink and paused, the mug still at his lips. A tall man with a long ponytail stopped outside the hone. He looked straight into Isaac's eyes, and then walked on.

Eryn suddenly spun around, looking out to the crowded

square. She turned back to Isaac, her stare intense. Her hair was dirty, and dried smudges stained her cheeks. She narrowed her eyes as with contempt. He shrugged, setting down the mug. She jumped from her stool, walking quickly out into the square.

"What did ya do, lad?" Garlock asked. A bite of steamed bun sat un-chewed in his mouth.

"Not a clue."

30 LUNCH WITH THE KING

Breezy and Mirrah were led to the end of the large hall, where the man in silk spoke with some men in hushed tones. Breezy heard the name, Armadon. He then spoke a strange language to a man with a long, finely pointed goatee. The man nodded.

"I have other matters," he said to Mirrah. "My servant, Zevant, will take care of you." With that he slightly bowed, hurrying off with the other men. Mirrah and Breezy were left alone with Zevant and his long goatee.

"Ziss way, pleece," he said with a strong accent. Breezy wondered where he might be from and then chided herself. Who knows where he's from in this world? He probably doesn't even know.

They walked through what seemed like endless halls and corridors. It reminded Breezy of the palace in Kharlome. This one was airy, bright and clean. The birds that hung high in the rafters and vaults echoed their voices to each other, filling the halls with beautiful sounds. The fragrance, not strong but sweet, would waft by ever so often bringing a feeling of peace, calming her anxious heart. She would breathe deeply whenever it drifted by.

Zevant walked at a steady, graceful pace, always upright and controlled in his movements. He stopped beside a door, turned the handle that looked like bluish jade and swung the large door open. He motioned for them to enter. Breezy hesitated, but Mirrah gently bowed and walked in.

"Yoo vill find all yoo need. Eff not, pleece call." He bowed and gently closed the door. Breezy immediately turned the handle and opened the door.

"It's not locked," she said, confused. "Maybe this will be okay."

"I am not sure what is happening. But you… you must not do that again, understood?" Mirrah was like a mother who just saved her child from a terrible accident.

"I'm sorry, Mirrah. I was… I'll try to keep my mouth shut." They embraced as Mirrah breathed a long, steady sigh.

"I wish I could see something, anything."

"I wish you could, too."

They walked into a large marble lined bathroom at the side of the room. A round bath of white was inlaid into the marble floor. Steaming water ran into the bath from blue-jade pipes mounted in the wall above. The room smelled like a hot spring and Breezy suddenly went weak at the knees. She realized how awfully long, absolutely horribly long, it had been since she had a good bath—a real bath.

"You go first," Mirrah said, seeing Breezy's excitement.

"You sure?" she asked, already getting undressed. Mirrah smiled, but Breezy saw the worry. She remembered Bella, and suddenly the bath seemed only a necessity, not something she could enjoy. "Will we find Bella?"

"Yes. We must."

After baths, they washed their clothes. Mirrah sat by the window letting her long hair dry in the sun and wind. Three stories up, their view was glorious, overlooking the city below. Breezy wondered how it could be since they had not walked up any steps. The room was luxurious with fine wooden furniture carved and inlayed with colorful stone.

"I feel like a princess." Breezy twirled in her underwear.

"You do not look like one right now," Mirrah said, and

they giggled together like little girls.

As the sun lit the room, Breezy watched Mirrah's hair waving in the wind. "Why do you wear your hair so long?"

"I am Pharen."

"So?"

Mirrah chuckled. "Pharens do not cut their hair. It is our pledge. Some say we lose our power to see."

"Really? Do guys grow it long, too?"

"Of course."

"But you said it comes from Ariel—the seeing thing."

"It does, but our hair is a way of showing our pledge to him, as to our...."

Breezy knew she was about to say 'husbands.' She somehow, instantly understood it as a sign of loyalty and faithfulness. In that moment, she wanted to grow her hair long, as long as she could—for Mirrah, for Bella, for the others.

"I wish I had hair like yours." She touched Mirrah's hair as it floated with the breeze. "It's beautiful."

"As is yours." Breezy's hair had grown more than she had realized. She pulled a lock of her wavy curls down straight. It went to the bottom of her shoulder.

"How come you haven't been able to see much, I mean since we arrived at your home?"

"I wish I knew."

When they had dressed, they wondered how to call Zevant, for they were feeling mighty hungry.

"Maybe you pull this." Breezy pulled a long braided cord. It came down a few inches, but nothing happened. She went to the door to look for Zevant, but as soon as she reached for the handle, it turned.

"Here, miss?" a young girl opened the door. She reminded Breezy of Sherrabella. Her hair was pulled back into a ponytail tied with a ribbon. She wore a simple but clean outfit of loose white cloth.

"Hi. Could we get some food?" Breezy asked, "if it's not too much trouble?"

"Yes, miss. Sorry, miss. You'll be... you will be dining in

the main hall in a fifth, miss. I will take you there when it's... when it is time, miss." The servant girl kept bowing as she spoke. She looked quick at Breezy's clothes then dropped her head and backed out the door.

"She is so sweet," Breezy said with eyes misting.

"Brielle, I do not know this king. We need to be alert and careful with our speech."

Breezy dropped her head. "I will try."

When the servant girl came, they followed her to the main hall, which was like the entrance hall but with much more decoration. Beautiful scenic tapestries and banners hung on the walls. Strange animal heads mounted on brass plates peered down from between the tapestries. Some had tremendous horns or antlers; some were grotesque while others quite beautiful. Breezy gasped when she saw a Perlin head with tufted ears and beard like Nusa mounted on a brass plate. She then noticed the tapestries were scenes of hunts and places of interesting beauty. They must tell the story of the hunt, she thought.

In each corner of the great hall was a large animal, fully stuffed in a terrifying pose. She gasped rather loudly, clutching Mirrah's arm, when she saw a huge cave gorron just like the one in the smelly cave. It stood so high with its large three fingers and stubby thumb reaching out to grab any passer by. Its mouth hung open with fangs stained red and a terrifying look in its eyes. It took her a moment to steady her heart as they stopped to gaze up at the beast.

"Cave gorron," came a gentle voice behind them. It was the handsome man in silk. Dressed now in bright loose cloth, an ocean blue that flowed gently with his movements, he gestured toward the beast. "Killed that one four rings ago on the isle of Tregoria. Not the brightest of beasts. A source of grief for the herdsmen, eating more than just goats."

"How did you kill it?" Mirrah asked.

"The only way—through the eyes. Its armored skin stops the fastest bolt." Breezy's eyes went wide. A little shiver went through her as she saw the cave scene, the beast grasping at its eye, its screams echoing through the cavern halls.

"Wouldn't want to meet one of those," Breezy said, with a long sigh. She was surprised at her own words.

"Wouldn't want you too, either. That's why I killed it." He gave a polite little smile. "Shall we eat?" He held out his hand toward a long table lavishly set with not only foods but also flowers and works of art.

They joined others who casually walked into the great hall talking and laughing, finding seats around the long table. No one seemed to notice them or think anything unusual.

"Please sit here, next to me," he said to Mirrah and Breezy, speaking so polite and calm. Breezy wondered why he did not introduce himself, and she dared not initiate, since Mirrah had addressed him as 'Your Highness.' She scrunched her face as they were seated. Huh? I thought I was his slave.

They were near the head of the table watching as people continued to come and sit. A little chime sounded, and those still standing and talking quickly found their seats. A moment later, a man stood near a large red door and announced the arrival of the king.

"Friends of the king, I give you Qwo-Raldy bel Morgalith the IV, king of Hether Dawn." Everyone stood and very softly tapped their right fist into their open left hand as if playing rock-paper-scissors. It sounded like babies running barefoot.

"Not even a golf clap," Breezy whispered to Mirrah.

"Hush."

The King was an average man in his late fifties, maybe. Breezy watched as he made his way along the table, randomly greeting the people as they stood waiting for him to be seated. He wore clothes like the handsome man, light silky loose garments that flowed as he walked. His hair was dark gray, long and wavy, his smile wide and gregarious. He went to his seat at the head of the table, signaled for everyone to sit, and then took his seat. The handsome man was at the king's right with Mirrah and then Breezy. An older man with a long scraggly beard sat next to Breezy.

The king reached and took a piece of leg from some small roasted creature, and as soon as he brought it to his mouth, the people began to talk and laugh, helping themselves to the food. Breezy dug in like a wolf at a pig roast. Mirrah had to gently kick her several times.

"So where are you from, milady?" asked the older man next to Breezy. "Are you in journey?"

"Ahh," Breezy looked to Mirrah who was in conversation with the handsome man. "I'm from... Kansas. Yeah, and I'm on a really long journey... yeah."

"Kansas? My deepest apologies, I know not this land."

"Oh, no prob, most people don't, even back home." She gave the old man a big smile and turned to listen in on Mirrah hoping he would not ask any more questions.

"From Kharlome?" Breezy heard the handsome man ask Mirrah. "To where were you sailing?"

"To an island in the southeast."

"I see. You had business there?"

"Historical research, actually."

"And this spirited young maiden is your assistant?"

Mirrah nodded. "Like a daughter to me, Your Lordship. I am grateful for your mercy and—" He silenced her with a raised hand. Breezy felt stupid again for acting up at the slave auction. But, come on, it was a slave auction. She listened as Mirrah told him how helpful this feisty girl had been. Breezy sighed. She thought back to how she had bonded with Mirrah the night they met. Again she wondered, how would they ever say goodbye?

She looked around at all the people talking and eating, laughing and enjoying each other. Was this real? Home seemed so far away, she rarely thought of it anymore. She realized how little she missed her family and friends. It was weird, but then again, things had been weird ever since they climbed out of the marble courtyard.

"You were quite... amazing this morning," the man said to Breezy. "You gave us all something to remember." He chuckled.

"Really sorry about that, sir… sire… Your… Honorship. I didn't know. I didn't mean to—"

"So who are these guests?" The king's voice rose above the clamor of conversation. He nodded to Mirrah and Breezy.

"This is Mirrah of Myrrh and her assistant, Breezy of Kansas, I believe."

"Breezy, how charming. I like that. Mirrah of Myrrh? Have we met before?"

"No, Your Kingship." Mirrah gracefully bowed her head.

"They were being sold in the market this morning," the handsome man continued. "Shipwrecked and taken by Boondas." The king gave out an uproarious laugh. Everyone stopped to look for but a second or two, then, as if nothing happened, rejoined their conversations and feasting.

"Those Boondas will sell anything. I go myself sometimes just to see what's there. Found our head cook that way—shipwrecked like you." He let out another laugh. "So where does your quest take you?"

"Back to Kharlome, Your Highness." Again Mirrah bowed her head as she spoke.

"Stay as long as you like; my kingdom welcomes you." He started to laugh but took a monstrous bite from a leg of ham, or something that looked like ham. It seemed he was going to choke but managed to chew and chuckle while nodding to other guests.

They continued to talk with the handsome man who they learned was the king's son and went by the title, Prince Calygrey. Mirrah was careful to keep her answers innocuous, not even mentioning Bella or the others. He invited them to stay as long as they wished and would be happy to help them secure passage to Kharlome. His mannerisms were so refined and pleasant that it was hard for Breezy to keep up her guard. Mirrah promised to repay the debt of the auction, to which he waved his hand. He has to be too good to be true, Breezy told herself. But he is so good-looking and such a gentleman.

When they all finished eating, and the king made his exit along with the others, leaving as casually as they had come, their little servant girl came and asked if they would like anything. She offered to show them around the palace or take them to the gardens that overlooked the sea. The gardens seemed good, and since they were not sure what else to do, they followed her out.

In a corner of the palace kitchen, a large man with a calloused, triangular nub on his forehead spoke quietly to a round little man with rosy cheeks. A young servant girl, new to her job, mopped the floor outside the kitchen doors.

"Make sure… this goes into their drink… or you'll never… wet your thirst again."

"Yes, My Lord."

"No one… shall know of this matter."

"Yes, My Lord."

"The Pharen… and the girl."

"Yes, My Lord."

31 A MYSTERIOUS LEADER

Isaac, Garlock and Alle-Encer sat in the Grimal hone for quite some time before Isaac suggested they go after Eryn.

"She's a big girl," Garlock said. He swooshed his mouth, spitting into an empty mug.

"Why would she leave like that, without telling us where she was going?"

"Cause she be a Pharen, laddie, and a girl. Probly drank too much mulger."

"I think something's up." Isaac stood and slung the pack over his shoulder.

"I think he's right." Alle-Encer gave the last piece of meat to Tercel.

They went out into the square and turned left, the way Eryn and the man with the ponytail had gone. Nusa went on ahead turning another left into a small side street. They walked the stony street never thinking to question Nusa. It narrowed into an alley, slowly climbing upward, until it became a dead end with doors on each side. Nusa stopped, sniffing the cobblestones like a bloodhound before looking toward a wooden door on the left. She looked at Alle-Encer. Tercel gave a little whistle.

"Shall we?" Alle-Encer walked up to the door. He knocked,

his claw-like nails curled into his stubby fist. It opened, freely, just a crack. Alle-Encer stepped back. Nusa pushed forward as the door swung to the side. Isaac stepped up to look into the dark room. Only one stream of light cut through from a window on the left. The light fell on a seated figure, tied to a post near the back of the room.

Isaac stepped in and let his eyes adjust. The figure shook its head and moaned loudly. Isaac stepped closer. Something inside told him to stop, but he needed to know more. He strained to see in the dim light. It was Eryn, her head wildly wagging back and forth, mouth bound with rags. Isaac saw her eyes screaming at him. He looked back at the others still outside. Nusa gave a low rumbling growl.

He stepped toward Eryn.

Wham! He tumbled forward, sprawling out, his head landing on Eryn's feet. Glittery lights filled his eyes. He tried to focus. Eryn was yelling at him through the rags, but he only heard telephones ringing. Why are phones ringing? Probably Mom calling. Then pain rushed, pulsating through his brain.

Nusa lunged into the room and stood beside Isaac and Eryn. Isaac rolled and tried to get to his feet. Four tall men dropped down from a loft above holding long staves. Each stave had a baseball-size knob on each end. Isaac watched Garlock draw his sword, but as soon as it came out he was struck on the back. He stumbled into the room. Half a dozen men stood outside in the alley surrounding Alle-Encer.

Isaac's head pulsed with pain. He stood up next to Eryn, his hand over his shoulder, clutching his sword but waiting to draw. The room spun in opposite directions at the same time. Nusa rumbled in her throat, but it was different. Isaac noticed, but there was too much happening to give it thought.

"Hold your place or die young," came a voice from the dark.

"What do you... waannnt?" Isaac sounded drunk. Garlock tried to get to his feet, but a knobby staff held him down. The men outside ushered Alle-Encer in and closed the door.

"Who are you, and why have you come?" A black

silhouette moved closer. Isaac turned toward the voice. He tried to stop the spinning. "I will ask only once more. Who are you and why have you come?" Isaac looked to Eryn. She shook her head, staying silent. Alle-Encer stood motionless. Tercel was gone.

"I am Isaac... the Mighty... and I... I... don't have a stinking clue why I'm here. Now... who in the blazing... buffalo chips are you?" He steadied himself on the post above Eryn

"Isaac the Mighty?" A murmur spread among the men. "You are a boy. Where are you from?"

"You wouldn't know... and why should I... whoa... tell you?"

"Because death awaits you, boy."

"Is this your custom... kill strangers to your city?"

"We kill Sasson spies, you drog." This voice came from the other side, a low rough voice.

"Sasson spies?" Isaac paused. He wanted to tell how they had been pursued by parlords and a Sasson vessel, but this could be a Sasson trap for them to reveal their allegiance. What allegiance? I don't even know who I am fighting for. Or is it 'whom'? It's 'for whom,' you idiot. I haven't met either party. Shouldn't have any allegiance till you meet the... whatever. He decided not to answer any more questions. He put his hands on his head, trying to make the spinning stop.

"If you cannot tell us where you are from," came the first voice, "and why you have come, we will do what we must. Bind them."

Nusa gave a loud warning growl as figures moved in the dim light. Isaac wondered why Alle-Encer or Garlock weren't saying something. Two men moved toward Garlock, and again Nusa gave out a chilling snarl. The men froze. Isaac yearned to draw his sword, but there were too many and nothing stood still.

"Tell them." Isaac heard a voice that made him stand up straight—the voice from the Isle of Moss, that night on the rock, the gentle female voice, low and soft. "Tell them who you are." Isaac looked at Nusa. Her eyes met him like that night on the rocky knoll.

"I'm not a Sasson spy... I've been sent by Ariel. I have come to your world from mine—not sure how or why... but I know that Sasson seems bent on stopping us." Sudden silence held the room. Isaac waited.

"You lie, you drog." It was the other man.

"What is a drog, for Mulder's beard and Arnon's mire? I don't even know what you're calling me. I'm not lying, you... you slick and slimy kroaken-gagger."

Muffled talk and whispers filled the room, and then the first voice called for lamps. Several lamps filled the room with yellow light as their wicks drew fresh oil. The sooty smell of burning oil wafted about for a moment, as silhouettes became men.

Isaac took his hands off his head. The spinning slowed. Eryn shook about in her ropes and gag. She was uttering something to Isaac, and it did not sound pleasant.

A man with a dark cloth across his face, revealing only his eyes, walked up to Isaac. He did not even look at Nusa. He stared straight into Isaac's eyes. Isaac held steady as the yellow light reflected in the man's dark eyes. They were intelligent eyes, discerning and wise.

"Isaac the Mighty..." The man held his stare. "Sent by Ariel."

Nusa acted quite peculiar, as if wanting to approach the man, but held herself back. Isaac glanced back to Eryn. Her eyes were furious. She fought the ropes and gag. Isaac noticed that no one else wore a cover over their face, only this man, the leader, the one asking questions.

"Prove to me so I can believe you," the man said.

"Prove?" Isaac looked down at Nusa. He then nodded toward her. "She is my proof." Eryn fought furiously at the ropes, yelling through the rag. "Yeah, Nusa is my proof."

The man stepped backward, bumping into the man near him. Isaac heard him softly say the name of Nusa. There was silence as everyone waited for the leader. He looked carefully at

Isaac, Nusa, Eryn and the two Grimalkyns.

Pointing to Alle-Encer he asked; "And you are who?"

"I am Alle-Encer of Sol Yorne."

"Alle-Encer?" Again the man seemed stunned. He walked over to Eryn who kept fighting hard, shaking the post so much that dust drifted down from the rafters. The man looked at her from the side. He reached for her neck, with both hands gloved in black leather. She tried to jerk herself away from his touch. He gently took the chain about her neck and lifted the stone out from beneath her clothing. He held it in his hand turning it to catch the light. Eryn did not move. He let it slide back down inside and stepped away.

There was a moment of silence before he pulled a man close to him and spoke in a hushed voice. The man listened, straightened upright, then looked at Isaac and nodded. The leader turned to Isaac.

"These men are loyal to Ariel. They will assist you. I cannot stay, but we will meet again. May Ah-Ra-El give us all wisdom and strength." He turned to Eryn who was now perfectly still. "Cut her free when I am gone." With that he slipped out a door at the back of the room.

Isaac did not wait for the men to cut Eryn free. He sliced the cords about her feet, then about her hands. She quickly reached up and tried to pull the gag from her mouth. She breathed heavy through her nose, fighting Isaac as he tried to help untie the knotted rag. She flung it to the ground and spit. Isaac stepped away, rubbing the growing welt on the back of his neck.

"You took that blow well," said the man to whom the leader had spoken. "My apologies. Sasson is crafty. We assumed you were his spies."

"Why would ya be thinkin' that?" Garlock growled as he stood.

"The parlord Armadon came yesterday," the man said. "You have come today, the same day as Mirrah of Myrrh, wife of Bain Sarro. We assumed you were part of whatever is planned."

"Mirrah is here?" Eryn said, shaking herself."

"She was sold in the market this morning with a young girl who defied the king's son, overpowering his personal guard."

"Breezy." Isaac shook his head with a smirk.

"They were taken to the palace. We believe they are here to infiltrate our cords."

Eryn stepped toward the man. He tightened up. "Mirrah is not here to infiltrate your cords. Why would you think that?"

"She's the wife of Bain Sarro, Sasson's drog."

"Bain Sarro? Beetle dung! She is the widow of Tesoro of Yorne, who died in Skone Lor. Who is this Bain Sarro?"

"They are one and the same."

"Are you bitten?" Eryn shuffled her feet like a bull offering challenge.

"Tesoro of Yorne has betrayed the Pharen code. In Hether Dawn, he calls himself, Bain Sarro. He has become a Sasson drog." The man readied himself. Eryn reached back for her sword, which was not there. She lunged toward the man. He raised his knobbed staff. She stopped and glared at him, her jaws tight. The man stepped further back. "He has the king's authority—to seek out Pharens in rebellion to Sasson. He is—"

"Dead." Garlock held his arm out to keep Eryn back. "Tesoro died in Skone Lor. Ya all be mistaken."

"He is not dead. He is Sasson's horl, sanctioned by free kingdom law, to hunt down Pharens in Hether Dawn."

"You lie!" Eryn said through clenched teeth. She glanced to Isaac's sword. He quickly backed away. She scowled and then moved toward the man like a stalking panther. Nusa leapt and spun around, blocking her way. "Nusa!"

"Eryn," Isaac spoke gently, "trust Nusa." She glared at him as Nusa nudged her backward toward the wall. Isaac addressed the men. They all had long braids and ponytails.

"Mirrah is not here on Sasson business. She is with us." The men murmured among themselves. Isaac rubbed the back of his head. It throbbed like someone beating a drum between his ears.

"She believes her husband is dead," he continued. "If her husband, Tesoro lives, and is truly this guy, Bain Sarro..." Eryn reached for Garlock's knife, but he grabbed her hand and held it tight. "We need to get her and our friend out of the palace. Is that possible?" The men did not answer. Isaac turned to Alle-Encer.

The old Grimal stood in a corner listening. He cleared his throat. "Life is real." He looked toward the door through which the leader had gone. "Life is earnest, and the grave is not its goal. I believe that today, we must use wisdom, for things are not what they seem. Do you have someone inside the palace?"

"Yes, but he only speaks with our leader, Dulac."

"Dulac, the Black Rose?" Alle-Encer asked.

"Yes, you've heard of him?"

"A little. When will he come back?"

"We never know."

Isaac looked around the room. A table sat beneath the window. He went over, pulled out a stool and sat. They all watched him closely.

"Suppose no one's got some aspirin, huh?" He rubbed his neck, groaning. "We're here for a reason. Your leader, the Black Rose guy, saw that. I have to find my brother; then I'm going to the palace to find Breezy and Mirrah, before her dead husband does, then I'm getting a ship and—"

"Is your brother the young lad traveling with her?" a man asked, nodding toward Eryn.

"Yes, but Armadon took him."

"We think he is in the palace," the man said. "Calygrey's soldiers took him from the parlord. He had the lad wrapped in a rug, heading for the harbor. It almost started war."

"Parlords cannot take prisoners in free kingdoms," the man in charge said. "Only Bain Sarro can." He eyed Eryn, his hand on his knife.

Isaac sat holding his head. How did they get into this? A woeful heaviness came. He pushed it aside. "Tell me everything I need to know. How do we get into the palace?"

He looked to Eryn standing in the shadows. "How do we contact your leader... and... why does he cover his face?"

32 A PARLORD, A POISONED POEM, AND PRISON

Breezy and Mirrah returned to their room. It had been refreshing to walk the beautiful gardens and look out over the sea. Breezy flopped down onto the big square bed. Her pillow was plush and felt so good compared to everything she had been forced to call a pillow over the last few weeks.

"This feels so flunderful," she said. "So fluffy, so wonderful." Mirrah smiled. Breezy rolled over and put her hand between the pillows. "Hey, what's this?" She sat up holding a small dirty rag. "Mirrah, look at this."

They both went to the window and looked at the small rag. Written with a charcoal stick were the words: 'du not drinc.' They turned it over and saw a crude drawing of a chalice with a large X crossed over it.

"It's a warning." Breezy said, with goose bumps rising.

"A warning not to drink." Mirrah turned the cloth over several times.

"I knew this was too good to be true." Breezy looked around the room. "The room's probably bugged."

"Bugged?"

"Ah, fuddy muddle cakes! I was just starting to feel good."

Mirrah washed the cloth clean. They stayed in their room, afraid to walk about. They talked quietly about the others, about finding Bella and getting back to Kharlome. Breezy told Mirrah things about her world. At first, Mirrah seemed doubtful of what Breezy told her.

"Your people sound like the Mersans. They had such things, things we do not understand. Tools and weapons now lost."

"Really? What happened?"

"Mersha was an amazing land, even during the Sasson wars. They kept back the Sasson army using their complicated weapons and thunder balls."

"Thunder balls? So what happened?"

"They grew selfish. Pleasure ruled their lives. Discipline, diligence and wisdom—the way of the Pharens, was not their way. They served no god but self, growing lazy and careless. A sickness came. They all died. That was long ago. The Vogans live there now—horrid people."

The sun was near the horizon when their servant girl tapped on the door. She led them down for dinner. Breezy wondered if she had left the warning.

"Can you write?" Breezy asked her.

"Miss?"

"Can you write words?"

"Sorry, miss."

"Can you write your name?"

She shook her head.

They came into the great hall again, but this time elaborate decorations of all colors and kinds hung everywhere possible. Again seated near the king, Breezy looked warily at the large metal chalice in front of her. Guests strolled in as before as did the king after his announcement. He came in, greeting people, smiling and laughing with thunderous bellows. Appetizers filled the table, as the main courses would come later.

A large company of circus performers juggled all sorts of things while others formed human pyramids and others flew through the air, launched from strange contraptions. It was all quite amazing but Breezy and Mirrah could only pretend to enjoy the show.

The handsome prince, Calygrey, had not yet arrived. An empty chair across from Mirrah seemed to stare back at her. As the performance came to a close, the prince came and took his seat, apologizing to Mirrah for his tardiness. As if a prince has to apologize for being late, Breezy thought. If I were a princess, I wouldn't apologize, would I? She began to see herself sauntering around the palace in flowing silk, doing as she pleased.

Suddenly, Mirrah gasped and looked down at her plate. Across the table, a large man, over seven feet tall, in a coin-like chain mail vest, pulled out the empty chair and sat down hard. His dark hair, long and wavy, hung free to his shoulders. His eyebrows were thick and heavy. Although his eyes were dark and intense, even severe, it was the nub on the center of his forehead that drew Breezy's gaze. It stuck out an inch and looked like a horn that had been cut off somewhere in the distant past. The man stared directly at Mirrah, and then Breezy, who also became very interested in her empty plate.

"Lord Armadon," the king said, a bit startled and void of all his usual cheeriness. "What a surprise. I was not informed. I assume you're just passing through. I hope that's all you're doing." He muttered the last looking down at his plate as well.

Armadon did not take his eyes off Mirrah. "Sasson's greetings… King Morgalith. I am passing through. You needn't fear… my intentions." He spoke from the side of his mouth as if his jaws were fixed shut, breathing short, shallow breaths.

"You missed the tumblers—quite good, be assured."

"I'm sure they were." He nodded to the prince. "Calygrey."

The prince was not pleased to see the parlord at his table. He was visibly tense but spoke boldly. "Passing through or collecting young victims? You violated free kingdom law. I could file for retribution."

Armadon chuckled returning his dark gaze on Mirrah. "Mirrah of Myrrh… wife of Tesoro of Yorne." Mirrah looked up with her eyes. The parlord smiled from the corner of his mouth. "What brings you… to Hether Dawn? Are you just… passing through?"

The king, having just taken a bite of roast lamb, its juice dribbling down, garbled out the words: "Tesoro? Sounds familiar. Is he nice?" He gestured to Mirrah, his cheeks bulging red. He swallowed too much and choked, but only for a moment.

Armadon leaned forward. He was huge. "Well, Mirrah, have you come… to visit your husband?" Mirrah shot her gaze upward to the parlord and then to the prince, her face turning deathly pale.

The king swallowed his half-chewed meat and almost choked again. "Does he live here?"

"I wonder?" the parlord continued. "What business… brings you? Would he approve?" The parlord smiled like a cat with a cornered mouse. Mirrah was in complete confusion. Prince Calygrey pushed his chair back.

"Are you now bringing charges against my guest?" His voice was firm but tense. "This woman was shipwrecked and did not intend on visiting our shores."

"Yes, convenient, isn't it?" Armadon sneered at Mirrah. "Sailing to where and with whom? Long way from… Yorne, are you not, lady Mirrah?"

"You are making charges," the prince said. "This is a free kingdom. I ask that you adhere to the law and let us dine with dignity and beneficial conversation."

"Be careful, young prince. Your guest… and this girl… bring trouble. They are here to rally defiant Pharens." Numerous gasps descended down both sides of the table. All chatter had stopped to listen to the strained conversation.

"Lord Armadon." The prince grew angry. "We have complied to neither aid nor harbor defiant Pharens. Bain Sarro, your lord's ambassador, has been given access, to move unhindered throughout Hether Dawn. These women, unlike you, are my guests. Would Mirrah honestly come with devious intentions—under the watchful eye of her own husband? I find your accusations dubious."

Mirrah slumped back in her chair, head swaying. The prince sat back with a huff, eyeing the huge parlord. "I suggest you stop ruining our meal and eat something. You look thin." The king, with a mouthful of food, chuckled at his son's boldness.

Poor Mirrah, her husband alive—in charge of seeking out 'defiant' Pharens—going by the name of Bain Sarro? The tall, elegant woman's hands trembled. Breezy felt sick—nauseous sick. Her heart sped fast, thumping like someone pounding a door.

"If you let me ... question them..." Armadon leaned even closer. His breath smelled like an old damp basement full of spider webs and bugs. "I will expose their devious plans." He glared at the prince. "If treason be found... I am entitled to take them... to Skone Lor."

Mirrah closed her eyes and bowed her head.

"So that is your charge? Treason?"

"You question me, Prince? I am never... in error." The parlord held up his chalice. "I smell treason. I can see it... from afar, like a carn... on the wing."

"Enough." The prince stood. "Your actions here are violation of your own law."

"I can prove their guilt even now." Armadon held his chalice toward the king. "By the horns of Morten... let my charge be tried."

"Horns of Morten? Nonsense!" Prince Calygrey slammed the table. A thud echoed through the hall.

"If nonsense, what do you fear?" Armadon raised his chalice higher. "Dear king, shall we?"

A boiling tension churned inside Breezy. The strange nausea grew stronger. Words pushed at her tongue. She held her lips tight, breathing fast through her nose, her mind screaming. Told you it was too good to be true. The bath and bed were just to tease you. Should have run when you had the chance.

The king had grown weary of the parlord, but held up his golden goblet, inlaid with small stones. The prince reluctantly joined in, as did Mirrah. The parlord looked to Breezy and nodded with his head for her to raise her chalice with the others. She slowly lifted it into the circle. The king rolled his eyes and began to chant:

"By the horns of Morten,
The king doth declare,
By the beard of Arnon,
Let liars beware.
If the words be spoken,
And the words be true,
Drink the cup of Morten,
Live the life through.
But if they lie,
Then let them sleep,
Until they die,
In darkness deep."

He finished with a sigh, mumbling something about hoping he got it right. They lightly clanged their cups together and brought them to their lips. Breezy's hands trembled, as did Mirrah's. The parlord brought the chalice to his thin pale lips—his face too gaunt for such a large man. He smiled at Breezy. Chills ran through her skin.

"If you speak truth... you have nothing... to fear." He coughed a laugh that seemed to come from everywhere except his mouth. It echoed far too long throughout the room. "Drink," he said. "Let truth be known."

Breezy stared into her cup. A young girl's face stared back, her eyes wide with dread, one blue, one green. "Why? Why me?"

A commotion near the entrance by the gorron stopped the zany ritual. Zevant, with several guards, came toward them, walking briskly, leading a young servant girl by the arm. She was crying. The king had emptied his goblet and swiped his silk sleeve across his mouth. Breezy and Mirrah still had their cups to their lips. The parlord's eyes narrowed.

Zevant came and whispered something into Calygrey's ear. The servant girl was behind Zevant, hiding her face from the guests. Calygrey spoke to Mirrah and Breezy who now had two guards standing behind them.

"Do you know this girl?" Zevant pulled the girl out from behind him. Breezy gasped. Standing with her hair in ponytails, in a cute white dress, with tears pouring down her face, was Sherrabella.

"Bella?" Breezy's mouth hung open. She clunked the chalice onto the table.

"Apparently so," the prince said. "She claims she's traveled with you from Kharlome. Is this true?" Mirrah nodded. "Says you were in Barthowl's palace before leaving Kharlome."

"Yes… true." Mirrah spoke so soft it was barely audible. It revealed how quiet the great hall had become. The prince paused. He looked back and forth between Bella and Breezy, contemplating the scene before him.

"She says you are spies from Kharlome, sent to study our defenses."

"Bella!" Breezy rose from her chair but got pushed down by the guard's strong hand. "Bella, how could you say such things?" Breezy stared at Bella who dropped tears onto the green marble floor, her head hung low as she cried. Breezy turned to the prince. "It's not true. We're not spies." The prince did not respond. Breezy slowly slumped back into her chair. How could this be happening—her little sister, Bella, accusing her of being a spy for Barthowl?

"Enough! We are troubling the king." Prince Calygrey stood. "Put them in a cell. I will deal with this later."

Breezy glared at Bella as they were jerked from the table. Bella glanced up, her rosy cheeks wet with tears. "I'm sorry, Breezy," the words hardly audible. "Please… the soul is dead that slumbers…"

They were led out from the great hall down several corridors and then spiral stairs into a basement, no, a dungeon. The temperature dropped as they walked down the damp cold stone steps.

They were led through dark halls lit by burning torches that smelled like burnt tires. The various odors grew stronger, making it hard to breathe. Breezy tried to use her sleeve to cover her nose. At the end of a hall their escort stopped. He used a four-sided skeleton key to open a thick wooden door with a small round hole at eye level.

It creaked open, revealing a room of stone with straw scattered on the floor. Two wooden beds, no mattresses or bedding, were on each side. A small window with iron bars was at the end. Although the window was six feet off the floor, it sat level with the outside ground. A rat-like creature scurried off as the door slammed shut. Chills crept over every inch of Breezy's skin. Drops of rain began to fall, bouncing on the stone, sprinkling into the cell.

A form lay motionless on the bunk to the left. The twilight sky shared little of its light. A dull yellow beam shone through the hole in the door. It was more than damp and musty—the air tasted like something, something dark and horrid.

They sat cautiously on the rickety bunk to the right. Breezy tried to keep control, but when Mirrah put a limp arm around her, it all gushed out in cries of anguished woe. She cried like she had never cried in all her life. Together they sat, drowning in the pains of cold betrayal.

In all her sorrow, Breezy still tried to not wake the person on the other bunk. She peered up from her hands. The sleeping form lay still. A shock of terror suddenly ran through. A body? We're in a cell with a… She again, buried her face into her wet palms and sobbed.

Zachary's head finally stopped swirling. He found himself inside a dark box—a musty box with dirt and rock—a square hole—the sarcophagus hole at the tombs of Dross! Panic flushed, his skin tingled. He kicked with his feet, but they met solid rock. He tried to push upward. It too, was solid. He slid an arm forward—empty space. He inched ahead, scraping elbows, unable to rise and crawl. He saw one stream of light come through cracks around a square opening. He crawled on, fighting to stay the panic. He reached the light and pushed. A large stone dropped away from the opening, falling in silence.

Bright light blinded his eyes.

A vast green valley with distant mountains came into view. He looked down and quickly scurried backward into the tomb. Far below was the valley of green, but he lay in the side of a massive cliff. He heard the stone shatter on the rocks below. He crept forward and peered out the tomb. Sheer rock wall spread out in every direction with a thousand foot drop to the lush valley below.

He cranked his neck to see the top. It too, was a thousand feet or more of sheer cliff face.

"How did I get here?" Dread swept over him, making him dizzy. He looked out over the valley. Thunderclouds of dark blue hung over the mountains. The fresh rain in the valley below glistened in the evening sun. The scene was beautiful but horrid. How do I get out of here?

He looked around again, determined not to go back into the dark hole. A large bird came out of the clouds over the mountains, flying out of the rain. It loped left and right but came steadily toward the mountain face. Then with incredible speed it came racing toward him. He could see its eyes locked onto his tiny hole in the cliff. It was an eagle or hawk, a raptor the size of a hang glider.

Zac tried to squirm back into the hole but his feet struck rock. How can that be? It's pushing me out the hole.

The bird came to the cliff face and hovered, pounding its massive wings straight at the rock face. Dust storms swirled with each voluminous stroke. Zac covered his head with his hands as dust swirled, pushing and pulling the stale air from inside the tomb. He waited for the beak to tear him from the hole. He lay their trembling, helpless.

"Do not fear me," came a loud voice. "I am here for you."

Zac tried to peer out between his arms and see if the bird had really spoken to him, but the dust made seeing impossible.

"When I rise up, grab the cord about my neck." With that, the giant raptor flew out away from the mountain face. It dropped down toward the valley and made one vast loop that sent it back up the cliff face toward Zac. It turned about as it soared up the face, its back toward the cliff. Zac peered down to see it rising up toward him. He could see the cord about its neck. No way!

Then, as if in slow motion, the large bird passed in front of his small hole in the rock wall. He saw his own hands reach out and grasp the soft rope of braided gold and purple. Somehow he shot out from the tomb hole onto the back of the bird. It leveled out away from the cliff wall and soared over the green valley below. Zac lay fully stretched out on the raptor's back, clutching the cord, knuckles white.

The dust from the tomb flew from his body. It left his hair, face, shirt and jeans. The moisture, still in the air from the recent rain, washed over his body like a cleansing mist. He felt joy flood his deepest being, a new joy, strong and steadfast. He was riding on the back of a giant hawk over a valley of green. Who gets to do that? Tears washed his eyes, rolling off with the wind that raced over the bird's back. Zac's smile was more than wide—it was deep like the joy, coming from far down inside.

The sun glittered off the river below that wound through the valley. "Where are we going?" Zac asked, shouting into the wind. The bird slowed to a gentle glide.

"Wherever you think we should go."

"I don't know where to go." He looked side-to-side, his cheeks pressing into the feathers on the neck. "Can I sit up… on your back?"

"Are you a prince?"

"A prince? No. Why?"

"Only kings and princes sit on a seraph's back."

"So I just lie here?"

"Not if you are a prince."

"I don't have a kingdom—need to have a kingdom to be a king or prince."

"What of your own heart?"

"What do you mean?"

"You are king of your own heart, are you not?"

"Not always."

They dropped suddenly making Zac's tummy feel like it got left on an air current. A vast city spread out up ahead. The hawk slowed to an even smoothed glide.

"Sit up now."

Zac pulled himself up to a sitting position as if riding a horse. It was surprisingly comfortable, even natural, like he was born to ride hawks.

"So what's a seraph?"

"I am a seraph, in service to Ariel, sent for you."

"Wow... so... am I a prince now?"

"You cannot rule others if you cannot rule your own heart—cannot lead if your own heart will not follow."

"Yeah, that's true. But I—"

"Let Ariel guide you."

They flew down low to the city. On the other side sat the harbor and the open sea. A bluish white palace with flags and banners flowing from spires sat on a hill overlooking the city and harbor. They circled over the city and palace, the people looking like small creatures scurrying here and there. Zac's vision intensified. He could see details far below. They dropped low and followed a street off from a large open square. The street narrowed, and he watched a party of three walking up the alley, a large animal leading the way.

"That's Nusa." Zac leaned over so far he almost slipped off the seraph's back. "That's Isaac and Alle-Encer and Garlock. Where are they going?"

"To meet with a Pharen who will guide you. He will be your rescue."

"Rescue? From what?"

They cut to the right and drifted near the palace. Three people walked in a garden down below, a garden of patios with fountains and benches to sit looking out over the city and the sea. Again Zac's vision cut through the distance and he could see plainly that it was Mirrah and Breezy walking with Bella. No, it wasn't Bella. They were talking and Breezy would spin around, arms out wide. It was good to see her happy. The bird suddenly cut back to the left and they zoomed toward the earth so fast it made Zac's stomach suck up into his chest.

"This is where you get off," the hawk said, as they leveled for a landing. "Trust Ariel. Do not doubt. Be strong and do what is right."

"Do you have a name?"

"I am Kee-el."

The seraph suddenly put his talons down into the turf. It jolted Zac forward. He tumbled over the bird's great head onto the ground, tumbling end over end, over and over until he finally lay face down.

He heard someone crying, sobbing. He rolled over and looked. The sky had turned dusky, almost dark. Two figures sat on a bed. They held each other close, crying.

Am I dead? Are they crying for me? He lifted his head, feeling woozy from the fall. He saw he lay on a bed. "Are you two okay?" he asked, dropping his legs over the side. He looked around. "Prison cell?"

The two figures lifted their heads and stared.

"Zachy?"

33 REUNITED—DISUNITED

"Breezy? Mirrah? What are you guys doing here? I just saw you. What am I doing here?"

"Zachy, I can't believe it's you." Breezy pulled him up off his bed and smothered him in a hug. "I thought you were a… body." His head twirled and his stomach swirled. He was either very hungry or nauseous from whatever the Grimalkyns used to knock him out. The dream had been so real. He strained to pull himself from the sleepy, dreamy state.

Breezy held him a long time. In all his years of being with Breezy, they had never embraced. He had pain for her, for all she had been through. He also felt grown up inside, not because he was being hugged by a girl, it was much more. They had a bond that was beyond the silly boy and girl stuff at school.

Mirrah put her arms around them both. Zac had warm tears on his cheeks, tears of joy, but he had to sit back down, his stomach was simply not happy. They sat together on Zac's bed and talked about all that had happened. He told them what had happened from the shipwreck to the alley full of dirty Grimalkyns.

He also told them of the vivid dream—it seemed so real— of seeing Isaac, Eryn and the others walking. "They must have found each other," he said. "I am so glad Isaac and Alle-Encer are alive—and Nusa."

"It was only a dream," Mirrah said. It was so unlike her, the one who kept telling them to trust and hope, the one who believed in dreams.

"I also saw you two walking in a garden overlooking the sea. You were with a girl that looked like Bella, but it wasn't."

"Mirrah!" Breezy jumped up. "That's not just a dream. We were in the garden this afternoon, walking with our servant girl. She does look a lot like Bella." Breezy's face tightened. "Bella…"

"Where is she?" Zac asked.

Breezy held her lips tight, breathing heavy through her nose.

"She… didn't make it?" Zac asked in a whisper.

"She betrayed us," Mirrah said, her voice mechanical.

"What?"

"Said we were spies—Barthowl's spies."

"Bella said that?"

The rain outside fell heavier as twilight turned to dark. Breezy painfully told all about the dinner with the king, the prince and the parlord. Zac listened carefully as she described Armadon and his accusations leading to the drinking poem of Morten and Arnon. Suddenly, she sat up straight.

"The note—the warning note—could Bella have given us the note?" She went on to tell about the crude note written with charcoal. "I taught Bella how to write."

"But why would she warn us?" Mirrah's mind was somewhere else, her voice apathetic. "To then betray us?"

"I don't know." Breezy fell silent for a while, replaying the whole scene. She shook her head. "And why'd she say; 'I'm sorry, Breezy, the soul is dead that slumbers.'"

"Sherrabella said that?" Zac leaned forward.

"It didn't make sense."

"'Tell me not in mournful numbers,'" Zac said the words carefully. "'Life is but an empty dream. For the soul is dead that slumbers and things are not…'" he stopped and smiled.

"'Things are not what they seem.' She gave you a clue, a hidden message."

Breezy crossed her arms. "How would Bella know those were the next lines?"

"She loved my poems. She learned some lines—really fast. I think—no, I know—she was telling you something."

"If she hadn't said something, we would have drank and… if something was in our drink…"

"I think she tried to foil Armadon's plan to take you to Skone Lor."

Mirrah listened. A little light came back into Mirrah's eyes.

"You should tell him, Mirrah," Breezy said very gently. Mirrah just stared, eyes blank. "Can I tell him?" Mirrah did not answer her.

"Tell me what?"

"Mirrah, would you mind?"

Mirrah just moaned.

"Breezy?" Zac had never seen Mirrah like this.

Brielle leaned over and whispered into Zac's ear. She told him about Mirrah's husband, Tesoro of Yorne, who now went by the name Bain Sarro, the Sasson drog. That he was not only alive but worked for Sasson to find and stop any rebel Pharens operating in Hether Dawn. Hether Dawn was not under Sasson's control but was in some agreement to not harbor rebels.

"It's something like that," she finished by speaking out loud. Zac did not move. His heart ached. He wanted to hold Mirrah, to say something helpful. He just sighed a very heavy-hearted sigh and sat in silence for a long time—a time of mourning.

A rat poked its head through the bars. Zac watched it sniff about. Not finding anything interesting, it scurried off. "*So— Tur—Faln.*" He said the words out loud. Three will certainly come—three bring destiny—three embrace… He stared out the small barred window. He wondered about the book. He wondered about Isaac and the others. Will he ever see them again?

Small footsteps came down the stone hallway. The bolt turned, and the servant girl stood in the opening with an armful of blankets and pillows. Her cute little face peered out from behind the pile. A large guard behind gave her a shove.

"Sorry, milady. Prince Calygrey sent me." She handed Breezy the blankets and pillows with a little smile and backed toward the door. With a bow, she winced as in pain, and then was gone. The clunk of the iron lock echoed down the hall with an air of dreadful finality.

They sat in silence for a while, and then Breezy gently pushed a pillow into Zac's face. "It ain't over till the fat lady sings." Zac pushed it away. He admired her effort to be strong. She often cried, but she had courage. She swung the pillow, smacking it square into his face. "Take it."

He laughed. "You're amazing."

They spread the blankets out on the hard rough planks. It was not comfortable, but it was better.

"So if I saw you guys in the garden," Zac said, "and you really were in the garden, then maybe I really saw Isaac and the others?"

"I think so," Breezy said. Mirrah did not answer. She lay on the bunk across from Zac. Breezy sat on the edge of Mirrah's bed, facing Zac. The rain splashed into the cell, and sometimes a cold, wet wind blew in, rustling the straw at their feet.

"Kee-el said they were coming to—" He stopped and wrinkled up his face. "Why did they put you in here with me?"

"I dunno."

"Grimalkyns captured me, and you're Calygrey's prisoner. Dungeon shortage?"

"I dunno."

Zac motioned for Breezy to lean forward. He leaned toward her to whisper into her ear. Her hair tickled his nose, so he pulled away and gave it a rub. "Could they, could he, Armadon, be wanting us to talk?" he whispered.

Breezy sat up and looked at him. "I think you're right, is what I think."

Zac motioned for her to lean forward again. "Kee-el said they were coming to rescue me. He didn't say from what, but I think it's pretty obvious."

Breezy sat back again. "I think you're right, again." She gave a little smile. Zac was amazed at how quickly she could go from dark despair, to silly, even giddy. He returned her smile. He wanted to ask more about Mirrah but knew it would be wrong. If Mirrah wanted him to know, she would tell him.

"We better be careful what we say," he whispered one more time. She nodded.

Isaac watched the flames wondering about Zac.

"Your brother is being held in the palace dungeon, with Mirrah of Myrrh and the girl." The Pharen leader, Sol Darin, spoke to Isaac without emotion. He was second in command of the rebels under Dulac, the Black Rose. A spy inside the palace had passed the news to a runner. "They are being charged as Kharlome spies."

"Spies? From Kharlome?" Isaac wrinkled his brow. "That's crazy."

They sat around a fire in a large cave. Eryn was on Isaac's right and Alle-Encer on his left. Several Pharens sat across from him. They had eaten and were discussing plans when the messenger came. Smoke filled the cave's open chamber above. Meats and cheeses hung on racks curing in the smoke.

The cave was in the cliffs by the sea. Its mouth was hidden with vines and vegetation, planted intentionally by Pharens years ago. Weapons of all kinds leaned against the walls. Men would come and go from different parts of the cave.

"A young servant girl made the charge," Sol Darin continued. "Armadon was pressing to have them, to take them to Skone Lor."

"Why would a servant girl do that?" Isaac leaned his head back and stared up into the smoky racks above. "Why spies from Kharlome? Are they at war?"

"Barthowl is a horl paw for Sasson. He'll strike whenever told. War looms, plaguing every land. Sasson feeds on war, he loves death." Sol Darin sat near the fire. "Hether Dawn remains free, under the terms that Bain Sarro, be allowed to hunt out rebels. But Sasson is coming—he wants it all. He knows we are here."

"How many free lands are there?" Isaac asked.

"Hether Dawn and Bellock. Cavl and a few others far south."

"And we Pharens are the only ones willing to fight," said a man across the fire.

"Aye, don't forget us Grimalkyns." Garlock stood by the weapons, rubbing rust off an old thorne.

"Hard to know you, Grimals," the Pharen said. "Some be for us and some against."

"And all Pharens be loyal?" Garlock huffed. "Suppose ya no choice."

"We have a choice, and we use it wisely. All Pharens are loyal."

"Except Tesoro of Yorne," a man in the back shadows muttered. Eryn got up and went to join Garlock looking through the weapons. She picked up a felkin and pulled the rubbery straps. The familiar fwoot sound reminded Isaac of their days on the Silver Blade. Those were good days—learning to shoot the thorne and throw swords and knives, eating dinner on the deck as the sun set, listening to Garlock with his flute and tales of adventure—those were good days.

"Have you a plan?" Sol Darin asked through the smoke and flames.

"Plan?" Isaac came back from The Silver Blade.

"To rescue your brother and the girl?"

"And Mirrah," Eryn said loudly from the far wall. She had trouble with these Pharens. Tesoro was a father to her. It did not help that she had been tied up, was the only girl, and now Isaac had command given him by a man with a mask.

"I don't know the palace," Isaac said. "You guys do. What would you suggest?"

"If you strike tonight," Sol Darin said, "while they are unsuspecting, you have a better chance."

Isaac looked to Eryn. She turned away. "That sounds wise," he said, "What else?"

"The challenge is not what to do but what we risk. We would risk much for such questionable—"

Eryn slapped a sword against the cave wall. She then turned to the men sitting around the fire. "If you have not the bowels then let us be—we will get them out. Just show us out of this... this boonda rat burrow."

"And mind we use some of these rustin' weapons?" Garlock slung the thorne over his shoulder. Nusa came from the back of the cave. She stood looking straight at Isaac. She was so much more than a giant lynx. Isaac wished she would give him some advice.

"If you go your own way," Sol Darin said, "your quest will end... in a pool of blood."

Eryn tossed a quiver of arrows to Garlock. "At least we will have shed our blood."

Isaac looked to Alle-Encer. He had been very quiet since meeting the Pharens and the Black Rose. Isaac wished the wise old Grimal would say something.

"Did the runner say where in the dungeon?" Isaac did not like the words coming out his own mouth.

"No." Sol Darin picked up a stick and stirred the coals.

Isaac waited for the Pharens to persuade them to not attempt an attack alone. He knew the sun would be almost set now, and they did not know the city let alone the palace and its dungeon. He felt the eyes on him. Why was he suddenly the decision maker? This wasn't even his fight—not even his world. He stood, his head feeling light and legs weak.

"I thought we were here to help you cowards. Thought this dusty book was supposed to be some key—" He looked at Eryn. Her eyes flared hot. Although they had not discussed it, he knew not to tell these Pharens about the book.

"What book is that?" Sol Darin looked up.

"If you don't want to help, we'll go alone—even if it means spilling our blood." Now he *really* did not like the words coming out his mouth.

"I asked you, what book?" Sol Darin stood and faced Isaac.

"It's nothing. Show us the way out… please."

"Should have killed 'em," came a voice further back from the fire.

"Why, because you're afraid we have courage, that we'll actually do something? What will you tell your mysterious leader—it was an accident?" He walked toward the weapons. "I hope you'll lend us a few weapons, since you can't lend courage." He picked up a thorne and a quiver, and then stood waiting, hoping someone would lead them out.

Tercel dropped down from a ledge and landed on Alle-Encer's shoulder. The elderly Grimal stood and adjusted his belt. "Your leader would have you guide us out." A long silence held the cave as no one moved.

Finally, Sol Darin spoke. "There are many passageways leading to different caves. They enable us to come and go undetected. I will take you to an opening near the palace." With that he walked past them into the dark.

Isaac felt sick as they followed Sol Darin. What had he done? What had Eryn done? They needed these guys. They had met for a purpose, and he blew it, big time. Nusa came up beside him. He put his hand on her fuzzy back. "Where were you?" he whispered. "You know more than all of us. Why didn't you tell me something?" Then he thought about Mirrah's seeing them before they arrived at her house that cold night. These guys are Pharens, why don't they see what's happening or what's going to happen? He looked again at Nusa. "Why do I hear you sometimes, but only sometimes?"

"What is that?" Sol Darin asked.

"Nothing."

"Climb up this passage and you will be near the palace. Make sure you are not seen and do not leave a trail."

"Thanks."

"May Ariel walk with you."

They climbed up a rocky passage to a small wooden trap door. Isaac pushed it open just in time to see the last of the sun drop behind a mountainous horizon. A sprinkling rain fell as he squeezed out the opening and crept away from the door. Kneeling in the middle of a grassy field, he could see the lights of the palace only several hundred yards away. He looked all around and whispered for the others.

As they spread out to not leave a trail, Isaac pointed to a large tree in the distance. They all nodded. The rain changed from drizzle to drops as they walked, lone silhouettes in the darkening twilight.

"I'm sorry about all that," Isaac said, when they gathered under the tree.

"For tellin' them kroaks they be cowards?" Garlock snarled out the words.

"But we need their help."

"No we don't!" Eryn said. "A coward's help is worse than no help."

"You said 'don't.'" Isaac smiled at Eryn. "You never use contractions."

"Contraptions?"

"Contractions, like, 'don't.'"

"Don't what?"

"'Don't' for 'do not'—a contraction." He gave a silly grin.

"Whatever. Let's get this done."

"You did it again."

"Isaac, please." She licked her lips, narrowing her eyes. "You've corrupted my speech."

Isaac chuckled. "This place is nuts, absolutely, totally, nuts."

"You found nuts?" Garlock looked about.

Isaac surveyed the palace. It looked huge in the evening light. "Can Tercel scout the palace and find out where they are?" Tercel bobbed his little head, opened his hooked beak and gave a short squawk.

"Then go find 'em ya little rooster." Garlock said. Tercel gave him an ear-shredding whistle. "Mugs of musty mulger. Do ya gots to do that?" Tercel made the laughing whistle sound as he leapt from Alle-Encer's shoulder into the drops of a darkening sky.

Alle-Encer had taken only a long staff from the cave. It had a natural wood knot on the end that was shaped like a hawks head. Eryn had an extra sword over her shoulder, presumably for Mirrah. She nodded to the pack on Isaac's back.

"Maybe I should carry the book."

"Why? It's not heavy."

"I just thought…"

"She thinks," Garlock tried to whisper but sounded more like an old cat's meow, "that she stands a better chance survivin' than you, lad."

"No, that's not what I thought."

Just then a large bird flew into the branches above them. They looked up but could not see it in the dim light.

"Whooo's beneath my treeee?" came a breathy voice from the branches. They all looked at each other.

"Did I just hear that?" Isaac whispered.

"I've heard of these, but never met one." Eryn peered upward.

"I said," came the voice again, "whooo's beneath my treeee." The bird then dropped down to the lowest branch just above their heads. It was a large white owl with long, black tufted ears pointing upward like the ears of Nusa. Its big yellow eyes stared at them rather blankly. "Can you speeeak or ooonly whisssper?"

"Ah… we can speak," Eryn answered. "I'm Eryn of Myrrh and this is—"

"None of your business," Isaac said. "Why should we tell you who we are? Who are you?"

"That's the laddie." Garlock whacked Isaac on the back.

"Isaac!" Eryn whacked him on the chest. "That's a dorby owl of Mersha."

"An owl? Why is it always owls?"

"They're rare like Nusa. They give advice. It can help us."

"Of course. Why didn't I know that?"

"Please forgive him," Eryn said to the owl. It stretched its wings out wide and gave a yawn. "We seek your advice." She stepped in front of Isaac and Garlock, who both shook their

315

heads.

"Ahhh, a wise one among fooools." The owl looked straight at Isaac.

He stepped in front of Eryn. "Tell us who you are and what's your business?"

"Why… should I… tell yooou?"

"Cause if you don't, I'll put an arrow through your fluffy white chest."

"Be cursed for liiife if yooou dooo. Ask the lady, she'll tell yooou. Your hooome will be cursed, your cattle and sheeeep, your dogs and caaaats, your ducks and geeeese, your fields and faaarms, your—"

"I get the point. And now you'll get mine." Isaac drew his thorne string tight. Eryn drew her sword giving Isaac the look. He relaxed the thorne with a sigh. "So tell me who you are so we can… get to know each other."

"I asked yooou first?"

Isaac re-pulled his thorne, and then relaxed it again. "That you did but I'm a human and you're an owl. In my land, owls always introduce themselves first. It would be dishonorable to them otherwise."

"Where dooo yooou come from?"

"Kansas."

"Is nooo land of which you saaay."

"How do you know?"

"I am a dorby owl of Mersha, I know everything."

"You don't know everything."

"I dooo."

"You don't know what's in my backpack."

"Yes, I dooo."

"No, you don't."

"But I dooo."

"Will you two stop it!" Eryn stepped forward. "Dorby owl, sir, can you help us?"

"Help yooou how?"

"We need to find our friends in the palace prison. We need to learn how to rescue them."

"Rescue? Why should I help yooou?"

"Because I asked you to."

"Would yooou follow my adviiice?"

"Yes, of course."

"Then yooou are a fool. Yooou do not knooow me."

"Let me shoot 'em," Garlock growled. "No wonder there be none left."

Isaac looked up at the bird. "Whose side are you on? Ariel's or Sasson's?"

"Whooose side are yooou?"

"I asked you first."

"That yooou did, but where I come from, we allllways let the mans tell us whooose side they are on, it's more hooonorable—"

"You're not a dorby owl, whatever that is. You're just... rude-noxious. Let's go." He shook his head. Eryn's using contractions and now I'm doing Breezy's thing.

"I do knooow what's on yooour back," called the owl as they walked back into the drizzling rain.

"No, you don't," Isaac called back.

"But I doooooo." The owl's voice turned into a long haunting hoot. They walked silently through the field, hoping Tercel would soon return with news.

"That was foolish." Eryn sheathed her sword with vengeance. "That owl could have helped us."

"You scold me for trusting Nusa and joining with the Pharens, your own people, and now you scold me for not trusting a rude and obnoxious owl of unknown origin or allegiance. He could have been a messenger for Armadon. Let's tell him everything we know—he's a dorby owl, whatever the heck that is."

"You should've never come to this land!"

"Girl, you got that right!"

"I'm not a girl!"

"Oh, yes you are."

"Well, you are... are... impossible!"

"Yeah, that's possible."

"No, I mean—"

"Aiya! Will you two kroaks put a bone in yeer jabbers."

34 ESCAPE AND CAPTURE

When Mirrah and Breezy were led away to the dungeon, Bella was left in the clutches of Zevant. Armadon looked intently at her, his dark eyes seething. She knew that he knew something was amiss.

"I will question... this wretch." Armadon rose from the table.

"Not in my dining hall," said the king, his voice squeaking.

"Then bring her."

Prince Calygrey rose to protest, but Armadon, with one sudden movement, drew his knife and had it pointed at the prince's chest. "If you wish to stay a free kingdom... you best stop hindering justice. My cup of tolerance... is full. Pray the wretch speaks... in your favor... little Prince."

He walked off. His large frame shook the marble floor ever so slightly. The guests watched in silence. Bella could not keep from shaking. Prince Calygrey wanted to question her, but dared not push any more confrontations with Armadon. He rose from the table, nodded to Zevant, who left with Sherrabella.

Armadon waited in a side room. Sherrabella stood in the doorway looking down, doing all she could to not cry. He studied her before dragging her in and closing the door.

"Servant drog," he said, his voice coarse and mean. "Born to serve... your masters." No kindness of any sort came from anywhere in his soul. He was a killer, designed to kill for his lord, Sasson. He towered above the quivering form. "Why did you say... they are spies? They are not spies for Kharlome."

Bella stared at her feet. Armadon slapped hard. She fell to the floor but did not cry out. "Stand... and speak." She stood, trembling, knowing she would die in his hands whether she talked or not. Armadon waited. Bella sniffled, biting her lip.

"No... you've been poisoned. You've been with the intruders. Who are they... why are they here? How did they kill... my two parlords? What power... do they bring?" His questions kept coming. She was so frightened she could not control herself, let alone speak intelligently.

"You deserve death," he said with disgust. He walked to the window. "You have hindered my plans... hindered justice. I should..." He rubbed the severed horn on his forehead, and then turned. "Bring me some food... and wine." He suddenly changed, speaking softly to her. He touched her hair. "I missed dinner. You will be... my servant. I will protect you... protect you from the strangers." He gently touched her head. "We shall be friends. Bring the best wine... you can find. I'll be good to you... if you obey." He lifted her chin to look into her face. Tears streamed down as lips quivered. "If you run off..." He slowly shook his head.

Bella forced a nod, then scurried out the door. Zevant was gone, so she gave a quick bow to Armadon, and hurried down the hall. She took off her cloth sandals and ran the marble halls in bare feet. It did not take her long to decide what to do. Armadon would only make her life horrid if she lived at all.

Her bare feet made little patters as she ran into the great hall. The servants were already cleaning the long table, helping themselves to leftover food. She came around the corner just as a man lifted Breezy's chalice to his lips.

"No!" she called from across the room. Everyone stopped and looked at her. They knew who she was from the incident. Some murmurs and whispers spread through the servants as she stood pointing. "Don't drink that."

"And why should I not?" the man asked.

"It's… " Bella looked about as she walked up to the table. Then whispering she said: "It's poisoned."

The man set down the cup. "Poisoned?" His voice echoed through the hall. A round little man with rosy cheeks put down what he was doing and came over to Bella. He pulled her aside.

"Just how does ya know it be poisoned?" he asked.

"I heard Armadon," she looked around quickly. "I heard him tell someone to poison it."

The man took Bella further aside and looked her in the eye. He then glanced side-to-side. "Ain't poison," he said in a hushed voice, "I couldn't do that. Just a sleeper. Ya best keep your pretty muzzle shut, or ya won't be needing it ever again." Bella nodded. "Now get your bein' busy."

She went to the table and put some food on a tray. "For Lord Armadon," she said. She then put the two tainted drinks on her tray. They all watched, but she knew she had little choice. Her mind was made up, and she could not go back.

Zac and Breezy continued to talk, sometimes in whispers, sometimes with quiet laughter. They were both amazed that they could laugh inside a prison cell.

"Remember that time Mandy Morgon took your lunch box and pulled out all your stuff, telling everyone what your 'mommy' made for you?" Zac said quietly since Mirrah lay sleeping.

"Mandy's a jerk."

"Yeah, but remember how it made you cry?"

"I wish she wasn't in our school."

"But look at you now. I'm trying to picture what would happen if Mandy did that again. I mean you took down a Prince's bodyguard, girl." Breezy smiled as she thought back to the incident. It seemed odd that it happened only that morning, feeling like days ago.

"I'm a little afraid to think what I might do," she said. "Remember that time you couldn't get your locker open and were late for math class? Peg-leg Saunders gave you detention. It was your first detention, so by the time you found the detention hall, you were late, which meant you got another detention." Breezy snickered and shook her head as she spoke. "I passed by and saw your eyes so red. I felt so sad for you."

"Yeah, sure is simple back home."

"Too simple. All I do is worry what they think of my clothes and stuff. Stupid, really."

"So are we all growed up now?" Zac said. He smiled big as Breezy giggled. He liked it when he could make her laugh.

"Auwk," came a sound from the barred window. A small blue-gray hawk with a brown speckled chest sat perched between the bars looking in.

"Tercel?" Zac stood. The little hawk bobbed his head and then flew off as quickly and quietly as he had come. "That was Tercel. Breeze, that was Tercel." He lowered his voice to barely a hush.

Breezy bowed her head. "Help them find us, please." She looked up. "Does Ariel listen to us?"

"If he's really God, he does."

Breezy looked back at Mirrah sleeping on the bed behind her. "We need to trust—even if Mirrah can't."

They sat in silence. The brief feelings of merriment gave way to the reality of the stone walls. Zac's stomach growled. He looked up to the window. I wonder if that really was Tercel. He then heard a noise outside the cell door, someone talking, and then the lock made its ominous clunk.

In the doorway stood Bella. She held a silver tray of food and pastries. The guard had a pastry in his mouth and a chalice in his left hand. He mumbled and gave Bella a push.

"Prince Calygrey sent this—" She gasped when she saw Zac.

"Bella!" Zac was just as surprised. Breezy did not say a thing but only stared.

"Ahh, I hope you enjoy these," Bella said. "I will come back... ah, long, long afterward... ah, if the tray is still unbroke." She handed the tray to Zac, looked painfully at

Breezy, and then stepped backward out the door. The lock bolted shut, and there was silence.

Breezy sat looking at the tray full of little meats and pastries. She did not know what to say. Zac took a bite from a creamy pastry.

"Oh, this is so good. Thank you, Bella." He looked over at Breezy. "Are you sure she's the one who called you spies?" Breezy tilted her head and gave him the look. "But what did she mean," Zac continued with a mouthful of oozing pastry, "long, long afterward—" His eyes suddenly got big, and then he smiled.

"What?" Breezy wrinkled her brow.

"'I shot an arrow into the air,

It fell to earth I knew not where.

I breathed a song into the air.

Long, long afterward, in an oak,

I found the arrow still unbroke.

And the song from beginning to end...'" He leaned forward to whisper into Breezy's ear. "'I found again, in the heart of a friend.'" He sat back. "You see?"

"See what?"

"Oh, come on. She said all that to show... you know."

Breezy just frowned, then her eyes lit up and a smile returned. "I didn't think she'd really..." She then leaned forward and whispered to Zac. "I knew she couldn't betray us." Zac was about to take another bite when they heard a loud thump and clanging outside their cell door.

Tercel came shooting out of the night sky, his wings made an eerie zooming sound. He again came straight for Garlock's head, making him duck. The little hawk then shot straight up and swooped around and landed lightly on Alle-Encer's shoulder.

"He's blind, I tell ya," Garlock sputtered. "Be but pebbles in his head." He adjusted his thorne and quiver. "Why me don't pluck his feathers, I lack the knowin's."

Isaac chuckled quietly.

"Sure, ya laugh like a night proxie, but ya'll be crying when he strikes yeer head, knockin' ya to yeer keg." This just made Isaac chuck all the more.

"He's found them," Alle-Encer said. "They be in a cell together, with yeer brother."

"Does he know which one?" Isaac asked.

"He's only a bird, I-zac. When we get near he will fly ahead and show us where to go. He can tell us where the guards be and be not."

Nusa walked on ahead, leading them through the various fruit trees that surrounded the palace yards. The rain came in large but scattered drops as frogs and toads filled the wet air with creeks and croaks. Isaac's clothes were soaked through. They came to a large stone wall over ten feet high. A lighted gate was far to the left with two guards holding spears. Tercel flew up and sat on the wall.

"Give me your hands," Eryn said to Isaac. He paused and then linked his hands together. She set her foot in his wet hands and he lifted her up the wall. She pulled herself up with little effort and peered over, looking left and right before dropping back down.

"It's darker down this way," she said in a low voice. "We can climb over and cross the open yard."

They slunk their way to the right and up she went again. She lay atop the wall with an arm and leg hanging down on each side.

"Grab my hand." She held her hand to Isaac.

"What about the others?"

"Just grab."

He reached up and grabbed her hand. Her skin was wet but her grip strong. She pulled as Garlock pushed from below. Isaac then lay atop the wall facing her. They held their arms down for Alle-Encer. Nusa groaned a lonely call.

Garlock lifted Alle-Encer, and they pulled him up and over the other side. He landed and fell backward on his 'keg.' Nusa stretched her fluffy front paws far up the wall and looked at Garlock.

"I'm not liftin' ya. Just jump, ya fur ball." Nusa shook her coat and walked slowly back away from the wall into the darkness. Suddenly, she was atop the wall looking at them.

"Get down, Nusa!" Eryn scolded the giant lynx like a naughty house cat. Nusa dropped silently on the other side.

Garlock's reach was way too short, so he took a run alongside the wall and leapt upward into Isaac's grasp. Garlock had to turn backward to find Eryn's hand so that he now faced out from the wall. They pulled him up, bending his back over the wall. When he passed over, he flipped his feet over his head and dropped down on the other side with a rough but spectacular landing. He gave a slight bow.

After Isaac and Eryn slid down, they moved across the grass, running in spurts from cover to cover. Guards walked with halberds, some with torches. They did not seem to be on alert as if expecting a break in.

Tercel flew on up ahead around a dark corner and did not return. They followed in silence, staying away from any light from the palace windows and doors. They were on the backside near the gardens. The croaking frogs mixed with oceans sounds, waves pounding endlessly into the rocky cliffs. Isaac thought back to the cave and the Pharens. It was stupid to have split off from them, just plain stupid. He wanted to put the blame on Eryn but he had made the decision.

The grass was soft and mushy beneath their feet. Isaac bumped a pine branch sending water onto Garlock who murmured his complaint and was hushed by Eryn. Tercel came back and circled overhead before flying off. They followed. Isaac thought he saw a large white form fly across their path in the direction of Tercel. Was that an owl? He paused and watched the sky. Garlock bumped him from behind.

"I ain't gonna carry ya, if that be yeer thinkin's."

They crossed the palace yards to a long stone building separate from the palace. Its windows were all barred, and only a few lights gave out their yellow glow. Tercel came back and sat on Alle-Encer's shoulder.

"How do we get in?" Isaac asked. "I don't see any doors on

this side."

They made their way around the building only to find that there were no doors, only barred windows. Two guards with covered torches made regular rounds encircling the building, one on each side.

"We can't even get close," Isaac whispered as Tercel flew to a small window near the ground.

"We go through the palace," Eryn whispered back. "There's no other way."

"Jolly, can't wait."

"Who is Jolly?"

"Not me, that's for sure."

"You're confusing." She sounded irritated, but Isaac knew she enjoyed being in charge.

They went back toward the palace, totally soaked and chilled. Two guards stood at attention near a door. Eryn dropped to one knee. They watched from beneath a large pine branch that spread out over the wet grass. She loaded her felkin.

"We can enter there, once we overpower the guards."

"How did I know you were going to say that?"

"Can you focus your boyish mind long enough to overpower one?"

"With my thorne?"

"Well, yes."

Isaac's stomach went queasy. "Kill him?"

She looked over at him as he kneeled beside her. She sighed and pulled the felkin back. Fwoot! The guard's head jerked backward. He staggered and his head swung in a small circle before he crumbled in a pile of arms, legs, and halberd. The other guard turned to look at him and then looked out into the darkness. A second fwoot and he too lay in a pile on the stone in front of the door.

"Let's go." Eryn sprinted out from beneath the pine bough. Just as they reached the door it swung open and there stood a servant girl with a large bowl of chopped food bits. Her mouth fell open as she looked at the four standing in the rain with two guards lying on the ground.

She dropped the bowl of slop and turned to run back inside. Eryn grabbed her clothing and pulled her close.

"You'll take me to the dungeon."

"Yes, milady."

They passed through the kitchen as the evening workers all stopped and watched them move through the piles of vegetables and hanging meats. Small children sat on stools pealing potatoes and turnips. Men chopped large sections of raw meat into strips and steaks. Isaac held his breath until they passed through into the bakery. Large stone ovens gave out warmth as breads and pastries baked inside. He wished he could stay and dry his soaked clothes. The aroma of the baking bread so contrasted with the pungent raw meat.

They came out into a hallway of smooth marble floors. The servant girl walked fast as if trying to lose the soggy party behind her.

"Where's Nusa." Isaac noticed she was gone.

"She'll be okay, lad. Don't be troublin' yeerself."

"And Tercel." He looked at Alle-Encer, who just shrugged. They turned a corner and there were three guards talking in front of a heavy looking door. They had no armor but held small spears with yellow streamers.

"What is this?" A guard stepped forward. The little servant girl quickly stepped aside and ran back down the hall.

"Ahh..." Isaac cleared his throat, "we are here to see... ahh, the prisoners, the three prisoners, right guys?" Isaac lowered his voice as he spoke, trying to sound authoritative.

"On whose orders?" the guard's voice rumbled.

"On the king's orders," Isaac lowered his voice even more and pushed out his chest.

"Show me the order."

"Fine, be that way. See if I care. You're not getting a star on your report card. I'll make sure of that." Isaac was not sure what he was saying. The guard wrinkled his face.

"Who are you?"

"I am... me!"

"Back away or we shall defend."

"I need to see three prisoners on order of the king, and you are not helping. How should I report that? Huh? How?"

"You have no orders, you wet frogs." The guards lowered their spears.

"Did you call me a drog? No one calls me a drog. Ya know why? Cause I still don't have a stinking clue what a drog is." Isaac pulled the thorne string as he backed away. Garlock did the same as Eryn readied her felkin. The guards stood dumbfounded. They had no defense against the arrows aimed at their throats.

"Lay down your spears! Get on the floor!" Isaac's voice became deep. The guards got down, keeping their eyes on the wet intruders. Alle-Encer went forward, taking their spears, and put his foot on the lead guard, pushing him down onto the floor.

"We'll watch 'em," Garlock said. "You two go find 'em." Eryn and Isaac stepped over the guards and opened the large door to the dungeon. A musty urine smell filled the air.

"Oh, come on." Isaac coughed and tried to hold his breath. Stone steps wound downward to the right. Before they took one step, heavy marching echoed in the hallway behind them. They looked back to see a full troop of palace guards running toward them. Isaac looked down the stairs. *Running into a dungeon to escape—why does there seem to be a flaw in that plan?*

"Put off your weapons," shouted the lead guard. Several men quickly grabbed Alle-Encer and Garlock. The guards on the floor rose, one reaching out and grabbing Eryn's braid. She fought, but stopped when a spear met her throat.

Isaac came out of the dungeon doorway, holding his sword out handle first. Two guards came and held him, one on each side. The lead dungeon guard came and struck his face. It burned. He grabbed Isaac by the head.

"Ya better pray they don't bring ya back to me."

They were marched down the labyrinth of hallways to the

large banquet hall with the various mounted heads and the cave gorron still looking fierce in the corner. A crackling fire blazed and snapped in a castle-sized fireplace blackened inside and out. Above it was a mounted head of some creature with a lion face and long fangs with forward pointing horns.

Sitting on the table, goblet in hand, was a large heavy man with long rust-red hair dressed in the armor of a parlord. A triangular nub protruded from his forehead. He sat watching the procession as the guards came and lined the four intruders before him.

Eryn trembled as she focused her gaze on the nub. Her lips barely moved. "Armadon." From a far corner of the great hall came a large white owl. It made a pass over the new arrivals, landing on the parlord's shoulder. A chill passed through the room.

"I understand... you have already met... my Supercilious." He reached over and stroked the owl between its tufted ears. The parlord's skin was dark bronze with patches of brown, like age spots but larger. The brass armguards were elaborately carved with black and purple lines. He leaned forward just a little and looked straight at Isaac, straining his eyes. "I'm told... you've greatly rippled... the air of Yorne. I have been searching... to meet you and your friends." He turned to the guard. "Bring up my prisoner, the one Calygrey stole from me... and bring the girl... with Mirrah of Myrrh."

"But your greatness, they are prisoners of Prince Calygrey." The guard lowered his head as he spoke.

"I am done with Calygrey. Bring them." Armadon put the goblet to his lips. He then lowered it to look intently at Isaac again. "What evil... has sent you, boy? From where... do you come?"

"I'm from... Kansas." Isaac's voice was weak. An evil dread, like the wetness of the rain, soaked through his skin. A cold, clammy fear pushed out life, seeping inward, invading his soul.

"Kansas? You lie, you mendacious lad. There is no... such land."

"There is. But I'm... really from Minnesota."

"Mines of Sootr? Lie again... and I'll cut a hole in your tongue... to put my finger through." His face flared.

"The land where I come from is called Minn-e-sota. That's not a lie."

The parlord did not respond as he eyed the lad. He took a drink and set the goblet down. "Release them," he said to the guards. Garlock gave a shake as they let him free. "Why have you come? Why are you here?"

"I don't know."

Armadon set his owl on the table. He stood, and taking a sharp iron poker, stepped to the fire, thrusting it into the coals. He walked over to Isaac, towering above him. With his right hand he grasped Isaac by the jaws and pulled his head upward.

"You have told me your last lie. Now why... have you come?" He jerked Isaac upward.

Isaac's flesh quivered. An evil pushed, taunting him to surrender, to succumb to the terror. His legs weakened as he glanced at the iron poker in the coals.

"I told you... I don't know why I'm here. If you want truth—that's it." Armadon still held him under his chin, his large hand cranking Isaac's head back and upward. Armadon peered into his eyes.

"You will go with me... to Skone Lor. Sasson... will be pleased with me." He jerked his hand away, jolting Isaac's head. He looked to the guards and growled, "Where are they?"

Just then, the guards came running into the great hall, their boots echoed as they pounded across the marble floor. They went immediately to their captain and spoke in hushed voices pointing back down the hallway.

"Where are they?!" Armadon barked, making everyone jump.

"My Lordship," the captain looked down as he spoke. "They have... they are..."

"Speak!"

"They are... gone."

35 INTO THE FIRE

Armadon narrowed his eyes and looked at the two guards. They dropped their heads. "What do you mean... gone?"

"They found the guards sleeping, but not of natural sleep. The cell door was open. The boy, the woman, and the girl are gone." The guard cringed as he spoke.

Armadon went into a rage. In two strides, he was at the fireplace. He pulled out the iron poker, its tip pulsating—yellow-white and orange. He held it to the captain's throat.

"Find them... now!" His voice crescendoed into a screaming rage. "They are mine! I will not lose them!"

Half of the guards rushed out of the great hall, clamoring to get away from the angry parlord. Armadon looked again to his four captives. He then spun and slammed the iron poker onto the table. The owl flew upward several feet and came back down with a low hiss.

"That servant girl," he growled. "She will beg for death... and find it not." The words came out with a deep, breathy hiss. Isaac shuttered. He tried to control himself, to keep the parlord from seeing, but his whole body quaked. He heard Garlock softly mumbling. Eryn breathed in sporadic breaths. Isaac was glad they had no weapons. He feared for what Eryn may try.

"Your satchel." Armadon turned back to Isaac, his hand held outward. It caught Isaac completely by surprise. Eryn gasped. She put her hand on the pack.

"No," she whispered, "you must not."

"Give that unholy bag... now!"

Isaac slowly took the pack from his back.

"No..." Eryn moaned. "Isaac, please, noooo."

As Isaac looked at the parlord's strong hand extending toward him, the brass guard over the forearm with its intricate black designs, a boldness, like electric anger, surged through him. "You want it? Go get it!" With a sudden toss, he flung his backpack into the flames of the large black fireplace. It landed square in the middle of the white coals and crackling flames. An eruption of sparks billowed out from the embers, popping and snapping their way up the chimney.

"No!" Eryn screamed, rushing toward the fireplace. Isaac grabbed her arm and jerked her back. She pulled at his arm and fought his grip. Armadon watched them squabble as the pack burst into flame.

"Take it out," he ordered a soldier standing nearest the flames. "You mindless drog," he said to Isaac. He picked up the smoldering poker and swung it backhand. It struck Isaac on his left shoulder leaving a dark charred line.

The guard stepped toward the fire but Isaac, still holding Eryn's arm, swept his leg into the man's feet. The guard hit the floor with a solid thud that echoed down the great hall. Armadon's face filled with rage, his reddish-dark eyes pulsed with evil. He raised the hot poker over Isaac.

"You! Take it out! Before I split... your puny head."

"I don't serve you," Isaac stood straight, looking up to face the parlord. He fought to stay steady, breathing through his nose, trying not to look at the raised poker. Silence filled the hall for a brief but revealing moment.

As the soldier got to his feet, Armadon held his gaze on Isaac. He then yelled at the man to pull out the pack. The soldier pulled his hand back as flames sprung from the nylon pack. Thick black ribbons of soot twirled up the chimney.

"Now!" Armadon shouted.

Isaac still held Eryn in his grip. She fought with eyes of rage. He squeezed her arm tight, knowing it hurt, but he dared not let her go. Armadon took his goblet of wine and dumped it on the pack. The smell of burning plastic mixed with scented wine. The soldier reached into the flames once more. He grasped the pack only to withdraw and see a glob of burning black goo stuck to his skin. He stifled a yell, shaking his hand violently.

Armadon watched. He bore the same expression as the parlord in Yorne who watched his worl struggle and die. The soldier put his burning hand between his knees. The pack was now nearly gone, reveling the brass box with flaming goo dripping down its sides.

Armadon reached with the poker to pull the box from the flames. Eryn sobbed and weakly struck at Isaac who continued to hold her tight. Garlock mumbled quietly, shaking his furry head. Alle-Encer stood silent.

Armadon worked at the blackened box with the poker, knocking it off the coals onto the stone hearth. Thick black sooty smoke continued to rise as burning nylon and plastic still clung to the box. Armadon tapped the box with the poker, studying Isaac and Eryn, who now seemed to give up on trying to rescue the precious pages. The parlord's face showed his confusion as he slowly scraped the blackened ash and burning goo from atop the box. Thick white smoke pushed out from the sides and seams of the box. The Pharrian script written on the outside seemed almost aglow as the large parlord leaned over just a little to study the writing.

Eryn wept—her strength leaving with the smoke that rose from the box. To have journeyed so long, enduring so much, to have found, read, and learned from the book of Hornin to now simply stand by and watch it burn at the hands of the beast who murdered her parents was beyond her ability to grasp. Her body went limp. Isaac now held her up more than restrained her.

Armadon went down to one knee, carefully keeping an eye

on Isaac. He blew the sooty ash from atop the box and turned his head to view the writing.

"Pharrian," he said to himself. He glanced at Isaac and Eryn then back at the box. "Middle Pharrian." He blew away a little more ash. "*So—Tur—Faln. So—Faln—Tur.* Three will surely come... will bring death." He tilted his head. "Death holds three. Hate this... cursed language." He looked one more time at Eryn then back at the script. "Three bring the end." With that, he stood up quickly and stepped back from the box. The room went silent.

"Bring water you drogs," he barked at the guards. They scurried about and finally came running with a small wooden bucket. The brass casing gave a long hiss as the water poured over its sides. Eryn continued to weep. Isaac released his grip.

"Trust me," he whispered. She scowled and clenched her teeth.

"Open it." Armadon watched them closely. A guard knelt and tried to open the brass box. The plastic and heat had melded the halves together. Armadon struck him with the poker. "Pick it up." The frazzled guard picked up the case and put it on the large banquet table. Armadon tossed the poker and drew his large sword.

Eryn cried out. "Please..."

Armadon grabbed Eryn by her braid, jerking her to the table.

"What is in this box?" A presence emanated from him—dark and daunting. He put the sword to her throat. It was clear that he had reached his limit. Eryn trembled and could not speak. He grabbed her right hand and pinned it to the table, fingers spread out flat. Raising his sword he spoke slowly. "I will start with your fingers and continue upward until you speak."

Eryn could not control her trembling lips. She fought to breathe, gasping as her whole body shook.

"Rocks, you idiot." Isaac was stunned by his own words. "I'm sick of this stupid game. Let her go, now!" He too, shook. Armadon did not move. "I said, let her go!" Armadon continued to stand, unmoved.

Then, he slowly raised his sword and looked down at Eryn's long fingers. He re-adjusted his grip on her hand. She turned away with a low, moaning cry.

"I'm done with this game as well." He glanced one last time at Isaac as if daring him to fight. Then fixed his gaze on Eryn's hand. "And you lose."

Before his sword dropped an inch, a flash of brown struck his arm, knocking him over the banquet table onto the floor. Eryn landed, sprawled out at the feet of Isaac. Armadon lay face down with a giant lynx tearing at his elbow.

Nusa had leapt from behind the gorron and struck the parlord with such force that she had pulled him forward over the brass box and down onto the floor. Nusa had slid across the table as her momentum swung her around landing in front of Garlock and Alle-Encer, still gripping the parlord's arm. A crunch sounded as Armadon let loose a cry of pain. The guards stood bewildered. Nusa turned and gave a loud, sharp snarl. A guard stumbled backward, his spear clanging on the stone floor. Again Nusa snarled and two guards ran toward the door. Garlock dashed for the far end of the table and grabbed his sword. By the time he reached it and spun about, the remaining guards were running out the door.

Eryn jumped to her feet as Armadon tried to push himself up. He groaned as he tried to use his right arm. He was speaking something in a strange tongue that did not sound friendly. Isaac quickly ran to fetch his sword as Eryn grabbed the brass box, holding it close to her chest with both arms. Armadon raised his head to stare straight into Nusa's eyes. She roared a snarl like nothing ever before. A warning, she's giving him a warning.

They grabbed their things and ran toward the door at the far end, far from Armadon. They took five steps into the hallway and stopped. Walking straight toward them came prince Calygrey with a host of guards. Directly behind him marched Mirrah, Breezy, Zac and Bella.

36   A PRINCE, AN ANGRY PARLORD,
AND A TRAITOR

"This way." Garlock waved his arms, running back into the great hall.

"We can't leave them." Isaac turned to watch him run. Eryn stood with Isaac. Alle-Encer was nearly clobbered, as Garlock and Nusa ran back out.

"We can't help 'em if we're in chains," Garlock shouted over his shoulder. He made a wide circle as another band of guards came pouring into the great hall. Garlock slid and ran for the other door. Guards filled the great hall like bees to their hive.

Isaac, with Eryn still clutching the brass box, backed up into the great hall, but there was nowhere to run. Spears, swords, and crossbows formed a wall of death.

Prince Calygrey stopped so abruptly, that Zac, with head down, bumped into him.

"Who are you?" the Prince called.

No one answered. Isaac stood staring at Zac and Breezy. He had sensed they were alive, but it was so different seeing them.

"Answer his Essence," the lead guard bellowed.

"They are with the spies." Armadon now stood behind them. He held his large sword in his left hand. Blood ran down from his right elbow under the brass arm guard. Rage oozed from his large frame. "They are rebel drogs. And they are all going with me... to Skone Lor." Isaac tried to see Armadon behind while keeping his face toward the prince. The prince continued to study the situation, slowly moving forward, his gaze shifting from Isaac to Eryn.

"Guards," Armadon shouted, "bind these traitors."

The prince held up his hand. He came straight up to Isaac and studied his eyes.

Again Armadon called to the guards. "Bind them... or I will crush your heads."

"I order the palace guard, parlord. You have no authority here."

"Traitors are mine. It is my duty... to take them to Lord Sasson."

"Sasson is not the lord of this land. If you are here to stir war, then I shall have you bound." Armadon roared in laughter. Calygrey knew the doubtful outcome of such an endeavor. But he also knew Armadon answered directly to Sasson and was now violating treaty agreements.

Calygrey scanned Isaac's odd clothing. "What is your business here?"

"I've come for my brother," he said with a nod toward Zachary. The others had moved closer, crowding the entrance into the great hall.

"Your brother? This boy freed the spies, poisoning my guards."

"He was kidnapped by Armadon this afternoon. He could not have freed the others. And they're not spies."

"And how would you know? You are not Pharen. Are you?"

"No, I am not." He kept looking over his shoulder.

"Guards." Calygrey motioned with his head. Several made their way past him into the hall. Armadon reluctantly stepped aside for them. Totally surrounded, Isaac and Eryn moved back into the great hall where the smell of burning plastic still hung.

The prince motioned for them to put their weapons on the banquet table. Isaac set his sword down. Eryn stood clutching the box. The air was tense. No one knew what to do or say. Mirrah looked so forlorn it was painful to watch her. Bella blinked back tears. Garlock and Nusa where gone.

"Why should I not give you to this parlord?" the prince asked Isaac, speaking slowly, thoughtfully.

"Because I am here for a reason."

"And what reason is that? Spying?"

"We are not spies."

"So what are you then?"

"We are… travelers."

"From Kharlome?"

"Yes, but not originally. We're from…"

"Where? Have you not posed as shipwrecked travelers, coming in by different routes, in separate parties, meeting with rebel Pharens, guided by none other than Mirrah of Myrrh, the wife of Bain Sarro? Did she plan the slave auction as an entrance into the palace?" He looked up at Mirrah who was not really listening.

"No," Isaac said. "We are not spies. We had to flee Kharlome, we—"

"Flee Kharlome? What reasons have you for that? Reluctant spies? In debt to Barthowl?"

"No, we are travelers… we are here to…"

"To what? Speak, lad."

"To help you."

"Enough!" Armadon slammed his sword flat on the table. "I am taking them, now! Guards, bind them."

The prince grabbed a sword. "I am not finished," he said, his knuckles turning white around the hilt. "They will do what I say."

"They will go with me now," Armadon countered. "If you wish to question them further… come to Skone Lor. Guards!" His voiced boomed through the hall. It reminded Breezy of the gorron's cry echoing through the caverns.

Calygrey stood silent. Armadon was not only a mighty parlord, he was Sasson's first—the first of the parlords. As a boy, the prince heard tales of Armadon defeating whole troops, slaughtering dozens. The prince sighed. He sensed something was awry but what more could he do?

The guards pressed in with spears pointing from all directions. Cording was brought, and they tied the prisoners' hands together behind their heads, wrapping the rough cord then up around their necks. Bella softly cried. Breezy pressed her lips tight. No one resisted, except Eryn, as they pried the brass box from her grasp.

The scene was piteous. They had not seen each other since the shipwreck and now together, bound as prisoners, doomed for Skone Lor. Pulsing waves of mixed emotions came with every breath. They were together again but for what? It was over. The end had finally come.

They came to Isaac last. He stood silent, his eyes fixed on the prince. The guard took delight in being rough, jerking the ropes tight. The other guards who knew of Isaac's defiance of Armadon watched with trepidation. No one challenged a parlord and lived—no one they had known. But this guard seemed to exalt himself, pulling the cording tight around Isaac's neck, making him struggle to breathe. The prince watched without a sound.

Armadon awkwardly sheathed his sword, using his left hand to slide it behind his back. "To the harbor." His voice boomed again through the great hall as he turned toward the door near the gorron. He suddenly paused, turned back toward Bella and then slapped her hard with his left hand. She fell to the floor in a heap.

"You... you gorron!" Breezy shouted. Armadon quickly raised his hand. Breezy flinched. He then drew his large hand slowly along her cheek. Breezy quaked.

"Take them out!"

They began moving toward the other end of the great hall

when suddenly, a tall man in dark clothing stepped through the doorway. Two men stood just behind on each side. He was older with streaks of light gray in his long black hair that hung behind, wound tightly into a long tail.

Mirrah gasped, her knees buckling. Eryn froze, gaping.

"Bain Sarro," the prince said, "you surprise." Armadon groaned, grinding his fist into the table. Bain Sarro did not speak as he surveyed the prisoners and then Mirrah.

"Are these the spies, Prince Calygrey?" He spoke with a sharp authoritative voice.

"They are the parlord's now. He insists on taking them to Skone Lor against my wishes. I feel this violates treaty."

"I heard they are spies from Kharlome."

"I sought to ascertain, but…"

Bain Sarro walked across the room with a strong athletic stride. He stood in front of Zachary looking into his eyes and then at Breezy, her eyes were red and swollen. The tall man reached out and wiped a tear off her cheek. Breezy stood silent. Her 'freakish' blue and green eyes caught his attention. He glanced quickly at Eryn and Mirrah, returning his gaze to Breezy, then to Isaac, as if he were looking for something.

"I can assure you, Prince Calygrey, they are not spies from Kharlome."

"How so?"

"I was in Kharlome the day they arrived. They were to be questioned about an event outside Kharlome."

"That," Armadon said, "would be the deaths… of Klonen and Garr… my parlords of Yorne." The prince and the guards were visibly stunned to hear this news. Some guards stepped back from the prisoners.

"Yes," Bain Sarro continued, "but they left the corlord's palace before I could question them. If they are spies, they are not from Kharlome. I have come now, to question them."

"You will have your chance… in Skone Lor." Armadon breathed through his nose like a bull about to charge.

Bain Sarro picked up Isaac's sword from the pile of weapons on the table. He took his time, angering the parlord all the more. "You, sir Armadon," he examined the handle, "have made matters difficult." He stepped close, showing no fear of the mighty parlord.

"Difficult? Because I'm doing your job?"

"If only you could. My men have watched this band since they arrived. I had hoped they would lure the Pharen leader, Dulac, into the open." At this Mirrah gave another gasp but caught herself. She breathed heavy with her gaze locked on Bain Sarro. The Pharen traitor calmly continued. "My men learned that this… Black Rose, as he calls himself—"

At this, Mirrah collapsed onto the floor. Breezy rushed to her, but the guards jerked her back. They pulled Mirrah to her feet, slapping her face. Bain Sarro watched, and then, as if nothing happened, continued. "We heard the Black Rose was plotting to kidnap Mirrah in hopes of securing some deal." He chuckled. "I watched the palace tonight, planning to catch them in their attempt, but you, sir Armadon, have spoiled all that."

"They are going to Sasson." Armadon gestured for the guards to move out. "You should quit playing games… and strive to please his Eminence." The guards moved the prisoners toward the door. Bain Sarro held up his hand and everyone stopped. Armadon slammed his fist again onto the large table. It echoed in the great hall. The tall Pharen spoke to the man on his right who then left immediately.

"Since you, sir Armadon, have befuddled things here, I shall sail with you to Skone Lor. I will have a ship prepared. We will sail within a lock." Armadon grunted his protest, but Bain Sarro obviously held some level of authority here in Hether Dawn. Mirrah was on the edge of hyperventilating. Bella and Breezy yearned to help her. Eryn kept her focus on the brass case on the table. "Was there not another Grimalkyn… and a Perlin of Mersha?" Bain Sarro asked. Armadon rubbed his elbow where the blood had crusted. No one answered.

They were led to the large entrance hall where Breezy and

Mirrah had walked through that morning. A beautiful rug with hunting scenes spread out beneath them. They stood in a circle for some time before Isaac sat down on the rug. It was hard to sit with hands tied behind the head. Weak and tired, his spirit began to break. The last two days felt like a month—the shipwreck, the journey to Hether Dawn, the Grimalkyn fight, Armadon, and now this.

He had hoped this Black Rose would show up with his men to help them free Zac and Breezy. Now he understood why they had not risked it. Bain Sarro was actually waiting for them. They were the last of the Pharen rebels being hunted by a Pharen—Mirrah's 'dead' husband, of all people. He wondered why she was so stunned when he mentioned Dulac's name and again when calling him the Black Rose?

He wondered about the masked man, Dulac.

Do his own men know who he is? Does Mirrah know something? Was this all a part of her plan? The Pharens could be grouping here, planning strategies. Am I helping or hurting? She obviously didn't know her husband was here, working against them. It's all too crazy. What does it even matter? I just want to go home.

He thought back to the night outside Kharlome, wondering if he were on the right side. Who is this Sasson? Is Ariel for real? Earlier that day, it all seemed to make sense—being part of something bigger—purpose, even destiny—and that he was helping somehow.

Sure didn't feel that way now. That was all a foolish dream, a wishful desire to find reason in the madness, purpose in this endless journey of trial and pain. Darkness pressed his soul. Gloom offered an exchange: for trust—spite, for faith—scorn, for hope—bitterness.

He watched a candle burning in a corner near the door. The flame flickered with the evening breezes, its light dancing on the walls. As he watched, a wind came and the light died, leaving nothing but a smoldering wick. How fitting, he thought. Then, the smoldering glow became a tiny flame. It rose back to burn even brighter than before, pushing back the darkness, filling its little world with light.

Alle-Encer leaned close. "It doesn't give up," he whispered, "just like you."

37 WHY WEREN'T WE RESCUED?

They sat with guards all around, as the cording cut into their necks and wrists. The weight of their arms pulled on the cording around their necks. Breezy whimpered, which made Bella pout, which made Alle-Encer moan, which made a guard slap Alle-Encer with the side of his spear. It knocked him over, and he just lay there, as it was too difficult to right himself.

"Where are Nusa and Garlock?" Zac whispered to Isaac.

"Shhh."

It seemed a very long time sitting on the floor with hands tied up behind their necks. No one spoke. They all knew it was not the time for questions or answers. Too many uncertainties and talking could only make things worse, if that were possible. Eryn kept sighing and talking to herself about the book. Zachary thought back to the dream of riding on Kee-el's back.

"He said we would be rescued."

"Shhh."

"To your feet," came a loud voice from the grand doorway. They were briskly pulled to their feet and led out into the drizzling night. Breezy thought of the plush bed in their palace room. What a day. She could not even wipe her eyes. She stumbled on a step as her vision blurred. *I cannot bear any more. I can't believe I lasted this long. Maybe I've gone crazy* and do not even know it. Maybe I lost my mind back on the island or in the sea, and now I think I am fine when I'm really loony. How would I know?

They were loaded into a wagon that bounced painfully over the stone streets to the harbor. Activity was everywhere as people ate and danced to flutes and pipes. Colored lanterns hung across storefronts, lighting the streets. Their reddish glow reflected off the wet stones. The rain turned to a foggy mist. Smells of a thousand things hung in the wet, night air. Steam from charcoal-fired kettles and woks rose like pillars into the sky.

Breezy winced at the sight of creatures skinned and hung in storefronts and restaurants. The smell of raw meat only added to her misery.

As they jostled along, the air turned fishy, and the sounds of gulls and soft waves replaced that of the busy streets. When the wagon stopped, they were drug out onto a wooden pier. Small boats of all kinds rocked in the waves, some with lights that dazzled across the bay. As the guards marched them down the slimy pier, they abruptly came to a halt, causing several to slip, jostling into each other.

"What's up?" Breezy asked, since no command had been given.

"Look." Zac motioned with his head. "Up there."

At the end of the peer, stood a man, or something like a man, but over twelve feet tall. He had heavy chains on his feet and wrists connected to an iron collar about his neck. He was fully dressed in worn out leathers with laced up boots like moccasins and thick leather armguards. His hair hung loose in golden-brown waves, thick and full. An oil light high on a pole at the end of the pier shone just below his face.

"A giant," Breezy said. "He's huge." He was not grotesque like one would expect a giant to be, but lean and muscular with a handsome face that bore a mischievous tint. A party of six guards stood around him in the yellow light. Some had crossbows while others simple spears.

"A Brone of Bellock," Alle-Encer said to Zac. "Not often

seen in these parts."

"Is he a prisoner?"

"He's chained hand and foot, lad."

Their lead guard walked the pier to speak to the soldiers around the Brone. He came back shaking his head. "He's to sail with us to Skone Lor." The guards groaned and spit. "Comes from port Gruel. Bind him to the mast. If he gives trouble, kill him and put 'em in the sea. Now get on." The men grumbled as they continued down the pier.

The giant Brone got prodded to the edge as they all passed by. They were loaded into a craft that would take them out to the vessel arranged and prepared by Bain Sarro, Mirrah's husband.

"How far to Skone Lor?" Isaac asked Alle-Encer as they rose and dropped with the waves. Four men in odorous rags rowed the party out into the dark water of the harbor. Lights from different ships and small craft created a broodingly beautiful sight. Waves of fog passed over them making Breezy and Bella shiver with sudden jerks.

"Do you know how far?" Isaac asked again.

"Six days sailing, a few days walking, if the weather's good."

"That long? Oh, God." His heart went sick.

"In a hurry to meet Sasson, lad?"

"It's just… I had hoped…"

"Hope is good."

"Not in this world."

"You were hoping to get back home."

Isaac gave one cynical laugh. "Yeah, actually stupid enough to believe it could still happen."

"It still could."

Isaac laughed again, a bitter, sour laugh. "Right. Thanks, but the dream's over." He watched Breezy and his brother. Sorrow and failure moved into his heart and set up house and home. He had lost. He gave his best shot… and he lost. How would he tell his mom and dad about Zac and Breeze? 'Sorry, I tried but couldn't bring them home.' You idiot, no one's going home.

"We need to trust." Allen-Encer's voice brought him back. "I tried that."

They came up to the side of a large multi-sailed vessel. A cage on a boom was lowered taking more than five up at a time. Breezy and Bella were shaking hard, and Isaac worried about hypothermia. He studied Mirrah, concerned for her mental condition, as she seemed to have collapsed on the inside. Can't blame her, he thought. In one night she learns her husband is not actually dead, but leads Sasson's secret police and was using her as bait to catch the leader of the rebel Pharens of whom she was hoping to help with the ancient book. And now she's bound for who-knows-what at Skone Lor.

"The book... it's up to you—"

A flat sword blade slapped him across the shoulder. "Move your carcass," a guard croaked. Isaac was the last to go up with the remaining guards. As the cage rose up the side of the ship, he saw another rowboat coming over the waves. It carried the Brone sitting at the stern. His large silhouette rose high above the small boat.

What's his story, I wonder?

They were taken below and locked into an iron cage with bars on all sides. Loose straw was spread over a rough wooden floor. A small guard cut the cording around their hands and necks as three guards stood watch about the cage. No one said a word as a code of silence had settled over them. They heard a rumble of chains and knew the anchors were being raised.

Everyone was tired except Zac who had slept most of the afternoon. Breezy and Bella leaned into each other but could not find comfort against the bars and hard floor. Brief sporadic sobs still came from one or the other. Eryn was forlorn and would not even look at Isaac. Mirrah was lost and confused. She would say something now and then to herself and shake her head. Alle-Encer just quietly observed. Zac sat next to Isaac and spoke so only those close could hear. He told him about their time at sea, the night on the beach, and the dream in the dungeon.

"Were you in a narrow alley, a dead-end street, with Nusa, Garlock and Alle-Encer?" he asked.

"Yeah, why?"

"I saw you from the giant bird just like I saw the girls in the garden."

"You said it was a dream."

"Don't know what it was, but Kee-el said you were meeting with a Pharen who would rescue me."

"Things didn't go well with the Pharens. Met the leader, Dulac. Seemed like a good guy, but then he left." Mirrah looked up, her face drawn and pale. Isaac turned away. He yearned to be happy, seeing his brother alive. They were together and with Breezy, but his heart stayed heavy—that weight of anxious woe. He forced a smile. "So Bella put Breeze in prison, then got you all out?"

"We didn't get far. Bumped right into Calygrey."

Isaac sighed. "Sorry, some rescue, huh?"

"Why'd the brass box look burnt?" Zac looked at Eryn. She gave a contemptuous glance.

"I threw it in the fire." He then leaned close and cupped his hand next to Zac's ear. Eryn watched him, her eyes red. When Isaac leaned back he put his finger to his mouth. Zac nodded. Alle-Encer slowly wagged his head at the boys.

"Speak of it no more," he said in a rough, stern whisper.

The ship began to sway as they left the harbor, the gentle motion bringing silence, and soon, all but Zac were sleeping. He thought back over the day. How could so much happen in one day? He thought of life back home—so simple—so controlled. He thought of his mom and dad. Search parties would have long given up, thinking they were dead. He thought of the ride on Kee-el's back, so real, so amazing, soaring so high, veering left and right, drifting, swooping, and then diving with his stomach going funny. He smiled. "I really saw them," he said softly. He lay down on the straw and sighed. "But why weren't we rescued?"

38 THINGS ARE NOT WHAT THEY SEEM

A loud clank broke the air as the door to the iron cage swung open, and a sailor with a long ponytail stood looking at the sleeping bodies in the straw. He stood for some time before Eryn awoke and sat upright. Straw stuck to her disheveled hair. She looked a mess.

"Would you like some breakfast, Miss Eryn of Myrrh?" As he spoke Mirrah awoke and sat up. She too, with straw in her hair, looked a pitiful sight. "It's time for breakfast," he said again. "Everyone up."

A chorus of moans came as they rubbed their sore arms and hips, straw sticking out from hair and clothing. He led them out and up the ladder steps to the open deck. The sun cracked the horizon to the port side sending long streams of early morning light. Breezy stumbled a little and then stamped her leg.

"Foot's asleep," she groaned. They stood on the open deck and stretched sore muscles and joints. The fresh sea air smelled good. Bella pulled straw from Breezy's hair, as did Eryn from Mirrah's. A thunderous laugh boomed across the deck.

"Ya look like taroons from Pelros picking each others' fur for ticks." Another thunderous laugh rumbled out. It was the Brone. He sat unshackled with his back to the cabin wall. He held a loaf of bread and a wedge of cheese. "Best of the dawn." He raised his left hand, the one holding the bread and chuckled, his voice deep and resonating.

"Where are the guards?" Zac asked.

Out from the main cabin door came Bain Sarro. He nodded to the Brone and then walked briskly to the disheveled group.

"Good morning," he said. "We thought it best to let you finish your sleep." He was met with many looks of confusion. "Come, have some breakfast." He turned back toward the main cabin door. The Brone again raised his hand with a smile as the group passed by. His hand, twice the size of Zachary's head, made it rather frightening to pass by so close.

Inside, a wood table lay set with fruits, breads and cheese. Wafts of steam rose from bowls of orange broth. Small cups with poached eggs sat by each plate.

"Poached eggs," Zac said with excitement, forgetting he was in the presence of one of the most feared men. He immediately pressed his lips together.

"Please sit and eat." Bain Sarro gestured with both hands. They all cautiously sat around the table but did not touch a thing. "Please, do not fear."

Breezy thought of the tainted drinks at the king's banquet. Her stomach growled. The broth smelled so good. They looked at each other hoping someone would know what to do. Mirrah kept her head down, sitting at the farthest point from her traitor husband who, sat at the head with Isaac and Alle-Encer on each side. A moment of still tension held the room, then Alle-Encer picked up a spoon and the bowl of broth and began to not only spoon it in but eagerly enjoy it. He looked up from his bowl with a goofy grin, broth on his beard, nodding for the others to eat.

"Mulger of Yorne," he said to Bain Sarro. "Praise to the cook."

"Glad you approve." Silence continued except for the robust slurping of Alle-Encer devouring his mulger. He quickly went to the poached egg and again looked up encouraging the others to dig in.

Mirrah's husband stood with his fingertips touching the table, his head touching the cabin ceiling. "You have endured much, especially you, dear Mirrah." He spoke softly. "Yet, by Ariel's hand, we are together." Everyone but Alle-Encer stared with open mouths and crunched brows.

"What I am about to tell you," he said quietly, "must not leave this room and must never be spoken of again." Alle-Encer finished his egg and set the small bowl down gently. All eyes were on the tall Pharen. Mirrah now focused intently on her 'resurrected' husband. "As some of you may know," he said, looking to Alle-Encer, "and some I had hoped would understand." He looked at Mirrah and Eryn, "I have been forced to play a difficult role." He paused to let his words sink in. "You know me as Tesoro of Yorne, the husband of Mirrah. Those in Hether Dawn know me as Bain Sarro, the Sasson drog. Very few know me as..." He turned again to Alle-Encer. "Are they one with us?"

Alle-Encer's little eyes followed Isaac, then Zac, and then Breezy. Stalks of straw stuck out beneath his brindled locks and beard.

"In all me doing's and learning's, I've never known finer." Alle-Encer smiled. "They have come by Ariel's hand."

The Pharen nodded and turned to Mirrah. "I am sorry," he said, "I could not tell you. But I have survived and kept the work alive." Confusion spread down the table. Alle-Encer just smiled. Mirrah seemed troubled.

"Mirrah," he continued, "surely you did not think I would side with Sasson?" Mirrah just stared, her face pale and long. "Mirrah." He leaned onto the table. "I am still your black rose." Mirrah slowly shook her head and went to stand only to collapse back onto her chair. He went to her side.

"Bain Sarro is the Black Rose?" Zac asked Isaac.

"Shhh."

He carefully touched Mirrah as the others just sat like mannequins. He pulled back her chair and picked her up. He carried her to a couch beneath the cabin window. The morning sun glistened through onto Mirrah's face. Tesoro gently brushed aside her hair. "I am so sorry," he kept saying. "So sorry."

Eryn stood and watched him. Her mouth hung open as tears filled her large, dark eyes. Suddenly, she was like a little lost girl who just got found. She stood there whimpering, as tears dropped to the floor.

"We trust." Alle-Encer pulled off a piece of bread. "Some days get dark—darker than soot on the kettle." He chuckled. "But no matter how dark a day gets, hope—and a good weapon—be still better than surrender."

"You knew?" Isaac asked Alle-Encer. "You knew Tesoro was the Black Rose?" Alle-Encer grunted, nodding his head and shoving in a piece of dried meat into the already bulging cheeks. "Why didn't you tell me?"

"Same reason ya be holding yeer tongue."

Isaac shook his head. "I suppose, if Sasson knew…" He looked around. "The guards… where are the guards?"

Tesoro embraced Eryn. She buried her head into his chest. He held her as he spoke. "The guards are locked below. My men were already aboard as sailors. Last night they took the ship, boasting loudly of having killed Bain Sarro, the Sasson drog, and tossed him overboard." He smiled. "So now I am once again dead, but this death brings new life."

Zac sat shaking his head. He thought of last night. Why weren't we rescued? A flush of joy filled his heart. Breezy's silly word came to mind. Funderful. This truly was fantastically wonderful, not much fun, but wonderful.

"What about Armadon?" Isaac asked.

"He was 'delayed' in Hether Dawn and seems to have missed his boat." Tesoro gave out a short laugh. "He will hear of my death from the guards when we set them adrift near Samonia. He will consider me the fool for falling into this Pharen trap." Tesoro paused to look into the eyes of Isaac, Zac, and Breezy, his face solemn. "He will not rest until he has taken you three to Skone Lor. I believe he was in Hether Dawn to spy on me, but now that he has seen you…" He sighed. "Many are searching for you. Armadon is relentless. He will pursue you or die trying. I pray it be the latter."

He caressed Eryn's hair, taking bits or straw from her tangled locks. "I knew my time was short. I took great risk to alert Prince Calygrey of Zachary's capture. So once again," he spoke very somber, "you must not address me any more as Bain Sarro, or Tesoro of Yorne. Last night, that man died and was thrown overboard. The guards will not see my face aboard ship and you must address me only as Dulac or the Black Rose." Mirrah had awakened and listened as her husband spoke. Eryn went to sit beside her. Tesoro, now to be known by his rebel name, Dulac, went to his wife.

Isaac went to the door. He had a million questions, but they could wait. "Come on guys, we can eat and talk later." They all made for the door. Zac copied Alle-Encer who grabbed food to take outside. Breezy and Bella were a mix of tears and laughter. They stepped outside in a stupor of awe and wonder.

"Short meal," the Brone said, as they filed out. "Not hungry, ho?"

They were not sure what to make of the Brone. They found some kegs for seats and sat looking out to the glistening sea, trying not to stare at the Brone. He had finished his meal and now cleaned his teeth with a nail, studying the boys and Breezy with a mischievous grin.

Tons of questions filled each mind, but no one dared speak about the breakfast events. So much had happened the past three days. Isaac thought back to the shipwreck and the night on the beach with Alle-Encer. Could two people have written the same poem? He thought of Zac's kidnapping and the Grimalkyns, the Pharens, the raid, and Armadon. What is this place? Now Mirrah's 'dead' husband has gone from traitor to rebel leader, and a smiling giant sits picking his teeth with a nail.

The Brone pulled out a large knife and a stone. He spit on the stone and began to hone the knife's edge. "Would you be the lad, Isaac the Mighty?" he said, his voice rumbling, hair waving in the wind. His large eyes blinked slowly as he eyed the sixteen year old. Isaac gave a quick chuckle. It sounded ridiculous, yet the Brone did not joke. "Be you Isaac the carn killer?" he asked again, drawing his knife across the stone.

"How do you know about that?" Isaac straightened up.

"So you are, ho?"

Isaac tightened his lips. He did not know what to think about this giant who just last night was in chains under heavy guard.

"Hmm." The Borne touched the knife's edge and then stroked it across his leather armguard. "Were you all wrecked on the reef the day before past?" No one answered. "Aboard the Fare Whether were you, ho? Pursued by a Sasson gray mast?"

"How do you know that?" Breezy rubbed the last bit of sleep from her eyes. The Brone laughed so loud it made them jump. "Be true, ho?"

"Who are you?" Isaac asked.

"'Ya be the talk of port Gruel." The giant flashed a huge smile. "A young lad, they say, brought down a Sasson carn. Young lad, like you, dropped it onto the ship's deck." He flashed another smile.

Alle-Encer hopped down off the keg. "Good sir, how you've come to know this?"

"Ho." The Brone breathed a small wind. "So it's true." He leaned forward, making the ship seem to move with his weight. "Are you then the one they call Isaac the Mighty?"

Isaac shrugged. "Isaac, yes, but nothing mighty."

The Brone sheathed his knife. "Tell me true—you killed a carn?" Isaac nodded. "Hortle-be-dunkin! Me legs in a pot!" the Brone shouted. Everyone jumped back. "That is mighty— brone mighty!" He sat back and looked Isaac over; his smile beamed in the morning light. "Says… 'twas but one arrow?"

"Who says?" Alle-Encer stepped toward him. The giant was about three times the size of the aging Grimalkyn. He took his time in answering.

"The Fare Whether's pilot says."

"The captain?" Breezy sat up straight. "The ship's captain?"

"He swears by the talon torn flesh of his chest."

"He's alive?" Breezy hopped off a large cask where she had sat with Bella. She balanced herself on the swaying deck, thinking back to the flooded cabin and the terror of the wreck, wondering why she had compassion for the captain.

The giant enjoyed the reaction. "He's the talk of port Gruel. Telling all ears of the lad who brought down a Sasson carn with just one arrow." Dulac came out with Mirrah and Eryn. He listened to the giant and then approached Isaac. He stood very earnest.

"Is this true?"

Isaac nodded.

"You killed a carn?"

Again, Isaac nodded.

"With just one arrow?"

He nodded again.

"And the parlord's outside Kharlome? Was that you, as well?"

"I just watched," Isaac said. "Mirrah and Nusa got the parlords; Zac shot the worl."

Mirrah told Dulac all that happened that day in the snowy wood of Yorne and how Zac killed Garr's worl. Dulac listened to every word.

"There is more," Mirrah said with a smile. It was so good to see her smile again. "We found…" She stopped. Rising on her toes she spoke closely into her husband's ear. He stood silent when she finished. Mirrah then told him about the knife of Yonnan.

Dulac bent down to speak with Zac. "You read the knife?"

Zac nodded.

"It led to the…" He looked around. "To the gift from Ariel?"

Zac nodded again.

"Where is it now?"

"The knife?"

"No, the gift."

Zac looked to his brother. Eryn stepped forward.

"With Armadon," she said with a scowl. "Isaac the Mighty gave it to Armadon."

Isaac sat silent, his thinking face on. How did they know this 'Dulac' was still not Bain Sarro, the Sasson drog? This all could be a ploy to find the rebel Pharens. This could be a trap! His heart started racing.

Eryn told Dulac, or whoever he was, about the events with Armadon and the book. Isaac just sat, lips tight, eyes following Dulac. If he deceived Sasson, he could surely deceive them.

I wish Nusa were here, she would know. Does he want the glory for himself, is that why he left without Armadon? Are we to be his trophies for Sasson?

"Why did you throw it in the fire?" Dulac asked.

Isaac kept his lips tight.

The tall Pharen kept asking questions as Isaac sat, quietly bearing Eryn's scorn. Alle-Encer came to stand beside him.

"Things are not what they seem," he said. "This be not the place, nor the time." He motioned toward the cabin door. "Shall we finish that spicy mulger?"

Isaac watched Dulac and Mirrah enter the cabin. They looked good together. He wanted to believe for the best. Maybe I'm too wary—too suspicious? It could be totally safe. No, it's never safe in this world.

Alle-Encer stayed back with Isaac, grabbing him by the upper arm.

"Do ya trust Nusa? the old Grimal asked. Isaac nodded. "Ya trust me?" Again he nodded. "Remember Nusa among the Pharens, yesterday, when Eryn be bound?"

Isaac looked out over the ship's rail. Light-blue sky and green-blue water filled the horizon. Red reflections painted the waves as the morning sun warmed the deck. A strong breeze filled the sails—a beautiful sailing day. He thought of yesterday among the Pharens, of meeting the masked leader. Nusa had been giddy, like a young puppy wanting to play.

Alle-Encer squeezed Isaac's arm. "I knew the masked leader was Tesoro—first by his... smell, then by Nusa. She knows the heart. I've known the man since I be young and foolish. He is Dulac. Trust him."

Isaac considered the Grimalkyn's words. He did trust Nusa—but she's a lynx. He chuckled. He knew if she were here, he would get the look. He breathed a long, heavy-laden sigh.

"Trust yeer heart," Alle-Encer gave a twinkling smile. "It knows truth."

"Thanks." He let the doubts go. Peace seeped into his soul. The morning breeze filled his lungs and he chuckled—just a little. Inside, he did know.

The giant had been listening. He flashed his brone grin. "Isaac the Mighty," he said, "You should've been born a Brone."

39 THE MOORS OF MYRRH

As they ate breakfast, Zac asked about Garlock and Nusa.

"Ah, Garlock's a wily one," Alle-Encer said. "Don't trouble yeerself. He and Nusa be fine. Tercel will keep 'em safe."

"He doesn't know about us though," Isaac said, "or about you." He nodded to Dulac. "He probably thinks we're going to Skone Lor." He looked out the window. "Where are we going?"

"To port Calesh," Dulac said, sitting beside Mirrah. "From there we will journey to the moors of Myrrh. My men will bring Garlock and Nusa to the moors."

"By the moors of Myrrh," Zac stared at nothing as he spoke, "the stone cutters, in candle light, carved the letters, on pillars white."

Dulac's mug hit the table with a thud, spilling some of the drink. "How do you know these words? They are sacred."

"From the pillar," he said with a shrug. "I just remembered—"

"What pillar?" Dulac asked. Mirrah had not told him about the pillars.

"The pillar by Garlock's place."

"In Yorne? You saw the white stone, the Lorian stone?"

"We all did."

"And you read it?"

"Just that part and some words about 'battles grim' and 'three ones will come.'"

Dulac sat back as the cabin groaned. "You, an outsider, read the stone." He paused eyeing Zac with that intense Pharen stare. "Could you take me there?"

Zac looked to Isaac.

"We're not sure where it is," Isaac said. "We were trying to get back to it when we found Garlock's place. Been lost ever since."

Dulac slowly rubbed his chin as he leaned forward. "Tell me everything, please."

Isaac glanced to Alle-Encer who gave a nod.

"Well, we were hiking in our back woods," Isaac began. "We found this little courtyard with a clear kind of white stone pillar, quartz-like." He told Dulac the events of that fateful day. Dulac listened patiently but with passion. He waited until Isaac told him everything.

"But how could he read the pillar?" Dulac asked Mirrah.

"How did he read the knife?" Mirrah said, then smiled, "if not by Ariel?"

Dulac got up and paced the tiny cabin. He muttered as he walked. "Wonderful... too wonderful, but how?" He stopped to look long at the disheveled weary teens. "It can mean only one thing. But the book—the book—we must retrieve the book." He walked to the window. "To read the pillars... we need that book." He came back to Isaac. "You gave the book to Armadon. Why?"

Isaac shook his head. "I didn't give him the book. All he got..." He again shot a glance to Alle-Encer who again nodded. "All he got was a box of rocks and grass. The book is safe."

Eryn's mouth dropped, her large eyes staring. The room sat still but for the subtle groans and creaking of the ship.

"Safe?" she said, barely audible. "Not in the box?" Eryn sat processing, her lips moving slowly. "The book is safe?"

Isaac nodded.

"Where?"

"Hidden."

"Hidden where?"

"Outside Hether Dawn."

"Why didn't you tell me?" her voice quivering.

"It wasn't safe."

"You just said it's safe."

"The book is safe. It wasn't safe to tell you."

"Why not?"

"Ahh, hello? Guys like Armadon…"

"You should've told me."

"Eryn, last night we were headed for Skone Lor—to the racks. If this book is what you say, then I figured it needed protection—and that meant hiding it and not telling anyone, even you." She gave him an exasperated stare. "Eryn, I did what I thought best. If I hadn't—"

"I should've never let you carry it."

"Carry it? I hid it before you… whatever."

Dulac watched them bicker. He turned to Mirrah and smiled. "Interesting. So who else knows?" he asked Isaac.

"Only Nusa."

"Nusa?" Eryn gave Isaac the meanest look she could muster.

Dulac raised his hand, ever so slightly. She lowered her head.

"Wise indeed, master Isaac," he said.

"Thank you, sir." Isaac wanted to give Eryn a smug little smile, but he just glanced her way.

Alle-Encer sat back and patted his little, round belly. "Garlock will find it. Nusa will show him." He muttered a prayer to Ariel for help and protection. "We did our best, now we trust." He raised his mug for the others to join in a toast to the 'virtues of hope and trust.' "May they always stand beside us and never leave us."

Isaac looked to Eryn hoping for some signal of peace. She squinted at him and mouthed the words, 'you should've told me.' He shook his head. She scrunched her face. He popped a small, red fruit into his mouth. It was sweet, then sour, then sweet again. His face contorted.

"What is this?"

"Enchanting grape." Dulac chuckled. "Some say it tastes of young love."

Isaac and Eryn each found something of pressing interesting at opposite ends of the table.

Breezy took a large bite of dark brown bread. It was very dry. "So what are these moors of Myrrh?" she mumbled out.

"A wasteland." Mirrah touched Breezy's arm. "Chew or speak. Do not do both."

She swallowed the bread before it was ready and her eyes bulged as she forced it down. She gave a silly smile, showing all her teeth. "So why are we going there?"

Dulac chuckled. "It is the birthplace of the Pharens," he said, "once a vast city of great beauty." He leaned back and looked out the cabin window. He continued as if telling his children some legend of renown. "The city lay between two snow-capped mountains; Seren Po to the north, Seren Ko to the south. A great river, the Encer, flowed through the city from the west, dividing into beautiful canals that followed streets, watering the plots and fields.

It was said to be the greatest of all cities under the wisest of all leaders during the happiest of all times. They knew of Sasson's tricks and guarded themselves to keep their land free. Mirrah and Eryn are direct descendants of its great leaders."

"So what happened?" Zac listened closely. "Why's it now a wasteland?"

"Strange events came. Early one dawn, Seren Ko shook and rumbled. A piece of the great mountain gave way and crumbled, blocking the Encer. The waters piled back into the city as people fled to higher ground."

"My forefathers sought to free the Encer," Mirrah said, "but could not. Its waters flowed until the great city was no more, hidden beneath a sea of blue.

"Then, the mountain exploded," Alle-Encer said, "smoke

hurling into the air, touching the sun." He gestured with his arms.

"But first, the Brone trees fell," Dulac said.

"Brone trees?" Zac looked toward the door. "Like Brones of Bellock?"

"Brone trees have trunks so large that fifty men could link hands and yet not circle the tree."

Mirrah looked up. "They say there was no grander sight than to walk the Brone trees of Seren Ko. When the leaves drifted down and the winds rustled the branches high, it was a sight and sound like nothing in all the land."

"So what do you mean they fell?" Breezy asked. She braided Bella's hair as she listened.

Dulac continued the account. "The sides of Seren Ko gave way, like the earth shook the trees loose. Brone trees slid down filling the waters of the flooded Encer. The mighty city lay covered by a ceiling of wood—a floating mass of tangled trunks and roots. It was beyond description. Then Seren Ko exploded.

Forty days, black ash gushed from the mountain, raining down upon the floating trees, hardening into stone." He paused. "Eventually the Encer flowed out but the roof remained. The city is still there, sleeping beneath the moors of Myrrh—land of sink holes and drogs."

"Drogs!" Isaac sat up. "Finally. Will someone please tell me, what is a drog?" The room was silent like he had not spoken. "Oh come on. I've been called one too many times."

"Beasts of gloom," boomed a voice at the cabin door. The Brone sat, filling most of the doorway. "Be wishing you'd never asked."

Dulac gave him a look. The giant sighed with a groan.

Zac countered with a pouting, puppy face, motioning the giant to answer his brother.

"They suck your blood," the Brone said. "Huge beasts like the jackals of Windlum, with hollow teeth. Hunt in packs and love the moors, only Ariel knows why." Dulac shook his head at the giant, but the deep voice carried on. "By Talbon the

362

Tough, they're ugly—wretched—from the doom pit, they are. Why they drink the blood before eating the organs, I don't know. Me uncle Whips tells of a time surrounded by a dozen of the hairy uglies. They moved like flashes, dashing in and out—"

"Enough." Dulac said, very calm but very stern. The giant went silent.

"So why are we going there," Isaac asked, "if it's full of blood sucking beasts?"

"As with the book, it is best you know not. I hope you understand." Dulac spoke respectfully to Isaac, as if to a fellow commander. Isaac nodded.

The conversation shifted to retelling all that had transpired since the night at Garlock's cabin. Dulac and the Brone listened intently to the tales of the parlords, the isle of Moss, the kroaks and the gorron. The Brone doubted the gorron account and asked many questions. He finally consented with a smile and a resonating 'hmm.'

It was good to talk it out—to laugh over that which was once terrifying. Even Eryn joined in, but still trying to stay sore at Isaac for not telling her about the book.

"Ariel is with us," Mirrah said. "He has watched and kept us."

"He could have watched a little closer," Isaac said, recounting his wounds. "Feels like we did a lot of fighting."

"He will not fight our battles for us," she said. "He will fight with us. He will give us strength of heart and minds to think, but we must do the fighting."

"Why? This is his fight, not ours. Why does he even let Sasson live? If he's so powerful, take the guy out—game over."

"He gave this world to us, his creation. Our ancestors gave it to Sasson; they were deceived, but they legally gave him control. Ariel will assist us, but the battle is ours. It is our responsibility to take it back."

Isaac paused to think over all Mirrah said. "But what about us? We don't have responsibility here. This isn't our world."

"Are you sure?" Dulac set his knife on the table and gave it a spin. The blade whirled around a dozen times before it stopped, the tip pointing at a bowl of fruit.

"What are the chances I could spin my knife and it would point at you every time, say ten times equal?" he asked Isaac.

"Well, we divide a circle into 360 points so just once would be 1 in 360, let's say. Ten times in a row? If you were not controlling the spin, nothing affecting the spin, so truly random, then the odds would be... crazy. It would never happen by chance."

"So unless there were some good reason for the knife to keep pointing at you, tens times over, it should never happen?"

"Right."

Dulac paused, as the cabin seemed to hold its breath. "I have listened to all that has happened, counting ten, no, eleven things very unusual, some only of the Lorian days. I ask you, are these by tossing pebbles? Or... do you three bring reason for such? A reason the knife keeps pointing at you?" Everyone sat in silence, pondering what was being said. "So now I am wondering... to which world... do you really belong?"

40   THE DAY OF THE STONE

It was well past noon by the time they moved back out onto the deck; the Brone being finally introduced as Dorian of Grelvn, seventh son of the chief Brone of Grelvn. He had been plotting with the rebel Pharens, hoping to form an alliance, but found an ornery parlord on his trail. Bain Sarro had him 'arrested.'

"I have been taking Pharens and Grimalkyns to the moors for almost a ring. Dorian is my first Brone," Dulac said in hushed tones. "I did not realize we were preparing for the great day."

"Taking them to the moors of Myrrh," Isaac asked, "under the pretense of prisoners to Skone Lor?" The Pharen leader nodded. "But, what about Sasson? Doesn't he suspect something? When you don't bring him anyone to question, or do whatever they do in Skone Lor?"

"I brought him those who had betrayed us, those in service to Sasson. I accused them of crimes against the kingdom and they were forced to... confess. Sasson loves withdrawing confessions."

"And he believed you?"

"He believed he had 'perfected' me, that I had become his model Pharen. As Bain Sarro, I delivered to him a leading

Pharen thought to be loyal—a gift of my allegiance. The truth was, I had learned this man was about to betray the Pharen code. To Sasson, I proved my loyalty, earning his trust. To Pharens, I had to bear the scorn of the very men who honored me as the Black Rose. None, but a few, knew my true identity." He chuckled. "Bain Sarro seemed to always know what the rebels were up to, but Dulac, the Black Rose, always seemed to intercept Bain Sarro and steal his prisoners. It was quite a game, which I knew could not last long. My true identity would someday be known."

"But you had to lie," Zac said. "I mean, I thought true Pharens and all that."

"No more am I true Pharen, but such is war. That game has ended. Now a new one has begun. Tesoro of Yorne is dead once again, taking Bain Sarro with him. Dulac, the Black Rose has triumphed."

Zac turned to face the afternoon wind. It blew the dirt and dust from off his hair and clothes. He stood lost in thought His hair blew across his face as he turned toward Dulac.

"What day?" he asked. "You said you were 'preparing for the great day.'"

"Yes, it is clear now."

"Preparing for what day?"

"The day of the stone—the last stone to be written—the beginning of the end." He waited for them to respond. The teens waited for him to explain. "Your presence here can mean but one thing." He looked at the teens like he had in the cabin. "The day has come—the day to fight—to restore what has been lost—to undo the works of Sasson—to free the land from his evil hand."

Zac turned to Isaac with weary eyes. Isaac looked at his brother, his hair long, tangled and flapping about his dirty face. He was not the same boy of a month ago. Dulac's words settled heavy on Isaac's heart. He just wanted to get his brother and Breezy home. He looked at Breezy. She sat on a barrel with Bella, braiding twine together as wind tossed their hair.

He looked back at Dulac and Mirrah standing side-by-side,

so tall and slender, their features dark and smooth. He looked at Alle-Encer, short and strong with his curly thick locks and bushy beard. And Eryn, the most amazing girl he'd ever been with, who could probably, no, most certainly, whip his butt in a fight, stood, still frowning at him, her beautiful long twisty hair waving in the wind.

Is this real? He looked at the giant sitting on the deck. Are we really here? Is this our world, our fight? "We're just kids. Why us?" He did not realize he had spoken the last words out loud.

"Why you?" Dulac said. "I do not know. Perplexing it is. Only a Lorian can find the stones. Only a Lorian of old can read its lines. To have killed parlords and a carn—you have shifted heaven. You have done what only the ancients could do." He shook his head as he spoke. "I do not know how this can be, but I know this is the day—the day of the last stone."

"But this isn't our fight." Isaac's voice cracked. "This isn't our world. We helped you find your book. Shouldn't we go home, now?" His heart beat faster with each word. "Haven't we done enough?"

Mirrah left her husband's side and wrapped her arms tight around Isaac. Warm tears touched his forehead, as the wind flung her hair around him.

"You have done more than enough," she said. "You have done more than we could have dreamed. You have shown us that Ariel is watching. He is here, with you, with your brother, with Brielle. We do not know why you three were chosen for this task, but you were chosen... you were sent." She put her hands on his shoulders and smiled her so gentle smile. "You have done your part. Now we shall do ours. We shall get you home. Oh-kay?"

Isaac sighed. "Okay."

It was a restful afternoon as the sun grew warm and several took naps. The women washed their hair and clothes. Zac got to gabbing with Dorian, asking many questions about the Brones. He thought of the large skeleton propped up outside the grotto—enjoying the view—guarding the cave.

The dinner meal was again a time of telling stories, asking questions, and making plans. Dulac did not want to share much about the work going on at the moors, but it was obvious that it was more than a vast wasteland.

After dinner, they sat outside on the upper deck and watched the sun turn the sky purple, orange, and red. Bella brought everyone a mug of hot, spiced drink. The bond between her and Breezy was unlike any the boys had seen. The two girls giggled and talked, often lost in their own world. Mirrah watched over them like a mother hen. Eryn was different now, sitting near Dulac as often as she could. Her tough tomboy image softened into a young girl with her father. They talked quietly with each other and with Mirrah. It was good to see them together.

"Dulac," Isaac said, as they sat together on stools, Dorian stretched out on the deck. "Why did you tell your men to help us that day? You didn't even know me."

"You were with Nusa. She would not stand with you in battle if you were not noble of heart." He smiled. "If half they say about you and your brother be true, then I too will stand beside you in battle, be it to victory or death."

Mirrah cleared her throat and nudged Dulac. "They are going home. No more talk of battles, war, and death."

"Of course." Dulac looked off into the sunset. "But there is news I must tell. As you are still in this world, you need to know." He paused. "Sasson knows his time is short. He too, knows the heavens have shifted—that the day of the stone is near. The halls of Skone Lor have filled with talks of war. Not like the wars of the past. Carns are being bred like never before. Troops are making weapons of massive size. Even drools are being trained for battle."

"Drools?" Isaac asked.

"Great beasts with legs like trees and backs like a ship's deck. They carry twenty men or more. Their hides are thick like gorrons. Their horns alone will crush a troop of men. Sasson is bringing them from the Plains of Mann. He knows something has come."

A wave of chills crept over Isaac's skin. A foreboding dread crept up with them, trying to seize his heart.

Dulac continued, "I will give my life to get you home. But I tell you this, as I believe your presence here is not by chance. In the day of the stone, Sasson's kingdom will fall. I am not the only one who believes it has begun. He knows why you have come. He knows his time is short. Forgive me, but I must be honest with you. I know you are young but Ariel has chosen you three—chosen you to usher in the last stone. Sasson knows this. He will seek your life."

The wind ruffled a loose sail. It snapped and fluttered till a Pharen pulled its line tight. The evening wind blew gentle but strong as the ship pressed toward the setting sun. It was all so beautiful. Why must war hang overhead?

Zac listened intently. His heart stirred with strange yearnings. He knew he was not the same boy. He had watched the changes in Isaac and Breezy and wondered. He felt, no, he knew they had a purpose here. He, like Dulac, wondered to which world they belonged. He had read the white stone. Something inside told him that he would help write the last stone.

"You said the last stone to be written... what do you mean?"

"There are five Lorian stones, one stands empty. The first stone stands in Mersha, somewhere, it holds the records of creation."

Eryn put her hand on Dulac's arm. "May I?" Her hair shone in the setting sun and wafted loosely about with the wind. Her face was calm. She thought for a moment then looked off into the sunset as she spoke.

> "'Hearty men, of strength and bold,
>   By silent night, in darkness cold,
> Set the pillars, the marble, the stones.
> Mersha be blessed, creation she owns.

Plains of Mann, with lands so vast,
Tell of the triumphs, the struggles, the past.
Wood of Yorne, most precious of all,
Tell of the Prince, his triumph, his fall.

Perrone of Kurhh, the ending, the sum,
Hold the secrets for things to come.
In land unknown, with trials be smitten,
Hold the red stone, yet to be written.'"

Eryn stopped, staring at Isaac, her face showing pain.
"'There is more.'"

"'Hidden by veil, the pillars and power,
Hidden from evils that destroy and… devour.
Be three that will come, three that will see,
Guided and led, to guide and to lead.
The times they will turn, the true to be tried,
Hearts will be tested, yet love will abide.'"

She nodded to Dulac.

"The fifth stone stands clear," he said, "awaiting the future to become history. It will record the end—the end of Sasson's reign—the return of the Great Prince. You three have rippled the air, you have started the end."

"But we're just us." Breezy looked up with a forlorn face. "What can we do?"

Dulac laughed. "Forgive me, but you three have ignited a flame that will spread till Sasson's kingdom is consumed. You have no idea what you have already done. The book will guide us to the pillars. From it, we will relearn the ancient words and read their script. The fourth, in Perrone of Kurhh, will show us how to fight."

Isaac, like Zac, had a war of emotions battling inside his heart.

"What if we aren't the real 'three' that will come? What if we try and fail?"

"Then, we Pharens will die—like the Lorians of old. He will seek us out and destroy us, till the land sinks into hopeless pain and darkest misery. His hatred grows. He rules by terror; he lives to torment. You do not understand what you have started. Two parlords in one day? A carn with one arrow? These are signs of the end and he knows it.

Ariel has protected you three. Sasson has been searching since the day you arrived. Scouts have gone out, parlords alerted. If the Silver Blade had not been sacked and burned by rue pirates, they would have tracked you to the Isle of Moss. Your weeks of abandonment saved your life. Sasson assumed you were dead. Then the carn—he sees through the eyes of the carns." Dulac sighed. "I am glad I found you when I did, yet I am sorry to be the one to tell you all this."

The sun touched the sea as they sat in silence for a long time. Isaac, Zac, and Breezy just looked at each other. The boys' hair had grown long. Isaac could almost pull his into a Pharen ponytail. Isaac pushed the bangs back off his eyes. He touched the scar on his forehead. The night in Kharlome flashed. Then everything flooded in. Vivid memories, in perfect detail, poured through. The images stopped in the great hall with Armadon holding the poker over Isaac.

"He was afraid." His heart sped as he recalled the scene.

"What's that?" Zac asked his brother.

Isaac sighed, calming his heart. "Nothing."

Dulac called Sherrabella to his side and whispered something to her. She ran down the planked steps and into the cabin.

"Enough of Sasson's plans," he said as Bella came running up with something wrapped in purple cloth. Dulac undid the cloth, revealing a polished Pharen sword and sheath. It was Isaac's sword, or rather Dulac's, which Mirrah had given Isaac that first morning. Dulac pulled the sword from its scabbard. The blade glistened red with the setting sun.

"I hear you have grown fond of this sword and used it well." Dulac slid the blade back into the scabbard. He held the sheathed sword out to Isaac with both hands extended. "Ariel has brought us together." He spoke slowly, reverently. "It is Pharen to pass the father's sword when a son becomes a man." He paused. "I would like you to have this sword, for whatever you face, in whatever land you journey. With it, I give my protection, my guidance, and my friendship."

No one spoke as wind and waves sang with the sun's last rays. Mirrah came and stood beside her husband. Her long hair flipped and floated about in the sea air. It was more than just receiving a really nice sword. Isaac reached out and took the sword with both hands. Tears pooled in his eyes. A dozen emotions flowed through his heart.

"Thank you," he said. "I…" He smiled as Mirrah reached out and pulled him into her embrace. He looked over her shoulder and caught Eryn's eye. She smiled, and then turned so the wind could fling her hair, hiding her face. A deep peace settled over his soul. The war inside was over. No matter what happened, it would be okay. He could trust.

Zachary stood and took Breezy's hand. With solemn ceremony, he quoted the last of Longfellow's poem.

> "'Let us then be up and doing,
>   With a heart for any fate,
> Still achieving, still pursuing,
> Learn to labor and to wait.'"

The sun flashed a glow of mellow-red, then sunk beneath the sea.

ABOUT THE AUTHOR

Lew Anderson lives and writes in Northfield, MN. He has an M.A. in Intercultural Studies from APTS in the Philippines and has lived and taught in China for five years, helping orphanages and remote mountain schools. "I miss living among different cultures."

He has three sons and one daughter. "The first stories were for them. When the last two boys were young, I started *Tombs of Dross*. One of the greatest joys in my life was to read fresh written chapters as they sat, eyes wide, wondering what would happen next."

Battles Grim, book two of *The Lorian Stones*, continues the journeys of Isaac, Zac, and Breezy, as they endure even greater trials and battles, find more wonder and excitement, while seeing their powers and gifts develop. Pursued by Sasson and his haunting 'death men,' they continue to 'shift the heavens,' wherever they go. From zeljin carns to riding perridons, an avenging worl and a Field of Blood, they continue their quest for home as the world around them takes on new meaning. Don't step into *Battles Grim* without a weapon at your side. "I hope you enjoy these stories as much as we did."